# If You Go

*A Tattoos on the Bay Novel*

by

**M.M. Tish**

Published by
**The Onyx Pyre Collective, LLC**
authormmtish.com

Cover Design by **Sage & Fable**
Edited by **Sabreena Rodgers**

**FIRST EDITION 2025**
**ISBN (Paperback):** 979-8-9938569-0-2

**ISBN (Hardcover):** 979-8-9938569-1-9

Cover Design by **Sage & Fable**
Edited by **Bennett's Bookshelf and Sabreena Rodgers**

Printed in the United States of America

10 9 8 7 6 5 4 3 2 1

If You Go

*A Tattoos on the Bay Novel*

by

**M.M. Tish**

*For the hearts that walked through hell and still chose love.*

*This is for you.*

Hello, and welcome to *Tattoos on The Bay*.
This book is not for everyone, and I want to make sure you know
what you are getting into before you dive any deeper.
If you are like me and have no triggers, you <u>may</u> still want to read
this to at least get a glimpse of what you are about to endure.
Because, that prologue? It's ROUGH. And it doesn't stop there.
Any of the triggers listed that are **BOLDED** means that they are
written in detail and may be more triggering
. If you would like a guide of what chapters to **SKIP** to avoid these
without missing anything, please reach out to me.

Abuse:

**Physical**

**Mental**

**Sexual**

**Domestic**

**Verbal**

Mention Past Childhood Abuse

**Blood**

Sexual:

**Rape**

**Explicit Consensual Situations**

Forced Breeding

Anal

Oral

**Light Breath Play**

Pregnancy:

**Pregnancy**

**Pregnancy Loss**

**Permenant Sterilization**

**Infertility**

\*THIS BOOK DOES NOT END IN PREGNANCY BUT THERE IS MENTION OF ALL OF THIS IN THE PROLOGUE AND SOME LATER CHAPTERS\*

Weapons:

Gun Description And Use

More Blood

Knife Description And Use

Tattoo Machines...

Sharks...

Bonus:

Mention Of Conversion Camps

Some More Blood

Suicidal Thoughts

Destruction Of Poor Innocent Buildings And Cars

Straight Up MURDER

*Contact me here for a customized reading guide:*

authormmtish@gmail.com

authormmtish.com

@authormmtish on Instagram

## Dedication 1

To *you*, dear reader. The ones who say trigger list? That's a SHOPPING list.

To *you*, dear reader. The ones that want the most fucked up shit. (Same)

To *you*, dear reader. Who has been through the thick of it and are here standing, having beaten it all. I applaud you, you deserve it.

To *us*, who have survived the partners or strangers or family members or humans who decided we would be their victims. We are not victims. We are **SURVIVORS**.

To *you*, who walked along side someone during recovery after the abuse. While they picked their life back up, and trudged to the top of the mountain once more. You are thanked and appreciated more than you realize.

Dedication 2

To my husband. Who walked with me during and after my recovery from abuse. Who supported me when a friend of a friend thought he could ruin my life. Who supported me through three pregnancies and births. Who has seen my best and my worst.

To my husband when you said _"I think it's really hot you're writing a book."_

To my kids, who are the best kids in the entire world. **And I don't care if I'm biased.**

To my family, who have NO idea I'm writing this book, but will soon enough. Sorry in advance. You might wanna skip some chapters.

To my friends, who are my sisters.

**_The Wellbutrin Club._**

_Smut Freak For Hire._

Let's get (more) matching tattoos.

### Surry O'Brien

Eldest Daughter of Stefan O'Brien. Heiress to the Irish Mafia in the Western United States.

### Stefan and Sabrina O'Brien.

Leaders of the Irish Mafia in the Western United States.

### Samuel, Surry, and Selene O'Brien.

Children of Stefan and Sabrina. Samuel was former Heir apparent.

### Surry's Friends.

Alisha, Richie, Hazel.

### Brenden Slater

Owner and operator of Slater Construction. Business Owner and Hit Man.

### Joshua Slater

Co-Owner of Slater Construction. Brother. Construction Manager and Hit Man.

### Corver Slater

Co-Owner of Slater Construction. Brother. Professional Coder and Hit Man.

### Friends of the Slater Brothers.

Gunnar, Arnie, Juniper.

~

### Slater Construction

~

*Serving the greater Seattle area for all your building, remodeling, and removal needs.*

**Ballard, Washington**

**Owner: Juniper Pierce**

**O'Brien Family Symbol.**

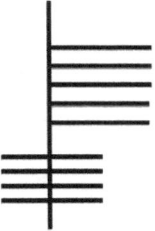

**Nion/Nin. Five straight lines.** A symbol of connections and creativity, and transitions between the worlds

**Eadhadh. Four straight lines in center.** A symbol of endurance and courage

**Gavin Kelly Family Symbol**

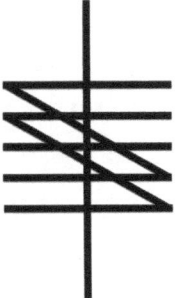

**Iodhadh. Five straight lines in the center.** Marker of Death and Endings
**Gort. Two diagonal lines.** Life goes on, in the endless cycle of life, death and rebirth

# If You Go Official Playlist

Devil In Disguise - Marino

Alkaline - Sleep Token

Heathens - Twenty One Pilots

Pretty Please - Dutch Melrose

Darkside - Neoni

Sun Killer - Spirit Box

Play with Fire - Sam Tinnesz

RUNRUNRUN - Dutch Melrose

BEG! - Vana

PSYCHO - HARDY

Death Of Peace Of Mind - Bad Omens

Take Me To The Beach - Imagine Dragons

I Put A Spell On You - Annie Lennox

You Should Be Sad - Halsey

Figure You Out - Violà

Blackhole - Architects

Pac Ave - Diggy Grave

Gethsemane - Sleep Token

Cry Evil! - Iluka

Let The World Burn - Chris Grey

Don't Look Away - The Plot In You

Lonely Day - System Of A Down

Violent Nature - IPrevail

Jaws - Sleep Token

Ordinary - Alex Warren

Link to Spotify

# PROLOGUE
## 15 YEARS AGO

**15 years ago**

I twirl pasta on my fork, sliding it over my lips and letting the rich, creamy sauce melt across my tongue. Across from me, Gavin grins the way he always does when I'm enjoying myself, the sharp lines of his suit catching in the candlelight. Just a blazer and button-up, slacks and polished shoes—nothing extravagant, but he always looks like he's in control of the room.

I smooth the soft grey fabric of my dress against my lap, the black lace catching faint glimmers in the low light. My long, bleach-blonde hair, curled loose to mid-back, brushes my shoulders whenever I lean forward. A touch of smoky shadow frames my green eyes, and the glass of red wine in my hand deepens the effect. I wanted to look beautiful for him, and judging by the way his gaze lingers, I've succeeded.

And as I sit there across from him now, I can't help reminiscing on the first time we met. That dinner wasn't really by chance at all—not that I knew it then. Our fathers had arranged it, Gavin had known, and I had been the only one in the dark. I thought I was stumbling into something spontaneous, a happy accident with a man who seemed to see me instantly. Gavin's smile that night, the way he kissed my hand, the easy laugh that made me feel like I was the only woman in the room—I'd believed it was the beginning of a love story only seen in the movies.

Nearly a year later, back at this same Italian place, sitting across from him again, it still feels like that to me. It all comes to the forefront of my mind as if it was yesterday.

*My father had insisted I come to one of his tedious "business dinners" at a private club in Seattle. I remember whining about it the whole drive, convinced it would be another evening of boring men in suits, talking numbers and tactics I didn't understand. Papa was the head of some insanely large security company, covering most of the US.*

*Instead, Gavin was there. Tall, handsome, with that*

*easy smile that made me feel seen the second he turned it on me. Our fathers introduced us casually, like they hadn't been plotting it all along.*

*"Gavin Kelly," his father said, clapping a heavy hand on his son's shoulder. "One of the best men we've got, Stephan. You'll like him."*

*I thought it was odd, the way my dad's eyes lingered on me before he nodded, like something unspoken passed between him and Gavin's father. But then Gavin reached for my hand and leaned in, kissed the back of it like some kind of old-world gentleman, and all my doubts melted.*

*We barely heard the others after that. Gavin asked about my favorite books, my favorite music, my dreams for the future including how many kids I wanted, and what my dream job was. He made me laugh until my cheeks hurt. He didn't feel like one of my dad's colleagues son's—he felt like someone who wanted me, not just what I could offer him with my riches.*

*By the end of the night, I was giddy, dizzy with the idea that fate had brought us together.*

Coming back to the present when Gavin asked the waiter for the check, this had been such a romantic evening. After dinner, Gavin took my hand, and instead of leading me back to where we parked the car, we began walking along the shoreline until we came to a cozy little beach side venue that had a large outdoor space facing the water.

As we ascended the stairs, I could see that my parents and my sister were there along with my best friend in the whole world Alisha. She and I have known each other since we were five years old. They all are watching me with excited expressions on their faces, causing me to be just a tad bit suspicious. Okay, a lot suspicious. Soft music wrapped around the space that I could just barely hear, it sounded like maybe a classical rendition of a Sleep Token song, which happens to be my absolute favorite.

Then it happened.

He got down on one knee. I couldn't breath, I didn't expect this at all. "Surry, from the moment you walked into my life, I knew you were the one who could make everything fall into place for me. You make me feel like the happiest man alive, and I want that feeling forever. Your kindness, your love, the way you make me feel like I belong–it's everything I've ever wanted. Please, do me the honor of wearing my ring and becoming my wife. Together, we'll be unstoppable. Will you marry me?"

I just stare at him. I couldn't breathe. My ears rang

with the waves and the soft music and my own heartbeat. This was everything I'd dreamed of. And yet, somewhere in my gut, something twisted.

This man has been my safe space for the past year. I hadn't thought he would propose so soon, but looking up I see my mother, sister, and Alisha all wearing shit eating grins that hadn't faded since the moment I walked up. I look to my dad, and while he doesn't look happy, he also doesn't look angry. His cuff links caught the light–gold knots, old-world heavy. I'd seen blood on those cuffs once, but chalked it up to an incident at one of his security holdings or something.

I take that predatory calm he always possesses as approval, and then go ahead to follow this man that I love into our future. I am shocked, but I know I will look back to this being the happiest day of my life. So I really only have one thing left to do as the sound returns to my hears, and the cool air brushes my exposed skin.

"YES!" I nearly scream at him, hardly able to contain my excitement but the nerves are definitely taking over. My words come out faster and faster as I continue to speak."I will marry you, Gavin!" The words tumble out of me in a breathless laugh, my chest tight with nerves but overflowing with joy. My hands are shaking, though I try to hide it by pressing them against his, clutching like he's the only thing tethering me to the earth. My heart hammers so fast I wonder if he can hear it, but all I see is his face is his smile, his eyes that seem to burn into me, like I'm the only thing that matters.

"I love you so much," I whisper, the truth breaking out of me in a rush, unpolished and raw. "I'm nervous—God, I'm terrified—but not about you. Never about you. About everything else. About being enough. About not messing this up. Because you're..." I swallow, the words catching in my throat before I force them out. "You're everything I've ever wanted. You make me feel safe, and alive, and like maybe I'm worth something after all. And I'm so excited, Gavin. I can't wait to spend the rest of my life with you. To build something together, to wake up every morning knowing you're mine."

I laugh again, half-teary, half-disbelieving, clutching his hand tighter. "So yes. Yes, a thousand times yes. I want forever with you."

He gives me his usual dazzling smile, and grabs my left hand, sliding a ring onto my third finger, but I don't look at it quite yet. He stands and grabs me around the waist and neck roughly, bending me backwards and kissing me deeply. It isn't until my family comes running up do I look down at my hand.

The ring is beautiful, it's a 3-carat emerald, coffin shaped, with little black diamonds all around it in a gold setting. It was exactly what I wanted. The emerald was dazzling, and it looks to be the exact shade of my eyes.

I am so enraptured by this man. I know that he is the one that I am going to spend the rest of my life with. He is my soul mate. People say not to get married so young, but I'm 20 now. I'm not a teenager anymore. I am in college with a 4.0 in a marketing program, I have a steady career online with brand deals and am a bit of an online celebrity. I decided not to move out so I could save money for a house, but part of me also wasn't ready to leave my sister alone after our brother had already moved out. I'm an adult, and I try my best to present myself in a manner befitting one of the richest families in the United States.

My mother, the beautiful and beaming Sabrina O'Brien, put her arms around me in a loving embrace. She always smells of pomegranate and teak wood. She didn't look like she was in her 50's. In fact, she looked closer to her 30's if anything. Her blonde hair is just starting to show the beginnings of grey, but it honestly fits her flowy attitude and attire.

My father on the other hand, was not so thrilled looking. But, he is always stoic. So it was hard to tell with him. Nothing matters more to him than family, and my sister Selene and I—his two daughters—were the light of his life. He's told us that more times than I can count. So I think he is just sad at losing his eldest daughter to marriage. I know he wouldn't have given Gavin permission to marry me if he didn't like him, right? My dad, Stephan O'Brien, was handsome, strong, and tall. All the girls in my high school told me I have a hot dad. Gross, but it is what it is.

I knew he wasn't like a normal dad, none of my family has ever been normal. Who else owns like ten houses and has housekeepers and staff at each one all year round even when we aren't there? But I loved it this way. He tried to keep it separate from us, but dad owned the largest, high profile security firm in the country. He was all about us being trained to protect ourselves as well, which I always thought just stemmed from what he saw at work. He did try to protect us from the dirty side of his work though but I saw what went on sometimes, late-night phone calls in hushed voices, the occasional stain on one of Dad's pressed white shirts that he brushed off as "work." He kept odd hours, disappearing for days sometimes, and yet somehow, Mom never looked worried.

He went a little overboard I think, teaching us how to read maps, trading routes of large companies, shooting and other weaponry training. I am really good with a bow, but I'm deadly with throwing knives now. It is so ingrained now that I can nearly do it in my sleep. But we always knew it was his way of showing his love for us.

It was just who he was, who we were. Different. Strong. Untouchable. My father's late-night calls, the mysterious stains he brushed off, the way strangers lowered their eyes when he entered a room–all of it seemed normal to me. It was simply the life I was born into, and I loved it.

So having them here, Selene, Alisha, and my parents standing proud–surrounding me on this perfect day, it was all I could ask for.

I looked into Gavin's eyes, blocking out everything else, and whispered, "I love you. You are the best thing to ever have happened to me."

He had that twinkle again, the smile that always made me feel chosen. "There is no one I would rather spend the rest of my life with," he said, and in that moment, I knew he was the one for me.

The celebration blurred after that–hugs from Selene, Alisha sneaking me a glass of champagne since she was already 21 and whispering that my ring looked like it belonged on a queen's hand. My mother's laugh carried over the music, my father's watchful gaze never left us. And then, like all perfect nights, it had to end. Bibbity boppity and all that.

Hand in hand, Gavin and I slipped out into the cool night air. The scent of saltwater clung to the breeze, carrying the faint sound of the waves from the beach. My heels clicked softly on the pavement as we crossed the lot to his sleek black car, the windows reflecting the glow of the venue lights. Gavin opened the door for me, ever the gentleman, and I slid into the leather seat, still buzzing with champagne and joy.

He started the engine, the low hum vibrating through me, and the radio crackled to life. A song drifted through the speakers–Devil in Disguise by Marino. I laughed, leaning back against the headrest.

"Of course this would play now," I teased, giggling. "Like the universe is testing us. We need a happier song I think."

Gavin just smiled but it didn't reach his eyes like it did before, one hand steady on the wheel, the other reaching over to grab my thigh possessively. I can't wait to be his forever.

**14 years ago**

This day could not be going any more perfect. My dress is exquisite, my hair is put together just how I imagined, and my makeup is absolutely flawless. The lace clung to my skin just right, the satin skirt swirled like a dream, and my lipstick hadn't smudged even though I kept biting down on my nerves. I knew everything going on outside the Bridal suite was going to plan because my mother or maid of honor, Alisha, had not come to talk to me. If anything was amiss, they were obviously able to handle it.

I sit at a white vanity with a broad mirror framed in glowing bulbs, the kind of light that flatters every angle. My long, pale blonde hair is swept into a low bun, woven with intricate braids that fold together like art. A few soft strands slip free to frame my face—messy, but in the deliberate, elegant way stylists seem to perfect.

My skin carries a warm glow from a spray tan, turning what is usually fair into a soft golden hue, like I've just returned from a week in the sun. My body is slim, delicate even, but healthy—toned in the subtle way that comes from movement and care, not vanity. My eyes are shaded in smoky blacks that make the emerald green shine, and my lashes sweep upward so high they nearly brush my brows. The gown draped over me is white with a hint of black lace peeking from the underskirt, traditional with just the right edge.

I don't think I've ever looked so beautiful.

In about 10 minutes, everyone would be seated in the little chapel just down the beach from where we had gotten engaged, Gavin and the priest are up there waiting for me. My dad is here now, waiting with me in the bridal suite until it's time to walk down the aisle, looking as impassive as ever. His suit was pressed, his hands folded behind his back, but the air around him carried a heaviness I didn't understand.

"Are ye sure dis is what ye want, me sweet Surry?" My dad asked, his voice low and steady.

Never once in the last year had he asked me if I was making the right decision. So this made me nervous. Was he having doubts?

"Papa, I am very excited to spend the rest of my life as Gavin's wife. Mrs. Gavin Kelly. Doesn't that sound so nice?" I was thrilled, and I think I overdid it to compensate for the nerves I was feeling at my dad ruining my perfectly smooth morning.

"Aye, me sweet Surry. Dat sounds beautiful, so it does. But ye remember dis—yer mam an' I'll always be here for ye, any time at all. Do ye understand me, girl?"

Okay, now I was definitely nervous. His eyes looked softer than usual, almost pleading, and that scared me more than if he'd been angry. I don't think in my twenty one years of life has he ever looked at me like this. I stop looking in the mirror and turn in my chair to face him.
"What is going on, Papa?"

"Dere's somethin' I should've told ye long ago. Somethin' I kept back. But now, on dis day, ye must know it, for it'll shape yer whole future."

My inner monologue was going haywire. I cannot believe he is dropping a bomb on me, on my wedding day. Is he a spy? Is he into drugs? Is he leaving my mother? What is happening right now?

"Ah, me sweet Surry, I'm not in private security, no matter what yer mam an' I've told ye all dese years. Ye know well our family runs straight back to Ireland. Yer grandparents brought us here when we were still nothin' but young ones ourselves. For we were promised, betrothed from birth, so we were. All to keep de bloodline pure an' see to it someone'd take up de family business—"

I interrupt, my voice sharper than intended. "Family business? What is the family business? I always thought you were in the security world."

"I'm de one all de Irish men answer to here in de Western States, Surry girl. Mafia. Yer mam's me right hand—me partner in life an' in business both. Tha' security firm, it was always jus' a front—fer what we truly do behind the curtains.. An' now, wit' Samuel steppin' away, wantin' nothin' to do wit' it, ye're de heiress to it all. Soon enough, once ye wed into de Kelly clan, ye'll be tied to Gavin, an' to de work he does for me. He runs one o' de smaller crews under me name."

I am spinning. Is it really hot in here? Why won't someone open the window? The veil on my head felt too heavy, my bodice too tight. To some degree, I am not shocked. I knew whatever he did wasn't normal; he, for one, didn't keep any sort of regular hours. Two, I saw him come home with blood on his cuffs and other parts of him before. Yet to hear it out loud—it was not something I expected. Especially not the head of the mafia! Not today. Why didn't he tell me sooner? Why didn't Gavin tell me?

I can't stop myself from asking, "Why was I not told about this sooner?" My voice sounded much stronger than I felt inside, thankfully.

"'Cause, me sweet Surry, I was hopin' dis day'd never come. I never wanted ye marryin' inside de business, so I didn't. Until ye met Gavin an' started courtin' him, then got yerself engaged, I'd been lookin' at other ways o' findin' an heir. Other avenues, other hands dat could take it on. But now..."

"You should have told me before. What am I going to do now, with all this information?"

Was I spinning? Did I want to be a Mafia wife? THEE Mafia wife? I've only see it in movies, and...well I guess I haven't *only* seen it in movies. My mother made it seem like it was a happy life; I never suspected anything like this from our sweet mother. My father seemed happy. So why couldn't Gavin and I be happy in this life? I am sure he knows what to expect.

My father looks at me like he is about to say something, but I interrupt. "I am going to marry Gavin. He is the love of my life, and he can teach me. I just want to be with him. If that means I join the family business, I will be honored to make you and Mama proud. Thank you for telling me now, instead of afterwards. I suppose." I grimace at that last part, and my dad smirks.

"Whatever ye say, me sweet Surry. Now, let's get ye down de aisle—yer future's waitin' on ye. But mind dis, girl: ye can always come to me, about anythin' at all. Even if ye're movin' off wit' him, ye're never alone. Not while I draw breath."

I look at the clock on the wall and realize I was supposed to be at the altar ten minutes ago. I hate running late, it makes my ADHD feel even more chaotic than normal, and I begin to sweat a bit.

Papa takes my hand and guides me to the door of the Bridal suite, giving my knuckles a brief kiss. He does not let go of my hand from the time we link together in the suite, all the way to the end of the aisle.

The church is beautiful. It is all white and tan, most of the tans coming from wooden beams and pews. The ground is a smooth cobblestone, worn with age. It was probably once red, but now a gentle brown, but still looks clean.

We get to the altar, and the first thing I see is Gavin. He is not looking at me like I hoped he would. He is smiling, yes, but there is something in his eyes. Cold, unreadable, like a shadow under the light. I look at my father, who is glaring at Gavin. He then gives Gavin a look that I can't discern. Instead all I can focus on is the priest as he begins to speak, announcing why we are here and who is giving away the bride. I then shift my eyes toward Gavin who has still not looked into my eyes yet.

Gavin gives a curt nod and takes my arm, a little forcefully, from my father. Once my hand is in Gavin's, his eyes soften just a touch. We turn to listen to the priest as he continues on with the ceremony.

"Dearly beloved, we are gathered here today in the sight of God and these witnesses to join this man and this woman in holy matrimony. It is a sacred bond, not to be entered into lightly, but with reverence and devotion."

Gavin squeezes my hand tightly, almost too tightly. I manage a small smile, though my nerves flicker under the weight of his grip.

The priest's words fade into the background, his blessing echoing through the church as Gavin's grip tightens around my hand. He looks at me then, his eyes almost soft, though the iron beneath never wavers.

When it's time for the vows, Gavin doesn't repeat the priest's words. Instead, his voice carries through the silence, steady and commanding:

"From this day forward, you'll be where I say, when I say. You'll not speak unless given leave, and you'll follow my rules without question. Nod if you understand, and accept me as your husband."

The room doesn't flinch–not here, not among these men and women who know what power looks like. To them, it sounds like devotion, strength, tradition.

My throat tightens, but I nod. The priest accepts it as though it were holy. Gavin's mouth tilts in satisfaction before he slides the ring onto my finger.

My eyes have gone wide, but the priest doesn't seem to notice, or at least he doesn't care. A shiver runs down my spine and just when I am about to turn to look at my father, Gavin squeezes my hand so hard I am shocked I don't hear my bones crack. I give a small nod as tears run down my face.

"Good, now act like you are the happiest bride in the world, marrying the love of your life. Because that is what I am still, am I not?"

I turn to look at him, really look at him. I give a flat smile, and another nod. I always thought your wedding day was supposed to be the happiest day of your life. Why did mine feel like the beginning of a nightmare? I then begin to repeat the vows the priest has asked me to.

### 12 years ago

"Gavin! Stop! It hurts, please stop!" I scream, and I scream, and I scream. The hits he gives to my stomach, my legs, my back. They are all I feel anymore.

"You will listen, you will shut up, and you will do as you're told. Now, are you going to give me the child I need to solidify this union with your family, or must I force it?"

I don't understand. I am not preventing any pregnancy. I have never been on birth control. I track my cycle with several apps and test strips, even taking my temperature every morning. I eat as though I am pregnant already to ensure that I never mess it up if I do get pregnant. The supplements I take are expensive and endless. "I am doing my best, I don't know what you want!"

At that, he rips my arm up, pulling me to a sort of stand where my legs are not supporting me, only my arm in his grip is. He spins me around, takes his hand, and places it on the back of my head. He forces my face into the bed, and with the other hand, pulls down my pants and underwear. When I feel him thrust into me, I cry out.

He grunts into my ear, "You will give me a son, and you will take it every day until you do so. This is how I expect to find you when I get home from now on. Naked, face down, and bared open to me. Do you understand?"

But I can't breathe. I can't answer. He grips my hair with his fist and yanks my head backwards, all the while still ramming into me with force that is unnecessary. I am half his size. What does he think I am going to do?

"I understand," I answer in a whisper so quiet, even I

can barely hear it, because I know that is what he is looking for.

He shoves my head back down and nearly suffocates me until he empties himself inside me. He lets me fall to the ground, tucks himself back inside his pants, and kicks me in the side.

I hunch over and cry into my arms, hoping he will just leave. The beatings started a few months after the wedding. So did whatever this sex was called. I know it wasn't love. He only needed me for a broodmare. I hear the door click shut, and I stay huddled in my little ball for a while, hoping that I will wake up from this never-ending nightmare.

### 11 Years Ago

Another year later, and still this has not ended. Morning and night, he came. Morning and night, I lay there and took it. A room stripped of everything—bed, dresser, mirror, bathroom—nothing else. My world shrank to four walls and a door that only opened for him.

For the first few months after we were married, we stayed in the same bedroom, as a normal married couple would do. But after failing several times to get or stay pregnant, I was removed from his room as he decided I wasn't good enough to stay with him. Now I stay in an empty room, it is even more depressing. Morning and night, I stay in this room, being used as he sees fit.

Outside of that, I don't see him anymore. Today had been a good day. Bleach on my hands from scrubbing the oven, the quiet hum of the fridge, the smell of soap. Alone. For a moment, I felt almost human. I had already prepped meals to feed us for the week, deep-cleaned the kitchen and living room, ensuring the entire house was spotless. Outside of bearing children, that is my only other job, according to Gavin. So when he barges into the kitchen in the middle of the day with some of his goons, I am shocked by the intrusion into what is normally my alone time.

They had walked in on me cleaning the oven on my

hands and knees with a scrub brush and some soap. I remained sitting on the floor, lowering my eyes and being as submissive as possible.

"I have had enough of you, you fucking cunt. You won't give me an heir, so I am done playing games and waiting on you."

"No—please, Gavin, don't say that. I'm trying, I swear I am. I can go back to the doctor, I'll do whatever they say. Just... don't leave me." The words spill out before I can stop them, fear flooding me, because I know when he says he's done, it never ends well. "No, you stupid bitch. I am not giving you up. How do you think I will take over the entire Western region if I don't stay married to you? Your father will never give it to me if you aren't my wife." I am in shock, completely appalled by what he is saying to me. He never really loved me, did he?

"Instead, I am going to have you filled with cock all day and night to ensure that you don't forget your most important job."

I slowly stand and begin backing away, around the island and toward the back door. I don't know what he means by this. But before I am able to grab the door handle and escape, his goons grab me and throw me onto the floor. Gavin walks up and kneels behind me, removing his knife slowly from his pocket and unfolding it. The creak of the metal raking down my already frayed nerves. He places the knife between my skin and pants, slicing down. The knife is sharp, and the side that touches my skin burns as he cuts into my skin.

I begin to scream, thrash, and pull my arms away from them, but no matter how hard I do, they don't let go. He shoves me onto the floor and straddles me from behind and I hear the belt he was wearing slip through the loops and the zipper of his jeans come down before he is entering me swiftly and painfully. It is made worse by his men holding me down, arms and legs, watching me suffer.

When he finally grunts his finish and gets off, I am thankful it is over. Thinking that he wanted to make a point that he is in charge and always will be. I feel two hands pull me up by my upper arms, and I am sagging between them. My feet and shins drag across the floor and my head hangs heavy down toward my chest as they move me over to the living room.

"Wha-t are you doing?" I ask, but no one answers me. "Gavin, please stop. Please. I can do better next time!" My voice turns into a shrill scream toward the end and I begin to sob.

"Okay, Neil, your turn." I freeze. My breath halts on

my lips. I second-guess that's what was said until Gavin is grabbing my arm, shoving it behind my back and up toward my shoulder, nearly breaking my arm. Then I feel someone behind me.

When Neil enters my body, my soul leaves me just as suddenly. No. Not now. If I can just... his hand—knife—burning my skin. I can't breathe. I cannot believe this is what I was meant to do. I cannot believe this is what being in the *family business* was supposed to mean. I cannot believe this was what my life's purpose is, to be raped by my husband's men.

He thrusts into me so violently that if Gavin and the other man weren't pinning me down, I would be sliding across the carpet. Regardless, I am sure I will have a rug burn everywhere that my skin touches the floor. Once Neil is done, I feel his body replaced by another, and then another, continuing on until long after the point I gave up counting.

As they all continue to have their turns, Gavin takes off more and more of my clothing. The carpet was hot and made me sweat, scratching my skin to a degree of pain I wasn't aware was possible. Someone's shoe squeaked. My hair stuck to my face with sweat. I tried to swallow, but my throat was dry as chalk.

Finally, the thrusting ended when several women walked in the door, dressed in almost nothing. The one on the left is tall, with olive skin and slightly slanted eyes. Her makeup is dark and smudged, her long dark hair falling pin straight to where her mini skirt sits on her waist, if that is what you can call it. Her top is a bandanna, a literal bandanna, that is tied around her, and she has heels on that cause her to be probably six feet tall, but it's hard to say from where I am lying on the floor. The one next to her is dressed nearly the same, skin tone maybe a bit lighter, and her bandanna is pink instead of red like her friend's. I can smell the overwhelming scent of their floral perfume from where I am pinned down.

They begin to panic, seeing me lying on the floor and bleeding, fully undressed, with multiple men surrounding me. The one in the red screams and begins to back away, and the one in the pink holds up her phone and snaps a picture, made obvious by the shutter sound, before they both run out the door. I am not sure what she is planning on doing with the picture, but at this point, who cares? It's the least of my concerns. Gavin grabs my hair at the root and begins to drag me across the house and shoves me into my room, leaving me there to rot.

That is, until I hear sirens outside. Why are the cops here? Those girls that ran out must have called them. I hear a struggle outside, but my door is locked from the outside, and I can't go and see, so I just listen while I wait.

Soon, I hear a voice on the other side calling "is there a woman here? Do you need help?" I begin banging on the door. This is it. My chance to escape this hell that was supposed to be my fairytale.

After a moment, I hear him say "stand back," and I do as he says, sitting on my bed in nothing but an oversized t-shirt I found on my floor, blood and cum still all over my legs. I had just been dragging myself to the shower to wash it off when I heard the sirens. I am thankful I didn't get that far, because I may not have heard the officer. The door bangs open, splintering at the frame, and the officer looks me over before reaching to his shoulder and speaking into his radio.

"10-23, found her. I need EMS, Code 3." Then he looks at me again and puts his hands in the air, palms outward.

He takes one step toward me. "We received a call that a woman needed help here." He glances down and sees the blood streaming down my bare legs. "Is that you?"

I nod, unable to form words. I don't know if I can trust this. If this is really a cop, or a figment of my imagination. I can't believe those women called the police. I am so incredibly thankful, but I wouldn't have blamed them if they had high-tailed it and simply never looked back. It doesn't seem like it was something those types of women would do.

"What's your name?" He asks me. But I simply cannot speak. I just shake my head, and silent tears begin to pour out of my eyes. "Okay, that's okay. Do you want me to call someone? Your husband?" He must have noticed my ring.

I shake my head and speak for the first time. "C-can I ca-ll my m-mom?" My voice is shaking.

He hands me his cell phone, and I punch in the numbers that my muscle memory thankfully knows, her voice flowing through the speaker after only one ring. A damn inside of me breaks as she speaks, sobs wrenching free from deep inside of me. It takes everything I possess to squeeze out the smalled of words. "M-m-mom. It's S-s-surry, I need help."

"Is that your name, Surry?" The officer asks, and I nod, holding the phone with my frantic mother on the other end out to him. He puts it to his ear just as an EMS crew walks into my room. I see the officer put his hand on the chest of the male medic, but he allows the woman to walk into my room. She nods at him, something flashing on her face before she looks back at me.

"Hi, honey," she greets me in a warm, slow, low tone. "My name is Elise. I am here to help you. Can you tell me what happened?" I shake my head, and I see her do a once-over of my body with her eyes. "Can I get you to come with me into the ambulance?" I don't answer. I see the officer lean over and whisper something to her.

"Okay, honey, Officer Martin here says he will come in the ambulance with you if you would like. Just you, him, and myself. Would that be okay?" I nod. I still can't tell if this is real. But if not, it is at least a nice figment of my imagination and an oddly comforting thing that an officer will still be around.

"Okay, let me get you a blanket, and we will take you to the hospital to get you checked out."

I nod again, and she takes a few slow steps toward me, holding up something I didn't notice before. She stops before me and places a blanket around my shoulders, and then hooks her arm around my shoulders to keep it wrapped around me. We make our way out of the house and to the ambulance, and just as promised, it's just me, Elise, and Officer Martin. None of us speak. Elise starts my work up–blood pressure, pulse ox, and temp. She asks if she can look under my shirt, but I just close my eyes, answering her with my silence.

When we arrive at the hospital's Emergency Department bay, I can hear someone screaming in a heavy Irish accent, using words that are old Gaelic, which she only uses when she is top-level furious. I know it's my mom. My eyes go wide as I search for her. Officer Martin obviously hears it, since he also has ears, and looks at me.

"I will go get your mom, Surry. She will be back with you as soon as possible, okay?" I nod again and speak to him finally. "Thank you." It's all I can manage, and it's barely above a whisper.

He smiles at me, and goes to pat my hand, but changes his mind mid-reach, before he stands up and leaves the ambulance.

"Okay, honey, we have to wheel you into the ED on the bed. Will that be okay? I do need help from my co-worker. His name is Chase and he is very kind. He has a wife and two little girls at home. I promise he won't touch you." I nod, because what other choice do I have?

Chase, I presume, walks up to the back of the ambulance and stands there waiting for Elise. She hops out and tells him that I agreed to be wheeled out, but that he wasn't to touch me. He looked sad, then faced me.

"Hi, Surry, I'm Chase Montgomery. I will be helping Elise take the bed out, but I promise, unless you fall out, I won't be touching you. Okay?" I again nod. He and Elise pull out the stretcher out, the wheels clattering as they lower me to the ground. Once steady, they start wheeling me toward the hospital doors–but not before Elise takes my hand and gives it a reassuring squeeze. I look at her and my eyes fill with tears once again. I didn't know I was capable of creating any more.

Once inside, my mother and sister race over to me with Officer Martin hot on their heels, as they begin shouting at everyone around to help me. They were frantically asking what happened, and then incomprehensible words started to come out of their mouths, but my ears began a ringing that was so loud I couldn't hear. That was, until it all went black.

It is in the hospital that I learn I was pregnant, again. The nurses ask me what happened. But I don't answer. The doctor, as well as the police, they all ask. I don't want to be hurt anymore. If they send me home, and Gavin learns I talked? My life would be over, or just somehow more impossibly miserable.

A baby. Why? Why is this happening? He finally got what he wanted, only to cause a forced miscarriage with the gang rape I just endured. Well, that is, until the doctor said words that I will never forget.

My mother and sister got to the room and listened to the doctor tell them what happened from the clipboard in his hand, and then he exits to leave me with my mother and sister. I tell them everything. They're both sobbing, and promise I will never return. I will never have to see his face again.

I let out a heaving sob of breath and face my mother before closing my eyes. Willing it all to vanish.

Present Day

The smell of saltwater drifts in through the cracked balcony door, mingling with the faint aroma of last night's pizza. Seattle mornings always carry a kind of damp hush, the streets below glistening from the rain that never really ends. From my spot at the counter, I drum my fingers against the black marble, its cold polish grounding me. My father insisted on the marble —"durable, timeless, Irish stone"—as though the apartment was meant to last centuries.

It's a beautiful kitchen. Spacious, open, tall windows letting in just enough gray light to make the place moody, cinematic. But the illusion is ruined when I see it.

Underwear. In the sink. *Again*.

"RICHIE!" My voice ricochets off the walls, sharp enough to wake the dead. Or at least the idiot who left his boxers next to yesterday's dirty dishes.

Heavy footsteps thud down the hall, and moments later, Richie appears, hair sticking up, tattoos spilling across his bare arms, a smirk already tugging at his mouth. He's six foot two and full of trouble and charm, a Greek god if a Greek god wore shorts that left nothing to the imagination and had gauged ears the size of a dollar coin.

"What you want, girly pop?" His tone drips with mock innocence.

I jab a finger toward the sink. "Explain that."

Richie leans past me, plucking the offending underwear with two fingers like it's evidence from a crime scene. He twirls them on his index finger, amused and unbothered.

"Oh relax. These aren't mine." He lifts them proudly, like he's presenting a trophy. "They're Tommy's."

"Tommy doesn't live here," I snap.

"Details." He waves his hand flippantly and saunters off, swinging the boxers like a flag of victory before throwing them over his shoulder proudly.

I pinch the bridge of my nose and close my eyes, stifling a laugh. Living with Richie is like living with a chaotic older brother—if that brother also worked out six days a week, collected tattoos like candy, and had zero shame.

"Besides, babe," he calls over his shoulder, "if they were mine, you'd know. Silk, not cotton."

"Too much information!" I yell, but my laugh betrays me.

When I turn back, Hazel is sliding onto a stool at the bar, mason jar in hand. She's the complete opposite of Richie. Tiny, soft-featured, cardigan energy wrapped in five feet of kindness. Her hands and arms are smudged with ink stains from sketching designs, hair tucked into a messy knot. Always glowing, even while sipping what looks suspiciously like liquefied lawn clippings.

"You should really eat actual food sometime, Surry," she says, eyeing the pizza box I've already opened. "That stuff doesn't count."

I press a finger against her lips, shushing her dramatically. "Shhh. Don't ruin this for me."

She rolls her big brown eyes but giggles, swatting at my hand.

"Just because you don't want it to be true," comes another voice, rich and teasing, "doesn't make it not true."

Alisha strides in, phone in hand, hair already perfect. Where Hazel is quiet sweetness, Alisha commands the room without trying. My rock since childhood, my sister. Not by blood, but in every way that matters. She plants herself against the counter with the ease of a queen taking her throne.

"You're officially thirty-five, love," she says smugly.

I groan. "RICHIE, they're bullying me again!"

A laugh booms from down the hall. "You are old, babe. Wear it with pride!"

I flip him off—whether he can see me or not doesn't matter—and turn my accusatory glare back to Hazel and Alisha. Hazel sips her juice serenely; Alisha smirks over her phone. My chest aches suddenly, sharp and sweet. They don't even realize how much I owe them.

The coffee maker hisses and sputters its last drop into my mug, and I close my eyes at the smell, grateful for the small mercies of caffeine and chosen family.

Hazel sets down her juice, and my gaze lingers on her. She's beautiful in the quiet way—freckles scattered across her nose, lips soft and unpainted eyes that laugh even when she doesn't. She doesn't know it, though. She brushes off compliments like they're jokes, laughs when someone calls her pretty. She has no idea that her presence saved me the day we met.

Years ago, Alisha, Richie, and I wandered into Tattoos On The Bay on a whim. Young, reckless, searching for something we couldn't name. Hazel was the artist who took us back, her laugh contagious, her voice steady. We ended up with matching stars tattooed on our big toes. Dumb, random, perfect. Hazel thought it was so hilarious that she tattooed one on herself, too. That single stupid moment stitched her into our lives forever.

Alisha and I go back even further. Childhood summers, scraped knees, whispered secrets. Her dad worked for mine, so we grew up glued together. She has always been the one who saw me clearly—through the smiles, the silence, the lies. During my marriage, when I wasn't allowed to talk to her, she knew something was wrong. She fought for me even when no one else listened. The day I landed in the hospital, broken, she stormed in and never left my side. My family already loved her, but that day she became more than my best friend—she entered the family as one of our own.

And Richie. God, Richie. Our glittering storm. Tenth-grade gym class, striding across the gym floor, announcing to the world that he was gay. No hesitation. No shame. Just bold, beautiful truth. We didn't know it then, but his bravery gave us all permission to be more ourselves. We claimed him immediately. He's been ours ever since.

So when Hazel needed a place to stay after life tilted sideways, it wasn't even a question. My father, in his security-obsessed way, built this apartment complex for us after I left Gavin, making sure only Irish families lived here under his watch. Everyone knows the Mafia owns the building, but with rent this cheap and security this tight, no one complains.

Four bedrooms. Four best friends. Four broken souls stitched into something whole.

I sip my coffee, the warmth grounding me, and hum as I stir in cream, sugar, and a dollop of cold foam. When I turn back, Hazel and Alisha are watching me expectantly.

"Sorry," I laugh. "Got lost in my brain. What did you say?"

Hazel perks up. "Oh, right—I have to go into the shop today. Outlining a sleeve for one of our regulars. He's on this mission to get tattooed by every one of us. So we each called an appendage. Juniper called the fifth one."

She wiggles her brows, dead serious.

I nearly spit out my coffee. "GROSS!"

We all scream-laugh, stomachs aching.

"Why would she tattoo his dick?" I manage between gasps.

"Because it's Juniper," Hazel says with a shrug.

And really—that's all the explanation needed. Juniper, the fiery redhead who owns the shop, curses like a sailor and surrounds herself with men who look like they stepped out of magazines. Every time I'm there, temptation flirts with me in the form of jawlines, tattoos, and leather jackets. I'd be lying if I said I hadn't thought about letting one of them ruin me for a night. Just once.

Alisha raises her brows at me knowingly, like she can read my thoughts. She probably can.

"Well," she says, pushing off the counter with a smirk, "I don't have anything to do today. What about you, Surry?"

I sip my coffee and sigh. "I've got filming to do. A new product came in. Need to record some ads."

Hazel groans dramatically. "Ugh, influencer life. So hard," she says with mock annoyance.

"Hey," I shoot back, grinning, "coffee, content, and chaos. That's the job description."

"Okay," Alisha claps her hands together like a general. "Then let's all go get ready. If we're wasting time, we're doing it hot."

We peel off into our rooms, each of us drifting into our little corners of the apartment to change. It's muscle memory now, the way we split up only to come back together again. Like satellites, orbiting our own small worlds, always drawn back into the same gravity.

My closet greets me like an old friend, the racks heavy with blacks, greys, and the occasional muted jewel tone hiding like a secret. Compared to Alisha's closet—an explosion of color, sequins, silk, textures that scream confidence—mine looks like it is in mourning. Richie's wardrobe is even louder, packed with neon gym shorts, glittering accessories, and floral shirts that cling to every inch of his carved chest. Hazel falls somewhere in between, a balance of cozy sweaters and edgy pieces smudged with ink stains from work.

But me? I've always felt safest in shadow. Black is armor. A language that says, *don't look too closely. Don't see what I don't want you to.*

I pull on ripped black jeans, a fitted crop top, and my high-top chucks—comfortable, easy, familiar. A sliver of tattooed skin flashes at my stomach when I move, but even that feels like a rebellion against the years Gavin tried to erase me. My jacket waits for me on the chair, leather and worn, soft at the edges, a gray hood stitched in. It smells faintly of smoke and rain. My life distilled into fabric.

I glance in the mirror, and for a second, my own reflection startles me. Tattoos bloom across my skin like armor, color and blackwork twining together, covering what they can. Every piece chosen carefully, deliberately, until the story of my survival became something beautiful, something no one could take from me. Only one scar remains uncovered, the one slashing from my eyebrow into my hairline. A souvenir Gavin carved into me. I've tried fading it, tried creams and laser treatments, but it lingers—faint, but stubborn. I can hide everything else. Not this.

*The kitchen smells like butter and frying potatoes, the kind of heavy warmth that sticks to the air and clings to the walls. I set the last plate down on the counter, my hands trembling a little with nerves but also pride. I've spent hours perfecting this—boxty with rashers and cabbage, just like the recipe I begged from Mama. The potatoes are golden, the cabbage tender, the meat crisp. It looks perfect. I want it to be perfect for him.*

*I balance the plate carefully in my hands and carry it toward the table where Gavin sits waiting, his expression already impatient. My heart hammers, but I force a smile. "I made something special tonight. It's one of my family's favorites. Thought you'd—"*

*The edge of the plate slips. My fingers lose their grip. Time slows as porcelain crashes against the hardwood, shattering into white shards. Food splatters across the floor, sauce staining Gavin's trousers and dripping onto his polished shoes. My breath catches in my throat, cold terror spreading through me before the sound even fades.*

*Silence. Then the scrape of his chair against the floor. He rises slowly, deliberately, his jaw tight. My words tumble out in a panic. "I—I'm so sorry, Gavin. I'll clean it up, you can have my plate—please, it was an accident."*

*His eyes are sharp and cold. He crouches, not to help, but to pluck a jagged shard from the wreckage. He turns it over in his hand, watching the light glint along the broken edge, and then his gaze snaps back to me.*

*"Accidents," he says softly, almost a whisper, "are lessons."*

*He moves faster than I can recoil. His hand fists in my hair, yanking my head back, and before I can scream, the shard bites across my temple, carving up through my brow and into my hairline. Fire explodes under my skin. I taste blood before I even feel it spilling warm down my cheek. My eye goes blind as blood flows down into it, causing me to scream. My body jerks, but he holds me still, his lips brushing my ear as his voice drops into something dark and final.*

*"Next time, maybe you'll think before you fuck up again." He licks the blood from my cheek, then runs his tongue along his now blood stained lips. His eyes flashing something dangerous.*

*He shoves me away from him and I collapse to the floor among the shards, clutching my face as the blood runs between my fingers. Gavin sits back down at the table like nothing has happened, calmly wiping sauce from his shoes, while I tremble in the ruins of the meal I'd been so proud to make.*

I drag myself out of the memory with a sharp breath, my pulse racing as though it just happened. My scar stares back at me in the mirror—faint, but permanent. A reminder carved into me, no matter how many tattoos I build around it. *Accidents are lessons.*

I continue getting ready, running a hand through my pale hair, white-blonde strands catching the light, and my emerald eyes stare back, too sharp, too haunted. The mirror doesn't lie. Some days, I still see a ghost.

I shake myself loose, grab my lotion, and smooth it across the ink that covers me, ritualistically. Taking care of what once felt like ruin. One small way of reclaiming this body.

When I'm dressed and ready, I make my way to the bathroom slowly. Bathroom time is sacred time. It's not just a space with mirrors and counters and tile—it's a chapel, a confessional, a therapy session wrapped in steam and hair products. In this room, everything is allowed. Everything is heard.

The three of them are already there, clustered in our familiar chaos. Alisha's perched on the counter in leggings and a tank top, her hair twisted into rollers, already scrolling TikTok with one hand while sipping coffee with the other. Hazel's sitting cross-legged on the floor with her makeup bag spilled out like treasure, carefully blending foundation into her skin, her concentration absolute. Richie—God bless him—is shirtless, fussing with his eyebrows in the mirror like they're a work of art, humming Britney under his breath.

I linger in the doorway for a moment, taking it in. These people. My people. This bathroom has heard every secret we were too afraid to tell anyone else.

Alisha's came first. Her voice shook when she finally admitted what her uncle had done, words dragging out of her throat like they'd been buried under rocks for years. She couldn't even look at us, her eyes fixed on the tile as she confessed how he stole her safety long before she even knew how to name it. She told us about the nightmares, how she still sometimes wakes gasping with phantom terror in her chest, her body remembering what her mind tries so hard to forget. We cried with her that night, holding her between the counters and the mirror, promising her she wasn't broken, even if the world had tried to make her feel that way.

Hazel's confession came later, softer but no less jagged. She told us how her father's hands left bruises, but it was his words that cut the deepest. How he could take her apart without lifting a finger, how his disappointment carved holes into her that she still tries to fill with ink. She admitted that even now, every time she finishes a tattoo, a tiny voice in the back of her mind whispers that it's not good enough, that she's not good enough. She whispered all this while twisting her hands in her lap, her eyes shimmering, and for once, we couldn't fix it with jokes. We just sat with her in the silence, letting her know she wasn't alone anymore.

And then Richie. Loud, unapologetic Richie, who somehow still carries the weight of scars no one can see. He told us about the conversion camp his parents forced him into between ninth and tenth grade—how the counselors preached shame like scripture, how they tried to scrub the truth out of him with prayers and punishment. He said he can still smell the pine needles from the woods that surrounded the camp, still hear the way his own sobs echoed in the thin mattress at night. He said they told him he was broken, and he believed it for too long. But then he looked up at us—smirking through tears—and said he doesn't believe it anymore. That we are the proof he was never broken in the first place. We all cried happy tears that night. For healing. For us. For our little chosen family.

And then there was me. My turn. I told them everything Gavin had done, every bruise, every scar, every way he broke me down until I thought there was nothing left. I spoke the words I had never dared to say out loud—that the man I had married had treated me like property, like a body to control, like a cage to keep his power in. I told them about the nights I begged him to stop, about the mornings I could barely get out of bed, about how I learned to smile through bloodied lips so no one would ask questions. Alisha had known some of it, suspected more, but even she hadn't known the full truth until that night. I thought they'd look at me differently once they knew. Instead, they held me, cried with me, and reminded me that what he did was not who I am. That I was still here, and that mattered.

We made this space holy. A sanctuary in a world that doesn't give women, queer kids, or survivors safe places. This is ours.

I move into the room, sliding into my spot by the sink, and the chatter dips for a moment before picking up again. Hazel's telling Alisha about the client today, the one who wants each of them to tattoo him. Alisha makes a crude joke that has Hazel blushing so hard she nearly drops her beauty blender. Richie cackles, tossing his head back dramatically.

I laugh with them, but my chest aches, my mind snagging on the words still burning a hole in my pocket. This was supposed to be where we bare it all-our sacred room of redemption-but I'm clinging to a secret. A text. Not just any text, but one from him. From Gavin. After years of silence, his name alone feels like a wound reopening, tearing through layers of scar tissue that I had spent years healing. I had rebuilt myself, reclaimed my life, survived what he thought would kill me. His words slithered through me like poison last night, dragging nightmares back into my sleep. I thought I was free. But monsters don't stay buried forever.

I know I need to tell them. Not just for me—for them. For their safety. If Gavin is back, he'll use anyone he can to get to me. The thought makes bile rise in my throat.

I stare at myself in the mirror, watching my friends in the reflection. Hazel's focused. Alisha's confident. Richie's exuberant. They're light. They're *my* light. I can't bring Gavin's shadow into this space. But if I don't, it'll creep in anyway.

I open my mouth to speak—

—and before I can utter a syllable Hazel shrieks, the sound sharp and panicked. My heart lurches, and I whip around, adrenaline spiking.

Her phone is clutched in her hands, her face going pale.

"Oh my God, guys!" she gasps. "June just texted." She looks up, eyes wide with disbelief. "The shop was BLOWN UP."

*RING RING RING*

The sound of my phone slices through the dark, loud enough to rattle my skull. I groan, roll over, and squint at the screen. Juniper.

Shit.

She doesn't call me before nine. Ever. Says I'm "as foul as a three-legged donkey" in the mornings. If she's calling now, it's bad.

I swipe and put it to my ear. "Hello?"

Her voice comes fast, panicked. "BRENDEN. The shop. It's wrecked." Then a sob cracks her words apart.

Juniper doesn't cry. Not anymore. Not since Mikey.

Mikey was all bluster and cheap leather jackets, thought he was the king of his little street gang. Not to mention, the fucker thought women were punching bags. By the time she ran into me—literally—she was half-blind from the last beating. She tried to lie, her story changing several times–it was an accident, I'm clumsy, he didn't mean to–but one look at her busted face and I knew. An accident with fists doesn't leave someone's face looking like that. I dragged her to Corver and Josh, sat her down, and didn't let her leave until she talked. Names, drugs, weapons. Everything. Needless to say, Mikey never saw another sunrise.

She used the money that came out of that mess to open her dream—Tattoos On The Bay. She lived for that place. If someone's gone after it, I'll burn them to the ground.

"What happened? You okay? What about the girls?" I'm already hauling jeans up, grabbing a white t-shirt, and my jacket.

"I think it happened after Hazel left. Around two this morning. I just got here. Brenden, everything's splintered and charred—windows, furniture, and there is a large spray paint something on the wall. It's ruined. It literally looks like a bomb went off, but I mean that for real."

My stomach knots. Not Mikey's crew. Too much time's passed, and they don't have the means to get anything big enough to do something like this. No reason for them to circle back. This smells new. Bigger.

"Go to your car. Park a few blocks away. Don't go back in. I'll be there in ten."

I hang up, grab my Glock, and pull my leather jacket over it so that it is covered. Not fashion—utility. Steel blades and weapons are neatly hidden in every pocket. I brush my teeth fast, tie my hair back low. It's grown darker this winter, heavy brown instead of sun-lightened. Doesn't matter. I'm moving.

I pound on Joshua's room, but it's empty as I open to check when he doesn't answer. Figures. Corver's already entering the hall when I go to bang on his door, black jeans and jacket matching mine.

"Josh woke me. Said something about June. Didn't explain."

I grunt. That's Josh. Always halfway gone before you get the story. I think he takes shoot first, ask questions later a little too seriously.

He's in the kitchen, lacing his combat boots with sharp, practiced pulls, before grabbing his helmet and tucking it under his arm. "Did you hear from June?" He asks as he heads toward the door, ready to go. "I'm heading out."

"Take a car," I cut him off. "Not the bike. We might need to move her. A bike is too dangerous if we have people on our backs."

He doesn't argue—just slams the helmet down, grabs the Lotus keys, and storms out. My teeth grind. The Lotus Evora is fast, sure. But if he dings it, I'll kill him myself.

Corver and I pull on our boots, the floorboards thudding beneath us, and snatch the keys to the 5500 utility truck. Time to move.

We make it downstairs, and we watch Josh roar off and damn near laugh at the sight. The kid's got fire—always has—but he's reckless the way a man is reckless when he thinks nothing's fragile enough to break him. Corver slaps the truck's side with an easy hand like it's an old friend.

"This thing'll take lumber or bodies," I say, because we always say that when we grab the 5500. It's a joke. Mostly. "We'd know what fits and what doesn't."

Corver snorts and pops the back open, the canopy lifting with a practiced push. "Depends on the size of the body and the shape of the paperwork."

We both grin, but the grin's flat. There's a long history under that kind of joke—years of hauling timber and trouble. Anytime anyone asks, we always tell them Slater Construction started dumb and honest enough: three kids with calluses and a van, flipping houses, changing kitchens, making a name in the one neighborhood that didn't mind our brand of hard work.

Corver was the kid who could bend a circuit board and teach it to sing. At eighteen, he was already stringing networks and sewing cameras into jobs so tidy you couldn't tell they were there. Josh and I did the heavy lifting. Josh was twenty when we kicked Slater off for real; I was twenty-three and stubborn enough to keep swinging a hammer until the sun set and the last nail held. We did kitchens, we did basements, we did the floor-to-ceiling remodels nobody else wanted. Word spread. People with money liked the way we showed up quietly, did a job, and left their house cleaner than we found it.

Money brings opportunities no one asks for. We were young and hungry, and the doors opened—little ones at first: a back room here, a basement safe there. Then a job on a high-rise and another connected job beside it. The business grew up with us, slow and mean and legal on the books. Slater Construction had invoices and permits, and an office with a nice receptionist. But it had other ledgers too. Corver kept those records smart: contracts that explained nothing to anyone who didn't need to know, shell companies with names that sounded boring on paper and dangerous in practice, that sort of thing.

When I was twenty-five my ma started seeing a new man. She'd always been soft for the wrong ones—no father around, no lessons on how to spot the rot. This one was worse. He hit her, once, then twice, then to the point that her voice stopped sounding like the safe place it used to be. One night the beating didn't stop. She died on the kitchen floor with his hand around her throat. There was no talking, no police that would help. So we did what we had to.

We found him and we ended it. Quick. Clean. No trial. No headlines for our house. After that the lines changed. We got more careful. We got smarter. We watched girls walk into bad situations—June was one—and we broke the men who thought they could do that kind of damage. Word got around. People with the kind of problems that couldn't be solved by lawyers started finding our number. They came with cash and names; they left with nothing but a receipt that said Slater Construction did a remodel.

It kept growing. The legit jobs paid the bills; the other work padded the accounts in ways banks liked to call "discrepancies." We learned how to make the books sing. Corver learned how to make a ghost company look like an LLC that paid taxes. We learned how to move money through Slater's invoices and real estate flips. Now? We're quiet billionaires in suits nobody ever sees except when they need a floor plan or a favor. The cars, the building, the whiskey—yeah, they're signs, but we hide them behind a contractor's license and a smile.

"And we still show up in a truck," Corver says, slapping the tailgate shut. "Because men use hands before they use phones."

It's the truth. Hands still solve most problems. Fingers on triggers, on phones, on tools—different jobs, same muscle memory.

On the drive over, I'd filled Corver in. His laptop's already open on his knees, fingers flying. Tech's his kingdom—cameras, systems, digital paper trails that fool governments. If someone left a trace, he'll find it.

"You thinking Mikey's old crew?" he asks.

"No. Too long has passed. This feels... targeted. Check for leaks. If anyone traced her back to us, I want to know."

"I'll have answers by the time we're there."

"Has this been on the police radar?" I ask. I don't want to have to explain it too much to anyone on the outside. Especially since we don't know exactly who is behind this.

"No, the cops on the payroll made sure to bury it just like they do with anything connected to us. Faulty something or other inside. They took it off the scanner already, I got alerted right before Joshua pounded on my door.

We drive in silence the rest of the way, the truck's engine growling. My gut gets tighter the closer we get.

When we roll up, the Lotus is there, spotless thankfully for him. He would be dead if had fucked it up. Josh is leaning against it, Juniper crushed against his chest. He's got an arm around her waist, rubbing her back while she sobs. Seeing her broken makes my chest ache.

Looking around, the ground is covered in debris. Beams, glass, chairs, random ink bottles, and a few animal skulls that I know were hanging inside the shop. I know, because I hung them up. And they are now twenty feet away from the front door. Or, at least, where the front door used to be.

We'll do what we do. Slater builds. Slater protects. Slater collects. No one ever called us saints, and that's the point.

I am halfway out of the truck when the sound of engines pulling up becomes louder, getting closer to where we are parked. BMWs. Three, no—four of them. They slide in smooth, boxing us in like wolves.

The doors open, and seven men step out in near-perfect sync. Suits pressed, faces marked by old violence. Eyes flat and practiced. Six-two, six-three–still shorter than my six-six stature. But height doesn't mean a thing against men who've already killed. And judging by their stance, their calculated movements, they have definitely killed before.

I slip my Glock out slow, keep it low. Corver does the same.

One steps forward, no weapon in his hands. His voice confirms what my gut already guessed.

"Good mornin', lads. We're here t' look inta de wee... accident dat's befallen dis fine establishment."

Irish. Thick as whiskey.

I square my shoulders. "What exactly can we help you boys with?" My voice stays calm, but I'm ready.

Juniper storms toward them, right past Corver and I, Josh following closely after her, all five feet of fury, wiping her tears and fixing a feral expression on her face. She's got a dagger at her ankle. Won't use it unless she has to, but she's not afraid to. We made sure she knew how to use it well.

"I didn't call anyone," she snaps. "So who the hell are you?"

The Irishman inclines his head, amused. "We know, lass. We're here on orders from Stefan O'Brien. Surry's da'."

The world freezes. Stefan O'Brien. Irish Mafia.

Juniper blinks, stunned. "What does—"

"Dat's not fer me t' say," he cuts her off with a half-smile. "We'd like t' take a look 'round. Collect evidence. Help wit' de rebuild."

Juniper crosses her arms, glare sharp enough to cut steel. "First of all, stop calling me 'lass' or 'ma'am.' My name's Juniper Hall. And I'm not fifty."

His smirk deepens. "Fair enough, Juniper. May we step inside?"

She sweeps an arm toward the shop. "Be my guest. Not like there's anything left to break."

They move toward the shattered doors. Juniper follows right behind, heels clicking, close enough that, yup, I think she did actually just step on his heels. He twitches, but says nothing.

The Irishman glances back. "We've dogs t' sniff fer

accelerants. Lab lads t' swab residue. If dere's danger left behind, we'll find it."

Joshua edges closer to me, phone out, thumbs flying. He's already texting Sam O'Brien, we met him a few years back with a home renovation in Seattle. He wanted a nice remodel, but with some secret rooms to hold weapons and leather. If you catch my drift. Corver mutters something about "footage" and peels off toward the truck, lost in his screens.

I follow Juniper inside. The crunch of glass under our boots sounds like bones breaking in the silence.

When we enter, I am even more stunned. The shop is completely unrecognizable. June was right. It does look like a bomb went off. I think that might have been what actually happened.

The front windows are jagged holes, glass scattered across the floor like ice. Spray paint covers the walls in thick black slashes—words scrawled, threats I don't recognize, symbols that look more ritual than random, almost like Runes. Stations overturned, chairs split, ink bottles smashed and smeared like bloodstains across the tile. The smell of chemicals hangs heavy, sharp, and wrong.

Juniper's hand shakes as she lifts a fallen frame—what's left of one of her first drawings. She presses it to her chest, shoulders trembling. Josh hovers too close, jaw tight, ready to swing at shadows.

The Irishmen fan out, moving as efficiently as soldiers. Which I suppose, they are. Two bring in dogs, sleek and lean, noses pressed to the ground while another snaps pictures. Another crouches near the counter, swabbing what's left of the charred residue. The leader strolls slowly, scanning everything, hands in his pockets like he owns the place, an unbothered king is what Juniper would typically call someone like that and I snort at my own thoughts.

I step closer, my voice low and clipped. "What does this have to do with you?"

He looks at me, eyes sharp, smile thin. "Yer askin' de wrong question, lad. Ye should be askin' what it has t' do wit' her." He jerks his chin toward Juniper—then toward Hazel's name scrawled on the wall in dripping paint.

My stomach drops. Hazel.

Josh's phone buzzes. He glances at the screen, his face hardening. "Sam says this isn't random. His sister's car was torched last night. Threats came through after. This was aimed at her. Juniper and Hazel are collateral damage."

The Irishman hears him and nods once. "Aye. Ye're in deeper dan ye know. Stefan's already movin'. Keep yer eyes open, lads. 'Cause dis... dis is only de beginnin'. Dis is war."

The words hang in the wrecked air, heavy as ash.

Images from old mafia reels flicker through my head–families warring in the shadows, vendettas carried out in alleys and back rooms, blood always spilling where it shouldn't. There's never just one target. Collateral damage follows like smoke after fire. Businesses burn, wives weep, sons inherit grudges older than themselves. I used to watch those films and think they were stories, exaggerated, distant. But standing here, glass still crunching under my boots, it doesn't feel like fiction. It feels like foreshadowing.

And for the first time since I was a twenty five year old kid, I feel the ground shift under me.

Heading down the elevator with Alisha and Hazel to rush over to the tattoo shop, panic tightens in my chest. The text message from last night burns like a brand in my pocket. I keep rehearsing how to tell them, when to tell them, but every version ends with their faces breaking—hurt, betrayed, angry that I kept it from them. But by the time the doors glide open to the underground garage, I've talked myself out of saying anything. I'll just... keep holding it in.

The elevator doors slide open, spilling that harsh glow of fluorescents across the garage floor. For a heartbeat, I think maybe the light's just too bright, maybe tha's why it looks wrong. But as the four of us step out, the silence hits first. No hum of the air system. No dripping pipes. Just...ruin.

The car sits in the center of the garage, or what's left of it. My *car*.

The hot pink Audi RS6, my pride and joy. The present I receive from my dad just two months ago. It isn't a car anymore. It's a crush can, a half-flattened skeleton of metal and glass. The roof's cave in as if something dropped straight form the sky. Every window has exploded outward, glittering shards scattered across the concrete like spilled diamonds. One Tire's complete shredded; the others sag, the rubber split and melted form the pressure. The front half looks...pulverized. Like it was run over by a goddamn tank.

Hazel gasps beside me. "Holy shit. What even—what could've done that?" But I can't barely hear her, let alone see her. What I do hear is the shrill sounding echo reverberating in my brain from the cavernous walls in the garage.

Alisha's hand flies to her mouth. "Was anyone down here?" she whispers, scanning corners as if expecting someone—or something—to still be here.

"No." My voice sounds foreign. Hollow. "I parked it last night. Nobody's been down here since. Or, I wasn't alerted to anyone else, anyways."

Richie crouches by the wreckage, squinting. "The tires didn't burn out. They *burst*. From inside out. That's pressure. Like it got...crushed." He runs his hand along the hood, then pulls back when his fingers come away smeared with a dark oil stain. "Whatever did this wasn't human hands. It was a machine of some kind."

I step closer, glass crunching beneath my boots. The smell of coolant, oil, and something burnt—rubber maybe—hangs thickly in the air clogging my throat. Or maybe those are the tears I haven't let fall. My heart hammers in my chest. Not fear, exactly. Just that sharp, crawling awareness that *someone's been here*. In my space.

Then I see it, somehow untouched by the surrounding debris.

A single sheet of paper lies dead center of the roof, pinned beneath a fragment of the wind shield. The white stark against the mangled metal, the handwriting unmistakably shark and deliberate.

A note. With my name on it.  In handwriting that brings a chill to my spine.

I stare at it for a long moment before moving, as if it might explode if I get too close. The others try to grab me, telling me to stay back. But I can't do nothing. My pulse pounds in my ears as I slide the glass aside and lift the page free.

Up close it's the same. Untouched by the surrounding oil and dust, it had obviously been placed after the damage.

My hand shake as I unfold it.

Once I finish reading it, I snap a photo and fire it off to my dad—Stephan O'Brien, the almighty leader of the Western US Irish Mafia—with nothing but that stupid squirt-gun emoji. The one I always use when I want to say blood without saying blood.

The garage isn't some casual lot. Dad had it built like a bunker—cameras in every corner with overlapping angles, infrared beams that read heat signatures, license-plate readers at the entry, bollards that drop if the code doesn't clear, magnetic locks on the pedestrian doors, key-card gates for vehicle access, PIN pads on the service doors, motion sensors under the soffits, and vibration sensors embedded in the concrete that would scream if somebody tried to jack a car out from under it. There are motion-activated lights, a redundant fiber optic loop for the cameras, and an off-site monitoring service that mirrors everything in real time. Even the elevators have biometric checks to get from the residential level down to the garages. It's all logged–timestamps, who swiped what card, which license plate rolled through at what second. Nothing here is casual. Nothing is easy.

So whoever did this didn't just walk in. To bypass it, you'd need one of a few ugly options: a cloned key-card and a tailgater, a direct physical breach with heavy equipment (and enough time to not trip the seismic sensors), or serious cyber-foo to blind cameras and scrub logs–which means someone with real hacking skills. Or you need someone on the inside to open a door and look the other way. None of those are simple. None are cheap. None are quick. And none are likely unless you have resources, balls, or friends in low places. Which means this wasn't random. This was planned. It was precise. It was personal.

When I look back down at my phone, I see my dad replied. *Five minutes. Go back upstairs. Tell Hazel to stay home.*

He must have already been in the city.

"Dad says head back up. Don't touch a thing. Hazel—he said don't go to work. I am assuming he wants to talk to you about the shop since we heard about it from June already."

Hazel's face drains of any color. "That's not ominous," she mutters, pulling out her phone. She types fast, texting Juniper that she isn't coming—my car was destroyed, and apparently, we're all grounded.

The three of us trade a look, silent, wide-eyed, then hustle back to the elevator. None of us breathes until the doors close.

Upstairs, Alisha makes a beeline for the wine fridge like a soldier to her weapon. She pulls out four bottles and doesn't even bother with glasses. Hands us each our own, opener included, then cracks hers and drinks half in one go. Hazel and I follow suit, collapsing on the couch, gulping down liquid courage. Richie not leaving his spot between the front door and kitchen as he chugs his entire bottle before striding into the kitchen and grabbing four more. Words don't come. Not even curses. Just silence, heavy as the texts from Gavin sitting in my pocket.

I wonder if there's a word stronger than furious. I'll have to Google that.

Now I feel like I do need to tell them. This doesn't just affect me. Not that I ever expected it to only affect me in the long run. It's Juniper and her shop. It's Hazel and her work. It's our garage. It is all of our safety.

"Hey, so I have been meaning to tell you something. I have just been really afraid. Also, I think I have been avoiding it.

But I go–"

*Ding.*

The elevator chimes.

Alisha and Hazel look expectantly at me. "It's my dad I'm sure. I'll get it. Then I can tell all of you at the same time. I need more alcohol though." Hazel gets up and moves toward the kitchen to grab more. For everyone. Third bottle of wine in a row, damn we are going to be drunk before I can even tell them.

"Oh, a stór, yer beautiful car!" Mama's voice breaks the air as she rushes from the elevator, skirts rustling as she half-runs toward me. She knows how much I loved that car, and it's nice to have those feelings validated. I know it's just a car. But, it was something that I loved. A lot.

"Mama," I choke, tears spilling fast. I don't even know what I'm crying for—fear, grief, rage. Maybe all of it.

She gathers me into her arms, whispering, "Sweet girl, we'll sort this."

Behind her, my dad steps in, broad and calm, but his voice carries the weight of command. "Sweet Surry, we need t' talk. But since it seems t' touch all four o' ye, ye'll all stay put." His accent thickens when he's tense. He scans the room seeing the open bottles in our hands. "Fetch s'more bottles, will ye?" He directs at Richie. "We'll be needin' it before this is done."

His guards, Darragh and Finley, linger by the elevator, their faces lit by the glow of their phones. Fingers fly, tapping furiously. Not normal. Not casual.

"Papa, I—" My voice falters. Shame prickles hot. "I have something to add. I should've said it earlier."

He holds up a hand. "We'll get t' it, mo stór. Let me speak first."

He paces, his voice dropping lower. "We checked the garage footage. Wiped clean, as I expected. Finley's workin' on diggin' it back. Darragh's speakin' wit' the others about the note. I assume ye know the hand. The symbol's been altered." His jaw tightens. "Hazel, lass, the shop's been hit as well. Likely 'cause Surry spends so much time there. My men are on it, searchin' fer anythin' left behind. 'Twas the same mark on the wall as the one we found on 'dis letter."

I pull the note out of my pocket and hand it to my dad, glancing at it before I do so. I hadn't noticed the symbol was different until now.

TO MY LOVE, I AM SO SORRY TO WRECK
THIS CAR, AS I SAW HOW HAPPY YOU
WERE WHEN YOU RECEIVED IT. BUT I
WILL BUY YOU A DOZEN MORE WHEN WE
ARE FINALLY REUNITED.

PLEASE DON'T MAKE ME RUIN ANYTHING
ELSE.

NEXT TIME, IT WON'T JUST BE INANIMATE
OBJECTS.

It's his. Gavin's. Always marked with Gort—the two diagonal lines. Life goes on. But now it's changed. Eadhadh. Five straight lines. To conquer.

He intends to conquer his obstacles. His adversaries. Now it's me. Us. My family.

My dad's eyes bore into mine. "Has he contacted ye?"

The truth claws out of me. "He texted me. Last night. I panicked—I didn't know how to tell anyone. I'm sorry."

I hand him my phone, shame burning in my chest. He reads. Mama leans in, Richie hovering, Hazel too. Alisha doesn't. She's staring at me, hurt deep in her eyes. A different kind of wound.

I drain the rest of my wine, slamming the bottle down with a hollow clunk. My hands shake. My breath won't even out. Before I have set it down for the long, Riche is handing me his, I didn't even notice he had walked over. He squeezes my arm and kisses the top of my head before going to the couch and sitting with Alisha.

My mom's voice cuts through, soft but firm. "Ye'll

stay here. Don't leave. Not until we say."

I nod, because what else can I do?

Ding.

The elevator. Darragh and Finley move instantly, weapons drawn, aimed at the door.

A woman screams. A man swears. "Fuck, what the hell, guys?"

"Sorry, sir. Sorry, miss," Darragh mutters in his thick brogue.

Then—"SISSY!" My sister's voice pierces through. Selene barrels into me, knocking me back until my shins touch the couch and I fall back with her on top of me. Alisha piles on top, hugging us both, silent tears cutting down her cheeks. She's angry at me, yes—but she's terrified for me, too. Always has been. Always will be.

Samuel enters behind them, broad-shouldered, steady. "Sorry we're late. Selene had to pack." He smirks when she rolls her eyes.

Then he looks at me. Just one word: "Surry."

The sound of it breaks me. I squeeze out of the group hug and stumble into his arms and cry harder than I have in years, my brother whispering low Gaelic words into my ear, so soft I doubt anyone else hears. Words only meant for me.

Mom joins, wrapping us both, Selene too, then Dad. Hazel and Richie pile in before he cracks a filthy joke about threesomes at the club that makes us laugh through tears. Everyone is used to his quips by now.

Wine flows again when we break apart. Thankfully, we keep a well-stocked liquor cabinet. Selene hands out bottles like communion. For a moment, it almost feels normal.

Until Richie asks, "Okay, so now what? I'll go stir-crazy sittin' here."

My dad clears his throat. "We'll cover bills. Hazel, lass, ye'll not worry about the shop. My men'll see t' it. We'll take three days t' gather intel. Then we'll act. Gavin's made moves. Word is he's taken over the Russians. We'll find out if it makes him stronger—or easier t' burn."

Talking about the Irish mafia and the Russian mafia brings me back to the time I had told everyone in the sacred bathroom about my dad being the head of the Irish. It was a hard conversation, but something they needed to know. To know that I'm not normal.

The memory hits me like cold water.

*The bathroom. Our sanctuary, our confessional. Steam still clung to the mirrors that night, curling around the edges as if the walls themselves were listening. We'd been sitting in our usual spots—Alisha perched on the counter, Hazel cross-legged on the floor with her makeup scattered around her, Richie fussing over his brows in the mirror. All of it the way it is every morning, basically. I'd been leaning against the sink, silent, chewing the inside of my cheek until I finally blurted it out.*

*"My family isn't... normal," my voice shaking in a way that wasn't like me. Their chatter died instantly. Alisha leans forward, brows knitting, Richie frozen mid-pluck, Hazel sets her mascara wand down so slowly you can barely hear the tiny clink against the tile. I tell them about my father. About the O'Briens. About what Mafia meant in real life—not the polished movies, not the glamor, but the weight, the blood, the expectations. My words tangle, heavy and raw, until the silence in the room was louder than anything I'd ever heard.*

Alisha already knew. Her dad works for my dad, so the truth had lived in her house long before I ever admitted it in mine. She kept quiet while I spoke, calm and steady, never once interrupting. When my words faltered, she smoothed them over for me, filling in the blanks I couldn't manage to say out loud. She added how she was connected, filling Richie and Hazel in on her life as well. Her quiet nods, her unshaken presence, told the others this wasn't just some wild confession—it was real. And because she stayed grounded, I did too.

They didn't run. They didn't look at me like a monster. Hazel's lip trembled, Richie muttered, "Well, that explains a lot." But I could see it in their eyes—that shift. They finally understood why I always carried shadows on my back. Why danger followed me like smoke. And for the first time, I let them see me for what I was: the daughter of a king. A kingdom of crime.

I'm brought back to the present by the clap of my brothers hands. Samuel speaks. "What about the Russians? How do you know?"

Papa looks at him gravely. "I sent ye an email. Ye can watch it now if ye like. But be warned, son—it's graphic. Disturbing. Not all o' ye will stomach it. An' I wouldn't blame ye if ye didn't."

Safe here. Safe here. I keep chanting it in my head like a prayer.

"Tell me more about what the connection to Surry is," Juniper presses, arms crossed, her tone sharp enough to cut through the wreckage as we step deeper into what used to be Tattoos On The Bay.

Joshua drifts closer to her side, a silent wall ready to grab and run if shit hits the fan. He's coiled tight, like he's waiting for the first crack of thunder. My gut agrees. This isn't a shop break-in anymore. It's war walking in the front door.

I've heard the name Surry before—Hazel mentioned her, and I'd seen one picture at Sam's house years back. Pretty girl. Sister. Protected. That was all I knew. I never bothered asking more, because Sam O'Brien's family was Sam's business. Now, standing here in the ruins of June's shop, her name's the only one on anyone's lips.

The Irishman clears his throat. Broad shoulders, a suit that actually fits, and a look in his eye that says he's used to walking into blood and walking back out of it.

"Aye, Ms. Hall. First off, de name's Kegan. I work fer Mr. O'Brien. Dere was a threat made agains' Miss Surry dis mornin' as well. We believe de incidents are connected." This guy, Kellan or whatever, is confirming what Joshua heard from Sam.

"We knew that already, man," Joshua cuts in, his voice tight. "Sam O'Brien's already brought me into the loop with the basics. What we want is more detail."

His eyes don't leave Juniper. The second K—Kirian? That's not right. When whatever his name is said threat, she'd pulled out her phone, scrolling like she wasn't even in the room anymore. I know that look—June's not ignoring him, she's building a wall. She does that when something cuts too close, when she doesn't want anyone to see the crack.

"No wonder Hazel texted me saying she couldn't come in," Juniper mutters.

"What'd she say?" Josh asks.

"That Surry's car was demolished in her guarded underground garage," June answers, flat, like she doesn't want to let the weight of that land in the room.

I take over. "Josh, take Juniper home. Full lockdown. I'll stay here with Corver in the truck. June, we'll get this place back on its feet. Just hold tight."

She nods, reluctant. She puts her phone down and looks around the space. A single tear falls over her lashes, spilling down to her cheek. Josh reaches out and wipes it before it can go any farther, and then leads her out toward the Lotus. Corver slides up next to me, arms crossed, his eyes scanning, calculating. He's already halfway inside the data by the time he reaches me. That's how Corver is though: Quiet, lethal, always two steps ahead.

I follow the Irish guy through the shop. My boots crunch on glass that used to be neon signs of tattoo supply brands, windows that lined the walls to the outside, and mirrors that leaned in corners. Two days ago, this place buzzed not just from the sound of the tattoo gun, but with life and loyalty.. June's personality on full display in the most artistic way possible. Now it looks like a bomb went off in a thrift store.

I stop in the middle of it all. My chest tightens. I've been in plenty of wrecked places. Bars after brawls, houses after hits, back alleys after we left bodies cooling. But this? This was a home for June. Her dream. I can see her laughter in the now ruined paint, her fingerprints on every displaced shelf. Now it's not where her heart resides, it's just, ash.

We step over the busted mahogany door that used to guard June's office. I paid for that door myself, heavy as a coffin lid. Now it's on the floor, hinges torn clean.

"Would ye like ta go first, Mr. Slater?"

"How do you know my name?" My voice is sharp before I can stop it.

He smirks, not in arrogance but in confidence.

"'Tis our business ta know. Anyone who's close to the O'Brien's, we keep watch on. She's had a dangerous past, Miss Surry, an' it ain't finished wit' her yet."

"Close to the O'Brien's? But I'm not? We're not?"

"Ah, now, but ye are. Yer brother, Joshua Slater, he speaks wit' the young Mr. O'Brien on da regular. An' Ms. Hall, she's close t' Ms. Surry. So by connection, lads, ye're close t' de family. We know who ye are, what ye do. An' truth be told—we're impressed. Not many can do what ye three do, an' walk away clean."

I let that sink in. They know who we are, who we really are. And what dangerous past? My fists clench. I thought this was about the shop, maybe someone had become ballsy enough running with Mikey's old crew. Or maybe someone had decided to get at us for something we had done, seeing us here regularly. But no. Not even close. Not even to do with June at all by the sounds of it. June is just collateral damage.

"So this isn't random?" I mutter the question. Not knowing what else to say to the guy.

"No, sir. Not random. 'Tis personal. An old enemy crawlin' out o' de grave."

We get into the office and the desk is splintered, drawers kicked in, safe dented but intact. Atop the wreckage, one piece of paper sits dead center of the desk. Too perfect. Too intentional.

I motion to it. The haughty Irishman leans over, visually scans it, takes a photo, then bags it with tweezers like he's done it a hundred times before. He leaves it on the table so I lean over and take a look to see what it says.

MY LOVE, YOU KNOW THAT I WILL GO TO THE ENDS OF THE EARTH IN ORDER TO GET YOU BACK. IT HAS BEEN LONG ENOUGH. COME BACK HOME TO ME. IT IS TIME TO TAKE OVER THE KINGDOM. JUST AS I ALWAYS SAID THAT WE WOULD.

COME NOW $URRY, BEFORE I HAVE TO HURT MORE THAN JUST CARS AND BUILDINGS. ALISHA IS LOOKING BETTER THAN I REMEMBER.

While he works, I let my eyes sweep the room. Juniper's crystals, gone. Hazel's sketches, shredded. Whoever did this wasn't just sending a message—they were stripping away identity. Making it clear that nothing sacred stays untouched. It's a good lesson never to fuck with someone who owns RPG's or other heavy ballistics. It's obvious this goes deeper than simple revenge. If they're after Sam's sister, Surry, then they're clearing out her circle first—isolating her.

Kellan or whatever pulls his phone out and straightens before walking over and slides me a card with his information on it.

"Mr. Slater, I'll leave ye now. Mr. O'Brien wants dis rebuilt. He'll front de cost, send men, tools, whatever ye need. Credit card arrives tomorrow."

Before I can answer, he's gone. Efficient. Brutal. Irish to the bone.

I nearly collide with Corver coming in, his face pale, his phone glowing with red codes.

He looks like the devil himself just texted him.

"We got trouble, brother. Big trouble. Surry's ex. Name's Gavin Kelly."

"Okay. What about him? Do we know him from somewhere?"

Corver's voice is tight. "He just took over the Russians."

He hands me the phone and the video begins to play. I assume it's Gavin's face that fills the screen initially, smug, sharp, alive with malice. Behind him sits Serge Romanov, bound, gagged, bloody. Natasha—his daughter—on her knees. My gut sinks into the floor at seeing her.

Serge Romanov. I'd met the man before. We'd done a few renovations for him over the years—one of those off-the-books projects where money was no object and discretion was everything. He was Bratva, the head of the Russians in Seattle, and everyone knew it. Didn't hide it, didn't flaunt it either. For all his reputation, Serge was surprisingly laid-back. A whiskey drinker, a card player, a guy who could sit in silence with you for an hour without it being awkward. I respected that about him. There aren't many men in this business you can say that about.

His daughter, though—Natasha. Christ. Just as mean as she was beautiful. Jet-black hair, lips like sin, eyes that cut sharper than glass. She'd walk into a room and scorch the paint off the walls with that attitude of hers. And yet... I'd catch Corver, my quiet, level-headed brother, looking at her like she was a fire he'd willingly burn for. He never said a word, not once. But I saw it. The way his mouth would twitch, like he wanted to smile when she snapped at him. The way he'd linger a second longer than he needed to when he handed her something. My calm, calculated brother falling with a live bomb of a woman. It would've been funny if it weren't so dangerous.

The reno itself was one of the more intricate ones we'd pulled off. Hidden panels, reinforced walls, safe rooms tucked behind bookshelves—you name it, we built it. Serge wanted his fortress to look like a gentleman's estate, polished wood and marble floors, but underneath it all was pure steel. I still remember him clapping me on the back one night, whiskey in hand, while Corver and Natasha argued in the corner about whether or not velvet curtains were "tacky."

*"Brenden, you build like a Russian—solid. Strong. Won't fall, even when the world does,"* Serge had said, his laugh low and warm.

And Natasha? She'd crossed her arms, glaring at Corver with that sharp little smirk of hers. *"You think you know style, techy boy? Stick to your computers. Leave the beauty to me."*

Corver hadn't flinched. Just raised a brow and fired back, calm as ever. *"Velvet's impractical. Collects dust. Not efficient."* Of course that was his argument.

The sparkle in her eyes said she'd never met a man who told her no. And the flicker in his? That was the moment I knew he'd never forget her.

A loud sound on the phone brings me back to the video. I think it was Natasha yelping. My gut clenches as Gavin takes her throat and shoves her down. I can see where this is going, and I am not sure I have the stomach to watch it all.

Gavin proceeds to rip Natalia's dress up her body and rape her on camera, in front of her father. She is crying, and her father is screaming, although he is fully tied to the chair with a gag in, he is putting up a valiant effort at getting free nearly knocking himself over at one point. Gavin continues pumping into her, laughing, grabbing her hair, and pulling her head back in a way that looks like he might snap her neck. After what feels like an eternity, he finishes, and I can see blood on her legs as he discards her on the floor. She lies there, so still I initially think he killed her, until I see her eyes blink and her mouth scrunch up.

Corver doesn't flinch. He's already watched it. The anger in his eyes is something I have only witnessed from him once before. When we killed the man who murdered our mother. I force myself to keep my eyes on the screen. Every brutal second. Gavin laughing, demanding acknowledgment.

"Now, Serge, I have officially consummated my relationship with your daughter, who was a virgin until just now, solidifying our marriage in God's eyes. Your only child and heir. This now makes me heir apparent. Do you agree?" He takes another knife from his pocket, his pants still undone. The sick fuck didn't even put away his still-hard dick. He opens the knife and runs it over Serge's face. Serge makes a noise that sounds like disagreement. Gavin laughs, reels back, and punches him as hard as he can in the face.

Serge's head snaps back, and I am shocked. What is Gavin trying to do? The other man with the knife taps Serge's face until he looks back at Gavin once more. "Again, I will ask you. Only one more time. Serge, do you agree that I am the heir now that I have consummated my marriage with your daughter? Or do I need to go get your wife as well?" Serge's eyes go wide as Gavin speaks, and he looks to his daughter. She nods just subtly, and Serge does the same. He pauses, eyes closed, gathering himself. When they open, the heat in them could scorch the earth. He nods once. Then he pins Gavin in place with a stare sharp enough to carve bone.

Gavin laughs a bitter, evil laugh. The kind that makes your heart fall to your stomach and fills you with dread. "You hear that, my love! I am the new heir, and I am now your husband. Which means..." At that, the other man slits Serge's throat. Holy Fuck. Gavin Kelly just became head of the Russian mafia. An Irishman just took over the Russian mafia. Gavin watches as Serge gurgles, blood sprayed down the front of his already bloodied shirt, dripping down onto the floor. It begins to pool at his feet and form a stream toward Natalia. To her credit, I almost forgot she was there during all the chaos because of how silent she was.

Then Gavin looks at the camera. At us. At me.

"Stefan," Gavin said, slow and sure, "I'm head of the Russians now. Bratva runs through me. I'm your equal–but I'm not finished. I never will be until I have back what's mine: my wife, my child. If I must, I'll take your daughters, your wife, and your empire. I'll get Surry back. Remember that.

He turned, address the room. "Boy's–enjoy yourselves. Until she is pregnant, she's up for grabs." The men moved in around Natasha like vultures.

He laughs. The kind of laugh that stains the room as Natasha lets out a blood curdling scream.

Corver cuts the video before the rest can play. "You don't want to see it."

I stare at the blank screen, rage burning hot and sharp in my throat.

This isn't just a turf war. This is personal. It became personal the moment he decided to hurt a woman-one we know only making it one hundred times worse. He checks every box for the kind of scum we take care of. The kind we load into the back of our truck, and haul away with the trash. A vendetta dressed as empire building. And now, whether I like it or not, I'm in it. Because when men like Gavin move, they don't stop at bloodlines. They take friends. Families. Anyone within reach.

And I just realized we're within reach.

# JUNIPER

The smell of smoke and broken plaster still hangs heavy in the air, even though the fire's long gone. I stand in the middle of what used to be my kingdom, Tattoos on the Bay, and all I see is ruin. Broken glass crunches under my boots with every step, like bones snapping. The neon signs that once bathed these walls in pink and blue light lie shattered, their wires sparking faintly in the corners.

I can almost see it the way it was—the way it should be. Black marble floors polished to a sheen, raw wood walls that smelled faintly of cedar, shelves lined with everything that made this place ours: taxidermy foxes with sly grins, animal skulls bleached white, potted plants that Hazel used to fuss over, and books—God, so many books. The memory makes my throat tighten.

I built this place from nothing, just a dream and the boys. When Joshua, Brenden, and Corver Slater showed up, everything changed. I'd run into Brenden first, all six-foot-six of him, looking like he'd been carved out of stone. Then his brothers —the quiet genius Corver with his watchful eyes, and Joshua with that wild streak you could smell a mile off. They didn't just help me put walls up. They made this place strong, safe. My family of choice, before I even realized I'd accepted them.

I remember the day Hazel walked in, portfolio in her trembling hands. She was barely out of her apprenticeship, green as hell, but I saw her talent in every line she'd drawn. Her stars, her shading, the way she captured softness in her tattoos—I couldn't say no. Everyone told me I was stupid for hiring someone so new. I told them to fuck off. Hazel was mine. And I was right—she bloomed fast, faster than anyone I'd ever seen. Clients lined up for her delicate work, and it wasn't long before Inked magazine was calling us for features. We weren't just another shop anymore. We were *the* shop.

Now? The cabinets are splintered. The stations smashed beyond recognition. My crystals are ground into glittering dust across the floor. All the memories, all the late nights and belly laughs with clients who became family, all the blood and ink and stories poured into these walls—it looks like none of it ever mattered.

But it did. It still does.

I run my hand across one of the broken chairs, fingertips catching on jagged wood. This was where Hazel tattooed her first full sleeve, hands shaking so bad I had to hold her wrist steady in the beginning. This was where the boys, Hazel, and I toasted with whiskey after landing the first magazine spread, the five of us drunk on success and hope. This was where I carved out a life I could be proud of, after all the shit I'd crawled through.

The bastards who did this don't know me. Don't know us.

This shop isn't just walls and ink and neon. It's blood. It's family. And if they think they can scare me back into silence—they're dead wrong.

Without any real answers, I agree to go home with Josh. He has been my safe place for quite a while now. But I haven't told him. Not yet. I can't. I don't want to ruin what we have now. Stolen glances, soft touches in the dark. Something is there, but I'm too afraid to go forward with it. And I know he is too, or else he would have said something by now.

Josh grabs my hand, leading me out to the Evo. This is Brenden's favorite car, and I know he loves me if he let Josh drive it. He is reckless, not careless. But he is willing to push the boundaries on anything and everything.

"We will get this sorted, June," he says to me as we trudge over broken pieces of my home.

"I know." It's all I manage to say. Because what else can I say? I really would like a drink. "Just take me home, Josh."

He nods at me, and opens my door so I can settle into the supple leather seats. I buckle my seat before he gets to his door and fire off a text to Hazel, see what the fuck is going on over there. She tells me what the car looked like. I know Surry loved that car, and how big of a shock it would be to find it that way. Especially in a place that was supposed to be so guarded. We agree to check in later, Surry's dad is just getting there now.

Josh puts the Evo in drive, and we take off at lightening speed toward the apartment to hunker down, and wait for this to be over.

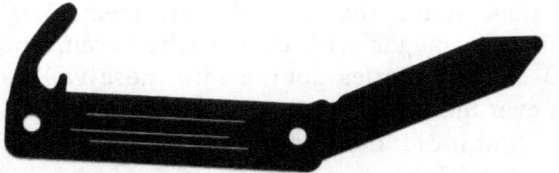

The ride back is quiet at first. Josh doesn't push, doesn't prod—just keeps his hands steady on the wheel of the Lotus Evora, the engine purring low as we cut through the wet pacific north west streets. The car smells like leather and faintly like him—cedar, smoke, and something warmer I can't place. My nerves finally start to ease, like the hum of the engine is pulling me out of my head.

I glance sideways at him. His jaw is tight, his knuckles flexing against the wheel, the dashboard lights cutting harsh shadows over his face. He's thinking—always thinking—but he doesn't spill it. Josh carries it, lets it eat at him until it shows in the set of his shoulders, the sharpness of his gaze.

By the time we pull into the garage, the silence has shifted from heavy to... comfortable. Familiar, even. He kills the engine, and for a moment we just sit there listening to the tick of cooling metal and the steady rhythm of our breaths. Then, without a word, he's out of the car and around to my side, opening the door. He is always like that. Always a gentleman, even when his whole body looks like a storm barely held in check.

Inside, the tension thins. He tosses his keys on the counter, shrugs out of his jacket, and disappears down the hall. When he comes back, he's holding a plain black T-shirt, worn soft from too many washes. He doesn't make some joke or ask if I need it—just hands it over, his eyes holding mine for one beat too long. Like he knows I'll take it. Like he knows I'll wear it.

I slip it on in his bedroom, the hem brushing my thighs, the fabric warm from his hands. It smells like him, too, and for a second I have to press my pointer fingers to my temples, steady myself. It's ridiculous—how something so simple, so small, can feel like more than it is.

When I walk back out, he's already on the couch, remote in hand, scrolling through channels like he's trying to find anything that won't remind us of blood, fire, or loss. When he lands on some half-forgotten sitcom rerun, he doesn't look at me, just pats the spot beside him.

I curl into his side without hesitation. His arm comes around me automatically, solid and protective, pulling me close. I'm tucked in under his arm, his hand resting at the junction between my thigh as ass. The laugh track fills the silence, but neither of us are really paying attention. My head rests against his chest, rising and falling with each steady breath. His thumb traces idle, absent circles on my thigh, and I don't think he even notices he's doing it.

For the first time since I walked into the wreckage of my shop, I feel like I can breathe. Like maybe we'll be okay, if only for tonight. That's the dangerous part, though—how safe he makes me feel. Safety like this is a luxury. It lures you in, makes you forget the world outside is made up of teeth and claws.

So I close my eyes, let the sound of his heartbeat and the warmth of his arm around me be enough. Just for now.

"Have your fill, boys. I won't need her for long."

The video echoes across the room, the voice a dagger to my chest. Even from where I sit, the sound is clear enough— too clear. The sick laughter, the muffled cries, the breaking of another woman's spirit. I can hear the sound of skin slapping. My father and his men stand near the TV, faces grim, eyes narrowed, the glow of the screen painting their features in harsh blue light. I should look away. I should plug my ears. But it's too late—the memories already claw their way up from the pit I keep them buried in.

*Seven months after marrying Gavin.*

*The stick shakes in my hand. One line. Not pregnant. Again.*

*The door crashes open. His shadow fills the bathroom. My breath freezes.*

*His hand clamps around my throat before I can hide the test. I choke, nails digging at his wrist, but he just laughs—low, cruel. "Seven months and nothing. Can't even give me a son."*

*My back slams against the sink. His fingers squeeze until my vision spots. He yanks me down by the hair, dragging me to my knees on the cold tile. His pants unzip. "Get me hard," he snarls, shoving himself into my mouth before I can even breathe. My jaw aches, my gag reflex kicks, but he doesn't care. Drool runs down my chin, my eyes water. I do it anyway, sloppy, desperate, because if I don't—*

*"Useless." His fist knots in my hair, ripping me back to my feet. My scalp burns. He pulls me behind him, my feet barely staying under me until we reach the bed. Then I'm thrown onto the bed, face smashing into the duvet. My lungs seize, no air. He shoves down on my back of my head, pushing my face into the mattress harder and harder, until all I taste is fabric and salt and panic. I hear the sound of my underwear tearing, the cotton cutting into my skin before it gives way. The pain when he forces himself inside me is white-hot, blinding. I can't scream. I can't breathe.*

*"Good for nothing whore." He spits out. I am thrashing, trying to snag any air I can. "Only job you've got is giving me an heir. My heir. You hear me? That's your only fuckin' purpose." If I could breathe, I would be crying.*

*The creaking mattress mocks my silent sobs within the coils. My chest burns, my body shakes, and somewhere far away I hear myself breaking. Every thrust, every word, every second is a brand seared into me. And when he finally leaves my body, when he pulls out and leaves me collapsed and gasping, I don't feel relief. Just emptiness. Just shame. Just silence.*

That poor girl. She's me on that fateful night when I finally escaped. Eleven years ago, I was her. Pinned down. Passed around. Screaming into the floor until my throat was raw, and no one came. My stomach lurches. I grip the edge of the couch until my knuckles ache, the urge to vomit clawing up my throat and my body retches.

Maybe I should just give myself back to him. Hand myself over, let him do whatever the hell he wants, as long as it stops here. As long as he doesn't touch Selene, or Alisha, or Hazel, or June. As long as he doesn't look at my mother with that smile again. I could end this. I could.

"I can see the look in your eyes."

The words hit me like a slap, yanking me back. I hadn't even noticed Richie slide into the seat beside me, hadn't felt the couch shift under his weight. He places a garbage can in front of me. He's good like that—slips in quietly when he wants to, despite his larger-than-life energy.

"What?" My voice comes out sharper than I intend, defensive. I clear my throat and try again, feigning innocence. "What look?"

He leans forward, elbows on his knees, looking at me from the corner of his eye. "That one. The one that says you're about to do something really fucking stupid. Then I heard you audibly gag."

I open my mouth, ready to deny it, but the words freeze in my throat as if I swallowed a rock. My jaw hinging as I open and close it like a fish out of water. He doesn't need me to answer; he already knows.

"Yeah," I breathe instead. "I just... the video. I was her once. I can't—" My chest tightens, tears burning my eyes. I bury my face in my hands, elbows digging uncomfortably into my thighs. "I can't let it happen to anyone else. Not again. I need to stop it."

Richie doesn't flinch. He lifts me up easily and places

me in his lap, rubbing my back and placing his chin on my head. This should soothe me, but only makes me want to scream. "Babe, there's nothing you can do. Not like this. Your dad's got it. They'll take his ass out. And then? Then we start something real. A non-profit, a shelter, something. You want to stop him? We stop all of them. Deal?"

His voice is low, steady. Grounding. He believes it—I can hear it.

But my body doesn't. The adrenaline is a wildfire in my veins, the panic shifting into rage. Fight, not flight. I lurch to my feet; the wine bottle rattles on the table when my knees clip it, and I hit the floor unsteady before finding my balance. My eyes lock on my father's across the room.

The days bleed together. Three of them. Maybe four. It's hard to tell anymore. Time doesn't feel real—it stretches, folds, collapses on itself. We sleep in shifts, jump at shadows, flinch when the elevator dings. Every noise feels like a warning. Tonight we're gathered at the kitchen table—Alisha, Hazel, Richie, Samuel, Selene, and me—the weight of the video still hasn't lifted. It clings to the walls like smoke that won't air out, no matter how wide we open the windows.

The table is littered with half-eaten Thai takeout, chopsticks abandoned on styrofoam boxes. One of the few good things about Washington: you can throw a rock and hit a restaurant with food worth dying for. Thai, Korean, Chinese, Japanese—you name it, it's all here. Normally, the smell of red curry and basil would have my mouth watering. Tonight, it's just background noise to the silence.

After my parents left, their men posted like shadows in the garage and outside the elevator. A wall of security. Safe, but suffocating. I glance around the apartment we've carved out for ourselves, the one place that feels entirely ours. Black and white everything, with splashes of hot pink like rebellion stamped into the walls. The LVP flooring looks like dark wood grain, and the bottom cabinets are black with sleek gold handles.

The upper cabinets? Painted hot pink. A joke that turned out to be brilliant. Alisha and Richie spent days with paint rollers and terrible music, while Hazel and I handled the lower cabinets, installing all the hardware. We bled and cursed into this kitchen until it looked like us.

The dining room stretches from the kitchen, anchored by our ridiculous twelve-person table. Black chairs, checkered rug, pink and white decor running down the center like we're hosting the world's oddest art exhibit. Past that, the living room glows faintly from the TV, the massive black couch piled with pink pillows, the wall behind the fireplace painted in deep, dramatic black. It doesn't look like grown-ups live here. It looks like an eclectic art teacher threw paint and furniture together and called it home. But we love it.

When I finally tear my gaze back to the table, everyone's watching me. Everyone but Alisha. She keeps poking at her noodles like they might give her answers she's too afraid to ask.

"What?" My voice comes out sharp, brittle.

"What's going through your head?" she asks without looking up.

"He texted me the night before everything happened," I admit. The words tumble out before I can second-guess myself. "Like right after we went to sleep. I wanted to tell you, but I didn't know how. Then the car... and the garage... and I panicked. I couldn't speak. I'm sorry. I never meant to keep you out of it."

Alisha's head lifts slowly. Her eyes catch mine, and the fear in them slices me open.

"How could you?" It's all she says, and it rips me open, my chest an open wound from the hurt she put into the words.

"Lish, I'm sorry. I was scared. I'm so so sorry." I outstretch my hand toward her, although shes across the table from me, and I can't reach her. Sam looks at me with sorrow in his eyes. He knows how much I'm hurting, but with his hand placed on Alisha's shoulder, I know he is with her on this. They have always been close, not as close as her and I. But there has always been something between them. Even when we were kids.

"You knew you were in danger. You know what happened last time he got his hands on you. How you have changed forever because of him. And you still let it go. Didn't say anything. I get you were scared. But I guess I thought we were closer than that? Have you forgotten that I was there? I had to sit there at your bedside and watch you recover, black and blue everywhere, stitches, and wounds, and that's not to mention the internal injuries. The ones here." She points to her head, indicating my mind.

I shake my head, my lips parted as if they wish to say something. But I have no idea what. Sorry isn't going to cut it, and I know that. Alisha begins to rise before Sam grabs her hand and pulls her gently back into her chair.

"She's sorry Al, you know that. If I can see it, I know you can."

Everyone else sits in uncomfortable silence, watching us argue from all the way across the table from one another.

"STILL!" She yells at him, at me, and everyone and no one all at once. "Still, she should have told me. Told us."

"How, how can I fix this?" I whisper, my voice barely audible. She just shakes her head, looking down at the table, unblinking.

Sam, who scoots noticeably close to Alisha, places his hand on her arm. I think he feels her fear as well. But the look in his eye says more.

"You won't lose me," I whisper. "I'm not going anywhere."

Her lips press together, but she doesn't answer. She doesn't need to—her silence says enough. Sam removes her hand and starts rubbing her back.

"Yeah, as long as you don't go getting all self-sacrificing," Richie mutters, trying to cut the tension.

I roll my eyes. "I'm not sacrificing myself."

The cold smirk on Alisha's face tells me she knows better. She's always known better.

Selene leans forward, resting her upper half onto the table and looking back and forth between all of us. "Well, I for one want to do something. You think Dad's goons will let us? We've been stuck here long enough and nothing has happened."

Richie lights up like a firecracker. "Ooooh, let's go! I was thinking of getting some blackout done. Anyone up for a tattoo run?"

Hazel snorts. "Can't. Shop was taken out too. Courtesy of the rapist fuck face."

The room stills for a second. We'd forgotten to check on Juniper.

"Shit. Is Juney okay?" Selene blurts.

"She's with the boys," Hazel answers. Relief flickers

across all of our faces. "She said we could come by last night, but I wasn't sure anyone would want to leave so I didn't bring it up. I can see if she is up for it tonight?"

Selene grins. "We can. We should. Right?

"If it's the Slaters, Dad will be fine with it," Sam replies. "They're just as scary as the Mafia... well, almost as scary."

The Slaters again. He always brings them up. Hazel and Juniper have talked about them, but I have no interest in meeting any men outside of the ones I already know. I causally date here and there. Not much though. Hookups, sure. Quick and empty. But dating? Trusting? Never again. Eleven years isn't long enough to erase the scars Gavin left, or least isn't long enough for me to want to see if they are. So meeting any of them has been a low priority for me.

Eventually, after too much begging, I cave. We scatter to get ready. I swipe perfume on my neck and wrists, tease my hair back to life, and slip on my classic, checkered black and white Vans—the one comfort I will never give up. Then I change my baggy t-shirt out for a cute tank top, and make sure my black skinny jeans don't have any stains before walking out.

The Suburbans are waiting downstairs, all bulletproof paranoia courtesy of my father. I slide into the passenger seat, Samuel and Alisha in the far back, Hazel, Selene, and Richie in the middle row. Two nameless guards flank us like shadows.

The drive takes forty minutes due to evening traffic, city lights flickering past the tinted windows. Seattle hums with life, oblivious to the war brewing under its skin.

Inside the Slaters' building, Hazel leads us down polished halls, past art, plants, and even a working rotary phone on a side table. I lift it, curious, and grin when the dial tone buzzes in my ear. Half the kids in this city wouldn't even know how to use it.

The elevator takes us to the top floor, and Juniper answers the knock, looking whole, thank God. She ushers us inside, demanding to know what we want to drink. She has got on a long black t-shirt, and from what I can see, nothing else. Interesting. Hazel and Richie vanish with her toward the kitchen, leaving me, Selene, and Samuel in the living room.

Then a man approaches—tall, broad-shouldered, hand outstretched. "Hey, Sam. How are you?"

"Great, Josh. How about you?"

Josh. That's the name. He's better looking than I expected. Selene catches my eye, and I know she's thinking the same.

Another one follows. Just as tall, just as magnetic. He greets Sam, then glances at us. "And you must be Selene and Surry."

Josh cuts in, eyes flicking between us. "So which one's which?"

"I'm Selene," she says, flashing her smile. "This is Surry. And no, we're not twins." She laughs and rests a hand on his arm. "We get asked that pretty regularly."

Juniper appears out of nowhere, sliding her hand through Josh's and tugging it free. Message received: no touchy-touchy.

"This is Joshua and Corver," she announces. "Brenden's being a pussy in his room. Claims he's calling it a night, but he'll probably wander out when he gets FOMO."

Sam frowns. "What the fuck is FOMO?"

I roll my eyes. "Fear of missing out. F-O-M-O. How are you thirty-eight, and don't know that?"

Linking arms with Selene, I turn to Juniper. "I need a drink. A strong one."

Juniper smirks. "Oh babe, I got you."

Later, the drinks blur into laughter. Sugar and rum buzz through my veins, a heady mix that makes the room dance in soft edges.

"JUNIPER! I NEED THE POTTY!" I yell, voice tipping into a whine.

"Down the hall, first door on the left!" she shouts back, perched on Josh's knee, playing charades like a queen.

I wander the hall, distracted by the empty walls—bare, not a single picture, not even art. The apartment feels so put together until you enter this area, like it was forgotten. As if they had made it all the way to this point and either didn't care or didn't know what to do.

At the crossroads, I hesitate. Light seeps from under

the left door. The right one is dark. Logic tells me left is occupied, so I twist the knob on the right and step inside.

And I freeze.

My sugar and alcohol induced haze evaporates in an instant. Standing before me is a man, no. A god. A towel slung low on his hips, long dark hair dripping water onto a chest carved like marble, ink scrawled over muscle. The overhead light is off, and just the lamp on his desk remains on, explaining the darkness under the door. His eyes catch mine, sharp and unyielding.

"Enjoying the show, darling?" His voice is low, gravelly. Dangerous. His hand loosen's on the towel slightly, causing it to highlight the sacred V-line and light trail of dark hair that disappears under the white material.

Oh, fuck.

This man. This beast. This GOD. He growled. He called me DARLING. I don't know what to do with myself. All I can do is stare at him.

He has long, shoulder-length dark brown hair that is freshly wet from the shower. His body is chiseled from marble; there is simply no other explanation. The deep V that cuts down into the towel leaves little to the imagination. Especially when I can see the uh, the outline, underneath. He is absolutely enormous. Has to be bigger than six foot four, is my bet. I am sure I look insane now, just staring at him. But what else is a girl to do.

# ᛒᚱᛁᚾᛏ

Once we left the tattoo shop, we met Joshua and Juniper here. They were asleep on the couch. It was clear that the immediate threat was not to us, nor June, but we wanted to keep an eye on her anyway. She will now be taking up residence in our guest room for the foreseeable future.

I had seen them first so I kept quiet, but Corver hadn't seen them so he was loud and talking plans as we walked in, waking both Joshua and June up. They scooted away from each other, trying not to be obvious they were just wrapped up in one another seconds earlier. We both didn't say anything, it wasn't the time to give Josh shit. Honestly, we were all too tired to tease each other right now anyway.

I went straight to the kitchen to grab a drink, pulling out a Redbull that had been calling my name since the glass first crunched under my boots at the shop.

Juniper is the only person who sleeps in our guest room, but I have a suspicion that she doesn't actually sleep in there. Instead, I think she is actually staying with Joshua. But that's not on my list of things to worry about. They can worry about that themselves. My only focus is to keep them all safe, not worry about their love lives if that's even what you would call it. But anyone with eyes can see that they have a thing for each other.

We settle in for the night, ordering dinner and then watching a movie before heading off to bed to hopefully forget the day that we had.

Four days pass in a blur.

Not quiet, not peaceful—just... suspended. Like we're all waiting for the next hit to land.

Corver's barely left his office in all that time. The door stays half-shut, blue light leaking through the crack like some kind of warning. The sound of typing, the occasional clatter of a dropped pen, and the steady arrival of takeout bags are the only proof he's still alive in there. If he's cooked a single meal, I haven't seen it. He says he's "researching," but we all know that means he's obsessing.

Josh and Juniper made a quick run to her apartment on the second day—mostly to check on her plants, which she swears have abandonment issues. She came back with half a duffel of her things, though she hasn't worn any of them. Every time I've seen her since, she's been swimming in Josh's shirts, her hair a permanent tangle, her feet bare against the hardwood.

She's restless, pacing from room to room like a caged cat. But if you look at Josh—really look—you can see it's heaven for him. Her chaos is his calm. The man's never looked more content in his life than he does sitting on that couch watching her wear holes into the floorboards.

When Corver finally emerges this evening, his eyes are bloodshot, and he looks like he hasn't slept since the dawn of time. He just mutters something about "needing more coffee" and disappears again. Typical.

I drop onto the couch beside Josh with a sigh that feels like it comes from somewhere deep in my bones. The cushions mold around me, claiming me instantly. "If I move from this spot, assume I've been abducted," I mutter, leaning my head back.

Juniper breezes past the hallway at that exact moment—freshly showered, hair scraped up in a wild bun, wearing yet another one of Josh's shirts that's too big to be decent. She looks relaxed, smug even, which makes me suspicious immediately.

She pauses, eyeing me with that mischievous glint I know too well. "Oh, by the way..." she singsongs, grabbing a Red Bull from the fridge like she owns the place. "I invited everyone over. Hope you don't mind, B! Love you!"

I groan and lift my head just enough to glare at her. "Juniper, if by 'everyone' you mean anyone who breathes, I *do* mind."

She flashes me a grin over her shoulder. "Too late. Already texted them."

She saunters past, humming, and I sink deeper into the couch. The same couch that's been my second home for the past four days.

"Again, who is everyone, June Bug?" Using the nickname that she despises gets her attention immediately. She stops what she's doing and fully turns to look at me.

"You know. Hazel, Richie, Alisha, Sam, Selene...Surry." She whispers Surry's name hoping I won't hear, but I'm not as old as she pretends as I am.

"You invited Surry here? That is a really bad idea,

June." The last thing we need is Gavin to be keeping an eye on her, and for her to come here. Which also then makes Surry and the others my problem. My problem to keep safe.

"Oh no, how come?" she asks, and I think she means it. Does she just not think about consequences like this, or is it just me who has these types of fears. I just stare at her, blinking slowly, as if we didn't just get through explaining to her what is going on.

"What if Gavin is watching her? Or tracking her? You saw what he did to the shop. Heard what he did to the car. Her coming here will lead him right to our door, putting a target on more than just Surry, but you, me, Corver, and Joshua also. You cannot be serious."

"Well then let's go to my place? I am okay with him targeting it. I need to move anyways."

I roll my eyes at her, honestly shocked she didn't think about this. All we have talked about the last several days is who did this, how bad they are. You would think with Corver's obsession she would see how serious this was.

Juniper places her empty cup under the ice machine in the fridge, the cubes dinging against the inside as they tumble down into it. "Do you really think he would follow her here? Target us?" She yells over the ice machine.

I watch as she finishes, then moves from the fridge to the counter, grabbing the Malibu and pouring two shots of in it. "Yes, I do. It's why he targeted the tattoo shop. She is there so often it was somewhere she enjoyed being, obviously."

"Aww, you really think she loved being at the shop?" She finishes her drink off by filling it the rest of the way with Pepsi, turning to look at me with a softness in her eyes before looking back at her cup and topping it with a maraschino cherry, all with a happy, almost dreamy, smile on her face. I don't understand the drink, but it's her guts, not mine.

I snort a laugh. As if Surry loving the shop is the top of our worries.

All of a sudden, heavy footsteps sound beside me, and Corver walks in, he still looks like he hasn't slept. Ever. "There are people coming up the elevator, Brenden."

"Okay. June, you're up. They are your friends. I am going to take a shower. I may or may not come back out." I peel myself from the couch and begin trudging to my bedroom.

She pouts at me, but makes her way toward the door to greet her friends. I pass Joshua in the hallway on the way to my bedroom.

"Hazel and all of them are coming over." I say.

"That's a bad fucking idea," he looks at me with raised eyebrows, as if I am the one who thought to invite them.

"I know it is, but they're already here. See to it that you keep an eye, and that Corver turns up all the security, please. I am going to take a shower."

"Oh, come on, old man. Come hang out with us. They're already here, so you might as well hang out. You never do anything fun." He punches me in the arm, then looks toward June. I catch him staring at her ass.

"I'm good, have fun." I wink at him and continue on my way toward my room. My room is the first door on the right, so that way I am closest to the door. I prefer it this way. I am also right across from the guest bathroom, which means I can keep an ear on everything as well. Not that we have any visitors outside of June.

The hallway stretched out in front of me, long and bare, the kind of empty that spoke more of indifference than design. No pictures, no art, not even a clock. Just white paint over drywall, scuffed here and there from boots or moving gear. A bachelor's stretch of wall, really.

We'd never bothered to fill it with anything—too busy building other people's towers and tearing down other people's demons. The silence of it made every footstep echo sharper than it should, and for a second, I caught myself staring at the blank space, thinking maybe we should hang something there. Then again, we never really cared. The place wasn't about being lived in—it was about being secure.

I walk into my room and shut the door. The video of Gavin keeps replaying in my mind. I am not really sure what to do. What the next move is. I texted Michael, our lead foreman for the construction company, the day after the shop blew up and let him know he will be running the show for the rest of the week at minimum, informing him it is locked down, no strangers in the compound, no new clients.

I walk into my closet and strip off all my clothes before walking through my closet to the bathroom and turn the shower on. While it begins to get warm, I look at myself in the mirror.

Tattoos stretch over me like armor plates, black and grey winding into each other, stories inked deep into my skin. They look good under the light—menacing, deliberate—but all I see is what came before.

I wasn't always this.

Back in high school, I was tall but not filled out—six foot and maybe a buck fifty, lanky as hell, invisible. Easy target. The scrawny kid everyone thought was safe to shove around. Nobody said my name unless it was followed by a laugh. Nobody thought I'd ever be more than a shadow.

Then I grew up and started to try and get my life figured out. That was easy until Mom died. And the shadow turned into fire.

That's when Slater Construction started. Out in the open, it was a way to build something real. A roof we could all stand under. We worked ourselves to the bone—Corver at nineteen was already running the books, having taught himself code and fraud systems on a shitty laptop when we were teens. Josh and I hauled lumber, hammered nails, did the grunt jobs no one wanted. We clawed our way up from remodels and drywall patches to skyscrapers and city contracts.

And behind that shiny mask? I hunted men like the one who took our mom. Predators. Wife-beaters. The kind of men who smiled at church and signed contracts by day, then left bruises blood behind closed doors. I didn't do it for the thrill or for money—we already had more than enough of that. I did it because someone had to. Because justice, as the world saw it, never came fast enough for people like us.

I carried the weight of every woman I couldn't save, every cry that came too late. Sometimes, I'd see it flicker behind my smile—the cost of being the kind of man who plays savior and executioner in the same breath. My hands were steady when they shouldn't have been. My eyes stayed soft, even when the work hardened the rest of me. And maybe that's what scared me most. How easily I could be both—the protector and the storm that burned everything unsafe out of our path.

The reflection in the mirror now is that of a man—six-six, three hundred pounds, built from fury and survival. I box. I fight. I choke men out until their lights go dark, then I walk away and sleep fine. Because I know the world's lighter without them in it. My body's not just muscle. It's purpose. Every scar and inked line is a ledger of what we've done, what we've built.

The mirror fogs as I step into the shower, water hammering down on me. For a long minute, I just stand there, letting it batter my shoulders, letting the pain of the last few days wash down the drain. The heat loosens the knots in my back but not the ones in my chest. Gavin's face is still there, grinning. The sound of his laugh still drills into me. The sound of Natasha's scream carved into my bones.

Shampoo. Rinse. Routine movements that give my hands something to do when my head won't shut off. I add the conditioner and then close my eyes, pressing my palms against the tile, forehead leaning into the steam. I add face wash to my hands and begin to scrub my face and beard until my skin feels a bit raw. I think about Natasha—Corver's face when he saw her in that video. The rage there. The helplessness.

I rinse my face and the conditioner at the same time. I think about Juniper, tucked into the guest room, pretending like she isn't shaking when the lights go out. I wash my body methodically, my brain still circling all the information we've learned over the past few days. I think about Gavin promising he'll take everything from Stefan O'Brien. And I think about Surry —whoever the hell she is—caught in the middle of it all. I don't like it when women are the means men use to get what they want.

When the water runs cold, I twist it off and grab the towel from the hook. I drag it over my skin, rough, quick, before shaking droplets from my hair and wrapping the towel around my hips as I step back into my room to check my phone. The cool air slaps me, raising goosebumps on my arms.

That's when I notice my door.

It isn't closed anymore.

And in the frame—like some apparition I conjured with my thoughts—she stands.

A blonde. Not just blonde. Bleach-white, long, loose, falling like silk over her shoulders. Eyes green as a storm-lit wave, the kind that drags sailors under, wide, startled, locked on me. Her lips part on a tiny breath, the sound barely audible over the pounding of my own pulse.

I collect myself quickly, because whoever this goddess is deserves me at my best. And I'm going to give it to her.

"Enjoying the show, darling?" I let the words roll low, gravel in my chest.

Her gaze dips—to where my hand grips the towel low. It lingers. I let my fingers loosen just a bit, dropping it just a bit to show my V-line to her a bit more. Her pupils widen. She doesn't run. Doesn't even blink.

"I-I'm sorry. I thought this was the bathroom." Her voice shakes, but her feet don't move.

She's frozen. Prey caught in the stare of a predator. And I can't look away.

My eyes drag down her frame, greedy. Black ripped jeans cling to long legs, her bare ankles showing off tattoo sleeves. Checkered Vans—scuffed to hell at the toes—pull it all together. A black tank top that simultaneously shows off her arm sleeves and chest tattoo, a Medusa, and dips just enough to tease curves she probably doesn't even realize she's showing. Her lips are pink and soft, trembling as she swallows. There's heat in her stare, buried under embarrassment.

I step forward, slow, deliberate. She presses back until the door frame catches her shoulder blades. My arm plants above her head, forearm braced on the wall, caging her in. My other hand is hanging from the top of the frame. My body towers over her, close enough to feel her breath stutter against my chest.

Then her scent hits me—sweet, feminine, something floral twisted with earth and smoke. It winds into me, dangerous, addictive.

"Like I said, Siren," I look into those emerald eyes, trying to see into her soul, leaning over so I can murmur against the shell of her ear, my breath grazing her skin. "Are you enjoying the show?"

"I-I-I—" she stammers, lips trembling. Her eyes flick from mine to my mouth, and back again. That stare alone could set me off.

"You keep looking at me like that, and I'm going to put those lips to good use since they can't seem to get any words out."

Her breath hitches. Her chest rises. And fuck, I want —

"SURRY!" A male voice bellows from the kitchen, snapping the string taut between us.

She jolts, eyes wide.

"Sorry," she mumbles, dragging her gaze away like it costs her something. "It seems I'm being summoned."

Fuck. This is Surry? If, if I had known. Fuck. I open my mouth to say something, but I'm not sure what. I close my mouth again while I think and look toward the hall with what I assume is an expression filled with disdain, but inside I'm already replaying every second.

I point to the door across from mine. "That's the bathroom. But I've got one in here if you'd rather use it." I wink, letting the heat linger between us. I can't just let her walk away if I can help it.

Her cheeks flush a shade of pink I'd kill to see again. She spins away and steps into the guest bath. But before the door clicks shut, she glances back once more. Green fire, lust, embarrassment, all tangled into one.

The lock snicks.
And I know it, certain as blood:
I will never let anyone touch that girl again.
She is mine.

"SURRY!"

Thank God for Richie. Because I was about to make some decisions that I may have regretted in the morning. But one thing's for damn sure: that man's body will haunt my dreams tonight, probably every night for the rest of forever. When he was made, angels cried and then immediately passed out. There has to have been songs written about his abs alone. Because there ain't no way that all of that was an accident.

The man—Brenden, it has to be—locks eyes with me as I slide the door to the actual bathroom shut. His stare is a physical weight, burning into my skin even after the lock clicks. It isn't until that moment that I remember I actually need to pee really badly. I rush to the toilet, thighs trembling, breath uneven.

When I finish, I pad over to the sink, turning on the water. That's when I notice the soap dispenser. I can't help but laugh—it's shaped like a tiny Harley, all chrome and detail, sitting there like a knick-knack. These grown ass men who own this place have almost no decorations, but this one soap dispenser. This has to be the cutest thing I have ever seen, and now I want one. I snap a photo with my phone. Tomorrow I'll wonder why the hell I took a picture of a motorcycle soap pump. But tonight? It feels like a small victory to cling to something so normal.

I dry my hands, straighten my shirt, and step out. The bedroom across the hall is obviously empty now, the door left wide open, and the lights are off. But his scent—clean, dark, masculine—still lingers.

I turn toward the dining room and begin my trek through the empty hallway, but freeze when I enter the large room that holds both the living room and dining room.

Sitting at the table, beer in hand, is Brenden. Shirtless, tattoos coiled across muscle like armor, those glacier-blue eyes tracking me. Not blinking. Not moving. Just watching. His fierce, sky blue eyes scan me from head to toe, and back again, causing me to shiver. His stare feels like fingers tracing my bare skin, leaving goosebumps in their wake.

My stomach swoops. Maybe Hazel and June were right. Maybe I should've met. No. Bad Surry. Bad vagina. I don't need a man. I've had enough of that to last a lifetime. My rogue vagina needs to sit down and shut the hell up.

I nod, feeling my cheeks heat, and make my way to the living room. Everyone's lounging around, laughing too loud, movements slow–definitely drunk or at least close to it.

Alisha, drunk and starry-eyed, is draped across Sam. "SURRYYYY!" she shrieks, dragging my name out like a song. "WHERE HAVE YOU BEEEEEEN!" She tries to get up off of Sam, but he holds her down. I'm not sure she could walk anywhere at the moment anyway. She was already too drunk about three bottles ago.

"I was in the bathroom, Lishy. Do you need anything?" I continue walking toward her, noticing her face is a bit pale and green. "Water, or maybe a garbage can? Are you ready to go home?"

"She can sleep here in the guest room," comes the same gravel-deep voice from right behind me. He leaves no room for argument, or at least he thinks he does. The sound vibrates across the base of my skull, and my panties dampen instantly. My pussy is a real, real problem.

I spin around, head tilting back, and back, and back, until I meet his gaze. Holy hell, he's massive. How did I not notice how much taller he is than me, oh wait, probably because I wasn't focused on his face to realize how high up it was. There was a much more distracting view directly in front of my eyeballs. But that face. It takes my breath away nearly the same.

"We're perfectly fine to head home, right guys? I think it's about tha—"

My words die as Alisha retches.

"She's fine to take the guest room, Sam," he repeats, eyes locked on mine, not even bothering to look toward the sound of impending doom for his carpet.

Sam disappears with her down the hall, Corver trailing behind them, holding a waste basket in one hand and a bottle of water in the other. He is making some jangling noises, so I assume he has some headache medicine on him. Selene snores softly with her head in Richie's lap, Hazel next to him with her head on his shoulder, while they both scroll on their phones. June and Josh are nowhere to be seen.

Which leaves me here. Alone.

With him.

"Come with me."

Not loud. Not a request. A command. His hand finds mine—firm, steady. Not trapping, but leading. And I follow. I know in my gut that if I said no right now, he wouldn't make me do anything. But apparently, my rogue vagina is in charge tonight, and I allow him to lead me away from the living room.

He guides me down the hallway, placing my hand around his bicep. My fingers don't even cover half the muscle. He leads me straight into his bedroom, shuts the door, and pins me gently against it.

"I'm sorry I didn't know who you were before. I should have guessed."

"I wouldn't have expected you to know me," I answer, how could he have known? He leans in and kisses the shell of my ear, heat rising into my cheeks. When he pulls away his eyes blaze with a fire that screams lust and desire so loudly I can nearly hear it audibly.

He leans down, his stubbled jawline grazing the sensitive hollow where my neck meets my shoulder. His nose traces a path up to the curve of my ear, where he inhales deeply, deliberately. The growl that escapes him is low and primal as he exhales my scent, like distant thunder trapped in his chest. It reverberates through my skin, sending electric currents down my spine, causing my already damp underwear to completely saturate. I'm shocked they haven't begun to weigh me down due to the moisture coming from my pussy. The heady, musky scent of my arousal mingles with his cologne, creating an intoxicating perfume that seems to thicken the air around us.

"Your smell will live in my dreams from now until the day I die. I never want to be able to smell anything but you in here, ever. Stay the night with me."

How the hell do you argue with that? I mean, I can blame it on the alcohol right? The sugar from the soda and juice? But also, do I really need an excuse? I deserve to feel good for a minute, and I am pretty sure he can do just that.

I slide one arm through the fabric of the tank top, then the other, never breaking our shared gaze. The cotton whispers against my skin as I pull it over my head, revealing inch by inch the bare flesh concealed beneath. His jaw slackens, his full lips parting with a sharp intake of breath. I stand before him, vulnerable yet powerful as the discarded garment pools like spilled ink at my feet. My eyes travel deliberately from his flushed face down the taut lines of his body, lingering on the visible evidence of his desire, before the ache building inside me becomes impossible to contain.

"Fuck it," I whisper, reaching up and yanking him down by his biceps, and crash my mouth against his.

His lips freeze for a heartbeat before his arms wrap around me, pulling me impossibly close to him. His hands glide down my body and cup my ass, lifting me up, and I instinctively wrap my legs around his waist. He never takes his mouth off mine, and our tongues begin to get acquainted with one another, tasting each other, creating a dance that is only for us in this moment.

I run my fingers up from his biceps to his shoulders, exploring each muscle as I go, eventually making my way to his neck. They continue their journey with my left hand crawling up and tangling in his thick hair, and my right hand goes to explore his jaw line, mingling with the short beard he keeps there. The hair, both on his face and head, are soft and smell sweet and sharp like citrus, and the woods outside my home growing up. The smell makes every nerve in me more alive.

I tug on the long strands on the back of his head and he moves his face backward, temporarily removing his mouth from mine. I am half his size, but it is so easy to maneuver him, as if I were the one who is double his size. I have never felt more powerful, honestly.

I trail my lips across his cheek and over to his ear, licking the outer shell and blowing lightly. He begins to turn and walk more into the center of the room before I am disconnected from him entirely when he throws me into the air. For a moment, I am weightless, looking at the man who tossed me, until I land on his soft bed. It smells of whiskey, soap, and leather.

He wastes no time climbing on top of me, his large muscles caging me in as he puts an elbow on either side of my head and uses his muscular thighs to spread mine. He presses his groin into me through our pants, and that is when I feel it. Hard. Heaving. Straining against my inner thigh. He is just as ready as I am, but I am not sure if I am going to be able to accommodate the enormous size of him. My eyebrows jump at the thought, my heart missing a beat.

He moves one elbow down, running his fingers along my face, down my neck, and onto my collar bone, before encircling my throat with his hand. Not tight, I can still breath, his hand barely a whisper on my sensitive skin. He is looking into my eyes, and then he gently places a light kiss on my lips before pulling away again, squeezing the sides of my throat ever so slightly, before loosening once again.

"Do you like to be choked, Siren?"

And I have no idea what I expected him to say, but that wasn't it. The words sink into me like a hook. Siren. My green eyes. I've never had anyone compare me to a mythological creature before, but I kind of like it. Sirens are known for singing men to their doom, before eating them. And I know I would love to swallow him...

"I—I..." My throat dries.

His grip tightens just slightly once more, sending a bolt of heat down to my core. My thighs clench, tightening around his hips that are pressed against me. My cheeks flame.

"I need you to say it," he rasps. He has a look in his eye that reminds me of a feral animal that has been caged. Barely contained, and once let loose, will destroy everything around it. Who said asking for consent was boring. Because this is anything but.

"Yes." My voice cracks, but it's enough. I don't even know why I said yes. I have never been choked when it wasn't forced. I should have said I don't know, but then again, I've never been *asked* either. But it seems my vagina is also doing the talking tonight. The only times I have ever been choked were not during sex. Never. I never let any other man get close enough to me to even ask that since I left Gavin. And Gavin never choked me during sex. He barely looked at me, always flipping me so my face was buried in the bed as he pushed down on the back of my head.

And I don't know how I know, but I've known since the second he grabbed my arm that if I had said no, he would stop. Five minutes ago, or five minutes from now, I know it in my gut.

"Fuck," he groans, and I feel his hips shift against my pussy, lining up his cock near my entrance. That is when I decide there are far too many articles of clothing between us. "You look beautiful in pink."

My pussy weeps as he kisses me hard, tongue sliding against mine. My hips buck, chasing friction. He groans into my mouth, grinding down with his cock, knowing exactly where to push and rub.

Just as quickly as it began, he sits up on his knees and looks down at me, tattoos flexing across every line of muscle on his chest. My eyes drink him in—scars, ink, the sheer size of him. I reach up to touch his chest, and run my fingers along his chest hair, raising goose bumps everywhere I touch.

Without warning, he reaches down and yanks me up by the throat, without ever cutting off my air, unhooks my bra, and slides it away. He lays me back down on the bed with a light toss and leans over me once more, scooting lower, before his mouth latches onto my nipple, sucking hard, teeth scraping.

"Oh my God!" I screech in heavenly bliss. I can't control my volume.

His hand pinches my other nipple, pulling, rolling, twisting. Pain tangled with pleasure until I can no longer tell which is which. I reach my hands up and tangle them in his hair, my hips rising to only find air between them.

He lets go of my nipple and moves his face slightly to look up at me. "I don't know why you're crying out to God. It's just me in here, Siren."

I let out a frustrated growl and lie back until he pulls my sensitive peak between his lips once more, and I move my fingers down his head to his shoulders. I rake my fingernails down his shoulders and arms, leaving trails. He groans into my breast, his body beginning to vibrate.

He releases my nipple with a wet, audible pop that sends shivers racing across my skin. His lips trace a burning path down my trembling stomach, leaving a trail of goosebumps in their wake. When he reaches the waistband of my jeans, his fingers work the button with practiced precision, the zipper's metallic hiss cutting through our heavy breathing. He peels the denim and my soaked panties down my thighs inch by torturous inch, exposing my aching center to the cool bedroom air. I gasp, back arching involuntarily when his hot tongue parts my slick folds, the electric touch against my swollen bud making my vision blur before sitting back up to focus on fully undressing me.

After wrestling my jeans past my ankles along with my mismatched socks, he flings everything carelessly aside, his eyes never leaving mine as he grips my knees with strong, possessive hands, positioning my feet firmly on the rumpled sheets.

He looks at me, waiting to see if I make any objections. I shift my hips, silently asking for more contact, and he accepts that as my answer. He lowers his face once again, his beard tickling my inner thighs, and begins to feast on me. His tongue dips once again into my swollen lips, and begins to flick my clit, causing my hips to buck. The immediate pleasure that courses through me is something that should be studied.

I reach down and rethread my fingers through his hair. I pull slightly, which only serves to egg him on. He increases his ferocity, moving lower and entering me with his tongue, and I think my soul might have left my body the moment his tongue entered it. Feeling him move inside me brings me quickly to an edge I haven't felt in quite some time. Maybe, ever. He must sense it, and his pace continues to increase, now thrusting into me with his tongue. My moans are becoming much louder and erratic, my breathing near hyperventilating, until I begin to see stars, and my head falls back, and I hold onto his hair for dear life. The scream that leaves me probably woke neighbors in the next building, but I can't bring myself to care.

He continues his ministrations until my walls cease pulsing around him, and I let go of his hair. He removes his tongue from me and sits up on his knees.

"Fuck, Surry. That might have been the best meal I have ever had in my entire life." He uses the pads of his large fingers to wipe his beard before placing each one in his mouth and sucking off the wetness. That has to be the hottest thing I have ever seen.

He then stands, and I realize he is still in his sweats. Grey sweats. Every girl's favorite article of clothing any man can own. And seeing the absolute monster that is in no way concealed inside has my eyes popping open wider than I thought possible. There is no way that thing can fit in me. He senses my eyes and smirks at me when I make eye contact again.

Smirk still on his face, he turns to his left and walks toward his nightstand. Picking up his phone, he pushes a few things and a sound bar under the TV across the room lights up before music begins to play. A song I am not familiar with turns on, but it is obviously music someone would pull up if they search *baby making music*. I have to say, I'm a fan. Before returning to me he reaches his hand into his bedside draws and pulls out a small square.

He saunters back over to the bed and stands before me, the lighting in the room enhancing the cut abs running down his front, giving him an almost eerie look about him.

Standing there looking down on me, he looks like a god from those smutty books women read, before reaching both hands to his waistband. Before I know it, he is lowering his sweats until his cock pops free.

I take it back. My pussy will fit whatever the fuck I tell her to fit.

He moves his thighs up and back down, one at a time, stepping out of his sweats before kicking them away. Then his large fingers deftly tear open the small square package, pulling out a condom and tossing the wrapper onto the floor. He places the end onto his tip and begins to roll it down his shaft, pinching the tip with one hand, and sliding it down with the other. Once the condom is fully seated, he places a knee onto the bed, directly under my thigh, and then follows suit with the opposite. His hard member pushing lightly into my inner thigh, so close to where I want it, but not close enough.

Leaning forward, Brenden places his upper body weight onto his elbows, his muscled forearms tensing on either side of my shoulders. He lowers his mouth to mine, his warm breath mingling with my own as he captures my lips in a slow, deliberate kiss that makes my toes curl. I taste the faint sweetness of whiskey and myself on his tongue as he explores my mouth, while simultaneously rolling his hips in a hypnotic rhythm, pressing the lubed head of his thick cock against my slick entrance. With each deep kiss, he applies more pressure, the sensitive tip parting my swollen lips, stretching me deliciously as he gradually works himself inside, inch by exquisite inch.

"That's it, Siren," he whispers in my ear when he removes his lips from mine. "Good girl. Take my cock like it was made for you. "

I whimper at his words. The feeling of him stretching me as he coaches me along. I never knew I had a praise kink, but I am absolutely loving this. His gaze meets mine, a question in there somewhere.

"I'm okay, it feels amazing. Keep going." My thoughts are jumbled from the mixture of pleasure and pain radiating from my stretched pussy. I am having trouble making complete sentences.

After several more languid thrusts, he is finally seated within me fully, and he pauses, both of us panting and sweating already.

"You are so fucking tight," he groans. "Surry. Holy fuck. I have to stop or I'm going to blow already." His body is trembling with the self restraint. The mixture of that and his words bringing me immense pleasure. To have done nearly nothing, and to have already brought this man to his knees, not only literally but figuratively. It does something to a girl's ego, that's for sure.

I begin to flex my inner walls, squeezing him tightly, and letting go, in rapid succession. He groans louder before he sits up abruptly and pulls my hips up with him. He is still filling me to the brim, and I never want to be parted from his body at this point.

He gives me a wild look before moving his hips back with his hands firmly around my waist, and slams us together, the head of his dick hitting my cervix like a battering ram. I gasp and he stops, looking at my face, studying me.

I look him in the eye. "It's... tight," I gasp.

"If it's too much, tell me. We've got forever."

Forever? He's insane.

"No. We have tonight. Fuck me, Brenden Slater."

He thrusts all the way once again. Hard. Deep. My eyes roll to the back of my head, my legs trembling already. He continues to move, fucking into me with deep, languid thrusts, each movement bringing me closer to the edge. My eyes close with the feeling, sucking me into my body as he brings my pleasure closer to the surface.

He abruptly stops once more before speaking to me. "Open your eyes, Siren," he commands in a deep, sultry voice, hand back on my throat before I even realize it. "Look at me when my cock is inside you."

I instantly obey. He lets go and our eyes lock as he begins to thrust into me once again, lowering his upper body to lay over top of me, and starts to kiss my neck. His tongue caresses my neck, the sensual movements driving me insane. He places his lips over the same spot and begins to suck. I'm sure I'll have a hickey in the morning.

He continues thrusting into me as breathy moans work up my throat and fill the room with the sounds of my ecstasy. Moving his mouth from my neck to my ear, he caresses the shell with his expertly trained lips and tongue. Brenden growls—a sound that vibrates through my bones—and then does exactly that. He stops and pulls out so quickly that I gasp at the sudden emptiness. Before I can process the loss, his strong hands grip my waist, fingers pressing into my flesh as he flips me over with practiced ease.

My palms and knees sink into the soft mattress, my hair falling in a curtain around my face. I freeze, muscles tensing, as he positions himself behind me, memories flooding my senses. The heat of his body radiates against my back before he enters me again in one fluid motion, stretching me deliciously. The feeling and the position working in tandem to both put me at ease, and cause anxiety to racket through my mind and body. His right hand slides up my spine, then around to my chin, tilting my face toward him. Our eyes lock, his pupils blown wide with desire, and something in his gentle yet commanding gaze anchors me to the present. This is Brenden Slater, this is not Gavin, I tell myself a few times before I take a deep, shuddering breath and the fog of memory clears. This is not Gavin. This is not eleven years ago.

This is now. This is a man who has never done a bad thing to me. Dirty, but not bad. I take another deep breath and let it out before arching my back and pushing into him as he thrusts even harder into my center, winding my orgasm up until I am nearly at the precipice.

His hand wraps around my throat, pulling me up and onto my knees, back against his chest. His cock driving deeper, harder. He slows, thrusts languid, kissing my shoulder. My walls flutter, milking him, but he knows what he's doing. My orgasm stays where it is, no longer building but holding steady.

"The moment I saw you in my room," he pants, speaking between thrusts, "I knew I should've taken you. But having you here, taking me like this—fuck." His movements become erratic the longer he talks. A song I know comes on, BEG! by Vana, and it is the perfect song to have him come to. I smile evilly.

I lean forward until his dick slips out of me and I sit up onto my knees before spinning around and facing him. I place my hand onto his chest and push him to the side until he is leaning up against the headboard, and he adjusts so he is sitting upright, back pressed straight against the black wooden frame. I crawl to him on my hands and knees until I reach his waist and then place my hands onto his shoulders and pull myself up to him, my front flush to his.

His skin is warm where it touches mine, and he has a light scatter of hair along his entire chest. I run my finger down it, enjoying the way it tickles my finger. I lean forward and lave my tongue from his pecs up to his neck as I situate myself to straddle him.

He looks down at my breasts and grabs them, pulling my nipples between his thumb and forefinger as I take position, placing my entrance above his throbbing erection. It twitches slightly as my smooth lips graze his tip so I begin to rock back and forth, teasing the tip. Brenden shudders and moans, before growling and giving me a look that tells me he has little patience left.

With the height difference he is still taller than me, my knees unable to touch the bed as I  straddle him. He bends down and places a kiss onto my lips, his beard both rough and soft against my flushed skin. His tongue tastes of salt and desire and me as it slides against mine, sending electric shivers down my spine.

"I want to watch you cum all over me," he whispers

hoarsely, his breath hot against my ear. I moan at his words, my back arching involuntarily. His eyes, dark and hungry, lock with mine. "I want to see your face when you fall apart. The way your eyes glaze over, the way your lips part. You're mine, Surry. Not just tonight but forever—every tremble, every sigh, every inch of you is mine."

He grabs my hips and lifts me, slamming me down, spearing his hardness into me again and again. My climax builds, his tip once again hitting deep inside me, driving me closer to the edge. I've never been taken like this—so deeply, so completely. Every thrust feels like he's claiming a part of me I didn't know was still alive.

"Brenden! I'm—fuck—I'm gonna—BRENDEN!" I can't form words anymore; my brain is mush. My arms barely hold me up, and my head lolls forward before I throw it back and scream my pleasure into the room. I ride him until I can't stay up anymore, my nails having implanted themselves into his shoulders before I go limp.

He snarls as soon as my hands begin to slip, thrusts jagged, roaring my name as he fills me. His heat pulses inside me.

We collapse together, sweaty, breathless. My head rests on his shoulder. His hand strokes my hair.

"Let's get you in the shower, baby," he murmurs into my hair, placing light kisses along my head and face. "Don't want you sleeping covered in my sweat.

I hum, too blissed out to reply, drifting in the safety of his arms.

I chuckle as I stand, rolling off the edge of the mattress. The sight of her in my bed—hair spilled over my pillow, mouth parted—hits like a clean shot of whiskey. New drug. Only one I'll ever need. I could never give her up. She's mine. And I'll make damn sure everyone knows it before they even *think* about testing me.

I stand there and look at her for a moment. She is beautiful. Quiet. She is peaceful. Even with her being testy earlier, last night I guess as I look at the clock and see it's about three in the morning now. It was adorable since she is so tiny compared to me. I have to have at least a whole foot on her. There is just something about her. The spice, the calm. She reminds me of someone. I can't place it. All I know is that I need her to be mine.

I cut through the closet into the bathroom and twist the shower handle hot—nearly scalding. Women tend to bathe in volcanic temps; no sense easing her into lukewarm. Steam fogs the glass in seconds.

On my way back to the bed, I snatch my phone off the nightstand. A stack of notifications waits—mostly from our group thread I renamed **DICK HEADS** because they earned it.

I glance over. She's asleep on her stomach, dead to the world, one hand fisted in my sheet like she's claiming the territory. Good.

I thumb the screen.

Good. They've got the perimeter. The second I laid eyes on this woman I knew that she would forever be mine. I can't let her go now, and I won't. But my nerves are fight me. I can tell that I became instantly on edge since the second she accidentally opened my door. My mind was already all over the place. But now? Now it is a constant stream of worse case scenario. I set the phone on the vanity. The bathroom's a warm cloud now, mirrors bleached white with steam. I close the door to trap the heat, then head back for my sleeping Siren.

I slide an arm under her knees and another under

her shoulders. She murmurs something and nuzzles into my chest on instinct. Light as nothing. I carry her into the shower and step under the spray, leaning us both into the heat slowly so I don't shock her awake.

"Mm." A soft sound against my collarbone. Yeah. She likes it hell-hot.

"Little Siren," I murmur, hands rubbing lazy circles into the swell of her ass, "let's get you cleaned up. Then we can go back to bed." Nothing. "Come on Surry, wake up, doll."

She squirms, more awake now. I keep my grip solid. Light pinches to her thigh earn me a tiny gasp and a blink up at me.

"Whoa. How did we get in the bathroom?"

"Carried you," I say, setting her down steady on the river-stone tile. "You fell out the second we finished." The sleepy haze she has on her face is driving me wild, but I'm sure she will be sore in the morning, so I hold myself back from showing her how undeniably attracted I am to her.

The shower space is built for men my size—no builder-grade box. Rounded gray-white stones underfoot; matte-black subway tile climbing to the ceiling; three adjustable heads in a triangle so there's no cold pocket anywhere. The rest of the room tracks with it—black fixtures, broad concrete counter, warm strip lighting. Industrial...clean...me.

I turn her gently, back to my chest, and pump shampoo into my palm. My cock jumps at the nearness of her ass, but I tell myself to cool the fuck off. But, I could easily hold up against the shower wall and fuck her again. The citrus-cedar scent opens up, bringing me back to what I was doing. I work it into her hair, fingertips moving slowly and firmly. She melts, head tipping back into me like a cat.

"As soon as we were done, I got the liquid fire temp water going, then  I scooped you up," I tell her, working the lather to the ends, while mentally repeating *don't get a boner* over and over in my head. "Figured you'd want the sweat off so you sleep clean."

I pivot her to face me and tilt her under the spray, rinsing until the suds are gone. Her nipples, hard at the contact, rub against my abs. The feeling oddly as comforting as it is sexy.

Chill Brenden. Conditioner next. The way the water beads on her shoulder blades is criminal. Her breasts press into my chest—tight, pink nipples begging for me to place my tongue there—and I tame the urge by twisting her hair into a loose bun to let the conditioner set.

She looks up, clear-eyed now. "Listen, Brenden. I don't know what you think this is," she takes a small step backwards not fully leaving the warmth of the water, "but I'm not looking for anything. This was just sex. And a bed. Thank you for... being kind. You have no idea what that means. But I'm not there. So we can shower and sleep, and then I'm going home. Got it?"

She thinks she's drawing the line. Cute. Her cheeks go the most delicious shade of pink when she's trying to look unbothered—nervous glint right there in her eyes. I can give her whatever version of control she needs for now. She'll learn soon enough: I'm not going anywhere. I belong to her now, just as much as she belongs to me.

When she faces me again, I nod once. "Yes, ma'am. Clean and cozy. Long day. We'll get you some peace." I look down and can't help my eyes wandering, but she must not notice since her shoulders drop a fraction in relief. Good call, Slater.

"Yeah," she says, voice unsteady. "My brand-new car got beaten to death. Juniper's shop got blown up. And I got a very threatening text and letter. I'm overwhelmed. Blowing off steam with you was..." She exhales. "Great. I appreciate it."

Picking up a loofah I flood it with the body wash that smells like dark florals and warm earth. I will never be able to smell this ever again without thinking of her. The way I am marking her with my own scents makes me feel something extra in that caveman part of my brain. "You have had an exceptionally bad day, I'll do the work. Just try and relax, okay Siren?" She nods her head, and closes her eyes. A small hum escapes her as I start to work.

I wash her head to toe—practical, steady. Neck, shoulders, arms. I drag the suds along her ribs and belly, between her thighs. She blushes and watches, biting her lip like she doesn't know what to do with being taken care of without strings attached. Or maybe she is as turned on as I am and doesn't want to admit it, maybe if I just...no. No, Slater. I continue, washing each one of her breasts and then move up to her chest and throat. Once I reach her chin, I hand her the face wash from the shelf.

"You'll want this. No sleeping in makeup."

Her mouth opens, stays there, then closes. "You have... face wash?"

I give her a mock insulted face, before asking "do I look like a heathen?"

She laughs—a small bell sound that hits low in my

spine—and works the cleanser across her skin. I loosen the bun, let her rinse everything at once, then step into a second head and rinse down myself—just conditioner through the hair, quick scrub of body. No need for a totally full shower since I just took one.

When the water stops, the room breathes steam. I reach for two towels through the glass and hand her one, wrapping the other at my waist. I step out and go to the cabinet, grabbing a third towel for her hair. Then a spare toothbrush for her. The small stuff matters.

I duck into the closet, grab her a soft, worn band tee —one that is short on me—and come back. She pulls it over her head and shakes her hair out of the towel. She's all clean skin and wet gold, her hair still dripping from the shower, leaving dark patches on the light colored band tee I gave her to wear. It clings to her curves and hits just below the crease where thigh meets hip, revealing a tantalizing glimpse of what lies beneath with every slight movement. My dick has opinions, jumping slightly every time I see a sliver of her smooth, firm, cheeks. I set my jaw and hang the towels instead of bending her over the counter like every cell is ordering me to.

Boxer briefs for me. Lights low. She eyes me again, but not in a way that screams she wants to jump on me again. She studies my tattoos, reaching out a finger and raking it down one of the blacked out portions on my forearm. Then she moves on to the ones covering my chest, running her hand lightly over my chest hair. It feels, intimate. I let her finish exploring me before I take her hand, lead her back to bed, and pull her into my chest. She nestles in like we've done it a hundred nights. Good. I hold her there and breathe her in until her weight goes slack.

She's asleep before my eyes close, but I'm not far behind.

My alarm bleats from the bathroom at five in the morning because Past Me is an idiot. I peel one arm out from under her inch by inch. She's starfished across my mattress, blanket strangled around one ankle, an arm flung over my ribs like she's keeping me in place. I slide free without waking her, kill the alarm, take a leak, and grab sweats and a cutoff.

When I step into the hall, the house is already breathing. Of course it is. I follow the smell of coffee.

Joshua and Corver are at the kitchen island—hoodies, bare feet, open laptops. Sam's there too in borrowed clothes, hair a mess that screams "slept on a sofa I didn't mean to." Although, I'm not sure where he slept exactly. Joshua lifts the pot toward me.

"Coffee?" he asks.

I nod. He pours. I wrap both hands around my favorite mug and inhale the burn.

"Sleep good?" I ask, meaning *no intruders, no ghosts of the past, no blood on the floor.*

Grunts all around. Good enough.

"Not great," says Corver. We all look at him. We know why.

"Did *you* get any sleep?" Joshua smirks. He's begging for it.

"Yes, you dick." I jerk my head toward Sam. "Her *brother* is sitting right here."

Sam stares up at the ceiling, visibly praying for the drywall to swallow him whole.

"Oh. Sorry, man," Josh mutters, bumping him with an elbow. Sam returns the favor with interest. Worth it.

I set the mug down. "Where are we with Natasha?"

Corver already has the laptop spinning. "Your best friend's encrypted servers got the video to Sam's father. I can't track Gavin. I can't track her. Nothing. I want her out." His voice is tight, clipped, controlled rage. "We need to get her out, Brenden. Now."

"I'm in complete agreement," I say. "But we need eyes. Call Arnie. See what he can drag out of the shadows."

Arnie's the brain—MIT freak who likes puzzles more than people. He and Corver run point on the data side when we hunt. Joshua has Gunnar for the other things. Gunnar's a good man with bad methods. We met him back when we first started the backdoor gig. He was on a similar job and we crossed paths. He is ex-Army. SpecOps. The guy is nuts, but genuine as fuck. The kind of guy that's hard to come by in this world. I wouldn't cross him for a kingdom, though.

"On it," Corver says, already walking to his office. "Text him a heads-up. I'm going to chew the line."

I pull my phone and type out a message to Arnie.

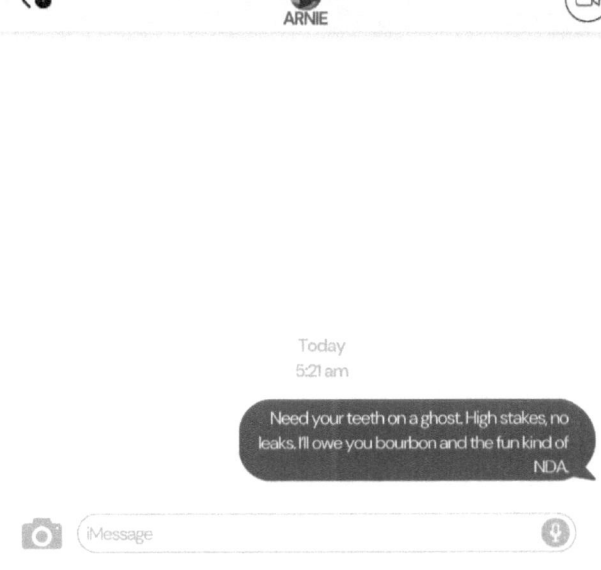

ARNIE

Today
5:21 am

Need your teeth on a ghost. High stakes, no leaks. I'll owe you bourbon and the fun kind of NDA.

iMessage

I set the phone down and hit the fridge, grabbing out all the supplies for a proper feast. If we're going to be under the same roof for a while, we're eating like soldiers before a fight.

Skillets go down. Flame up. Coffee brews a second pot while I run point on breakfast. By 7:15 the counter is a lineup —scrambles, crispy bacon, sausage links, toast, hot sauce, buttered jam, refilled cups.

Richie shuffles in with Selene—both wearing Corver's clothes like pilfering raccoons. They look wrecked.

"Morning," I say. "Coffee? Breakfast? Both?"

Selene grumbles. Richie answers for them. "Coffee first, brekky second. Us girls gotta wake up before we can eat." He winks at me, and I just smirk back. This guy is actually really funny.

I pour. Let them make bad decisions with caffeine before food. Not my stomach.

Once they down their liquid life, they eat. The living room swallows them. Joshua and Sam take the sofa; Selene drapes across the chair by the window like a cat in a sunbeam. The windows throw that big Seattle gray light across everything, and for a minute, it almost looks like a normal morning.

At 7:35, Alisha staggers out, hair like a storm cloud. Sam moves so fast he nearly dumps his coffee onto the floor.

"You good, Lish? You want breakfast? Coffee? Hair of the dog?" Sam fusses, already building a plate.

She swats his arm, eyes half closed but smiling. "Yes. All."

I sip coffee and look at the hall. Door still closed. Quiet. The room feels wrong without her in it. My bed smells like her. My shirt smells like her. I want the rest of the apartment to catch up.

I am not a patient man by nature. But for her, I can be.

My phone vibrates on the counter and I pick it up. A reply from Arnie.

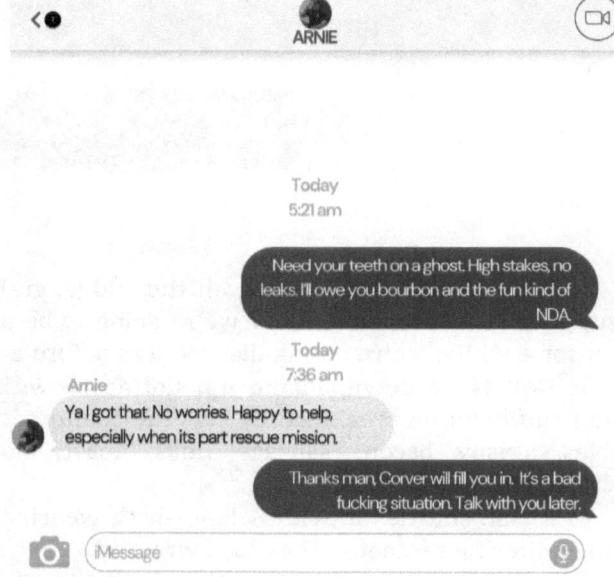

I grunt. "If Gavin wants a war, he picked the wrong coast."

Joshua nods into his mug. "We'll hit what we can see and make the rest visible."

"Good," I say. "We keep June under glass. We keep Surry here until her father finalizes the move. We are not the soft target."

"Already doubled cams, changed door pins, and set the garage to manual overrides only," Corver calls from his office. "Nobody gets in without a voice and a gun aimed at them."

My jaw loosens a fraction. That's our system: one hand builds, one hand breaks, both hands protect.

Now I just need *her* to wake up.

Just at that moment, I hear slight movement down the hall. A door closes, and I hear feet shuffling along the wooden floors.

I lean back against the counter, fold my arms over my chest, and wait for the woman who fell asleep on me to walk into my kitchen like she belongs there.

Because she does.

And I plan to make sure she never forgets it.

OH. MY. FUCKING. GOD.

What did I do last night?

I feel like I got run over by a bus and then the bus backed up to check if I was okay and ran me over again. I don't open my eyes yet—too scared of what I'll find—so I inventory with touch: sheet, duvet, cool air across bare thighs, the faint floral scent of someone else's soap. Flashes come back to me, piece by piece. Brenden's arms around me, his mouth on mine. The way he threw me onto the bed. The way his skin felt against mine. The warm bed after the shower. But now, no other body in the bed. No heat but mine.

I crack one eye, then the other. I'm in Brenden's room. His bed. The massive wall of shadow where his closet door stands and leads to the shower where we took me is ajar. I lift my head. He isn't in here, and the darkness of the closet leads me to believe he isn't here anywhere. I'm alone. Why does that make me feel sad? I wanted this. That's what I told him.

A stretch pulls through my hamstrings and lower back; a sweet ache answers low in my body, pulsing with each heartbeat. My skin still tingles where his beard rasped: neck, breasts, inner thighs. The pillow smells like him—cedar and soap and something warm, like sun on worn leather—and I bury my face in it for one breath, just one. I can't regret any of it. I won't. Not a single second.

I slip off the mattress, legs wobbly, and pad to the bathroom. Cool tile. Relief. Water, soap, the soft rasp of a toothbrush he'd set out like he knew I would need it. I catch my reflection—hair a mess, mouth kiss-swollen, the ghost of last night's flush still high in my cheeks—and I don't look away. I look...happy.

I make my way back in the bedroom, looking through his closet as I go. His closet is a mirror of my own. Black, grey, brown, some white. But no color. I see if I can find anything that might be closer to my side, but no luck. Great. Over sized band tee it is. Phone? I left it in the living room during charades. I smack myself on accident as I put my hand over my face. Of course I did.

I crack the door. The hallway beyond is bare as a bone —no art, no photos, just clean paint and a practical runner. It reads like a bachelor pad that never bothered pretending otherwise. For a second, I imagine frames here, a gallery of lives; then I remember where I am and who owns this place, and the blankness makes sense. Men who've taught themselves not to need anything that can be stolen don't hang memories on drywall.

Where I have created a small community, a family of sorts, Brenden has avoided that. He stays within what he knows. His brothers. His work. Where he is the rock the storm beats against, I am the waves. Perfect compliment, but also the making of an epic tragedy.

I step out of his room, and begin to pad toward the open room beyond.

Voices carry from the kitchen. Alisha and Samuel stand shoulder to shoulder at the island, digging into plates, both in borrowed clothes. Selene's messy bun bobs as she rummages in a cabinet, the too-long sleeves of someone else's shirt swallowing her hands. Looking around, it makes me feel better I'm not the only one waking up in clothes that don't belong to me.

Brenden sits at the far end of the counter, blue eyes on his phone, thumbs moving. The moment my bare feet hit cool tile, his attention snaps up. That grin—shameless, satisfied, a little dangerous—spreads across his mouth like he can still taste me.

"Good morning, Siren," he rumbles. It's unfair that a voice alone can stroke my entire nervous system with one simple sentence.

"Good morning. Um... is there coffee?" I can smell it, but I've learned not to assume.

He's already moving, chair legs scraping back as he rounds the counter. I catch a flash of the space while he pours: industrial-clean lines, matte black hardware, big windows spilling gray Seattle light. Joshua leans against the frame, jaw working; Corver is missing; Selene hums some upbeat riff under her breath that my brain, jittered by nerves and lack of sleep, tags as *Death of Peace of Mind* by Bad Omens—because of course my life would cue that right now.

I keep glancing around the room, taking silent inventory of my people. Hazel and Richie are back on the couch just as they were last night. Not sure if they slept there, or if they just migrated there again.

"Where's June?" I ask as he passes me a mug—heavy, handmade, perfectly imperfect. The glaze is a stormy marble that swirls dark into light. "And where did you get this? Is it handmade? It's beautiful."

"She was up and out here earlier, I think she's in the shower now," he says, softening. "Doesn't like the morning-after vibe. Thinks it gives Joshua the wrong idea." The corner of his mouth ticks. "And yeah—my mom made that. Years ago. It's my favorite."

He says *mom* and something bright and breakable flickers behind his eyes. I don't know if it's love or ache; I know better than to pry.

"Juniper? And Josh?" I echo in a whisper, Josh standing so close to us. "Seriously?" I haven't heard June talk about any man like that. I drift to the fridge and fish out some creamer. "Sugar?"

He's already holding a ceramic jar out to me when I turn. Of course he is. I doctor the coffee, stir, lift.

The first sip drags a sound out of me I can't swallow fast enough. I freeze at my own moan of pleasure, embarrassed that I did that in front of this enormous man. I look up into his face slowly, a flush spreading across my skin.

"Damn, girl, that's almost as good a moan as I got from you last night," he says, playful, wicked. "Had I known coffee could do that, I'd have added it to the menu."

I shove his arm, rolling my eyes, smiling despite the scrape of panic rising in my chest. Memory is a traitor. It offers heat and safety then turns on me with cold hands and whispers *what now*. He must see it flicker across my face because he doesn't crowd me—just steps in slow, the way you move with a skittish horse. Then his gaze travels down and back, deliberate as a touch.

"I respect you. And I respect your calls," he says, voice low and even. "But I'm not going anywhere. I'll prove it. I'm here for whatever you need. You say jump, I ask how high. But you...Surry O'Brien... you are mine."

"You say—" I go to argue but he cuts me off.

"And I am yours."

He closes the space. Left hand resting gently on the back of my neck; right hand settling warm on my hip. His breath is heat against the shell of my ear. "And I'm not letting you walk away from me, Siren. Do you understand?"

Oh. Fuck.

My brain freezes. My body doesn't. Everything in me leans into him like it's gravity and I'm just...falling. How dangerous. This feeling of desire. Of happiness. Of hope.

"I—I—"

Then the world rips.

A concussion-punch of air slams the room, the building, my bones. The sound is a white wall, a roar that eats everything. Light flares—then the kitchen folds, cabinets shuddering, glass screaming as it explodes. The floor bucks. Brenden is already on me, a full-body shield, driving me down. My spine kisses the cabinet. His forearm cages my head; the other covers his own. I can taste copper and dust. For a moment, there is no time, just heartbeat-heartbeat-heartbeat, a distant siren of someone screaming that I slowly realize is me.

The second wave hits—a rumble that bows the window frames and turns the far wall into a mouth of open air. Wind slices through. Something whines—rebar flexing, or a pipe. A hanging beam tilts, a shower of fine, glittering plaster dust turning the gray light into fog. Sparks spit from a torn electrical run—blue-white, vicious. The smell comes next, a dirty stack: burned plastic, hot metal, drywall, and the medicinal sting of fresh blood atomized into the air.

Then sound returns in pieces.

Yelling. Alarms. Boots on tile. Over it all, the wet keening that nails my ribs open.

Brenden hauls me up. The room tilts and rights. His hand finds mine and tucks me under his arm like I'm cargo he refuses to lose. My gaze darts, frantic—count them, count them, where is—

Selene.

"I don't see Selene. Where is she—where—" My voice cracks, small and savage at once.

Alisha appears like she's conjured, mascara wet tracks down her cheeks. "She's hurt, Surry, Selene is hurt!" She points, and that's when I hear the screaming. Not distant. Ours.

The living room is half living room, half catastrophic edge. Shattered glass glitters like diamonds across the marble floor. The window—no, the entire eastern wall—has been blown outward, leaving jagged concrete teeth and twisted rebar claws grasping at empty air. Thirty stories below, ant-sized cars crawl through gridlocked streets while the city's spires pierce a smoke-stained sky that feels close enough to touch. Joshua stands at the torn opening, his silhouette stark against the burning horizon, scanning the chaos below while barking rapid-fire orders to my father's stone-faced men in black suits posted at the elevator. Sam, wild-eyed with pupils blown wide in terror, kneels over Selene's crumpled form on the Persian rug now slick with something dark and viscous. The acrid smoke curls around everything, softening edges and distorting sounds, like a nightmare desperately trying to disguise itself as just a fading memory.

Richie's got Hazel locked to his chest near the hall, her face buried, his eyes wide and sharp over her head. He catches my gaze, flicks it to the door. I shake my head. No. I'm not leaving her. I'm not leaving *any* of them.

"Move," Brenden growls, steering me down the hallway. We hit his room and he releases me just long enough to vanish into his closet. The thunder of my pulse lives in my throat. I stand useless, shaking, while the house ticks and groans around us like a wounded animal. Wires spit in the ceiling; a sprinkling head coughs once, twice, and dies.

Thirty seconds? A minute? I don't know. My hands are vibrating, they shake so bad. I can't get my breathing under control, I feel like I might pass out. He reemerges with two duffels, a packet, two flip phones, chargers, and guns. The weight of the world reorders itself around the sight.

He drops the bags and strides over to me, grabbing my face firmly, but gentle enough to guide my eyes to his. With our foreheads together he takes a large inhale, causing my brain to mimic him. I reach up and grab his wrists tightly, as if they are a lifeline I didn't realize I needed.

"Wherever you go, I go," he says. "Here are your clothes. Do you need help?"

I don't answer. My hands are numb. He takes that as a yes—peels the shirt off me with efficient gentleness, slides my bra on, then my top, kneels to work jeans over my shaky legs, and socks onto my feet. No panties. Not asking. He's changed too: black slim cargos, fitted black tee, high tops, that brutal multi-pocket jacket. He looks like the thing men cross streets to avoid.

"Surry, have you used a gun before?"

I nod. My dad insisted beginning at twelve. Range days instead of recitals, another reason I should have guessed he was more than just *in the security world*. He places a pistol into my palm. Muscle memory checks the mag, the chamber, and the safety. Loaded. Safe on. It slides into my waistband like it was made for me.

The weight wakes something in me. I look up at him,

grab his shirt, pull him down, and kiss him hard—like lighting a match inside my own chest. He kisses me back just as fervently.

"Thank you," I breathe against his mouth. "I needed that." He smiles tightly down at me, going in for one more kiss, quick but firm.

Then we move.

Back in the living room, the air tastes like chalk. Joshua stands alone now, backlit by the torn wall; the others are gone.

"Where did they go?" I ask, throat raw.

"Corver took Juniper, Richie, and Hazel to our safe house," Joshua says, eyes still working. His jaw works when he says June, showing his clear disdain of being separated from her. "Your dad's guys took the other three to the hospital. Selene caught shrapnel in her abdomen. She'll be fine if they get there quickly. She'll likely need surgery, though. It bled, yeah—but it was red and steady, not that dark, pumping arterial—so I'm betting high odds." He finally looks at me. Steady. Grounding.

"Okay, so what are we doing?" I cross the dining room, snatch my purse from a chair buried in dust and glittering glass. My phone is inside, blessedly intact.

"We hang back," he says. "They'll assume you got pulled the second it went off. Let 'em chase ghosts while we breathe and think. Everyone's prepped. Don't be afraid."

I nod, but the laugh that punches out of me tastes like a sob. "Okay, so then what? Safe house? Mexico?" The laugh breaks. "I can't be taken. He can't take me. I can't be there again. I'll kill myself this time."

I'm not sorry I said it, and I mean it. I can't go back. I know I thought that would solve all our problems. But the time I endured with Gavin was more than enough for an entire lifetime. I look at Brenden. He doesn't look shocked by the declaration, simply serious. Josh on the other hand, his face is alarmed, but alert.

Brenden steps in behind me, arms gentle but iron, breath warm and gentle at my ear. "He can't take you because I won't let that happen. I'm right here. I'm not going anywhere."

"I'm not going anywhere either, shorty," Joshua's mouth crooks, having recovered from his shock. "You're stuck with that giant idiot, which means I've got your six like I've got his."

The panic eases its claws a fraction, barely. I nod.

"Okay. So what's the plan when we do finally leave?"

"We need to talk to your dad," Brenden says. "See

what he wants to do."

Easy. I thumb Dad's contact and put it on speaker.

"Oh, my sweet Surry," my father answers, his accent thicker—stress always drags Galway into his mouth. "I'm so glad ye're okay. Yer sister's just in the doors o' the hospital. Why aren't ye with her?"

"It's okay, Papa. I'm still with Brenden and Josh Slater at their apartment."

"Aye, good an' good. I've always admired th' lads." Brenden and Josh both shoot me a look. I can't help the smirk before shrugging. Seeing them so shocked is hilarious, but I am equally out of the loop on what that means.

"Yes, Daddy—I'm sure Samuel has told you lots about them."

"No, love, I've kept my eye on 'em fer a time now. Glad ye found 'em." That surprises me. I had no idea that my dad knew the Slater's more than just what Sam had told them. To know the Mafia has been watching them, I'm not sure if they should feel proud or terrified.

"Oh. Okay. Papa—where do I go? What do we do?"

"Go t' the place where the sky meets the sea, Surry. D'ye know the one?" His voice lowers, meaning threaded through sound.

"Yes. I know." The memories of salt and gulls, and the heavy scent of the sea roll through me like a tide. It's the code we use whenever we talk about it.

"Will I see you there?"

"No, m'sweet girl, not yet. We won't be comin' just now—we'll make for th' island house, it's nearer t' th' hospital. Keep them boys wi' ye, an' bring Alisha, Hazel, an' Richie, an' whoever else's needin' shelter. I'll ring ye later, aye? Love ye, m'sweet Surry. Yer mam's sendin' all her love."

"Okay, Papa. I love you too."

The line clicks.

Joshua blinks. "Okay, so what the fuck does *where the sky meets the sea* mean?"

I smile, a small stubborn thing that doesn't belong in the wreckage but insists on existing anyway. Memory surges: an island ferry riding whitecaps, the tang of kelp, the house with windows that face nothing but horizon. I can feel the sun on my face, smell the evergreen.

"We're going home."

"What the fuck, Surry, you didn't say we were going to be driving this long!"

Josh hasn't stopped complaining since Tacoma. The highway unspools in a gray ribbon, rain spitting on the windshield, wipers ticking a steady metronome against my nerves. The silence that is emanating off Brenden is heavier than the constant whining from the back seat.

"I know, it's nearly a six-hour drive. I'm sorry." I keep my gaze on the window, where firs and maples smear into a watercolor of green and slate. "But nobody outside my family—and now you two—knows about this place. So will you just shut up and deal?" I am, in fact, not sorry at all. And he is getting on my nerves at this point.

He huffs behind me. Brenden's fingers rest lightly on the wheel, his presence heavy. Mountains drift in and out between low clouds—Rainier a ghosted crown, St. Helen's a scab of history, Hood distant and clean. Being surrounded by the twenty four active volcanoes actually lowers my nerves, and brings me peace. The farther south we go, the more the world loosens—traffic drops, shoulders widen, trees thicken until the highway feels tunneled by pine.

Brenden doesn't talk much. He hums sometimes, a low vibration that seems to come from somewhere deeper than his throat. His knuckles rest loosely on the steering wheel, tanned skin stretched over bone. He's got the kind of quiet that fills a car like water filling a glass—complete, without bubbles or gaps. The center display glows cobalt blue against the darkness of the dashboard, illuminating the lower half of his face. When *Take Me To The Beach* by Imagine Dragons pops up, the entire cabin transforms around us. Not because of the lyrics—I don't even need them. Just the pulse of it, something yearning and salt-tanged, tugging the ribcage open like an insistent tide pulling at a dock.

I feel my shoulders drop, breath deepen into my

belly. I grew up following winding coastal roads that eventually surrendered to dunes and sand, the asphalt giving way to something less certain. I learned to read the choppy whitecaps and shifting wind patterns before I could solve for x or grasp long division. The song isn't ours, not yet, but the want inside it feels as familiar as my own heartbeat—like sun-browned hands outstretched toward cool, beckoning water. Before I know it, I'm signing along to the words as if they're carved into my soul.

The phone rings, silencing the music as Corver's name floods the screen. I lean forward, tapping the green circle to answer.

"Where is this place again, Surry?" His voice comes through the speakers before I can even say hello, clipped. I swear these men look really tough, but are the most impatient whining babies I have ever met. "Hard to navigate when the address is some state secret."

"Not a secret," I say, then sigh. "Okay, it's a secret. We don't say it over lines. Ever. My dad is strict. I watched him kill a guy for breaking that rule." I glance at the rain-gritted window. "Do you want to be next?"

Silence. A cough on their end that sounds suspiciously like Richie covering up a laugh. Even the song takes a breath.

"We'll meet at the gas station I sent you in Eugene," I add, softer. "Then you guys follow us for the last leg. Don't worry – I'm not leaving you lost."

"Alright then, I'll trust you, see you in Eugene," Corver replies.

"Good," Brenden cuts in, voice like gravel over heat. "See you soon, brother." The call ends. His hand slides down to my knee.

I should pull away. I do, kind of—turning to the window so his hand falls. I'm already melting, and I can't afford melting. Not when the calculus of everyone I love being alive keeps rearranging itself in my head. He just puts it back, palm warm against the inside of my thigh, and leans in enough that his breath ghosts my neck.

"You're mine, Siren," he says, low and certain. "You'll see. Hades himself couldn't keep you from me."

I swallow. He doesn't squeeze—just anchors. I tell myself I hate it. My body calls me a liar. Behind us, Josh mutters something about getting a room. I roll my eyes and keep watching the trees race north as we go south, and I pretend my pulse isn't syncing to the song.

Eugene smells like wet asphalt and diesel. We pull

into the gas station—a squat rectangle of buzzing lights and old coffee. I hop out, the air sharp with rain and petroleum, and call my father. I need Selene's voice. I need to know she's still threaded to this world with something more than stitches.

He answers on the second beat. "Hello, my sweet Surry. Are ye home yet?"

"No, Papa. Eugene. We're waiting for the others. Thank you for trusting them."

"They make ye happy, mo chroí. And I've vetted 'em. Nothin' in their closets I can't live with." A pause. "You didn't give the address over the line, did ye now?"

I laugh despite everything. "No, Papa. I wrote it for Brenden on paper, he unfolded just enough to read it, then we burned it. Like you taught me."

"That's my girl." I hear a shuffle. Voices. "Ye want to speak to yer sister?"

"Yes, please."

There's muffled sound through the line and then Selene's voice ricochets down the line—bright, breathless. "SISSY! Are you there? How is it? Did the apple tree bloom? How's Bridget? I'm so jealous! I want them to send me home already! I can't wait to see you. Samuel has asked about Alisha about twenty ti—OW! Don't injure me even more than I already am, Samuel!"

God, she's a hurricane. My chest aches with love and the shape of fear it carves.

"I'm in Eugene," I say, smiling helplessly into the rain. "I'll tell you everything when we get there. Do they have a discharge date?"

"Tomorrow, maybe the next. Extra scans, blah blah." She huffs. "Papa's ordering a med bed and a nurse on the Island. Once I don't need all that shit I can come down there and stay with you. Surgery went smooth, four hours, you know that. I want my own pillows. Oh! Mama—"

The line shifts and my mother's voice arrives, soft steel. "So, who's da handsome lad ye're wit'?"

"Mama. Not now."

"Ah, this's th' only fella we've seen ye wit' since ye left th' Compound. Humor yer mother, love."

"When you get here," I say. "I'll tell you then. I love you. Punch Samuel for me?"

"Aye, I'll do that, so I will. I love ye too, a stór."

I hear an outraged "What was that for?" and Selene's witchy cackle. My mother exhales a laugh. We say our goodbyes and then the line clicks off. A text from Selene lands immediately, full of hearts and knives and something about stealing Alisha's man as a joke that will definitely get her killed.

I look up. Brenden is perched on the hood, phone in one hand, eyes scanning the screen, although I am not sure what he is studying with such intensity. He changed when we realized how far we were driving, we all did. He's now in high-tops, slutty little thigh shorts, a T-shirt damp at the collar from rain, hair pulled into a low bun. He looks like temptation dressed in black cotton. I hoist myself onto the metal beside him. It's cold through my jeans. He, however, is not. He tilts his head toward me without looking, like he knew I was always going to sit here.

"Thanks for all of this," I say. The rain is finer now, a mist that clings instead of falls. "You guys don't have to stay. You weren't the target. It was a message. You're welcome to regroup there, but you don't have to play bodyguard."

"Oh, I hate to break it to you, sweetheart, and I apparently need to repeat myself hourly," he slides his phone into his pocket and turns, caging me between his thighs with infuriating ease. "But I will be guarding that body." He looks me up and down for emphasis, making me blush. I swear I am going to have circulatory issues from how often he does that. "From the moment I saw you in my room until my last breath. That body belongs to me now." He winks. Fuck.

He grips my hip and pulls me closer. Heat sparks—quick, all encompassing. "Did you forget?" His voice is velvet over barbed wire. "You're mine. And I'll make sure everyone knows it. You included."

My mouth opens and closes like I'm learning to breathe for the first time. "Okay," I hear myself say.

Okay? Who am I? My traitor body purrs. My brain throws up its hands.

"Good girl," he rumbles, and it vibrates across the metal into my bones. The words should feel like a collar. Instead, they feel like a promise.

He smiles like a wolf who just watched a door swing open to look in upon its prey. *I am not prey.*

"You're right, you're not prey," he adds. "You're fierce Surry—stronger than you know. Queen of the castle. Look how many people you assembled in a day. You're invincible."

"Fuck, did I say that out loud?" My words come out in a mumble, making me think I am starting to go crazy.

"You did." He looks almost amused. "One day, I'll punish the man who made you feel like prey. I'll wait. Till then,

I'll prove I'm nothing but your servant. To worship your body and mind until I die."

His phone rings. He ignores it. The chorus of *Take Me To The Beach* rises again—a haunt of tide and heat. Neither of us moves.

Headlights swing in. Two vehicles pull alongside Brenden's—an overloaded truck with off-road tires and the attitude of a siege tower, and a sleek BMW hatchback. Doors fly open and people spill out, stretching, laughing, shaking out the road from their bones. The air fills with shouts, the skitter of gravel, and the sound of relief people make when a long drive finally ends.

Hazel reaches me first, bone-crushing hug, Alisha slamming into us with an "oof!" and Richie wrapping both his long arms around all of us like a blanket. Somewhere in the mob is Juniper, swearing and laughing.

"That was a tight fit on the way here, damn."

A new voice cuts through—deep, smooth, with a grin threaded in it. I turn.

A tall man drops down from the truck's passenger side, rain glinting on the nearly blacked-out tattoos that sleeve his right arm from wrist to shoulder. A dark mustache, darker eyes, and the kind of swagger that says he's trouble wrapped in leather and good intentions. His gaze lands squarely on Hazel first.

"Please tell me someone saved me a seat near *that* one," he says, flashing a grin that could melt steel. "Or maybe we toss a few folks in the back and give and give us a chance to get acquainted."

Hazel's cheeks go crimson, her smirk betraying the flutter behind it. "You wish," she shoots back, playful despite herself.

He chuckles, unfazed, and then turns to me like the energy in his body just shifts direction.

"And you must be Surry," he says, voice dropping a register. "The one everyone's been talking about. Didn't think the stories would do you justice—but damn, they undersold you." He winks. HE WINKS!

That's when Brenden's jaw tightens beside me. His hand finds the small of my back in a move that's calm on the surface but all claim underneath.

The stranger's grin widens like he's just found a live wire. "Easy, big guy," he says, raising both hands in mock surrender. "I like breathing."

The tension cracks just enough for laughter to spill out—mine included.

He steps forward, extending a hand. "Arnie," he introduces himself. "Tech, logistics, and sometimes comic relief." I take his hand. He bows slightly and plants a quick kiss on my knuckles before winking.

"Jesus," Juniper mutters. "He's flirting like it's a contact sport."

"Only the best kind," Arnie fires back.

The truck's driver climbs out next—broad, quiet, weathered. "Let's get this circus back on the road," he says, voice even as gravel. "Name's Gunnar. These idiots are my family. If you're important to them, you're important to me."

He offers a massive, steady hand; I take it, grounding instantly in that calm strength.

Tears sting before I can stop them. I nod, and Brenden's hand finds my shoulder—steady, protective, no longer sharp. His smile looks like a bruise—dark with things he won't say out loud. He pulls me in close.

"I told you, Siren," he murmurs, low enough that only I hear. "Mine."

We reshuffle. Josh, Juniper, and Alisha pile into our car with us—wet hair, big opinions, elbows everywhere. Arnie, Hazel, and Richie stuff into Corver's. Gunnar rumbles along at the back like a patient bear.

The rain thins to gossamer mist as we turn off the concrete artery of the freeway and start climbing into a verdant cathedral of ancient pines. Dexter materializes through curtains of fog, nestled in a hush of moss-draped trees and obsidian water that reflects the pewter sky. The asphalt ribbon narrows, then narrows again, switchbacks tightening like a secret being whispered, until we're slipping into a pocket dimension that belongs only to us.

My stomach performs its familiar somersault, that weightless vertigo I've felt since childhood. The gates emerge without warning from the emerald gloom of the surrounding trees, twenty feet of wrought-iron filigree twisted into patterns of thorns and vines, black as a midnight promise. The brick wall on either side, the color of dried blood, runs off into primeval forest, its top crowned with gleaming anti-drone hardware disguised as ornate spikes and cameras nestled in stone falcons' eyes. The brushed-steel keypad waits like a small altar, its blue glow the only artificial light for miles.

I punch in 0-6-2-0-#—my parents' anniversary. The

gates swing inward as if pulled by old magic.

"If you ever need speed," I say, glancing at Brenden, "add a one before the code. It opens fast and slams shut faster. But it trips alarms. Don't use it unless you actually need it."

He nods once. I know he's memorized it the way he memorizes exits and faces and the weight of a gun.

We file through, one by one, the gates washing us back into a life I haven't touched in nine years. The main drive curls under immortal trees, the ground slick with needles. You can't see the house until you're almost kissing it; that's by design. We crest a last bend, and there it is—the courtyard opening like a stage, the manor rising out of rain and laurel. Lamps glow along the portico. Staff line the steps, still as chess pieces.

"Holy shit, lady," Josh says, craning around me. "You are like...a princess."

"I used to think that too, when I was little." Pretending to be a princess with Selene, Sam was our knight who came to save us from dragons, or other kingdoms. Little did we know, it was but a glimpse into what life would really look like so many years later.

"You are my Queen," Brenden says quietly. I look up. Something unnameable moves across his face, not love—it can't be love—but in the same constellation.

"Pull up front," I say, voice gone thin. "We'll unload. They'll park in the underground. If Gunnar wants to babysit his gear, have him follow down."

We stop. Before the engine even sighs off, I'm out—sprinting across stone into a pair of arms I've been missing since I was twenty-six.

"BRIDGET!" My voice ricochets off the stone. Bridget Doherty catches me like she always has, wraps me up in cinnamon and starch and the kind of love that smells like fresh bread. She's rounder now, softer around the edges, eyes just as sharp.

She pushes me back and squints up. "Me heavens, child," she says in an accent heavy enough to bend light, "what've ye done to yer skin?"

I laugh, throat tight. "Decorated my temple."

Her gaze warms, full and wet. "Aye, ye did." She casts her eyes down the steps, clocking every unfamiliar face like she's tallying the dead and the living. "Who've ye brought wi' ye? We knew to expect company, but how many beds am I makin'?"

Brenden's voice rolls smooth behind me. "Surry and I will be in a room together, so don't worry about me. I'll be wherever she's at."

I feel, rather than see, Bridget turn that gaze on him. It can peel paint. "Boyo," she says, stepping closer, "don't feck wit' me. The IRA's in me blood. D'ye think I'm standin' here 'cause I can make a stew?"

A couple of the lads cough-laugh and then stop when she flicks a look. Brenden doesn't flinch.

"Yes, ma'am," he says, hands open. "I understand completely. I'll sleep on the floor if I have to. But I won't be leaving her side." His eyes cut to mine, steady and unblinking. "Never again."

I have a hundred questions about those two words. None of them are for right now.

"Right, so." Bridget claps once, loud enough to make the line of staff jump. "Bring yer shite inside. We'll sort rooms. There's plenty o' sheets in this house and more stew than sense."

We cross the threshold. The black-and-white checkered floor is an old movie star of a room—grand ceiling, the chandelier I once hung Christmas ribbons from, the smell of lemon oil and history. The twin curving staircases gleam, carved banisters smooth under my palm as I take the right-hand flight. I don't look back. I follow muscle memory down the gallery, past ancestral portraits and newer frames, to my door.

The handle is cool, familiar. I turn it. The room is a held breath.

Same wide bed, same bookshelf bowing under weight, same desk with a shallow scratch where Selene tried to cut a lime at fourteen and botched it. It smells like dust and linen and the paper-dry perfume of my old notebooks. For a second, I am twenty-one, broken, angry, being folded into this room like a wing being set, and I want to cry from relief and grief in the same breath.

Footsteps. I turn. Brenden fills the doorway like an eclipse.

I take two steps and fist his shirt and drag him down.

This kiss isn't a spark. It's a tide going out and then rushing in again, salt in my mouth, hands steady on his jaw. It's steady and sure and slow enough to count the ways it could mean home. The room tilts; I don't care. The panic in my ribs loosens like a knot relieved of duty.

I didn't want a man. Didn't want a relationship. Swore off marriage, kids, the whole storybook. I built a life with hard rules and good locks.

And I want to break at least one of those rules for

him.

I'm his.
And—God help me—I think I want him to be mine.

# BRINT

The next few weeks blur together in the kind of calm that feels borrowed—like the world has pressed pause just long enough for us to breathe again. We arrived in early August, and the trees show proof that the end of September is nearing.

For the first time in what feels like years, there's no running, no screaming, no explosions. Just the soft hum of the forest that surrounds the Compound and the distant crash of the river somewhere beyond the tree line.

Arnie took off two days after we got here. The forty-eight hours before that, he was basically welded to Hazel. Don't think I saw either of them once, unless it was by accident—and even then, it was just her hair disappearing around a corner with him trailing behind. When he finally surfaced, he said he was heading back to Tacoma to get a jump on the intel trail. Gavin's network left fingerprints all over the state, and Arnie's the kind of bastard who can lift them clean with a keyboard and a cup of coffee.

He borrowed Corver's car since we've got Gunnar's truck for transport anyway, and drove north before the rest of us were awake. Said he'd hole up in his "office." That's what he calls the bunker he built under a fake business front—a full floor of servers, screens, and enough firewalls to keep God out if He came knocking. Every inch of it is wired into someone's secrets. Each room runs a different operation—some he monitors, some he manipulates, and a few he's already dismantled just to make a point.

Before he left, he tried to talk Hazel into going with him. She told him she wouldn't leave Surry. I respect the hell out of that—her loyalty, her fight—but part of me wishes she'd gone anyway. Not because I want her gone. She's good people. She brings light into this place. But if I could pull any of them out of the blast radius before Gavin's ghost starts breathing again, I would. It'd take two names off my *worry list*. And I'm running out of room on that list as it is.

We've only checked in without construction foreman a few times, but he said that lock down is running smoothly. So we haven't talked to him the past week. At least the business is working as it should.

Now, each morning I wake before everyone else. Habit. Years of staying alive by being first on my feet. The air is cool when I step out onto the back terrace, mist curling off the grass and rolling through the gardens. From here, I can see the first slice of sunlight breaking through the pines, painting the old stone walls gold. Somewhere below, I hear Bridget humming to herself in the kitchen—her accent floating up like a prayer.

By the time I wander back inside, Surry's usually there. Her hair is always tied up in that messy knot that somehow still makes her look like sin itself. She's wearing one of my shirts most mornings now, pretending it's *convenience*, pretending she doesn't notice that I notice.

She does.

She just doesn't want to admit how much she likes the way I look at her in it.

"Coffee?" she asks every morning, like it's not already sitting in front of me, black and steaming.

"Only if you're having some, Siren," I answer, every single time. Because there is not a thing in this world I want to do without her anymore.

It makes her roll her eyes—but she smiles while she does it.

Joshua and Gunnar have taken over part of the back field, building some kind of outdoor gym out of wood and concrete blocks. I think they know that there is an indoor gym, but I won't spoil their fun.

They train every afternoon until sweat glistens on their backs and the air smells like pine and iron. I think it started as a way to burn off nerves, but now it's a ritual—controlled violence against the ghosts that won't stop chasing us.

Juniper pretends she's just out there to "check their form," but she's not fooling anyone. She leans against the fence, sunglasses perched low on her nose, pretending to scroll her phone while her eyes track every flex and movement Joshua makes. She ended up bringing a sun tanning chair out there after a few days so she could "sun bathe" while they worked out. He knows it, too—the smug bastard. He moves more slowly when she's watching, deliberate, like he's showing off for her alone. It's all silent, unspoken, but the air between them hums like static.

And Surry... she drifts between all of it.

Helping Bridget bake bread one minute, walking barefoot through the gardens the next. Every now and then, she'll stop and just stand there, her eyes closed, breathing like she's trying to remember what peace feels like. Watching her do that wrecks me a little more each time.

At night, the house glows with amber light. Everyone gathers somewhere—the long dining table, the fire pit outside, the sitting room that smells faintly of whiskey and old leather tangled with coal. I don't think any of us expected to find something like this in the middle of chaos.

Family.

Blood or not, that's what it's starting to feel like.

Surry doesn't say much in these moments. She listens. Laughs when she forgets to be guarded. Sometimes she catches me watching her and pretends not to notice. But she always blushes. It brings peace to my soul when I see her be herself. I never got to see how she acted pre-all *this shit*. But now it feels like I am truly seeing her.

Bridget decided tonight that we all need a "proper Irish meal," her words said with that thick Irish bite, like food made in her kitchen can fix more than hunger.

The smell hits long before the food does: garlic, rosemary, butter, and something seared to absolute perfection. By the time we all sit down at the massive oak table outside, the sun is lowering just enough to set everything in honey hued light.

The chairs are heavy, carved from the same dark wood, with soft cream cushions that make you want to stay for hours. The clinking of silverware mixes with the murmur of conversation, the sound of wine being poured, and Bridget fussing at anyone who dares to skip seconds.

Surry sits to my left. Her hand keeps brushing my arm—*accidentally*, she'd claim.

I don't buy it.

I can feel the tension in her with every brush of skin. The worry for her family. The way she keeps checking her phone even when there's been almost no word since we arrived. Security is what we all say. We are keeping them and us safe. But every time she does, I want to reach over and take it from her, to remind her she's safe now. But I know better. She needs to hold on to something that feels like control.

So instead, I settle for letting my knee rest against hers beneath the table, solid and steady. A quiet reminder that she's not alone.

Dinner stretches on with the easy kind of noise that fills the silence between strangers-turned-family. The long wooden table glows under the string lights Bridget insisted be hung earlier, and the air smells like roasted garlic, butter, and the faintest trace of wood smoke.

Joshua and Richie argue over who drinks faster, their laughter rolling across the courtyard like thunder. Juniper, seated between them, keeps egging Joshua on—*"Go on then, Slater, prove it!"*—clinking her glass against his until Bridget threatens to take the bottle away. Joshua only grins wider, and Juniper looks downright pleased with herself, her cheeks flushed and her curls wild from the evening breeze.

Hazel and Alisha are whispering behind their hands, giggling over Gunnar, who sits at the far end of the table, pretending not to notice but clearly loving the attention. He keeps that stoic face, but the corner of his mouth twitches every time Alisha's laugh hits a higher note.

Corver, as usual, has his phone half-hidden beneath the table, the glow lighting his jawline as he scrolls through encrypted messages. But even he can't completely tune out the chatter. When Hazel leans in to share some gossip about one of Bridget's staff—something about a secret boyfriend in town—Corver actually snorts. A rare sound, quick and quiet, but enough to make the others stare at him like they've spotted a unicorn.

And through it all, Bridget laughs so loud it echoes off the trees, her joy filling the courtyard like a hymn. It's infectious—the kind of laugh that makes you feel like you've earned a place here. Like maybe, just maybe, you belong.

The sky deepens from gold to violet. The air cools, the first hint of autumn curling around us. Somewhere in the house, someone has music playing faintly—a mix of old records Bridget keeps in the study. The crackle of vinyl drifts through the open doors, soft and imperfect.

And that's when it happens—this quiet, accidental shift.

I look over and see Surry watching the sunset, her chin resting in her palm, eyes soft and far away. The song changes. A low, haunting female voice fills the air, smoky and electric.

*I put a spell on you... because you're mine.*

I know that song. I think everyone has heard at least one version of it. Don't know who sings this one, but the voice grabs hold of me.

I glance back at her, and she's still staring at the horizon like she can't hear it—or maybe she's pretending not to. Her lips part, barely moving with the words, and my chest tightens. The song feels like her. Wild. Dangerous. Inevitable.

Before I can stop myself, I reach out and trace a finger over her wrist, just a light touch. She startles, then looks up at me. I don't say anything, but I know she sees it in my eyes. The claim. The promise. The spell, whatever it is, has already been cast.

The noise of the table drifts around us—Bridget's laughter, the clatter of silverware, Richie and Joshua bickering again—but between us it's quiet. She takes a small breath, and for a heartbeat, I think she might lean into me. Instead, she looks down at her plate and pushes a bit of salmon across it with her fork.

"What's wrong, Surry?" I ask softly. "Food not good?"

Her head snaps up, eyes wide, like she didn't expect me to use her name. I can't help the small grin that tugs at my mouth.

"You called me Surry," she says, almost accusingly.

"Guess I did." I shrug. "Siren fits better, though. But you didn't answer the question."

She exhales and sets her fork down, shoulders slumping. "I'm just ... nervous. I won't feel better until my parents, Samuel, and Selene let me know what's happening. I have no idea what's going on out there. What Gavin's doing. Where he is. It scares me."

Her voice trembles on that last word. I feel it more than I hear it, like something sinking its claws into my chest.

"I get that," I tell her. "But you still need to eat. You can't run on fear." I reach under the table and give her upper thigh a gentle squeeze, just enough to ground her. "How about I see if Corver's heard anything? Would that help?"

She looks at me, her eyes bright and tired all at once, and nods. "Yeah. I ... I'd like that." She spears a small piece of salmon and finally eats it.

"Good girl." The words slip out before I can stop them, low enough that only she hears. Her breath catches, but she doesn't look away.

I pull my phone out beneath the table, thumb hovering over the screen. The message I send to Corver is quick, coded, the way we always do it when things might be watched.

A moment later, my phone buzzes once. I glance at it, then set it down beside my plate.

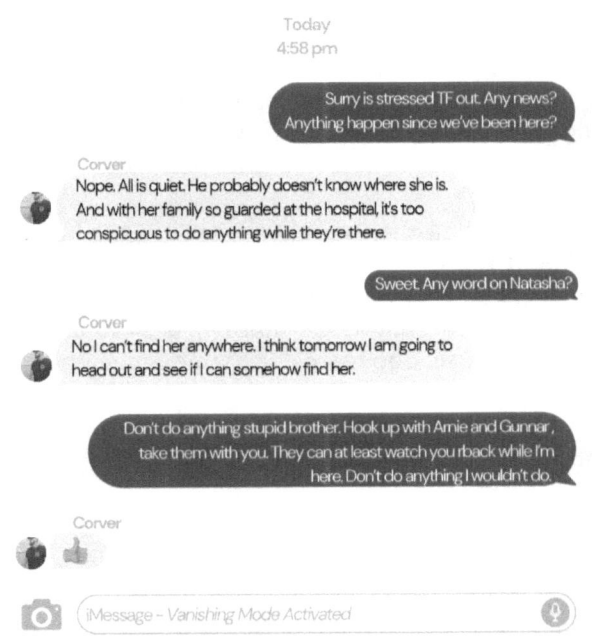

DICK HEADS

Today
4:58 pm

**Sumy is stressed TF out. Any news? Anything happen since we've been here?**

Corver
Nope. All is quiet. He probably doesn't know where she is. And with her family so guarded at the hospital, it's too conspicuous to do anything while they're there.

**Sweet. Any word on Natasha?**

Corver
No I can't find her anywhere. I think tomorrow I am going to head out and see if I can somehow find her.

**Don't do anything stupid brother. Hook up with Amie and Gunnar, take them with you. They can at least watch your rback while I'm here. Don't do anything I wouldn't do.**

Corver

iMessage – Vanishing Mode Activated

I lean closer to her, close enough that my breath brushes her hair. I tell her everything Corver texts me, keeping my eyes on her facial expression the entire time.

Her shoulders sag with relief, and she closes her eyes for a beat, whispering, "Thank God." When she looks at me again, the tension in her face has softened.

Apparently, when my girl is stressed, she doesn't eat. So I make a quiet promise right then—I'll do whatever it takes to make sure she never starves herself with worry again.

She picks up her fork and starts eating in small bites,

the color returning to her cheeks. I can't help the chuckle that slips out. "There we go. Knew you had an appetite in there somewhere." I give her thigh another squeeze. "Just make sure you don't get too full, Siren. There's still plenty for us to do tonight, and I can't have you in a food coma."

Her lips curve into that dangerous smirk I love. "Oh, trust me," she murmurs, her voice dipping low, "I won't be falling asleep. There's plenty I still want to do too."

I can't help the laugh that escapes me—low, quiet, rougher than I meant it to be. The kind that makes her breath catch again. The table noise fades into the background. All I see is her. The sunlight catches the loose strands of her hair, painting them a warm golden color. Her pulse beats visibly in her throat. The whole world could end outside this compound, and I wouldn't care.

I lean closer until our foreheads almost touch. "Careful, Siren," I whisper, my mouth just a breath from hers. "Say things like that and I might forget we're not alone."

Her voice is barely a whisper. "Maybe I want you to forget."

That's all the invitation I need. I tilt her chin up with my thumb and forefinger and kiss her, slow at first, then deeper when she sighs against my mouth. It's not the frantic kind of kiss we had before—it's steadier, claiming, a promise I don't even bother trying to hide. She tastes like wine and salt and something sweet I can't name.

We haven't done more than explore with my hands and minds since we have been here. So I am dying to taste her again.

And of course, that's when the peanut gallery around us loses their minds.

"Jesus Christ, can we not have a live porno at the dinner table?" Joshua's voice cuts through the noise, half-amused, half-brotherly disgust. "At least wait 'til dessert, yeah?"

Richie slaps the table, howling with laughter. "Oh, let 'em! It's about time someone broke in the new dining set. Been lookin' too damn polished anyway." He winks at us as Bridget swats his arm, muttering something about *manners* and *heathens* under her breath.

Alisha gasps theatrically. "Richie!"

"What? I'm just sayin', they've got chemistry." He leans back in his chair, smirking. "You can practically feel it vibrate off 'em. Hell, I think my beer fizzed."

Juniper chimes in next, stirring her drink with her

straw. "Careful, Richie. Keep talking like that and you'll be the next one blushing."

"I don't blush, sweetheart," he fires back, grin widening and a glint growing in his eyes. His eyes shift to Gunnar and Josh before winking at them.

"You do now," she quips, earning another round of laughter from the table.

Surry pulls back, cheeks pink and eyes wide, but she's smiling—really smiling. The kind that reaches her eyes and softens every sharp edge she's been holding onto. I swipe my thumb across her bottom lip, catching a faint trace of her lip gloss, and murmur, "worth it."

"Alright, you two," Joshua says, shaking his head, "if you're gonna keep makin' heart eyes, at least take it somewhere with a lock on the door."

"Gladly," I shoot back, standing and taking Surry's hand. She looks at me like she can't decide whether to laugh or hide under the table, but she lets me pull her up beside me anyway.

Richie raises his beer. "Don't do anything I wouldn't do!"

I pause, smirking over my shoulder. "Is there anything you wouldn't do, though?"

That earns me a chorus of laughter, Bridget clapping her hands in mock disapproval. "Now off with ye, ye eejits — out o' me dining room afore I have the hose on ye two, so I will."

I glance down at Surry, her face still pink but glowing in the low light, and she shakes her head, whispering, "They're all impossible."

"Maybe," I murmur, brushing a stray lock of hair from her face. "But they're family."

Then I scoop her up and throw her over my shoulder, slapping her ass for good measure. She laughs, pounding her tiny fists on my back as I continue to lightly pinch her ass, moving to caress between her thighs as we continue our walk toward the house. A tiny moan escapes her lips and she pauses her punching for a moment before we reach the house.

I set her down as we reach the French doors, the laughter behind us fading into the hum of crickets and the rustle of trees in the cooling night air as we slip inside. The sun's low enough now that everything's bathed in amber—the kind of light that makes the world feel softer, safer. Her hand's still in mine, small but sure, fingers curling tighter as we step into the house.

The hallways twist and wind like a maze, the kind of

place that's been added onto over generations. Every turn smells faintly of old pine and lemon oil. Shadows gather in the corners, thick and quiet, and the air hums with the distant sound of conversation still drifting from outside. Somewhere behind us, Bridget's laugh rings out again, muffled by walls and distance.

Surry doesn't say a word. She just leads—bare feet whispering against the cool tile, her hair spilling loose down her back. Every few steps, she glances behind her like she's making sure I'm still there. As if I'd ever be anywhere else.

We round another corner, and she stops at a set of double doors I haven't noticed before—dark wood, heavy, old enough to groan when she pushes them open. She steps aside and gestures me in first.

The air inside is cooler, smelling faintly of popcorn and leather and the quiet static hum of unused electronics. When I hit the light switch, the soft amber sconces along the walls flicker to life, spilling warmth across the room.

It's a home theater—but not the sleek, sterile kind you find in new builds. This one's lived-in. The far wall is dominated by a massive screen, the kind you could lose yourself in. Rows of plush recliners rise in tiers, each draped with worn blankets and throw pillows that don't match but somehow belong together. Down front, instead of the usual seats, sit three over sized daybeds—wide enough to fit two people each, covered in dark gray linen, the kind that feels soft even from a distance.

She walks straight for the middle one, the confidence in her stride completely at odds with the faint pink still dusting her cheeks. There's already a remote resting in the cup holder, like fate—or temptation—set the stage for her.

Without a word, she grabs the remote and plops down cross-legged on the bed. The springs creak softly under her, and she looks up at me with that half-smile that never fails to gut me. "Well?" she says. "You planning to just stand there, or sit?"

I close the doors behind us, the latch clicking softly into place, and make my way to her. "What are we watching?"

"Whatever I find first," she says, scrolling through the selections without even glancing at the screen. "I don't plan on paying attention."

She doesn't see my grin, but she hears it in my voice when I answer, "Damn right, you're not paying attention. I have a few ideas of what we could do instead."

I sit beside her, close enough that our shoulders brush. She's still flipping through menus when she stops suddenly, and a slow smile curves her lips. Then I hear it—the soft, sultry voice that spills through the speakers, low and spellbound:

*"I put a spell on you..."*

It takes me a second to place it, that smoky, aching voice—female, rich enough to taste in the air. I don't know the movie, but I know the song. It's what we heard out on the patio earlier. Now it fills the room around us, the visuals on the screen showing a woman in what is obviously the Pacific Northwest somewhere. It's the kind of sound that makes you think about danger and devotion in the same breath.

Surry sets the remote down, right there in the cup holder, and leans back against the pillows. Her head tilts just enough for her eyes to meet mine. The faint light from the sconces catches the gold in her irises.

"Guess we'll let that play," she murmurs.

I nod, throat dry. "Guess we will."

The song lingers in the air, haunting and slow, wrapping around the space between us until it feels almost alive. I turn slightly, close enough now to smell the faint trace of her perfume—something soft, like vanilla and smoke. She shifts toward me, legs brushing mine, her lips parting just slightly.

The air hums. The song swells. My pulse kicks hard against my ribs.

I lean down and turn, just enough to wrap my hands under the soft curve of her ass, feeling the warmth of her skin through the thin fabric as I pull her over to straddle my waist. Her thighs grip me tightly on either side, and I feel the heat of her core against my stomach. I place my lips onto hers—soft, plump, tasting faintly of cherry—and take full control over her mouth, using my tongue to trace the delicate ridge of her teeth before delving deeper. We kiss, tongues dancing in a slow, deliberate rhythm, her small gasps vibrating against my lips. My hands wander from her hips to her waist, fingers splaying across the dip of her lower back, while hers thread through my hair, nails lightly scraping my scalp, discovering one another at a leisurely pace.

I sit up with her still in my lap and flip us over gently, watching her golden hair fan across the white linen of the daybed. Her skin flushes pink where my hands press against her waist, her breath catching as I lower myself over her. The curve of her hip fits perfectly into my palm, as if sculpted by an artist who knew exactly what I would crave. Every inch of her—from the hollow of her throat to the soft dip behind her knee—calls to be traced, tasted, memorized. When her body arches up to meet mine, the contact ignites something primal between us, like two pieces of a lock finally clicking into place.

"What are you.."

She doesn't get to finish because I sit forward and place a finger in her mouth, pumping it in and out. Her eyes widen as she explores the finger that has intruded into her.

"Be a good girl and suck. I don't want to hear you talk unless it's 'yes sir', or your safe word. Which is red. Tap my hand if you understand."

She reaches up hesitantly and taps the hand that's still thrusting into her mouth. She sucks on it like such a good girl. I stifle a groan as she continues her ministrations on my finger. I wonder what she could do with my dick in her mouth.

"If you need to use your safe word but are unable, two quick taps will also be your safe word, tap me again if you understand." She once again taps me on the arm.

I use my free hand to start undoing the button of her faded jeans, tugging the zipper down tooth by tooth while my finger continues its rhythm in her mouth. The denim slides over her smooth thighs, taking her black lace underwear with it until both pool on the hardwood floor beside me.

When I withdraw my now slick finger from her mouth, a glistening thread connects us momentarily before breaking. I trace that wetness down to the pink, swollen bud between her thighs, circling it with deliberate pressure before dipping lower to where she's already molten and waiting. The sound she makes—half gasp, half moan—vibrates through her body as her head falls back, throat exposed, her weight still balanced on trembling elbows as she stares unseeing at the textured ceiling.

I pump into her a few times before removing my finger and placing it into my own mouth, sucking off the delectable juices she imbues them with. I place my slick fingers into my mouth, ensuring they are nice and wet before plunging them both into her hot slit. Surry drops from her elbows onto her back, closing her eyes and enjoying the feeling of me thrusting into her. Her hands reach above her head, fisting into the soft fabric of the daybed's comforter that we didn't bother to move before we sat down.

She moans, and so I  take her open mouth as an opportunity to put the fingers on my other hand into her mouth, going down her throat. Like a good girl, she automatically closes her lips around it, sucking and using her tongue to explore the sides of the intrusion. I continue fucking two of her holes with both hands as she relaxes more and more into the daybed. Leaning down, I nibble on her inner thigh, causing her to moan around my finger, so I continue with the bites from knee to inner thigh.

She begins making more noises in her throat—little desperate whimpers that vibrate against my palm—her eyes rolling back until only crescents of emerald remain visible beneath fluttering lashes. I know she is close. I pick up my speed, slamming my knuckles into her pelvis while my other hand continues forcing its way down the beautiful column of her throat, feeling her pulse hammering wildly against my fingertips. Before long she arches back, her spine a perfect bow, and moans so loud the sound seems to ricochet off the walls. I am sure the movie was pointless and our friends know exactly what we're doing in here. But I don't stop. I don't care.

"Good girl, Surry. Come for me."

She claws at the bed, thrashing and moaning, until she finally begins to come down, and I slow my movements with hers. She lets go of the bed sheets as I pull both hands out of her mouth and pussy and lies there panting. I only give her about a five-second reprieve until I can't contain myself any longer.

I lean down and press my face into her ready center, the heat of her radiating against my lips as I taste her slick arousal. She wiggles beneath me, her thighs trembling against my shoulders as a breathy moan escapes her parted lips. I trace slow, deliberate circles with my tongue, savoring the sweet-salt tang of her desire, letting her adjust to the sensation before I dive in fully. "You taste like honey and sin," I murmur against her tender flesh, my breath hot against her wetness. "I cannot wait until your scent clings to my skin like a second heartbeat."

With that, I move lower and place my tongue into her tight channel, and begin to thrust into her with my tongue, curling it up. If there was ever a time I gave thanks for having such a long tongue, now would be it. Surry is already clawing at the bed again with one hand, the other in my hair, pulling roughly at the strands she can reach.

"Good girl, Surry. Fuck my face," I say before I go back down to continue my feast.

She grips my hair tighter and begins maneuvering my face so it slides up and down, up and down. With her free hand, she circles her clit. I swat her hand out of the way.

"Well, if you aren't going to, then I am," she throws at me, her voice breathy but commanding. I love this version of Surry.

I nip at her skin, and she lets out an angry-sounding moan. Oh. So my girl wants a little pain with her pleasure, does she? I nip some more, working my way up to her clit. I take it between my teeth and start biting down just enough that I can tell she feels just a spark of pain. She lets out a moan so loud I know I've found it. I continue to work on her clit, and use my hand to enter her wet pussy once again, finger fucking her until she screams her orgasm to the ether around us.

"Your moans are damn near enough to bring me to my own finish. I want everyone to know how well I worship you." I grind my hand against her, and curl my fingers up within her while I speak, causing her to cry out in pleasure even louder.

The moment she has finished, I sit up and remove my own clothes before descending on her. I sit her up enough to peel her shirt up and over her head, and remove her bra. Grabbing her hips, I flip her over onto her stomach, welcoming the most beautiful view.

"This perfect ass is all I have been able to think about today, Siren. Your shorts were so short, they possessed my every thought. Did you pick them out on purpose?"

"Yes, sir." She replies, voice breathy. Coming out as nearly a moan.

"Were you aware that not only would I see your ass, but everyone else in the house?"

"Yes, sir," she smirked, her tone becoming firmer. "I hoped that it would drive you crazy enough to take me." She is so evil, I think I'm already falling for her.

"Well, my beautiful, dangerous Siren," I say before I spit on her tight back entrance," this will become mine tonight then. Have you ever had anything here before?" I ask her this as I rub my thumb on the entrance, just slightly pushing inward.

She gasps and throws her head back the deeper my thumb enters. "Yes sir, but..." I freeze.

"Tell me," I demand. I need clarification and triple explicit consent from her now. I am not going to do this unless she tells me to, in all the words.

"I told you I would try and open up. Please don't ruin this. I want this. In my ass, in my pussy, in my mouth. I want to explore with you. New positions, new places. Please take me." Her eyes are serious, but still full of lust. I reach down and grab her chin, turning her eyes toward mine.

"Say it again," I answer.

"I told..."

"Not that," I interrupt.

"I want you…"

"Good girl." That's what I needed.

The movie's long over. The credits have finished rolling. The only light left comes from the faint blue wash of the screen saver, flickering soft shadows across her bare shoulders.

Surry's head rests on my chest, her breathing slow but not quite steady—like she's still trying to come down from more than just what we did. My arm's around her, tracing idle lines down her spine, memorizing every quiet tremor of her body, every line of tattoo and scarring. I noticed that her tattoos are covering up various shaped and sized scars.

I can feel the weight of the words she's not saying. It's a tension I know too well—the silence that isn't peace, it's fear trying to stay quiet.

"Talk to me, Siren," I whisper into her hair. "Don't hold it in. Not with me."

She's still for a long moment. Then she exhales, long and shaky.

"It's not that I don't want this," she finally says, her voice barely audible against my skin. "I just… I don't know how to start something new when the last thing nearly killed me."

I don't speak. I just keep tracing her back, letting her pace herself. As long as she is talking, I'm happy to wait.

"My marriage to Gavin was—" she stops, swallows. "It wasn't love. Not real love. It was control dressed up as protection. Everything was a transaction. Every smile, every touch, even the way I breathed felt… managed. If I said the wrong thing, if I looked at someone too long, he'd find a way to make me regret it."

She pauses again. I feel her tense under my hand.

"I left eleven years ago. Since then, I haven't been with anyone longer than a night. Just… empty things. Things I could leave before they hurt me."

Her voice cracks. "And then you walked into my life like a hurricane and made it impossible to breathe without feeling something again. And that terrifies me, Brenden. Because if I fall for you, I don't know if I'll survive losing you."

I tighten my hold, pressing my lips against the top of

her head. Her words hit hard—not because of what they say about the bastard Gavin, but what they say about her. About how much she's carried and still somehow shines through it.

"You won't lose me, Siren," I say, my voice low. "I'm not him. I won't cage you. I don't want your obedience, I want your honesty. Even if it's messy." I pause, letting her feel the truth. "Especially if it's messy."

She shifts, looking up at me, her eyes glassy but fierce. "Then you'll get it. All of it. Just... not tonight."

"I can accept that, Siren. Just be honest, and tell me what you can, when you're ready," before reaching down and kissing her temple gently.

We lie there in the quiet, the only sound the soft hum of the screen and our breathing syncing together. I can feel her heartbeat through my chest, steady now, calmer.

After a while, I find myself talking without planning to. "My mom used to say love should never feel like fear."

Surry lifts her head slightly, eyes searching mine. "She sounds like a wise woman."

"She was." I swallow hard, feeling that familiar ache when I think of her. "She... she didn't get to live by her own words for long."

She doesn't ask, but she doesn't look away either. Her fingers now drawing soft circles against my chest, patient, waiting.

I take a breath, feel it stick in my throat. "She was the first person who ever taught me to fight for peace. Even when it kills you a little to do it."

Surry's hand stills, her eyes soft and open. "Tell me about her?"

I nod, staring up at the ceiling, the words coming slow but certain. "Yeah, I'll tell you."

The blue light flickers once, fades to black. The screen goes dark, but neither of us move.

And in that darkness, I start to talk. I tell her about my mom, the years of her trying her best, only to fall victim to a bad men more times than I can count, and how ultimately that is how she lost her life. I explain what Joshua, Corver, and I do outside of Slater Construction, and how we got to this point.

How we know Natasha, how we assume Surry's father knows us. I tell her everything. Because there is nothing more that I want than for this woman to know me. All of me. The light and the dark. The hard and the easy. I want her to have it all.

I wake to warmth and weight and the faint, sugary smell of buttered popcorn baked into the theater's walls. The screen in front of us is black having turned off while we talked last night; the speakers hum softly, waiting for someone to press play. My cheek is on Brenden's chest, the slow, even rise and fall, a metronome I didn't know my body needed. His arm is around my waist, heavy in a way that makes me feel anchored instead of pinned.

We must've fallen asleep talking at some point, I have no idea when though.

My mouth tastes like wine and his skin. My thighs ache in a way that makes me bite back a shaky smile. I don't move for a moment. I just listen—to the quiet of a house this big at dawn, to the distant clink of pans in Bridget's kitchen, to the hush that feels like the world pressed pause just for us.

Thoughts come back to me of last night. How great it felt the two of us entwined in every way. While the first night we spent together was hot, sexy, passionate, last night was different. It was exploration. It was sensual. It was intimate. It was what I always pictured love was supposed to be like.

*"I want you..." I had said, calming his nerves of my rejection.*

*"Good girl."*

*He pressed his thumb further into that back entrance that no one ever talks about. It felt weird at first. Not painful, but uncomfortable for sure. I had never had anyone warm me up before putting something in there before. The sensation tried to bring back memories, but I wouldn't let them rise. This is Brenden. Not Gavin. I had to repeat that to myself a few times. And I know Brenden could tell.*

*"You have to relax, Surry. I'll never get anything in there if you keep clenching."*

*This is Brenden. I take a breath. This is Brenden. I take another breath. I can feel his thumb enter inch by inch each time I take a breath. He pulls out slightly, and I feel his warm saliva land on my entrance before he pushes back in. This time, much further.*

*"Good girl, great job Surry. You've got this. I've got you." I take another breath. His praise easing me once again.*

*Once his thumb is totally seated within my ass, I feel his other fingers begin to strum my core, pressing two fingers within me, filling me completely. The sensation is magical.*

I blush at the memories. It was so hot, and so beautiful at the same time. Then I remember him switching to his cock at my entrance and the pressure I felt. Slowly, he had begun to enter me. That hurt more, but after what was probably ten minutes, he was fully seated and riding me, making me see stars. It felt so good. The soreness I feel between my legs, and the cum I can feel between my legs renews the throbbing in my core that I felt last night.

*"That's it, Surry, take my cock. Take it deep in that sweet, tight ass of yours. I'm gonna come, Surry. I want you to come with me." At that, I exploded, pressing back into him, screaming my release into the dark room, Brenden leaning forward, and roaring into my hair as he wildly thrust into me, filling me. It was thrilling and empowering, honestly.*

My thoughts are interrupted by the voice rumbling under my ear of the man who I was just thinking of.

"Morning, my Siren."

"Morning." My voice comes out ruined and soft, a blush creeping over my skin. "Did we—"

"—forget to make it upstairs?" He huffs a laugh. "Yeah."

We untangle slowly, carefully, like the wrong movement will shatter whatever fragile thing is hovering over us. He stands first, muscles stretching before placing his shirt over his head and pulling it into place, then offers me both hands like I'm breakable. I'm not, but I let him pretend. He grabs the blanket from the daybed and swings it over my shoulders, fingers lingering at my collarbone like he can't quite help himself.

"Shower?" he asks.

"Please."

We sneak through the quiet hallways like teenagers who absolutely should not be proud of what they did and absolutely are. We collect shoes, a stray sock, my shirt that somehow ended up draped over a sconce, and a hair tie from the floor like breadcrumbs as we make our way out of the room and back to my room upstairs. Inside, I grab clean clothes from the wardrobe, and the bathroom fills with steam in seconds. He kisses my forehead—just my forehead—and leaves me to the hot water and the quiet that hurts.

By the time I'm dressed—jeans, a soft black tee, my hair pulled into a damp knot—someone knocks.

"Don't open it," I whisper automatically. My heart does that cold flush thing it learned in another life.

Brenden squeezes my hip once before he strides to the door and opens it just a touch.

I see fiery red hair through the crack; it's just June.

She leans in the frame, sunglasses on her head despite the indoor lighting, a grin she doesn't bother to hide. "Well, well," she singsongs. "Did we have a nice little movie night?"

I internally die. "We watched the credits," I mutter.

"Is that what you call it?" She looks over my shoulder. "Slater, I see your shirt. I also see it's on the wrong person."

Brenden, traitor that he is, grins. "Looks better on her."

June cackles. "Josh sent me to come get you two. There's news about Gavin. And—" her gaze softens for a half-beat "—you probably want to hear it sitting down."

The folded feeling in my chest returns. The present tightens around the edges, color draining out. I nod once. "We'll be right down."

Juniper heads back down the hall. Brenden's thumb finds that spot at the base of my throat and presses gently. It's not restraint; it's reassurance—like he's telling my pulse to breathe. "I'm with you," he says.

"I know." I hate how much I mean it.

We take the stairs together, hands entwined. His are so much bigger than mine, we can't intertwine our fingers, but I think it's cute holding hands like an old married couple

The foyer opens into the long room off the courtyard, where everyone has gathered. Morning light pours in, pale and cold; it makes the dust in the air look like falling stars. Joshua and Richie lean over the big table; Hazel perches on the edge, fingers twisting the stem of an empty glass. Bridget hovers near the doorway to the kitchens, dish towel over her shoulder, eyes assessing all of us like she can will us full and safe.

Corver's there, too, jaw set, phone face-down in front of him for once. Gunnar stands at his shoulder—quiet, coiled, listening.

Brenden guides me to a chair with a hand at my back

—possessive, yes, but not performative. Mine, his touch says. Safe, it says louder.

Joshua doesn't waste time. "He's moving," he says, and those two words are enough to make my stomach drop. "Kelly made plays with the Bratva overnight. Not whispers. He's flashing teeth. Money moved. Muscle moved. They want a war. Arnie alerted us early this morning, and Corver confirmed it all."

Richie blows out a breath. "Of course they do."

"Sam and your dad are already mobilizing," Joshua goes on, looking at me like I might break and he'll catch me if I do. "Irish are prepping for counter-hits. They're not waiting."

It takes me a second to find my voice. "They're what?" The room blurs. "Sam got out. He—he left this. I dragged him back. I dragged them all back." I cover my eyes as the tears come.

Hazel is beside me before I can spiral further, her hand warm over my knuckles. "No, honey. You didn't drag anyone. We walked."

"Ran," Richie adds. "Toward you. On purpose."

Brenden's voice is low. "We do not blame the match for the gasoline someone else poured."

I look at him. He looks back like he means it.

Alisha comes over and grabs my hand, dragging my eyes away from Brenden, and locking with hers. "He was prepared for this, Surry. He knew it would happen the second he heard about the car. He isn't going in blind. Trust him." I nod, unable to find any words.

Corver clears his throat. "There's something else." He taps the phone without turning it over. "We found a thread. Natasha pinged a network that Gunnar and I can chase. It's dirty and buried, but it's there."

June straightens, all of her regular teasing gone. "You can find her?"

"We can try," Gunnar says, finally speaking. His voice is calm, which is scarier than if he shouted. "But it means leaving. Now."

My chest squeezes. Natasha. She's a wound and a map at once. "You think she'll lead you to Gavin?"

"Or to the money that keeps him moving," Corver says. "Same result."

Bridget slides a mug in front of me like she listened for the exact moment my hands started to shake. "Tea," she says simply. "Proper."

I wrap my fingers around the heat and nod. "Go," I hear myself say, before I have time to think it into a mistake. "If you can find her, if you can cut one of his legs out from under him—go."

Gunnar looks to Brenden. "You good?"

Brenden's jaw flickers, but he nods. "Find her. You taking Arnie with you?"

Gunnar and Corver nod at the same time, their movements miming one another.

Hazel turns to Corver, worry making her look younger than she is. "You'll check in?" She leans in and hugs him, saying something only to him.

"Every six hours," he promises. "Twelve if we're dark."

Josh rubs a hand over his face. "Route?"

"Back roads south, then east," Gunnar replies. "We'll look like contractors, not hitters. We'll leave half our comms here and run burn phones for anything we don't want traced."

Richie whistles. "Sexy."

"Not the word I'd use," June mutters, but she's smirking again, and the room exhales around her. But it's noticeable when she scoots slightly closer to Josh. They are like magnets, always drawn to one another.

Corver stands and pockets his phone, shoulders already shifting into go-mode. "We load in ten."

Gunnar squeezes Joshua's shoulder in passing. It's a small touch. It carries weight. Then they're gone—footsteps quick down the hallway, a door opening to the bright morning, the distant grind of tires over gravel.

Silence settles for a beat. Then Bridget claps once. "Eat somethin' before your thoughts chew holes in ya," she orders, and somehow I love her more for it.

I try. I pick at a slice of toast, a piece of apple from a plate someone set down without me noticing. It tastes like nothing. I want to be helpful. I want to be steel. I want to be anything other than a woman whose hands won't stop trembling.

Alisha edges closer and drops her voice. "Surry, love... I think it's time."

"For what?" I croak out. My throat knows before my brain does.

"To tell them," she says gently, eyes flicking to Brenden, to Joshua and June, and the others who are all pretend not to stare. "Brenden, Josh and June don't know why we're here.

It'll help them help you."

"I—" The room tilts. Words knot behind my teeth. Shame, old and shapeless, licks up my spine. It's stupid. I know it's stupid. Shame belongs to him, not me. But it lingers like smoke you can't wash out.

Richie comes to my other side, warm palm at my elbow, that soft look he gets when he's dead serious. "Start at the beginning," he says. "Like you told us. We're not going anywhere."

Hazel nods. "No judgment. No pity. Just us."

I look at Brenden.

He doesn't push. He doesn't prompt. He just tips his head the slightest bit, a yes that says I'll stand here as long as you need me to.

I turn toward the kitchen. "Bridget?"

She's already moving, clearing the end of the long island like she's done this with me before—because she has. Kettle on. Mugs down. Honey. A plate of shortbread, because sugar helps even if science says otherwise. The domestic sound of it eases something sharp in my chest.

We file in. Take places. The kettle sings. The steam smells like chamomile and safety.

"Where do I even start?" I ask the rim of my mug.

"With the beach," Alisha says, voice steady. "With how young you were."

So I do, but I go back even further.

"It started when I was seventeen," I say, and my voice doesn't break, which feels like a miracle. "Gavin Kelly was kind. He was—God—he was perfect at pretending. Flowers. Notes. He said I was his future. It felt... safe. Looking back, I now know he meant future as in the mafia, not the love of his life future."

I talk. The words feel like stones I have to carry from one side of a river to the other. I set them down, one by one. Meeting him. His family's shadows I told myself not to see. The proposal on the sand, the ring I thought meant forever, the wedding, the early sweetness.

"How old were you when you found out about your parents?" Joshua asks carefully.

"On my wedding day," I answer. "I thought my dad was in private security. Sam knew. Selene and I didn't. Looking back, that was the point." I take a breath. "We got married. At the alter, he threatened me, but I thought maybe it was the stress, or showing he was powerful tot he rest of the congregated mafia in the chapel. But three months later, what was left of the kindness curdled entirely."

I talk about the trying. The not conceiving. The first miscarriage. The second. The way he folded grief into a weapon and used my body to sharpen the blade. I keep my voice flat, because if I add feeling, I won't survive the paragraph.

"When I 'misbehaved,' he'd slap me," I say. "When I lost a baby, he'd make a show of it. Drag me out. Humiliate me. Sometimes worse." The room goes very still. "Some of his men tried to stop him. He made examples of them."

Brenden's hand finds mine under the counter. His palm is hot. His thumb rubs that slow, grounding circle again and again like he's telling my nervous system a story where I live.

"Eventually," I say, and the word tastes like blood, "a doctor said I was 'ready to try again' after the fifth miscarriage." Ready. Like a switch you flip. Like I'm a machine that just needed maintenance.

The next part lives in my throat like glass. I can't swallow it down or cough it out.

I stare into my tea until the leaves blur. The room waits. Alisha's hand is on my back, between my shoulder blades, an anchor.

"Do you want to finish, or do you want me to?" She asks quietly.

I shake my head, but it's not a no. It's an *I don't know*.

Brenden's voice comes from a softer place than I knew he had. "Siren." I look up. He holds my gaze. "We can step out. Just you and me. You don't owe anyone the worst parts unless you want to."

The relief that floods me is humiliating and holy. I nod once. "Okay."

I don't remember moving. I only remember arms—his —under my knees and behind my shoulders, lifting me like I'm not heavy, like this isn't. "Go ahead and finish with the story for them," he tells Alisha as he backs us out of the kitchen, and then we're in the hall, the cool air a mercy on my face, the noise of the house falling away behind us as he carries me somewhere quieter.

Brenden carries me down the hall like the floor might splinter if my feet touch it. His shoulder is solid under my cheek, his heartbeat steady and human in a way that keeps the world from spinning. The smell of coffee and rain through the open window hits as he steps into the smaller sitting room off the terrace, a song playing through the window. I would recognize it anywhere because it's been my theme for so many years now. *You Should Be Sad* by Halsey, her words hitting every single feeling I have had since that night in the hospital.

When we sit down, it's quieter than when we were next to the window—dim light, soft leather, the hum of distant conversation fading behind us. I let the lyrics sink into me for a moment.

*Oh I feel so sorry I feel so sad...I had no warning about who you are. I'm just glad I made it out without breaking down and then ran so fucking far. You would never touch me again. I'm so glad I never, ever, had a baby with you...*

He doesn't say anything. Just lowers me onto the couch, sits beside me, and waits. His hand stays on my knee—warm, unmoving. He has this way of making silence feel like permission, not pressure.

I stare at my hands. At the faint scar on my ring finger that's never gone away. "It's pathetic," I whisper. "How much it still feels like he owns parts of me."

Brenden shakes his head. "He owns nothing."

I laugh, sharp and wrong. "He took everything. You can't undo that."

He doesn't flinch. "Then we'll build new things."

The quiet stretches. The tea's gone cold in my hand. I keep talking because if I stop, I'll break.

"When the doctor said I could 'try again,' I knew what that meant. I knew what he'd do. But you can't imagine what fear makes you agree to until it's standing in front of you."

My voice thins to a thread. "He wanted a son. Another chance to prove he was worth the bloodline. He said if I failed again, there wouldn't be a next time."

Brenden's fingers tighten slightly on my knee—just enough to say *I'm here.*

"I hadn't taken a test yet, so I didn't know. It had been over a month since the doctor said I could try again. But I was pregnant. The sixth time. Early, but it was there."

Brenden's thumb was rubbing along my knee, his face looking pained. But not in a *she was knocked up by another man* pain. But more of a fear of what I was going to say next. And he was right to be afraid.

"*I have had enough of you, you fucking cunt. You won't give me an heir, so I am done playing games and waiting on you.*"

"*No—please, Gavin, don't say that. I'm trying, I swear*

*I am. I can go back to the doctor, I'll do whatever they say. Just... don't leave me." The words spill out before I can stop them, fear flooding me, because I know when he says he's done, it never ends well. "No, you stupid bitch. I am not giving you up. How do you think I will take over the entire Western region if I don't stay married to you? Your father will never give it to me if you aren't my wife." I am in shock, completely appalled by what he is saying to me. He never really loved me, did he?*

*"Instead, I am going to have you filled with cock all day and night to ensure that you don't forget your most important job."*

The memories flooding back from that night into my mind.

"He said he was done waiting, and if I couldn't hold his heir, he would make sure that-he would make sure that I at least held *an* heir."

Brenden's eyes darken, his face morphing into something more than angry. I look down once again and kept talking. Getting it out before I can't any more.

"I'm not sure how many of them there were. I think I stopped counting around twenty men. Back to back. They raped me on the floor, lying my face on the couch, my knees on the floor. I couldn't breathe. I had carpet burn for months afterwards everywhere. They tore me inside so badly I needed reconstruction surgery later on."

I pause, catching my breath, sipping my cold tea, trying to gain strength from the dregs.

I take a deep gulp of air and continue, feeling as though I can't catch my breath, the words coming out higher with tears accompanying them. "They kept pushing my face into the couch cushions."

I stop talking for a moment, catching my breath and wiping my tears.

"Finally, mercifully, these two random women walked into the house. They screamed and left, and I was then moved to my room and locked in."

"They gang raped you? He let his men fucking rape you? What does that accomplish for him?" Brenden's eyes are wild, his face still in something more than anger, he can't comprehend. It took me a long time to realize that it wasn't about getting an heir. Not that night at least. It was about control. I shake my head instead of replying to him, and continue the story, building up my nerve for this last part of the horror movie of a life.

"Next thing I know, I hear sirens, then a scuffle outside. I was locked inside, so I couldn't go find out. But then I heard the police calling for me and I started to pound on the door, knowing this was it. It was my chance to escape. I was bleeding. God–I was bleeding so badly. Officer Martin. I'll never forget him. He knew exactly what I needed, and couldn't handle. He was a blessing that night. They called an ambulance and took me to the hospital, where my mom, Selene, and Alisha met me."

The words scrape coming out. "I had passed out, and something went wrong. I was bleeding too much. They said they had to—" I stop. Can't say it. My throat closes. The memory is all metal and antiseptic and the smell of burned fabric. I can still hear and smell it now.

I press a fist against my mouth, shaking. He moves closer but doesn't pull me in; he lets me choose. I lean into him anyway.

"They took it," I say finally, the words muffled against his shirt just trying to get anything out. "Everything. I can't have kids. He made sure of that. I was hemorrhaging so badly, they had to take my uterus out."

Brenden's breath stutters once, like he's trying not to break with me. Then he exhales, slow and controlled.

"I know what people think when they find out," I say quietly. "They get that look. Pity. And part of why I never got close to any man ever since, outside of never wanting to be powerless ever again, I can never give a future partner any children."

He turns my face toward him, thumb tracing the edge of my jaw. "You'll never get pity from me, Siren. Only awe. For surviving that and still having enough left to care about anyone at all."

His eyes are fierce, his sky blue eyes now dark and glassy like bottled stormlight. "I don't want children out of you. I want peace with you. Whatever that looks like."

Something cracks open in my chest. "You're too good."

"I'm just learning from you," he murmurs.

We sit like that for a long time. My tears slow. His thumb keeps moving, patient circles over my skin. The window light shifts, washing the room in pale gold. For the first time in years, the ache in my ribs eases.

Brenden leans into my side, placing his lips against my ear, whispering only for me to hear. "I'm not going to let him keep living rent-free in the parts of you that deserve peace. We'll deal with him. On our terms."

I nod against his chin. The strength in his calm steadies me more than any promise of revenge.

After a while, I lift my head. "How do you do that?" I ask. "Sound angry and gentle at the same time."

He half-smiles. "Practice. My mom taught me."

"The one who said love shouldn't feel like fear?"

"Yeah." He looks away, eyes unfocused, voice low. "She believed it, even when it stopped being true for her. I was too young to stop it. Too young to understand."

He pauses, ruminating in the old hurt. "She used to hum when she was scared. Same three notes. Like she could drown out whatever was coming. I didn't get it then, but I do now. Sometimes, surviving is just finding a sound louder than the fear."

Something in me unclenches. The confession isn't loud or dramatic—it's simple, human. And it feels like he's handing me a matching scar to hold.

I touch his wrist. "Tell me more about her? About your childhood?"

He nods slowly. "Yeah," he says, and his voice goes quieter still. "I'll tell you."

The light outside fades to silver. The sound of the river threads through the open window. He starts talking—about her laugh, the way she burned every meal, the way she once punched a cop for yelling at Corver—and the world feels small enough to fit in the space between his words.

For the first time in forever, I let it.

# BRITT

I don't realize I've been holding my breath until her last word lands and it feels as if the world around us goes silent. The tea has gone officially cold, the couch now somehow feels scratchier compared to when we sat down. I can't control my emotions. Anger, grief, helpless fury, it all comes and goes across my heart and my face.

I take Surry's empty cup, set it down, and lift her—an easy scoop, one arm under her knees, one at her back. She's light, but the weight of what she said hangs off her like wet wool. I just sit there with her, letting her collect her thoughts, and deciding on what she wants to say next. But nothing comes. Not yet.

I carry Surry out. The hallway is cool and dim; the old plaster swallows sound. She doesn't cry—she's far past tears—but her hands are fisted in my shirt, not tight, just... anchored. Like if she lets go she'll float away.

"I'm not leaving," I say, finally. Simple. Not eloquent. The only sentence that matters.

She nods once against my chest.

Time passes in the way it does after a storm: quietly, the world remembering itself. Richie drifts by the doorway and doesn't enter, but he taps the frame twice—our version of a salute—before fading back into the murmur of the house. Somewhere deeper in the Compound, Hazel's laugh sparks and dies, a bright flare swallowed by distance. Joshua's voice rumbles on the back terrace; I hear the thunk of a kettle bell hitting packed earth. The place breathes.

When Surry finally lifts her head, there's resolve in her eyes that wasn't there this morning. Not the brittle kind. The forged kind. She slides off my lap, straightens my collar like she's smoothing the world back into place, and says, "I want a shower."

"I'll walk you up."

"Walk me to the stairs," she corrects gently. "I can do the rest."

"Compromise." I hold out a hand. "I will walk you up the stairs. Then I wait at the top."

She almost smiles. "Bossy."

"Accurate." I wink at her, letting her know I'm serious, but I want to help lighten her mood.

We move. The big house turns golden as the sun angles down; dust motes float like lazy galaxies in the stairwell light. At the landing, she pauses, touch ghosting my jaw, gratitude and heat and something steadier flickering there.

"Thank you," she says, and disappears down the hall.

I plant myself at the top step, shoulder to the newel post. I'm not guarding the hall to her room–she doesn't need a sentinel so much as a witness. A few minutes later, Juniper peeks around the corner, sunglasses on indoors like she's hiding from feelings.

"She okay?" she asks, voice carefully casual.

"She's showering."

"Right." Juniper's mouth quirks. "You should know Josh asked me to come check on you two, but... also to tell you he and Bridget are putting together dinner 'for morale.' His words." She flexes her pointer and middle fingers in bunny ear quotations when she says for *morale*.

I smirk at her use of air quotes. "He's learning."

"He's trying." Her tone softens. "For what it's worth, she did the hardest part today. It doesn't fix things, but sometimes saying it out loud makes it smaller."

"Sometimes," I say. "Sometimes it makes it real."

Juniper tips an imaginary hat and slips away. Water stops. Doors open. Footsteps pad. Surry returns in clean clothes—soft black leggings, one of my shirts she definitely stole, damp hair braided down her back. She looks like herself. Not the armor, not the silence—herself.

"Hungry? I guess Bridget and Joshua are making dinner" I tell her.

She hesitates, quirking a brow. Like at the combination of Bridget and Joshua and Dinner all in the same sentence. Then quietly but firmly says, "Only if you sit with me."

"Non-negotiable." I grin before grabbing her hand and leading us both toward the stairs.

Downstairs, the house is in that mellow evening swing where everyone is doing something and nothing at once. Bridget has orchestrated a meal that smells of rosemary, butter, and therapy. Richie's cutting bread, he absolutely does not need to be trusted with that knife; Alisha hip-checks him out of the way thankfully. Joshua pretends not to watch Juniper pretend not to watch him. Normal for them.

We don't talk strategy at dinner. Bridget wouldn't

allow it. She believes in "proper meals" the way field medics believe in tourniquets: you stop the bleeding first. Conversation finds air pockets that don't hurt—Richie's disastrously short "trucker tan," Alisha's claim that she can out-bench Joshua *(she can't, and the bet is set for tomorrow)*, Hazel's latest conspiracy about one of the groundskeepers having a secret twin in the village. Surry listens and eats, small bites, steady. That's a victory. I catalog it like numbers on a plan.

After, I check my phone. A single ping—Gunnar's coded check-in: wheels up in thirty, back tomorrow if the trail holds. He and Corver split leads at dawn; Arnie ran point into the nastier corners of the darknet afterward. They're pulling all threads that say Natasha. We're down a third of our muscle in exchange for the one person whose messages might unravel the whole thing. Worth it.

I show Joshua the screen. He nods. "War room after the kitchen's put to bed?"

"Yeah."

He jerks his chin toward Surry. "She gonna listen in?"

"If she wants."

"She'll want." There's zero doubt in his voice. "And she'll catch the details we'll miss. She's smart."

"I don't doubt it."

By the time the dishes are stacked and Bridget has chased everyone from her domain with a dish towel and a laugh, the sky is slate and the house is a low thrum of lamps and long shadows. We take the big round table in the formal dining room—not for ceremony, for surface area. Maps spread. Laptops open. A legal pad I'll never admit is mine sits under my hand, pencil ready. Joshua's on my right, already booted into our secure line. Surry curls into the chair to my left, legs tucked under, hair pulled over one shoulder. She looks small, but she feels enormous in the room.

The encrypted call snaps hot and clear: one tone, then Gunnar's low burr. "You alive, Slater?"

"Unfortunately," I say. "You?"

"Equipments live. Leads are mean." No hello, no wasted breath. "Arnie's digging on a shell company that paid out to a transport outfit we've seen on two Russian manifests. Corv's ghosting accounts that spin back to a network with three familiar IPs. Kelly isn't hiding—he's taunting."

Joshua leans in. "Natasha?"

"Not yet," Gunnar says. "But the chatter around her name spikes when we scrape an old Slavic forum tied to

Brotherhood business. We're on it in the morning, hard. For now: you tell me how our girl is."

I don't look at Surry when I answer. "She told us everything today. He needs to die, but by my hand, or hers, alone."

Static hums. Then Gunnar's voice goes softer, which isn't a thing he often allows. "Copy. Then we adjust." The command in his voice renews before he continues. "New plan: we make it cost him in pride before we take his body. Pride is his oxygen."

"Walk it," Joshua says.

We sketch. Fast, precise. Corver breaks in once from the background—low and clipped—about an email reroute that bought him an address he shouldn't have. Arnie's laugh filters through, dark and pleased: "He bought a yacht through a cousin's trash company. Of course he did. I can work with trash."

I give them what we have here—security rotations, staff we trust, staff we question but keep anyway because Bridget swears by them. Surry listens without interruption, then taps the edge of the map.

She leans in like she's laying out a fact, not a plan. "He won't bring his own men near my family," she says. "He'll hire disposable crews—blokes who burn out fast. Look for tiny rentals, temporary trucks: that's how he hides."

The way she says it—clean, unhesitating—makes the entire table pause. She's not guessing. She knows.

And I realize, not for the first time, that there's an entire part of Surry O'Brien most people will never see.

I lean back, watching her trace lines on the map like she's sketching muscle memory. Her finger moves through terrain, ports, supply roads—without hesitation.

"You've done this before," I say quietly. Not a question, a clear observation.

Her eyes flick to mine, and for a breath, I catch a flash of the girl she used to be—before scars and smoke and bastards with too much power. Then the commander returns. "Papa trained us," she says simply. "Not for fun, not for pride—because we had to know how to survive. His words."

Her voice goes softer, almost distant. "When other girls were learning piano, Selene and I were learning trade routes. Smuggling lines. Which ports could move goods fast, which ones had customs officers you could buy with a favor or a promise. He called it 'education.' Said if the men in our family ever fell, it would be us who rebuilt from the ashes."

Joshua's pen stills. Gunnar grunts his approval through the comm. Even Arnie whistles low.

But she's not done.

"When I married Gavin, he thought it was ornamental," she continues, gaze steady on the map, continuing to make x's and o's. "He never understood that I'd already been raised in a warzone—one with better manners, sure, but just as bloody underneath. He'd talk business at dinner like I was furniture, but I was listening. Every time he mentioned a name, a shipment, a port, I filed it away." She taps a point on the map. "That's how I know this one. He used to send cargo through here before he laundered the company into one of his Russian fronts. He thought he was clever. But I know his routes. I know his patterns."

Her jaw sets. "He taught me how to break him, just by thinking I wasn't just as knowledgeable as him. His mistake for underestimating a woman. The daughter of the Irish King."

I feel it—something old and lethal stirring behind my ribs. Pride. Awe. The sharp, clean heat of wanting to watch her burn the world that burned her.

"Jesus," Joshua mutters. "Remind me never to play chess with you."

Surry almost smiles. "Papa used to make us play risk instead. Said it kept our minds sharp and our hearts soft. You can't rule if you can't feel."

I glance sideways at her, a line of white hair slipping forward from her braid. I reach forward and tuck in while speaking directly to her. "You still feel, Surry."

She meets my gaze, unflinching. "That's the point, Brenden. I can feel and still fight."

And there it is—the difference between who she was and who she's become. She isn't just a survivor anymore. She's a strategist. The woman sitting beside me could take apart an empire with a highlighter and a grudge.

Gunnar's voice crackles back through the line, low and satisfied. "Hell of an asset you've got there, Slater."

I look at her, then back at the map. "Not an asset," I correct. "She's the plan."

Arnie's voice: "Send me a five-mile radius around your supply routes. I'll flag leases that smell like mercenary boarding houses."

Surry doesn't flinch at the word mercenary. She just slides the map closer and starts reading off coordinates like a second language. Her dad did well teaching her, without ever letting her know what he was teaching her. I think she, herself, blocked this information until now. A key unlocking a part of her that was buried under duress. Now, free from the secrets, she can unlock herself.

We talk for another half hour. When we finally break, the room is warm with intent. Plans have edges again. We have the next steps. It isn't a victory. It's momentum. Sometimes that's more valuable.

Joshua ends the call, pushes the laptop away, and rubs his jaw. "You know," he says to the ceiling, "I used to think construction was logistics. This is logistics with teeth."

"You always liked teeth," I tell him, a small smile on my face.

"True." He nods with a shit eating grin on his own.

I'm about to stand when my phone vibrates. No buzz pattern. No name. Just a number that carries weight like an anvil. I answer.

"Slater." Stefan's voice is iron and peat, no preamble. "He knows you're in Oregon."

Cold licks up my spine. "Understood. Orders?"

"Tell Bridget da word." His accent thickens on it. "Lockdown."

The line clicks dead. That's all. That's enough.

Surry's already watching me. She doesn't need the words to know. Still, I give them to her.

"Lockdown," I say.

She's on her feet before the syllables finish. No panic. No tremor. She moves the way a conductor lifts a baton—clean, decisive, absolute.

"Joshua," she says, voice carrying down the corridor like a bell, "east wing shutters first, then the galleries. Get Richie and Hazel to gather the staff inside, account for everyone, no exceptions. Alisha will go to the safe room with Bridget and ensure medical kits are staged at the foyer and the back terrace. Juniper can kill the exterior lights as soon as the last person's through the doors, then check cams for a sweep."

"On it," Joshua answers, already racing up the stairs to collect the others to give orders.

Bridget appears in the dining room doorway as if conjured—apron off, hair braided, a small laminated key card already in her hand. She doesn't ask questions; she has run this play before. "Go," she says simply, and tosses the card to Surry, who catches it without looking.

The house begins to change. Hidden panels hum. Steel sighs behind old wood. The glass that made afternoons glow honey-warm now reveals its real job, sliding into armored channels with a steady, expensive purr. Air pressure shifts. Somewhere above us, a metallic clank confirms the roof hatches have sealed.

I move with Surry—room to room, hall to hall—our steps in sync. I don't touch her unless she needs a passcode or a second set of hands. She doesn't need rescuing. She needs room to lead.

We reach the last set of shutters in the rear gallery— a long throat of windows that look down into the trees. She swipes the card, keys in the code, and I watch the final panel glide into place. The night outside becomes a reflection of ourselves.

Silence settles. Not empty. Primed.

Surry exhales once, slow and steady. She looks at me then, and all the steel in her eases just enough for the woman to step forward again. She steps into my space, presses her forehead to my chest, breathes me in like a reset.

"I'm okay," she says, mostly to herself. Then, more firmly, to me: "We're okay."

"We are," I answer. My hand finds the small of her back, holding there, steady as bedrock. "He doesn't get to touch what's ours."

Footsteps approach—Joshua, fast. "Outer perimeter's clean. No vehicles within a mile on our cams. If he knows we're here, he's not knocking tonight."

"He's watching," I say.

"Then let him watch us be ready," Surry replies.

There it is—that forged thing again. She turns, shoulders squared, eyes bright and clear, and starts walking toward the foyer where everyone will gather for headcount and a debrief. I fall in at her side.

I'm not naïve. This isn't over. It's barely begun. But tonight, the house is sealed, the people we love are inside, and the woman I walked into a room and chose is choosing this fight with me.

If he thinks that's a weakness, he's never seen what it looks like when a siren stops singing and starts steering the ship.

Brenden meets my eyes—steady, grounding—and then I turn down the hall following Bridget's lead. My legs move before my brain catches up, automatic, trained. The floor under my bare feet is cold, the hallway lit in the faint amber wash of emergency lights. I register the tiny details the way Papa taught us as kids: count cameras, count corners, count exits. My pulse stutters, then locks to a rhythm—inhale four, hold two, exhale six. Don't feed the fear.

The control room feels bigger than I remember. I haven't been inside since I was here recovering all those years ago. I used to lock myself in here when I would have panic attacks or nightmares; it was the only place I felt safe. It looks like the heart of something meant to outlive the people who built it—rows of metal consoles, cables running like veins into the walls, and the huge wall of monitors flickering with grainy night vision. Every angle of the house is here: the gates, the terrace, the pool, the forest. A schematic of the main manor hums along the bottom row—green where systems are live, steady amber where the manual backups own the line.

The air hums faintly with electricity and fear.

Bridget always said this room could survive a bomb. I used to laugh at that. Now, with my palms sweating and my heart in my throat, it doesn't sound like an exaggeration. The door is pure steel, thick as a vault, disguised on the outside to look like a wall. You'd never know it existed unless you'd built it.

"Right, loves," Bridget says, voice low and iron-calm, "eyes up an' mouths shut. If ye hear me say 'down cellar', ye move before ye think. D'ye understand?" Her brogue thickens when it matters. It steadies me.

Then the cameras flash, calling my focus to the wall of monitors. Headlights. Four cars at the gate.

They're just sitting there—engines idling, white light bleeding through the trees like ghosts waiting for permission. I don't recognize the vehicles, but my stomach knows who they belong to.

They haven't breached yet. Not yet. But we are ready for them, and something inside me says let them come.

"Stay here," I tell Bridget and the others. My voice sounds steady. That's good. It doesn't feel steady, but it sounds it.

Then I run.

Back through the hallway, across the polished floor of the living room, breath tight in my chest. Brenden's already there, pulling people out of their rooms, shouting orders in that low voice that makes people listen. Richie's half-joking to keep Alisha from spinning out; Hazel has both hands on Juniper's shoulders, eyes bright, jaw set.

"This way!" I call, waving them toward the hallway. "Down, then right. Open vault door—get inside!"

I start for the stairs, but Brenden catches my arm. The look in his eyes says what his mouth doesn't: Where the hell do you think you're going?

"I need shoes and real pants," I hiss. I glance down. Over sized T-shirt. Leggings. Literally nothing else.

His jaw flexes. "I'm coming with you." No room for argument. He grabs my hand and shouts for Josh to stay with Bridget, to get everyone inside and sealed.

We take the stairs two at a time, somewhere between a run and a prayer. The house smells like lemon oil and danger. My room feels too far away, every hallway longer than it should be. Papa always said houses remember footsteps; tonight the manor is learning ours again.

We burst inside. I grab the first pair of pants I see, socks, and a bra. Brenden snatches my shoes from the door. I'm bending to step in when—

Everything goes black.

The lights cut out. The hum of the house dies. For one heartbeat, the silence is total.

"Fuck." The word slips out before I can stop it. "They breached the gates. Power's cut—it's a failsafe. Everything runs on the mechanical grid. It'll slow them down, but not for long. We've got four minutes, tops."

He squeezes my hand. No panic in him—just motion. I drag the socks on, shove my feet into shoes. He slings my bra over his shoulder like it's a spare magazine, grabs my hand firmly, and we run.

The last stair is in sight when the first sound hits—cars, close. Too close. Tires on gravel, the growl of engines, the hiss of wet stone.

"How the hell—" I don't finish. We're already moving.

Josh is waiting at the vault, door cracked. We dive through, and he slams it shut. The lock thunders home, echoing through my bones.

"What the fuck," Brenden snaps, breath ragged. "How are they already at the doors?"

"Because they knew the road," Bridget answers, pale but focused. "Drove it like they'd done it before."

No one says it, but we're all thinking it: they've been here.

"Ye can't fly drones this close," she adds quickly. "The EM field blocks the signal, so they can't spy that way. This isn't random. They were told."

"Our phones," Alisha blurts out. My stomach drops.

"Possibly," Bridget says. She doesn't sugarcoat it. "Or the foreman on the outer road. People break under the wrong sort of ask."

The only light comes from the monitors, painting our faces in cold blue. The front of the house—headlights still, unmoving. Then, a flicker of motion. Shadows.

"There." Josh points to a smaller monitor—the back door off the kitchen. The old service entrance. They're in the house.

"They're already inside," I whisper. How the fuck did they get in without us hearing it?

"Kitchen door's a double seal," I murmur, brain flicking through schematics I thought I'd forgotten. "If the outer lock is jammed, the inner pin can be teased with a thin driver. Papa kept that flaw on purpose—'for family if the power goes.'" I swallow. "Gavin knows old Irish men. He'd guess."

I reach for the volume knob. "Turn it up."

Brenden's hand finds mine. He doesn't look at me, just holds on.

The speakers crackle, and then his voice fills the room.

"The house is too quiet," Gavin says, tone calm and cold as ever. "Are you sure they're even here? You said you had intel."

My heart twists. I know that voice in my bones.

One of his men answers, "We tapped into the brother's phone—Joshua Slater. Got the foreman at gunpoint. Used the signal to track 'em. Spoofed the ping. They're home."

The breath leaves the room. I glance at Josh—his face

is carved with guilt. No wonder we hadn't heard from him.

"Don't," I tell him. "You didn't know."

"Give me a minute and I'll make it hurt," he mutters, already hunched over the console. Fingers flying. "If they're still leeching my cell node, I can backbleed them. Static theirs, clean ours. Maybe pull a plate, a face. Anything." Josh told us he started learning the computer wizardry a few years ago in case we were ever separated from Corver and he and Gunnar left for Washington. I guess it's finally paying off.

"So where the fuck are they, Sawyer?" Gavin snarls. Glass skitters somewhere off-screen.

Josh's jaw tightens. "Keep them talking," he whispers to the air, like he can bend time.

More footsteps. A door opens somewhere upstairs— my door. The camera catches Gavin at the edge of frame, pale light across his cheekbones. He moves through my room like a man touring a museum, touching nothing until he does. He drags his knuckles along my dresser. Runs two fingers across my pillow. Smiles without joy.

The bile rises so fast I taste metal.

"How long has that camera been in there?" I hiss at Bridget.

"Since ye were just a girl," Bridget murmurs. "We never meant ta use it, love. But right now, I'm glad we can see what we're fightin'."

I don't answer. I pull the blanket tighter around me, curl deeper into Brenden's chest, and watch the monitor.

Gavin's face contorts, the vein at his temple pulsing. "This bitch doesn't have a single shred of proof we were married," he hisses, slamming his fist against the mahogany desk. "Little cunt should be ready to come back. Run the empire like we planned." He straightens his collar with trembling fingers. "She doesn't even know how good she would have had it. No one can give her what I can."

I almost laugh. He's delusional. He never understood the math of me: what I'll burn to keep my people warm.

Outside the room, his men pace the halls, frustrated and confused. One says, "They have to be in here somewhere. Maybe we wait them out."

"Fuck that," Josh mutters, typing faster. "Got him." He slaps a key. On the left monitor, a still frame freezes: a plate half-caught, mud-splashed. Another key, and a grainy face sharpens—a beard, a broken nose, a neck tattoo like a wire. "Richie, memorize it," Josh says. "Hazel, snap it. Bridget, record channel three always-on."

"There's another option," Bridget says, calm as ever. "An escape hatch. It's new—leads to a hidden garage a few miles off the property. Fully stocked. Fuel, food, backup vehicles."

Richie whistles. "Got a chopper down there, too?"

"Actually, yes."

We all blink at her.

"Well since none of us can fly a helicopter is there also like vans or trucks and stuff down here?" Brenden asks Bridget. She is about to speak when Hazel cuts in.

She raises her hand, "I can fly it." Sweet, sweet baby Hazel. How the fuck did I not know she could fly a helicopter?

Even in this nightmare, I can't help but huff a laugh. "Of course you can."

"Bucket list item," she says, unbothered.

"Right then," Bridget says, eyes bright and fierce. "We're not mice in a barrel. We'll leave the bastards chasin' shadows." She flicks a switch on the console—one I've never seen used. "Ghost walk."

A speaker upstairs clicks on. Footsteps start to play—recorded movement through the north gallery, the kind of creak you only learn if you live in a house long enough. A door shuts, faint. Then a woman's cough. Then silence.

On the monitor, Gavin's head snaps toward the gallery. He gestures, and two men peel off, guns up.

"Good girl, Bridge," Joshua breathes. "Let's go while they're idiots."

"...Isn't that, always?" I ask. Josh beams at me before nodding and turning the supplies.

We start packing—quiet, efficient. Gunnar's not here, but his systems are; Josh dumps the live buffer to an encrypted drive. Bridget queues the cameras to record on motion until the batteries die if the power doesn't come back on first. "If ye must leave a house," she mutters, "leave it watchin'."

We gather at the back panel—the one that looks like a bookcase. It hisses when Bridget slides the keycard and turns the hidden crank. Cold air leaks in. The passage yawns open—black, ribbed with old stone and new conduit.

The first step down always takes something from you. I tighten my grip on Brenden's shoulder and take it anyway. He insisted on going first so that if anyone falls he can catch us, but also if he falls he won't drag anyone else down.

The passage is barely wide enough for two people to

walk side by side. The walls close in, sweating damp against the low hum of emergency lights that flicker overhead. It smells like copper, wet earth, and old secrets. Papa used to joke the tunnel was from "the bad old days"—and every Irish child knows there are a lot of those—built first to move people, then to move contraband, then—when we tried to be better—to move our own safely when the world forgot how.

My blanket drags, the edge dark from the floor, but I keep moving. My heart won't slow down—it's in my throat, in my fingertips, in the echo of our steps. Each sound makes me flinch. It's too much like before—the hiding, the silence, the hope that staying quiet means staying alive.

Halfway down, a dull, heavy thud rolls through the stone—something above, something big.

We freeze.

Another thud. Closer to the study this time. Then a muffled voice: "Clear."

Brenden's thumb strokes the side of my hand once, a small, deliberate anchor. I lift my chin. I won't be small again.

"Go on, then," Bridget whispers behind us, voice soft and flint. "Lead us out, a chroí."

We move. One turn, then another, the tunnel pitching gently as it follows bedrock. We must have walked four or five miles at this point when finally a steel door looms out of the gloom—industrial, over sized, a wheel at its center like a ship. Bridget spins it. The seal sighs and releases. Cold, dry air rushes over us.

The lights flick on in stages—fluorescent strips blooming awake one by one. For a second I'm blind. Then shapes resolve: shelves of sealed crates, stacked fuel cans, pallets of MREs, tool chests, three covered vehicles gleaming under tarps... and at the far end, the chopper.

Hope, mechanical and loud, with rotors like razor-edged promises.

Hazel makes a delighted, slightly feral sound. "Hello, gorgeous." She's already moving—checks, switches, straps. Her hands are sure, practiced. Of course they are.

"Helmets," Bridget snaps, tossing them out like loaves of bread. "Ear pro. Belts on."

The rotors begin to turn, slow at first, then faster—wind tugging hair and clothes into flapping banners. Dust lifts in veils. Juniper whoops and immediately clamps a hand over her own mouth to muffle it. Alisha's fingers find mine, squeeze hard, let go.

"Buckle up, kiddies," Hazel says, voice steady as earth. "Mama's driving."

The floor shudders as the roof panels above us unlatch and peel apart like the petals of some black steel flower. Night air pours down—wet, sweet, full of pine and the ghost of river.

Then we lift.

Weightlessness snatches my stomach and sets it back down somewhere behind my ribs. The chopper rises through the open mouth of the bunker; the tunnel throat shrinks below us, the overhead panels sliding back into place with a soft hydraulic kiss. Hazel noses us sideways and up, keeping the pine canopy between us and the manor as long as physics allows.

We skim the treetops, drowned in rotor thunder. Through the open door, I catch the faintest glow—the manor's silhouette, blacked out and armored, holding its ground like an animal baring its teeth. Somewhere inside, men are opening cupboards and finding ghosts. Let them. Let him.

"Talk to me," Brenden says, mouth to my ear to beat the noise. "You okay?"

"I'm... here." It isn't eloquent, but it's true. The wind steals the rest.

We bank south, hugging the dark spine of the hills. The compound melts into forest, then forest melts into nothing at all. No headlights behind us. No beam raking the sky. Hazel flies low and dirty, the way a guilty thing flies when it intends to live.

On the far monitor bolted near Hazel's knee, a split screen runs from the house—motion only. Black and white ghosts drift room to room. I watch long enough to see Gavin pause in my doorway again, eyes sweeping the bed one last time, like a man convinced a sea will give back what it has already taken.

"Next time," I whisper to the wind that shreds the words before anyone else can hear, "we won't be the ones running."

Brenden's hand tightens around mine. I don't look away from the trees.

I don't look back.

# BRITT

The flight back to Washington is absolutely breathtaking. The world below blurs into ribbons of dark green and silver as we cut north through the sky. At this height, the Oregon forest rolls beneath us like an endless ocean, and when the coastline finally appears, the real one waits beyond—the Pacific stretching out until it curves with the earth. Down below, the small coastal towns glow like constellations scattered across the ground. It's beautiful, almost peaceful, like the world forgot what kind of hell we just ran from.

But my favorite part isn't the view. It's Surry. She's tucked in my lap, her head resting on my shoulder, her body rising and falling in the rhythm of sleep. I've got my arms wrapped around her within the blanket we're sharing, keeping her upright as we slice through the dark sky. I flipped off the comms on her headset an hour ago—she doesn't need to hear the constant chatter between Hazel and the others. Every few minutes, I feel her breathe a little deeper like her body's negotiating with the world and finally accepting the treaty: we're safe for the moment.

The cockpit glow throws a soft blue on Hazel's cheekbones as she flies—focused, steady, hands sure on the collective. Instruments hum. Tiny green numbers crawl. A faint vibration rides up through the skids, through the ribs of the bird, into my bones. I catalog it all the way I do on a run: RPM, torque, altitude. If Hazel needed me to take the stick, I could. She won't. The woman flies like she was born in a hangar.

Josh's voice breaks through the quiet hum. "Hey guys, I'm really sorry. I should have been more careful."

Juniper leans over and rubs his arm, soft and steady. She looks the most put together out of all of us—like chaos didn't just chew us up and spit us out. Her bright orange curls are loose, bouncing around her shoulders, and her blue sundress catches the dim cockpit light every time she moves. Tattoos shimmer against her skin like reflections off glass. She looks like she was on her way to something softer. A date, maybe. Then I notice Josh —shirt pressed, boots clean, hair slicked back like he was trying too hard.

It hits me. They were planning a date. The corners of my mouth twitch, and I catch Josh's eye. He flushes red as a warning light and looks away fast. I raise an eyebrow, mouthing, really? He scratches the back of his neck, trying not to grin. Even through exhaustion, I can't help it—I chuckle quietly. Leave it to my brother to make time for romance between gunfire and lockdowns.

"It's not your fault," I tell him, keeping my voice low so I don't wake Surry. "They didn't hack your phone. They went through our foreman. He's probably scared out of his damn mind right now... if he's even still alive."

Josh's jaw tightens. I pull my phone out, thumb flying over the screen as I shoot a message to the foreman—quick, coded, nothing traceable. A few tense minutes later, the screen lights up with a reply.

"He's okay," I exhale. "Shaken, but alive."

Josh nods once, eyes flicking toward the window, and leans back into his seat. Juniper rests her head against his shoulder. For a second, the noise in the cabin fades, replaced by the steady thrum of rotor blades and the faint crackle of the comms.

Behind them, Richie's sprawled like a dead starfish with his headset askew, one hand still wrapped around an unopened granola bar like he fought and won it. Alisha's got her knees hugged to her chest, chin on them, watching clouds scroll past like she's trying to memorize a new version of calm. Bridget —God bless her—is snoring in the jump seat, mouth slightly open, hands folded over a tote that probably contains a rosary, a multitool, and snacks no mortal can refuse.

Surry stirs slightly, mumbling something against my neck. I brush my thumb over her arm. She told me earlier this place—her parents' island—isn't somewhere she visits often. Once a year, usually, a summer trip with Richie, Alisha, and Hazel. A little pocket of peace she keeps tucked away. I'm hoping it'll still feel like that when we land.

"Haze," I say into the mic. "You good up there? Need me to sing to keep you awake?"

Hazel giggles through the headset. "I'm good! Haven't flown in a while, so adrenaline's keeping me plenty awake. You might wanna sing to Bridget, though—she's out cold next to me."

"She deserves it," I say. "But if you get tired, you yell for me. Got it?"

"Got it, boss."

We slide past a ragged smear of storm over the

water. Lightning spiders far offshore—silent at this distance, a light show with the sound turned off. It's about a 340-mile flight from Corvallis up to the Strait of Juan de Fuca. From this height, the night looks painted—streaks of navy and violet, the occasional pulse of lightning far out over the ocean. The world looks too calm for what we've been through.

Hazel flips a couple of toggles. "Crossfeed's good. We're sweet on fuel. ETA sixty-five."

"Copy."

At some point, Hazel flips on the cabin speakers. "Thought we could use a little noise," she says, grinning.

A few seconds later, a deep, atmospheric beat fills the helicopter—Pac Ave by Diggy Graves. The music hums low, pulsing through the metal floor, vibrating against my chest where Surry's heartbeat rests. It fits—dark, haunting, but beautiful. The kind of song that doesn't just play; it lingers. The words describing the landscape we can see now that we are getting closer to Seattle.

Everyone falls quiet. The hum of the engine and the low bass from the song weave together, creating a strange kind of calm. Surry's head shifts slightly on my shoulder, her hand brushing my chest in her sleep, and I swear I can feel her dream through the way her body softens.

"Hey, B?" Richie says after a while, voice half-asleep. "What's the breakfast situation on this island? Asking for me."

"Bread," Bridget mumbles without opening her eyes, pure Irish in a single syllable. "There'll be bread, boy."

"And jam," Hazel adds, because of course she does.

"Copy that," Richie says, satisfied like we've solved war.

We skim over a break in the clouds. Seattle's glow blooms far to our right, then drifts behind us as we angle toward a scatter of black rocks in silver water. It's a few hours later, judging by the sun's position when Hazel begins her descent. The ocean glimmers almost metallic under the early dawn light, and a cluster of small islands appears through the thinning clouds. Pines spear the sky. A white line of surf frays and re-stitches itself along the outer beaches.

Hazel lines up on a narrow crescent of concrete cut into the trees—the private helipad—and flares smooth. The skids kiss down. The rotors keep biting air as she spools down. Salt wind shoves at the open door, cold enough to sting.

I nudge Surry gently. "Good morning, beautiful," I whisper, tucking a strand of hair behind her ear. Her skin is soft and warm against my fingers. She blinks awake, stretching, the blanket slipping to her waist.

Then she sees them—her parents waiting near the helipad. Her whole face changes, blooming into something I haven't seen before. Light. Hope.

She unbuckles, throws open the door, and takes off running. Stefan catches her in his arms like he's been waiting years for it. Sabrina wraps around both of them, laughing through tears. Watching it makes something in my chest ache— the kind of ache that feels like wanting something you didn't know you'd missed.

Hazel kills the last of the spin. I pop belts, help the others deboard—Hazel, Richie, Alisha, Josh, Juniper, and finally Bridget, who blinks against the dawn, muttering about needing coffee. A small team in dark jackets and unobtrusive earpieces jogs in—O'Brien security, moving like a choir that knows the hymn.

"Clear the disc," one of them calls, polite but firm. We step beyond the painted circle as the rotor settles to a lazy fan.

A square-shouldered woman with a clipboard approaches, face weathered by sea wind. "Ms. O'Brien." She nods at Surry, then at me and Josh. "Welcome. I'm Aoife. We've got vehicles staged and warm. Luggage will be pulled and placed in your rooms." She says it like an oath, not a courtesy.

"Thank you," I tell her, "but we have no luggage. Just us." Aoife nods.

I walk toward Surry and her parents. Up close, Stefan is taller than I remember from photos, wearing a fisherman's sweater and the kind of authority that doesn't need volume. Sabrina is gentler at first glance, but her eyes could cut stone.

"Good morning," I say, offering my hand to Stefan. He grips it with both of his, his smile tight but sincere.

"T'ank ya for lookin' after me girl," he says softly. "Ye've done more'n ye know."

"I'll keep doing it," I tell him.

He nods once, eyes sharp and assessing, before gesturing toward the hangar. "C'mon now. We'll get ye all settled —there's folks waitin' fer ye."

As we walk, Sabrina falls into step beside me, her accent a softer music. "Ye kept her alive," she says, a simple statement. "That's the measure that matters, lad."

"Yes, ma'am."

The path from the helipad to the main hangar hugs

the tree line. Early dawn bleeds through fog; gulls wheel and shout. Inside the hangar, two private jets rest beside a smaller helicopter and what looks like a military recon plane retrofitted for civilian use. The O'Briens don't just prepare for trouble; they anticipate it. Tool chests gleam. A row of labeled pelican cases lines a shelf like squared-off soldiers: MED, COMMS, DRONES, WATER.

Stefan leads the way, his wife at his side, Surry tucked close under his arm. "We've been watchin' the feeds o' the compound since ye left," he rumbles. "They found the lockroom wi' their bloody heat gun—saw the cold shape o' the door plain as day. Tore up everythin' they could touch, but we've still a bit o' the network left runnin'. Praise be ye left when ye did."

"What now?" I ask. "You have a plan?"

"Aye," he says. "But I'll be needin' you an' yer brothers t' help. Are they willin'?"

Josh answers before I can. "Fuck yeah, we're in."

I grin at him. That's my brother. Always loud, always loyal.

A man in his fifties jogs over with mugs on a tray. "Tea an' coffee," he says cheerfully. "Fuel for the living." The mugs are mismatched, chipped in a way that looks like love, not neglect. Bridget snatches a tea like it owed her money.

"Well, it's nearly six in the mornin'," Stefan starts.

"Nearly seven," Sabrina corrects, elbowing him with a small smile on her face.

He sighs before smiling back at his wife. "Grand so," he says. "We'll talk the details after breakfast."

We file into the waiting sedans. The short drive to the O'Briens' home is quiet, the sound of gravel under the tires and distant waves our only soundtrack. The house rises out of the mist like something out of an old story—modern lines wrapped in ivy, walls of glass and stone. A pair of stone seals flank the entrance, noses lifted as if scenting weather. Inside, marble floors and pale walls lined with flowers lead us through warm light and quiet elegance. The air smells like wood smoke and lemon oil, like someone made morning on purpose.

We pass a long table already half-set—bowls of berries, a platter of smoked fish, soda bread cooling on racks, butter in crocks. A radio murmurs in the kitchen: some local radio host talking under the clatter of plates. Somewhere deeper in the house a clock chimes the hour, soft as breath.

Sabrina turns to Surry. "Ye know where yer room is, a stór. Show the others where ta go."

"Yes, Mama." They squeeze hands before Surry turns to me and grabs my own, leading me and the others upstairs.

"Oi," Josh whispers as we climb, taking in the carved banister, the way the hall opens to a library balcony. "If I get lost, do I yell 'Marco' or 'O'Brien'?"

"Ye yell 'Bridget!'" Bridget answers without looking back. "An' I appear."

Once we get to the top, we peel off in pairs. Josh and Juniper disappear into a guest room, doors closing with a hush only old houses know. Alisha ghosts down another hallway—probably hunting for Sam's last location via instinct and sheer stubbornness. Richie and Hazel vanish behind two more doors with matching tired smiles.

Soon it's just me and Surry left in the hall.

"This one's mine," she says, stopping in front of a door. Then, with a teasing tilt of her head, "You staying with me or do you need a babysitter?"

I smirk. "I was thinking Josh—"

She elbows me in the ribs, and I laugh, following her inside.

Her room is everything I expected—soft sage walls, one black accent wall covered in art, and a bed big enough for three people, dressed in emerald green and shadow. A glass door opens to a balcony where you can hear the sea argue with the shore. There's a stack of old books on the nightstand with a sprig of dried heather tucked between them. It smells like lavender and salt. Like her.

Surry toes off her shoes and pulls the elastic from her braid; her hair falls like a flag dropping to half-mast. We change quietly—her removing everything, while I slip off all my clothes minus my boxers since we didn't have time to grab anything. We crawl under the covers preparing for a well-deserved nap, and for the first time in days, my body remembers what rest feels like. I pull her close, her head under my chin, her breath warm against my chest.

"Sleep good," I whisper into the darkness.

"You too," she answers me also in a hushed tone, as if we spoke any louder, we would be found out by the evil we're running from.

"Mo chroí," I add without thinking—my heart. I've been looking into Gaelic so I could talk more with her dad, but also for more ways to tell her how I feel about her. It earns me a sleepy squeeze to the ribs.

That's the last thing I remember before sleep takes

me.

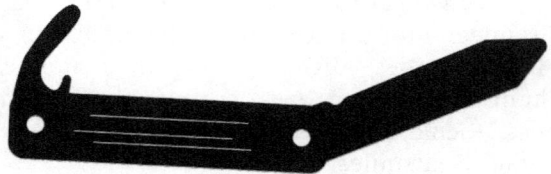

The dream starts softly. Then it turns.

*I'm back in the compound. Smoke everywhere. The sound of gunfire echoing down hallways that shouldn't exist. I can't find her. Surry's voice calls my name, sharp and panicked, but every time I turn toward it, she's farther away. Gavin's there—always just ahead, dragging her by the arm, his grin carved out of cruelty. I run, but my legs feel heavy, like the air's turned to tar. I reach for her, fingertips brushing hers just as he pulls her through a doorway that slams shut like a vault.*

*"Not again," I choke out, pounding my fists against steel. "Not again."*

*I hear my mother's scream behind it—the same sound I heard when I was eight, hiding in a closet while a man beat her nearly to death. The same helpless, suffocating silence when I was twenty-five, when another man accomplished the job.*

*I can't save her either.*

When I wake, I'm gasping. The room's dark, quiet except for the sound of Surry breathing beside me, her hand still resting on my chest like an anchor. I stare at the ceiling until my pulse slows. It's just a dream. Just a dream. But my body doesn't believe it.

The clock on her desk glows 9:00 a.m. Wind scrapes across the balcony rail, smelling of kelp and cold sunlight. Somewhere lower in the house, a kettle clicks off and someone laughs—Bridget, by the music of it.

I slide out of bed carefully, grab my phone, and slip into the adjoined bathroom en suite. The rug covering tile is soft under my feet. A painting of a storm at sea watches me pass like it has opinions. I make my way toward the sink to wash my face when I'm stopped dead in my tracks—the message waiting on my screen from Corver is equally good news and danger rolled into one.

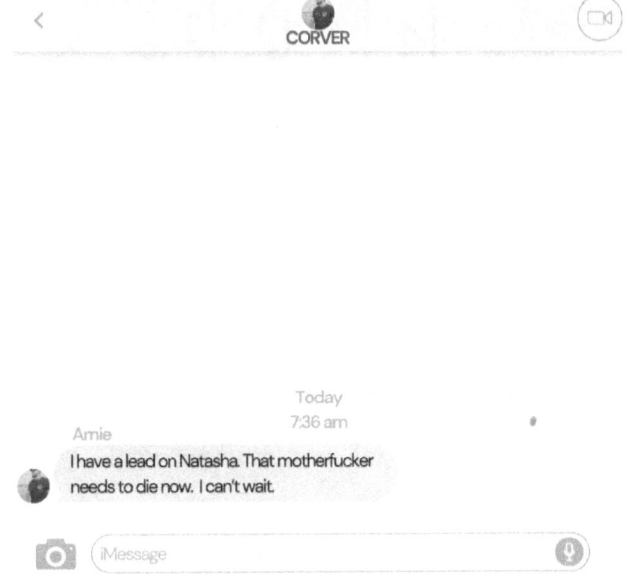

I stare at it for a long moment. The words are simple. The implications aren't. It's a choice wrapped in a threat, a time stamped demand pretending to be mercy. The kind of thing a coward sends when he wants to sound like God.

I look back at the closed bedroom door, at the woman sleeping inside.

"Not yet," I whisper.

I shoot Corver a reply telling him to wait until I talk to Stefan, then I tuck the phone into my palm like a blade and head for the balcony. The door slides open on oiled rails; the morning hits my face clean and cold. Pine sap, wet stone, the promise of rain. Out past the cove, a ferry carves a neat white wake through pewter water, ordinary people crossing from one piece of their lives to another like it's the easiest thing in the world.

I make a silent vow to the horizon: I will build her ordinary. I will carve it out of days if I have to, out of my bones if that's the cost. Let him bring the storm. We've learned how to fly through worse.

Waking up in my parents' house feels like slipping into a memory that doesn't quite fit anymore. Everything smells the same-cedar floors, salt from the sea, that faint trace of chamomile that lives in my mother's hair-but it feels smaller somehow. Maybe it's because there are more people here than ever before. Maybe it's because I'm not alone this time.

The giant man beside me changes the whole gravity of this place.

Brenden looks completely out of place in my childhood bed, yet he belongs here more than anyone ever has. He's in nothing but his boxers since he has no clothes here, and he's bigger than my dad or Sam. The morning light turns his skin gold, his hair sticking up in ten different directions. He's propped up against the headboard, phone in his hands, that furrow between his brows deep enough to drown in.

He doesn't even notice me watching him.

"What time is it?" My voice is scratchy, still heavy with sleep.

He doesn't look up. "Little after nine-thirty." His voice is rough, lower than usual-the sound of bad news wearing human clothes.

I sit up, pulling the blanket with me. I am wearing nothing, having gone to sleep completely naked. I didn't even put any underwear on before sleep. We tangled up together, legs wound and arms around necks, before we drifted off. Nothing happened but as much as I wanted it to this morning, his tone has cut that dream short. "What happened?"

He finally drags his eyes away from the screen. The small, soft smile he gives me is the kind that tries to hide the weight behind it. His thumb traces the line of my cheekbone, gentle, almost apologetic.

"Answer me, Brenden."

He exhales, long and hard. "Got some news. Corver texted. They got wind of her-Natasha. The Russian boss's daughter. Remember?"

The image flashes-the video, the screaming, the silence after. I nod. "I remember. I didn't watch the whole thing. But ... I know what that feels like. I hope she's ..." I stop when a phone rings, loud enough to jolt us both.

"My phone?"

He nods toward my desk. "Plugged it in for you last night. Was dead. Figured you'd want it charged. Though, honestly, I think your dad's gonna have all of ours destroyed before lunch."

He's probably right.

I pad across the cold floor, arms wrapped around myself as goosebumps explode over my naked body, and grab the phone. My dad's name flashes on the screen. *Why is he calling when he's downstairs?*

"Hi, Papa."

"Ah, me sweet Surry," his voice hums through the speaker, thick and warm with that Irish rasp. "Would ye come down fer breakfast, aye?"

I grab one of Sam's old Mariners shirts–two sizes too big, soft as sin–and nothing else. I crawl back into bed, wedge my icy feet under Brenden's legs. He yelps, and I grin.

"Yes, we'll be down soon. But why call? We're literally in the same house."

"I didn't wanna intrude, lass," he says, amusement in every word.

That's my father–a warlord who doesn't want to intrude.

"Brenden is just keeping an eye on me Papa, don't go putting a hit out on him for being in your daughters room."

He chuckles, a low, warm sound. "Ah, me girl, ye've finally found a man worthy o' ye. I'm glad he's here. Don't care where he sleeps so long as he treats ye right."

I smile at Brenden, who's half-listening, one hand scrolling, the other drawing lazy circles on my bare thigh drawing ever closer to my bare center with each swipe. "I did, huh," I murmur, mostly to myself. "Finally found a good one."

He looks up, curious. I shake my head. Later. His hand moves up several inches and grazes the junction between hip and thigh. He smiles evilly at me while I swat at his hand.

"We'll be down in ten, Papa."

Brenden mouths fifteen at me, then wiggles his eye brows. I roll my own eyes.

"Fifteen tops, Papa."

"Grand so. See ye then."

I hang up. "Welp, my dad loves you."

Brenden stares like I've just told him gravity's optional. "He does? I figured he'd be pissed I'm in here with you."

"Nope. He's thrilled. Said you're worthy. Which I guess is a good thing since you say you aren't leaving me."

He puts his phone aside, rolls toward me, wraps me up until I can't tell where I end and he begins. His breath brushes my ear when he whispers, "I'm happy I'm here too." He shifts me so we're face-to-face, noses brushing, eyes locked. "I can't keep it in anymore, Surry."

My heart stutters. I notice then at some point he has removed his boxers and I can feel his erection rubbing against my center. My blood begins to boil with need.

He stares at me, his light blue eyes boring deep into my soul, his calloused thumb tucking my wild copper strands behind my ear. I feel the rough pad of his finger trail down the sensitive skin of my chin, leaving goosebumps in its wake. "I love you." The words fall from his full lips like they've been waiting years, suspended in time even before he knew me, hanging in the air between us like delicate crystal. "I have since the first moment—you standing in my room, completely out of place but also looking like a storm that could wreck my whole world. I know it hasn't been long, mere heartbeats compared to how long I want to be next to you, and it's been one hell of a hurricane since the second we met. But it's true. I can feel it coursing through my veins every time I breathe, each time our skin grazes." He shifts his pelvis forward a bit, nearly entering me, but not quite. "You're it for me—my beginning and end."

Tears sting before I can stop them. This man, who could break mountains with his hands, is giving me his heart like it's the easiest thing in the world.

"People may call me crazy, because, well, I love you too," I whisper. "But I'm terrified. I've been hurt, Brenden. Ruined. I can't give you much—just my heart. And someday, I'll take over the family business, all of it. That's my life, whether I want it or not. So if you want me, you are going to have to find a way to fit in with all this" I gesture loosely at the room around us." But also, you will have to be patient with me, while I learn to trust again, while I find comfort in giving pieces of myself away to another that I fought so hard to get back from the last. No matter how much I want to say all of me belongs to you, deep down, there are parts I am still working on, pieces that won't rest easy until the one who broke them pays."

His hands cup my face, thumbs brushing away tears. "I know what I'm signing up for, Siren. And I'm not running. I want every part you're willing to give, and I will patiently earn the rest.

You're everything, my everything.." He kisses my forehead, right where the scar splits my eyebrow.

"You need to tell me how you got this."

"Later," I whisper.

His mouth moves to mine, hot and possessive. I open slightly, letting his tongue entry. He shifts forward once again, and he enters me in one motion. The feeling of fullness he brings is everything I could want. As if I was covered in cracks, and he closes them.

He beings rocking slowly back and forth, thrusting in and out of me in the most intimate display. "I love you, Surry." He thrusts again. "I will love you every day." Again. "Until the day I die." His speed picks up, not rough, just a little faster.

"I love you Brenden," I say between silent breathy moans. "There is no one else I would rather be here with. Healing with. Learning with."

Brenden lowers his forehead to mine, kissing my nose, before he once again picks up the pace. We are short on time, but we don't want to lose this moment. Our mouths meet as he continues to claim me, just as I claim him with the scratching and little bites I place on his shoulder and neck. I wrap my legs around his waist and lift my hips, allowing him better access.

"Fuck, Surry." It's all he has to say. He beings to grunt and I fall over the precipice. It is not a descent off the tallest mountain in the world, but it is warm. It's comforting. It's what my future will hold with him at my side.

Once finished, the both of us hop up and head to the bathroom, jumping in the shower for a quick wash before we head downstairs.

"We've got a few minutes to get dressed before breakfast. So tell me what Corver said–that's all the time you get." He lightly pinches my nipple, while simultaneously kissing my ear, trying to redirect my thoughts, but I won't let it.

While we wash, he tells me about what Corver has learned, and what he hopes to do. Just more issues and pain. Just more problems that I am at the root of.

We make it to breakfast barely on time. I'm in pajamas, Brenden's in the same jeans and t-shirt from yesterday. Richie, Hazel, and Alisha look fresh, wearing the clothes we all keep stashed here for emergencies–our "last-minute vacation" drawers. Poor Josh, Juniper, and Brenden aren't so lucky.

My dad stands when we walk in. "Mornin', me loves," he says, voice booming but warm. "Glad t' have such a full table, even if the reason's not a happy one. Bridget's gone out fer clothes fer ye all–took a few o' the guards with her. Our home's yer home. Treat it like yer own, aye?"

His hand rests on Ma's shoulder. She gazes up at him like she's still half in love and half exasperated–that's always been them.

"Thanks, Papa," I say, kissing his cheek before taking my seat beside him, Brenden on my right. Across from us: Richie, Hazel, Alisha. Down the table, Josh and Juniper whisper about something, probably each other. Empty seats wait like ghosts of who's missing.

Then–a familiar voice.

"SISSY!"

I whip around. Selene stands in the doorway, pale but smiling. For a heartbeat, I forget to breathe. Then I'm running, slippers silent on marble, heart slamming against my ribs.

I stop just short of touching her–scared she's still too fragile.

"Don't ye dare do that," she scolds softly, her Irish lilt matching Ma's. "Get over here, ya eejit."

Her embrace is careful but full, and I melt into it. She smells like rosewater and hospital soap. Relief burns through me so fast it almost hurts. Over her shoulder, I see Sam watching, waiting, standing behind Alisha with a hand on her shoulder. He must have come up after I had heard Selene.

"Hi, brother," I whisper.

"Hi, sissy." He squeezes my arm. His eyes look older somehow, tired but bright.

Then Ma's there, pressing into us, her curls brushing my cheek. Papa wraps his arms around the whole pile of us. The weight of their bodies, their warmth, their breath–it breaks something open inside me I didn't know was still locked.

"I'm delighted we're all t'gether again, though the reason's a dark one, God help us, " Ma says, voice shaking with that melodic Irish tilt.

"Us too, Mama," Selene, Sam, and I echo, voices overlapping.

When we finally untangle, I help Selene to her seat beside Hazel. Sam takes the empty chair beside Alisha. I wiggle my eyebrows at him–you like her–and he rolls his eyes. No confession today, apparently. I've been hoping and trying for years.

I settle back beside Brenden just as his hand finds my lap under the table. Warm, grounding. His touch reminds me of what he told me upstairs–Corver's update, Natasha, the cold trail. That he loves me. I can almost feel the storm waiting beyond the walls. As thrilled as I am I'm equally, if not more so, scared.

Mama's voice breaks through my thoughts. "How did ye all

sleep, then? I know it was't long 'nough"

Murmurs all around: *Good. Comfy. Dead to the world.*

"Perfect," she says. "If ye need anythin', ye come t' me, aye?"

The kitchen staff bring breakfast-Pancakes and eggs sizzle beside rashers and black pudding, bowls of berries gleaming under the morning light, and a loaf of soda bread still warm from the oven. The smell of strong coffee fills the room, cut with the richer scent of butter melting over hot boxty. It's calm. It's peaceful.

But the back of my neck still prickles. Peace never lasts.

Once breakfast clears, everyone drifts off to get ready for the day. Each of us constantly glancing over our shoulders, waiting for the next pang of alarm.

The house hums with movement-laughter in one hallway, footsteps in another-and for a moment, it almost feels like a home instead of a bunker.

Sam offers clothes to the guys since they all seem to share the same giant-gorilla build. Josh gets a pair of sweats and a faded band tee. Brenden gets one too— sweats that are a few inches too short and a black t-shirt with Sleep Token across the chest. It's snug, but I can tell it would normally be loose on Sam.

I blink. "Um. What?"

Sam grins, halfway proud, halfway waiting for the reaction. "What?"

"You like Sleep Token too?" I can't keep the disbelief out of my voice. My brother listens to moody indie rock-think Hoozier. Sleep Token is... not that.

"Hell ya," he says, already energized. "You do too?"

"Of course I do."

That's all it takes. In seconds, we're talking over each other about the newest album, the stage show, the absolute choke hold The Summoning still has on humanity. How Gethsemane is literally my all-time favorite song. He's animated, gesturing with his hands; I haven't seen him light up like this since before everything went to hell.

Mid-conversation, Brenden squeezes my arm and presses a kiss to my cheek. "Your dad wants to speak with Joshua and me," he says, his words still clipped in that coded calm he uses when things aren't quite fine. "I'll be back soon, Siren. Keep talkin' to your brother. I won't be long."

I nod. He kisses me once more and disappears down the hall. I already miss the heat of him.

Sam and I keep walking toward Selene's room, our voices

trailing through the corridor. The hallway smells like wood polish and sea air. The morning sun cuts through the tall windows, slicing everything into warm gold.

"Selene doesn't leave her room much," Sam says quietly. "Still hurts to move some days."

I nod, the memory of the explosion flashing quickly behind my eyes. "How bad was it?"

He exhales. "Shrapnel hit her side, nicked a few organs. Not bad enough to ruin anything long term, thank God, but she's still sore. Doctors said she would be for a while, but she's healing. They got her on a special diet, lots of protein."

When we reach her door, I knock twice before pushing it open. The sight makes me smile despite everything.

Selene sits curled up in a hanging egg chair identical to the one in my room. The entire space looks like a cotton-candy planetarium–pink walls, pink bedding, pink fuzzy rug, pink stars painted and stuck to the ceiling that'll glow softly when the lights go out. She's in matching pink pajamas too, holding a book that's bigger than her head.

Two words: *Pink Celestial.*

"Whatcha readin'?" I ask, snatching the book gently from her lap while keeping her place with my thumb. I'm not *that* evil.

She gasps, mock-offended. "Give it back!"

I tilt the cover toward me. "Dragons? Seriously?"

"It's *so* good," she says, sitting up straighter. "A girl goes to a school to ride dragons, and the hot guy has these crazy shadow powers. He's obsessed with her–in the good way. *I'm* obsessed with *him.*"

"Shadows?" I laugh, handing the book back. "Didn't peg you for fantasy, babe."

"Ever heard of a shadow daddy?" she teases, eyes glinting. "From the looks of you and all that muscle at the table during breakfast, pretty sure you'd be into it too. That, or reverse harem." She winks at me, and Sam groans before making mock wretching sounds.

I choke on a laugh. "Oh my God, *Selene.*"

She grins, but it fades when I really look at her — the circles under her eyes, the dullness around the edges of her smile. I kneel at her feet, leaning against the soft rug, studying her face until she sighs and turns away.

"What's wrong, babe?" I ask gently.

Sam edges closer, instinctively reading the shift in my tone.

She exhales, long and shaky. "I was so worried, Sissy. And I couldn't help. I just sat here while everyone else was fighting or running or bleeding. I was... useless. A burden." Her voice cracks on the last word.

That's all it takes.

Sam and I both move at once, climbing to our knees and wrapping her tight between us. She cries hard–body-shaking sobs that sound like they've been trapped in her ribs for days. There's nothing to say. We just hold her.

When she finally stills, we stay there a bit longer — three kids tangled on a pink rug, breathing the same broken rhythm.

Eventually, I pull back, wipe my cheeks, and grab her hand. "You're not a burden, Moon. Not even close. No one could've predicted what happened at Brenden's place. You did what you had to–you survived. That's enough." Our childhood nicknames, Sun and Moon popping out. They usually cheer her up.

She nods, her lip trembles. But not this time.

"We probably should've come here first," I admit quietly. "Would've been safer. What can they even do to us here?"

Sam looks uneasy but doesn't answer. The question hangs between us like fog.

Before either of them can speak again, there's a soft knock at the door frame. Our dad stands there, shoulders squared beneath his charcoal suit, the silver at his temples catching the light. Brenden looms just behind him, jaw clenched tight enough to crack walnuts, his knuckles white around the leather shoulder holster. Both of them look carved out of steel—Dad weathered and battle-scarred like an old naval destroyer, Brenden polished to a threatening gleam, all sharp edges and cold purpose.

The shift in the air is instant.

Something's wrong.

The knock on Selene's door was soft, but it might as well be thunder.

Brenden walks in first, his expression carved from stone. My dad follows, heavier, slower, voice low enough to make the air tremble.

"What. What happened?" My voice sounds too small.

"We just heard from Gavin." Brenden starts.

The name rips through me like glass. I flinch before I even register it.

"What?" My throat closes around the word. "What happened? I know it's bad–just say it." Sam grabs my hand. His palm is hot, grounding.

"He took Bridget," Brenden says quietly.

The floor tilts. My heart slams once, twice, then starts racing so fast I can't feel where one beat ends and the next begins.

"What do you mean he *took her?*" I'm standing before I know it, pacing. "How–how did he grab her? She had guards. You *sent guards*, didn't you? What do we do? We can't let him keep her. He'll kill her–he'll kill her, Papa!" My hands find his shoulders before my brain catches up. "Papa, what are we going to do?"

He grips my wrists gently, steady, but his voice carries the weight of too many plans.

"We've a plan, mo stór. Bridget knew da risk, tis part o' da job. That's why I called the lads in. We were goin' over what t' do if somethin' like this happened, and right then–" He sighs, the sound of defeat in his lungs. "Right then, the bastard reached out. We've already set things in motion, but I need ye t' tell me if he tries t' contact ye. Everyone else has burners, but ye–ye're the one he'll reach for first."

My hands drop. I can't feel them. I can't feel anything.

He wants me to *wait*. To be bait.

The room folds in on itself. The air thickens, pressing against my chest. I can't catch a full breath.

Brenden crouches down in front of me. I can see him, his mouth moving, his hand reaching–but the sound–

The sound is gone.

There's a ringing, high and sharp, filling every space in my skull. My vision tunnels until all I see are the edges of his face and the panic in his eyes.

My heart hammers against my ribs–too fast–too loud–too much. My fingers shake, and I can't stop them. My throat burns, but no air gets in.

*Breathe. Just breathe. Please breathe.*

I don't know if I say it or think it or if it's someone else entirely. I'm floating somewhere between the two.

Everything is blurry now–Sam's voice muffled, Selene's crying, my dad's deep tone somewhere behind it all. I think I'm crying too. I don't know.

Then–Alisha.

Her hands are on me. One behind my neck, the other pressing firm against my chest. Her voice cuts through the ringing like a thread of light.

"Hey, Surry. Look at me. Right here, love. Breathe with me, okay? In–" she exaggerates a breath "–and out. You're okay. You're safe."

I can't follow her at first. My chest jerks instead of expanding.

My hands claw at my own legs. The edges of the room flicker.

"Come back t' me, girl," my dad says somewhere above me, his voice raw and broken. "Ye're alright now, mo chroí. We've got ye. No one's takin' ye again."

The sound of his accent—thick, rooted, old as stone—grounds me.

I gasp, then choke, then finally drag in a real breath. My ears still buzz, but the world stops tilting.

"There she is," Alisha whispers. I can finally see her face clearly. Her eyes flick over mine like she's counting. "You with me?"

I nod, but it's shaky.

"They want me to talk to him," I rasp. My voice barely exists.

Alisha's head snaps toward Dad. "Absolutely not. I'll do it. He hasn't heard her voice in a decade. I can fake it. He won't know."

My dad shakes his head. "He'll know, lass. He always bloody knows, so he does. I'd not be askin' her if there were another road t' take. But only if he rings—aye? We won't force the hand. An' I'm doubtin' he'll call t'day. Not ta mention, we'll be here wi' ye, sure enough."

Alisha's jaw tightens. "Fine. But she needs a Xanax and rest *now*. I've seen her like this before. There's a way to tell her these things without sending her into a full spiral. Next time, you tell me first, Stefan."

He nods once, slow and shameful. "Aye. Ye're right. I should'a thought."

Alisha turns to Brenden. "Take her upstairs. Get her into bed. I'll come up and help you settle her."

Brenden scoops me up before I can argue, not that I would. His arms are strong, but his chest is trembling.

He doesn't say a word. Just carries me through the halls of my home, blurred at the edges, quiet except for the pounding in my head.

In my room, he sets me down gently, peels off my clothes with careful hands. Pants, socks, then bra. Alisha presses a pill into my palm, a glass of water against my lips. I can't believe I let myself get here. That I allowed myself to react to something as simple as his name.

"I'm sorry," I murmur to Alisha.

"Swallow, love," she replies instead of acknowledging my words.

I do.

"There is nothing to be sorry for, Surry. You can't help what your nervous system does. You went into fight, flight, or freeze. And this time, your body chose freeze. But there was nothing you could do to stop it. For now, just rest. It will help you wake with a clear head and we will plan. Alright?" She brushes my hair back from my face and kisses my forehead.

The world starts to soften. The edges blur again, but this time, it's gentle. Safe.

Brenden tucks me in, his hand smoothing my hair back as the blackness creeps in. I hear him whisper something — maybe my name, maybe a prayer.

Then nothing.

A ringing wakes me before the sun moves much. I assume two or three hours I was out. The vibrating get's louder somehow. Or maybe I'm just more awake. My phone.

For a second, I think I've had a nightmare. Then I remember: the *panic, the tears, Bridget...*

I sit up too fast. My mouth tastes like dust. My head's thick. I grab the phone without looking and press the green button.

"Hello?"

"Hello, Surry."

The voice freezes me mid-breath. Smooth. Familiar.

"It's been so long since I've spoken t'ye. Did you miss me, my bride?"

My blood turns to ice.

"Who is this?" My words come out too fast, too shaky. I had just gotten that slightly accented tone out of my head after eleven years of hearing it in my nightmares.

A soft laugh. "Ah, you wound me, mo bhean. It's me—your loving husband and father of your child. I've missed you somethin' fierce. Are ya ready t' come home? I think Bridget's ready for you to come home, too. And it's time to teach my son to rule with me."

There's screaming in the background—muffled, terrified.

"Gavin." His name is poison on my tongue. I don't say I don't have a child, I don't want to aggravate him any more than he already is. I take a deep breath before continuing. "If you want me to come, you have to stop hurting her."

"Now, now," he croons. "That's not how you speak to yer husband, is it?"

I swallow hard. The years fall away, the fear crawls back into my skin. "I'm sorry, sir. I won't raise my voice again. Please. Stop hurting Bridget. So I can come to you."

"That's my good girl," he purrs. "Can ye get off the island?"

"Yes," I whisper. Then correct myself. "Yes, sir."

"Grand. Then come to Seattle, Surry. Bring me my child. That's where ye'll find me–and yer precious Bridget. My men will pick you both up at the port."

The line clicks dead.

I stare at the phone, my hand shaking so hard it slips from my fingers and hits the floor.

For a moment, I sit there in silence. Then I move.

Fast.

I throw on clothes without thinking–black cargo pants, a black hoodie, socks, my trusty Doc Martens. My hands move like they belong to someone else. I shove my sunglasses and phone into my pocket, twist my hair into a messy ponytail, grab the small revolver from my desk drawer. I shove it in my bra, and make way way toward the stairs.

Every step down the hall feels heavier.

*Don't tell them. If you tell them, they'll stop you. Bridget dies. You can't tell them.*

The thought repeats, an anchor dragging behind me.

Outside, the air hits like ice. The world smells of salt and pine. My lungs still burn from earlier, but I keep going–down to the docks, down to where the smaller boats are tied.

There's one with keys still in the ignition.

I climb in, start the motor, and push off before I can talk myself out of it.

As the boat drifts away from the island, I glance back once–at the lights glowing in my family's windows, at Brenden somewhere up there in the dark.

"I'm sorry," I whisper.

I turn my phone to airplane mode so I can use it for music before shoving it in my pocket, and aim for Seattle. I turn my headphones on, and Gethsemane of all songs pours into my ears. Perfect.

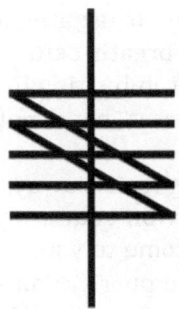

Finally, finally I have heard my Surry's voice after so long. That little cunt better get the fuck off that island. I am ready to take the throne. I will be the head of both the Irish and the Russian Mafia. Nobody will be able to stop me.

"She's comin'," I say to my second. That's what I call him— never cared to learn his name.

He grunts his acknowledgment before adding, "what must we do to prepare for her arrival?"

"Go to the port an' wait," I tell him, my voice low, calm. "See if she comes. I'll wager she'll be there in the next few hours. She's too soft-hearted for her own good — can't stand seein' anyone bleed on her behalf. That's why she kept her mouth shut until those daft bitches called the police." I handled the issues back then, the cops and medics never returning to their families after their shift ended minus that one cop that brought her to the hospital. Never found him, unfortunately.

"Yes, sir. I'll get men on it right away."

"Make sure they're the quiet ones," I add, letting my tone sharpen. "No guns till I say. I want her scared, not dead. There's a difference."

The man nods quickly, eyes wide. He won't forget that distinction — not if he values his life.

With that, he turns and leaves my office. Having her number, I am able to track her phone, so I will be able to see if she leaves the island. I'm not sure how she will do it. But I know she will. She is predictable.

I look under the desk to the slut that is down on her knees with my cock in her mouth. Tears running down her face, makeup everywhere. Just how I like it.

"Pick up the pace, bitch. I've someplace to be—and I won't be kept waitin'." Her head begins to bob faster, and I reach down and place the palm of my hand on the back of her head, then I plug her nose. Effectively, choking her on my cock. I hear her sputtering and she tries to push off to get air. I don't let go. Her fingernails drag down my legs as she tries, and fails, to get loose. The struggle turns me on more. Watching the life leave them is like my favorite drug. Although it would be a pity if she died. She has an excellent mouth.

I push down further, her thrashing is renewed in her panic, completely helpless. This is what causes my release, I shoot my cum down her throat, and she begins to hit my thighs and try to push herself off me even more. I don't let her go.

I hold her head there after I finish, my fingers digging into her scalp, the silky strands of her hair wound tight around my knuckles until they turn white. I count her desperate swallows, feeling each one against my sensitive flesh, before yanking her backward. She crashes to the hardwood floor, her pale body curling inward as she gasps for air, each breath a ragged symphony. Dark rivulets of mascara trace the contours of her flushed cheekbones, the black tears glistening under the dim light. Her lips, swollen and trembling, part slightly as she tries to regain composure. Beautiful. She is a masterpiece—vulnerability carved in flesh, surrender painted in tears.

"That will do," I say to her, excusing her from my presence.

She begins to push off the floor, fixing the slutty pink bodycon dress she is wearing, brushing her blonde hair back behind her shoulders, and slipping on her pink heels. She begins to walk past me toward the door when I stop her with my words alone.

"I'll see ye at the same time next week," I say — not a question, an order. She's paid well for her trouble, so I don't want to hear any whining..

She falters by the door, her hand reaching up to steady herself on the door frame. I hear her take in a sharp breath before she continues exiting. I hear her heels clap on the tile as she leaves, and hear another pair enter my office.

"Sir, there is a man on the phone for you. He won't give his name, and won't take no for an answer. Would you like to take it?"

Brittney? Maybe Ashley? I have no idea what her name is. I think it starts with a B or maybe an A. Don't matter, regardless.

"Yes, send it through. Did he have an accent—anything that stood out?"

"No sir, he didn't." Interesting. I wave her off so she can go put the call through to my phone. Within a moment, the phone on my desk has a red light next to the number one. I press it with my pointer finger, and use the rest of my hand to pick up the receiver. There is just something about a standard, old school office phone that makes my black, shriveled heart light up. Feels very Mad Men, and I like it.

I put the speaker piece of the telephone to my ear and grunt my acknowledgment of whoever is on the other side. "This is Gavin." I say nothing else.

"You think you have all this figured out, don't you?" Says the voice on the other end of the phone line.

"Well, I do tend ta only act when I know I'll accomplish the goal."

"You don't, but it's fun to watch you make all your moves thinking you know what the ultimate outcome will be." He says back. His voice is clean—flat American, polished. Too polished. I know that sound. I know exactly who this is.

"Are ye enjoyin' yerself with my wife, Brenden Slater—while I'm kind enough ta let her believe she's free?"

"You will never have her back, Gavin. She is a free woman, strong and independent. She is free to spend time with whomever she wants. But I know for a fact that is not you. Why don't you meet me like a man? We can settle this, between us."

"Ye truly think I'll agree ta that, do ye? As if ye wouldn't bring backup—try an ambush, maybe? No. I'll keep me own odds and plans, thank ye kindly. Have a *splendid* day, Brenden." I move to set the receiver back down when his voice cuts through again—low, amused, and far too calm.

"Wait Gavin, I'm not done talking to you. You'll never get what you want, you'll never lead the Irish Mafia. You are not a real man, Gavin, you're a child dressed as an adult." Then the line cuts out with the dial tone blasting through the speaker.

I'll show him. He thinks he is going to get what belongs to me. The mafia, the woman, this city? No. Once Surry is back in her cage, I will make it my main focus to see Brenden and his entire organization dead, or better yet, they will belong to me.

I stand and collect my things, and turn off the lamp that is sitting on my strong, oak desk. My office is styled after a 1950's office. Wood paneling on the walls that extend to about three quarters up the wall. The rest is painted black up to the ceiling with random, very expensive art pieces hung on three of the walls. I had told my assistant to get me the most expensive antique paintings she could find, so I really couldn't tell you what they are or what they are worth. Doesn't affect me, but it does make me look better to the businessmen who visit me here.

The final wall is full glass, looking over all of Seattle's downtown and The Sound. The Seattle ferris wheel is only two blocks to the south of my window. I turn the light off to my office, and shut the door behind me, locking it before stepping away.

Once I step outside, I look at my assistant. "What's yer name, then?" I ask, letting the question drag just enough to sound like a warning wrapped in curiosity. There's no point in pretending I give a shit about her name, but it's helpful to know what to call her.

"Callie, sir."

Wow, I wasn't even close. Oh well. "Callie, lass, ride home with me. I need ta go over my schedule—an' a few... *important matters*. I'll likely be outta the office for the next few days."

"Yes, sir." She stands and straightens her red pencil skirt style dress with phenomenal cleavage. She has long blonde hair, bright blue eyes, and legs that go on for miles. She will do nicely. I begin my walk to the exit, Callie trailing behind me after quickly shutting off the lights and snagging her laptop and purse.

The clack of her heels follows me out to the garage, where my car and driver are waiting. I stand by the back door, and the driver opens it for me. I let Callie get in first, and I climb in behind her. All my cars are blacked out, bullet proof SUV's. Which means that there is lots of room in the back. I had this specific SUV renovated to fit my style, my needs. The luxurious interior was fitted with seating around the edges, but with access still to the hatch in the back, allowing me to haul whatever I need still. The black interior always smells new as that is what I require from my driver. There is a minifridge on one side full of champagne, beer, whiskey, and glasses for each. It is especially impressive to business partners when I take them in this vehicle. Nothing screams money like having a top of the line alcohol fridge in your fully renovated car.

Callie slides in and goes to the back, quickly taking her laptop out of her bag and opening it up.

"I'm expectin' my wife ta join me today—after far too long apart. I'll be... *reconnectin'* with her over the next few days, along with takin' care of some business. Now, what meetings do I have within, let's say... the next week?"

If she is surprised that I said I have a wife, she doesn't show it. "You have a meeting with the owner of FerryCorp, Richard Ferry. That is tomorrow at one in the afternoon. I can call his office and reschedule that for you. The next day is a meeting with the Richmond LLC. I don't have any other details on that meeting noted.."

"Keep the Richmond appointment. I'll make sure I'm there for that one. It's about buildin' me new location—where the new office'll stand, with a penthouse sittin' pretty on the top floor."

Nobody knows this, but the "penthouse" will be a prison

essentially. I want to keep Surry close to me and not give her any means of escape. A house is too easy. Top floor of a monitored sky scraper with no escape unless you have a keycard, which she will obviously not possess; she is not likely to succeed no matter what help she receives, and there damn sure wont be any chances of stupid bitches walking in to call the cops At least, not without serious damage done.

"Yes, sir, otherwise your schedule is pretty open. I have *Warehouse* written on most of the days. I am not sure what that means, other than you told me to put it."

"Perfect. That's exactly where we're headin' now."

"Oh, I thought you said we were going to your home. No matter. What else can I do for you sir?"

"That'll do for schedulin' today. Tell me, how're ya likin' workin' for me—our little arrangement, hmm?"

"I am incredibly grateful for the opportunity to work for such an esteemed man, such as yourself sir. I am also very happy with our arrangement. Have I been satisfactory for you?"

"Yes, matter of fact, remove yer underwear and get on yer knees." I say nothing more, she knows what I am requesting.

She seems caught off guard. Maybe by the sudden change in conversation, or maybe my face looks angrier than usual. No matter.

"Uh, okay sir." She looks nervous, as she should.

"This is part of yer duty as me secretary. Car rides'll always require this. Would ya like to quit now, or keep workin' for Kelly Enterprises?" It's a simple question, really.

" I will do whatever you ask of me, boss." She looks compliant now. I won't need long to ruin that.

"Good, now take off yer underwear, get on yer knees, and face the back of the vehicle. I don't want to see yer face."

Her face falls a bit, but she does as I have commanded her. Good, she will make a great addition to my regular whores if she takes my dick well during these random events as she does my regular commands. She has been good about coming to my home to service me after work, but this is the first time during a workday that I have required her to give her body to me.

"Head t'the warehouse. We'll wait there for news," I tell the driver, my voice low and clipped. He nods, turns the key, and the engine rumbles to life as we roll toward the seedy side o' Seattle, where the city's shine fades and the rot begins to show.

With the prospect of being able to have my bride back in her cage, I am ready to go for round two, but a soft throat is not what I'm after. I want tears.

I take my dick out and begin to stroke it, but it was already hard so I don't require much stimulation to be ready to go. I yank her dress up and hear a tearing sound. Callie lets out a small shriek, but I ignore her. Her pretty pink pussy and her tight, apparently bleached, ass hole are ready and waiting for me. I spit on her ass, and then again on my hand to get my dick wet.

I don't warm her up or give her any warning, I shove my dick into her pussy to help get even more wet. She begins to moan and move with my thrusts, shoving her hips back into my groin, causing me to go deeper. But her pleasure brings me none. Before I can stop it, she lays her face down on the leather seat, her cheek pressed against the cool surface, and reaches behind her until her long fingers with a French tip manicure—pristine white crescents against pale pink—grab ahold of my shirt, bunching the fabric between her knuckles. She starts slamming herself onto me, greedy with need, her spine arching like a bow, hips working in desperate rhythm. For a moment, I let her, taking it as a challenge to thrust into her harder, the sound of skin against skin echoing in the confined space, until she starts orgasming on my dick, her body trembling, inner walls pulsing around me. I nearly lose my erection at this, my desire suddenly cooling like metal plunged into water.

I grab her hands, peeling her manicured fingers free of my silk shirt one by one. Now I will punish her for the audacity of thinking this was about her pleasure. I withdraw my half limp length from her slick, pulsating cunt and, without warning, drive myself to the hilt into her tight ass. Her piercing screams fills the leather interior as she claws desperately at the butter-soft seat in front of her, her body arching away from me like a frightened animal.

"Sir," she gasps, her voice breaking as I feel her body's resistance—that delicious tension of muscle fighting against intrusion. Sobs breaking free from her throat, she looks back at me with tears dropping from her fake eyelashes. "Sir, please stop," she begs through ragged breaths, each desperate plea sending electric currents of excitement through my veins, hardening me further inside her. She must be able to feel it because her screams renew almost instantly. I respond by gripping her hips harder, leaving crescent-shaped indentations from my own nails as I increase my pace. Through the privacy partition, I hear my driver's knowing chuckle. He's heard this symphony before. He knows precisely how I savor this moment.

"Shut the fuck up, bitch and hold still. Stop scratching me. You will take my cock up your slutty little ass hole, or ye'll be sent to swim with the fishes. What's it gonna be, then?" I say all of this with labored breath as I continue to fuck into her. She stops screaming but I can still hear her whimpering and painful moans. I grab her wrists and put her hands behind her back, using them as a hold to fuck her deeper.

"We're here, sir," my driver says as I feel him turn and then park the car.

"Good, open the door 'n let the men see the little hoor I brought them today as I finish," I say between heavy breaths and gritted teeth.

"Very good, sir."

The back hatch opens, and the seats fold backward so that the view of her crying face is in full view of all my men as they come out of the warehouse. Callie is crying again, but not struggling anymore, which nearly ruins my enjoyment. I yank her arms up her back a bit, causing her to cry out, which helps. I thrust into her a few more times, my dick going in and out of her abused ass, and blow my load deep inside of her. I unceremoniously pull out of her seeing blood stains along the sides, before using her skirt to wipe myself clean, and put my dick back in my pants.

"Thank you, Callie. The men will see to the rest of your pleasure now. Boys, make sure she's fit to work at the office tomorrow and that she gets home in one piece. Don't fail me." I say the last part to my driver. He will get his turn when he takes her home, that's always been the ritual. Although he likes to be a little more civil. He will take care of her, pretend he gives a single fuck about her. News flash—he doesn't. Then once she's asleep he will tie her to the bed and cut her clothes off with a knife, and fuck her until she wakes. That's how he likes them. Shocked, surprised, and scared. I only hire men who can appreciate women the way I do. I have been very lucky to find the men I have that now belong to my inner sanctum.

Once I am fully redressed, I grab my briefcase and hop out of the SUV and walk to the warehouse where I know the rest of my inner circle is waiting for me all the while listening to Callie scream from the car I just left her in with five men. The warehouse is just that, an old abandoned warehouse outside of downtown. It is over in the district where the football stadium is. It's the bad part of town, which helps keep all my dealings quiet.

I step into the front doors of the dilapidated building and feel as though I have entered another dimension. The warehouse is falling apart outside, or so we want you to think. Inside looks as if you walked into a spaceship from a sci-fi movie. There are screens up on one of the tall walls, about twenty of them. They are connected to cameras all throughout my holdings, as well as some public cameras to keep watch, such as the docks down where Surry is supposed to arrive. Beneath them is a chair, in it is Surry's maid, Bridget. She looks a little worse for wear. But she won't be getting out of here alive regardless.

"Hello, sir, we haven't seen her arrive at the port yet. We also aren't sure where she will come in, or how. So we will continue watching." I nod at them and go to my office to set my things down. Once my coat, briefcase, and hat are put away, I go into my private bathroom to change. I don't like to get dirty in my work clothes. I change into a pair of jeans, sneakers, and a plain white t-shirt. I like to see all the blood spatter, so I wear light colored clothing.

Before I go out to see the men and our newest guest, I decide to go see the most recent resident of the warehouse following my overthrowing of the Russian mafia. The Bratva. Dear Natasha, she has a nice pussy. Today I will have her take a pregnancy test, see if I'm going to be the daddy of the new Russian Mafia leader. I head down the hall to do just that.

"Ah, hello, love. How are ye this fine evenin'? Comfortable, are ya? They've been feedin' ya on time, I hope?" I enter the code to the door and walk into her...bedroom? Cell? Eh, same difference. It's more comfortable than a normal prisoner would get.

Natasha doesn't move, look at me, or make a single sound. She knows better. She just lies on her bed, staring at the ceiling.

"Up ye get, Natasha. Pee in the cup for me now—aye, that's it. Good girl." I grab her arm and pull her to a standing position, and then walk her to the bathroom.

"Take this," I hand her a medical urine collection cup, "pee in this cup." She grabbed the cup, and we walked together to the toilet. She lifts her dress up, and places the cup under her to catch her urine. "Good girl, Natasha." She fills the cup up, and then hands it back to me, finishes her business, and then stands to wash her hands. Once she is finished, she walks back to the room and gets back onto the bed, face up, staring at the ceiling. She immediately parts her thighs, leaving her pussy on display; she knows what will be taking place with my arrival, smart girl. I take my time, and place the pregnancy test into her urine, count to ten, and then place it on the counter and set a three-minute timer. This gives me time to go use Natasha as she was intended to be used.

"Ah, my sweet Natasha. When would ya like t' be wed, then? We're needing t' marry soon, love—can't have my child called a bastard, now can we?"

Natasha turns her head and looks at me, "How will you know it's yours? I have different men inside me every hour. There's no way to tell without a blood test."

"Ah, Natasha, ye forget—I don't give a shite what anyone says or feels. That child's mine, no question. So tell me, would ye like a fall or winter weddin'? Or hell, we could find a justice o' the peace an' have ourselves a summer weddin' tomorrow, if ye fancy it. Summer's nearly gone, but there's still time for a lovely day outdoors." I give her a nasty grin, knowing she is not happy with this arrangement. But I don't give a fuck.

"Lift your skirt more and show me the best part of you, Natasha." I unzip my pants and walk toward her. She does as she is bidden, pulling the dress over her breasts so that I can have a good view of them as well, and I climb on top of her, entering her in one swift motion. "If my son isn't in you yet, he will be soon," I say between thrusts. "I say we have a fall weddin', so I can make sure ye're knocked up beforehand — I won't be weddin' a woman who's unsuit-." I feel something on my dick, something sharp. "The fuck is that?" Natasha feigns innocence.

"What the actual fuck is that, inside your pussy, Natasha?" I roar at her, my dick still buried within her. At this, she gives me the grin of a Cheshire cat.

"I can't be pregnant, I have an IUD, мудак (ass hole)." This. Bitch.

I pull out of her and put my face to her pussy, and reach my fingers inside, stretching her until I can fit my four fingers inside her, feeling around until I can grab the string I know is inside her. Natasha begins to scream, but it's too late. Her legs are kicking and she is thrashing around, but I grab the string with one hand and use my free hand to push down on her stomach so she can't get away.

Once I have a firm grasp, I rip it out of her. With a wicked grin on my face I hold it up for her to see, returning her evil smile tenfold. She is screaming and crying now. I am positive that didn't feel good. I just simply don't give a fuck.

"You will give me a son, Natasha," I say between labored breaths. I look down and see the blood on the sheets. Someone will need to clean this up once I'm done. Can't have the mother of my child sleeping in blood. I reenter her and continue fucking her, hoping that the effects of the IUD will be instantly reversed. If not, she will learn her lesson. Natasha continues to hit me, causing my dick to slip out, and screams at me in Russian, which I understand none of. Too bad for her. I shove my dick back inside of her, despite her efforts to close her legs. I continue thrusting until I finish and empty my entire load right onto her swollen cervix. Hopefully, some of that will make it into her womb so that next time I give her a test, she will be filled with my son.

I hop up and put my now soft dick back into my boxers, and zip my pants back up. Natasha lay there crying, rolled over, still bleeding. I walk into the bathroom, see the test is negative, and begin to clean up, anger flooding me. I flush her urine down the toilet and throw away the cup and the pregnancy test.

"Okay, I'll see ya tomorrow, my love," I tell her as I walk out, locking the door with the code behind me. The bitch won't be leaving this room until my son is born. And then she will be moved to her plot in my family's cemetery.

I walk out of the hallway that leads to Natasha's room and into the large main room where my men and my captive wait for me.

"Hello, Bridget. How're you? Been a long time." I address her as I walk out of my office, holding a towel in my hand, and walk toward where she is tied up. Her left eye is swollen shut, and her clothes are torn.

She looks up at me through her one good eye, and when I get close to her, she spits in my direction.

I click my tongue at her, and laugh. Although I don't think it's a pleasant sound. Most of my men's shoulders rise up toward their ears when they hear it. Once I am right in front of her, I backhand her across the face.

"Ah now, don't be disrespectin' your host like that. Thought we were closer, back when I was still livin' with me wife." She lets out a slight chuckle. I don't think the old woman has energy for much more. "Tell me what I want t'know, an' I'll have ye out o' that chair an' into a proper holdin' room — a hot shower, a real bed, the whole bleedin' thing. Sound fair?" I try to tempt her. I need to move her out of here regardless, but this will hopefully be mutually beneficial.

"I won't tell ya shite, ya rotten gobshite pox bottle. Think I'd give you a single word 'bout my sweet Surry, ya scut? Feck off, ya wanker." Her accent is much stronger when she is angry. I don't remember it being so aggressive the last time I saw her.

Her words also drag the brogue right out of me; it slips through my teeth before I can bite it back, old-country vowels cutting clean through the calm I try to keep. "Ah Jaysus, I'd near forgot how sharp yer tongue could be. Alright then—are there any boats Surry can drive at her da's house?" I chuckle at my own words and how they sound now. Now I just want to see if she will say anything other than classless Irish insults.

"Yer thick as shite, and twice as ugly. Feck off back to yer hole before Stefan buries ya in it."

Nope, guess not. I backhand her again, and she lets out a scream. I grab a fistful of her gray hair and bring her face within an inch of mine, ensuring I spit a little when I talk to her.

"Tell me how she will be gettin' to the port, or you won't draw another breath to see her with yer own two eyes."

"Sir, we found her."

My men interrupt me with the best news I have heard in nearly ten years. I let go of Bridget's hair, pushing her backward until she falls over onto her back, still tied to the chair. See how the old cunt likes that.

As I walk toward the screens, I see the one they have highlighted. It's Surry, hopping off a small boat. Only took her two hours, and she dressed pretty well to hide from me, but she can't truly hide from me, not ever. She has her long, beautiful hair pulled into the hood of a too big black sweater, combat-looking trousers, and black combat boots, with a large orange life jacket and over sized black sunglasses. Even still, she's as easy to spot as if she had a beacon on her. I cannot wait to see how she has changed under those clothes, but I do wonder where my child is. What she did with him. It was well documented that she was pregnant when she arrived at the hospital that night, but the rest was buried under red tape and paperwork.

"There she is," I say, the first syllable catching the old brogue before I smooth it out, "go get her. Bring her to me. Bring me my wife."

"This is getting out of hand, we need to make a move. Now. Stop him before he does anything worse," Sam says, voice flat with that cold certainty that makes people listen.

We're crowded into Stefan's office-me, Sam, Josh, Stefan-elbows and maps and too much coffee. It's been hours since Surry's panic attack. She's asleep in her room; the girls and Richie are taking shifts watching over her so she won't wake alone. I told myself that was enough. That I could sit here and plan and then go to her and be the first thing she sees when she opens her eyes. But the idea of her curled up and fragile while we chase ghosts makes my teeth ache.

"Surry can't keep dealing with this," I say. The words taste like iron. "She's going to break if we keep dragging her through it. My job is to protect her — not just her body. Her mind too. We remove her from this. Full stop."

Stefan nods; Sam and I lock eyes. They offer no pushback, we're all in agreement. I feel the small, ugly thing at the edge of my chest-the thought that maybe I should have done more earlier. That if I'd been faster, smarter, this wouldn't be happening. I shove it down and look for action.

"Let's see if we can pinpoint a location if I give him a call," I say. I want to bait him, make him slip. Josh smirks because he knows me the way brothers know each other, the part of me that rants, becomes the part that moves. "Get Corver on the phone so he can tap in and hopefully find this bastard." Stefan snaps at one of his men, who opens a secure video line, and we get three for the price of one. Corver, Gunnar, and Arnie are on the screen looking at us, and we fill them in on what we want to do.

"What if it makes him angrier?" Sam asks. He's thinking of Bridget, of collateral. "He might do something worse."

"If we call, he has less leverage," I say. "He won't act until he thinks he can take Surry. He won't get her." I pace. I can feel hands on me, the steadying presence of people who know how to take a man apart and put him back together. I see Josh's hands holding my shoulder, and I look from him to the screen. Gunnar gives me a shallow nod, encouraging me as well.

I pick up the phone. Corver's fingers dance across a laptop screen-he's already pushing at Gavin's comms, trying to get a bead on the man. Five minutes and the line is live.

The receptionist answers exactly like I hate: polite, but a tremor under the surface.

"Hello, you have reached Callie at Kelly Enterprises. How can I direct your call?"

"Send me to your boss, and I won't take no for an answer," I say.

"Oh, okay sir, let me see if he is in," she says, and then the world's ugliest hold music pulses through the speaker. I can feel all of them leaning in.

"God, even his hold music is fucking ugly," I mutter. A few of them chuckle; Stefan rolls his eyes. Corver clears his throat and says he's got a line into Gavin's work phone; he's working on the cell. "Do not hang up until I say," he cautions. I nod.

I don't want to let the receptionist go, anyways. Her voice is frayed.

"Hello, sir, may I ask who is calling?" she asks when she comes back on.

"No, but trust he will want to talk to me, are you safe?" I can't help myself. I throw the offer out because I don't trust the cheap warmth behind corporate voices.

"I'm-I'm sorry sir? I don't understand your question. Safe from what?" Her voice trembles harder.

"Take this number down. If you need help, call me. Any hour. I or one of my associates will come for you. Do you understand? Take the number down. Now."

"Sure...okay." I hear a pen scratch, and I hope it's not just a habit. I'm not letting anyone be a cog in his machine.

"Now, I am ready to be transferred when you are."

"Okay, I will transfer you now, sir, one moment."

The hold music begins and then suddenly stops. For a beat, I taste the room's stale air.

He grunts, then a voice I despise comes through.

"This is Gavin."

The conversation unfolds like a choreographed dance where I already know all the steps. His voice—that particular blend of honey and gravel—slides through the phone and settles in my ear like an infection. Each word lands with the precision of a boxer's jab: calculated, measured, designed to wound without leaving visible marks. My knuckles whiten around the receiver as heat crawls up my neck, my jaw clenching so hard I can hear my molars grinding. The familiar rage builds not in waves but in concentric circles, expanding outward from my chest until my fingertips tingle with it. I did my part and kept him on long enough to serve its purpose, both for getting a location and to ignite the war drums in my soul.

"Got the location on his work phone," Corver says without ceremony. "It's a landline. I need more digging to find his cell. Also-weird-trackers are pinging on all your phones. All of yours are safe. Surry's phone shows a Seattle ping."

"Seattle?" Sam blinks; the word lands in the room like a thrown brick.

I run out of the room. My feet carry me to Surry's room, my heart a fist. The door is cracked, the light a sliver. I push it open, and the small world I've been holding-the covers, the scent of her-is gone. The bed is empty, sheets bunched over nothing. Her phone is gone. Her side of everything has been stripped.

"ALISHA!" I roar. The name echoes off crown molding, and within breaths, Alisha barrels in, breath ragged.

"What is it-" she starts, but then she sees the bed and the words leaves her throat sounding dry and cracked. "Where is she?"

"Who is supposed to be watching her?" Names spill out, panicked — Richie, Hazel, Juniper. They come running, faces ashen. Selene lurches in, limping, the sight of her sister's empty bed collapsing something inside her.

"Who was with her?" I bark. No one answers quickly enough. Hazel's voice breaks; she was in Selene's room. Time slipped. It's always time, slipping. Selene starts crying, and the house tilts. I don't have patience for anyone's grief right now. Surry is gone.

My knees hit the floor before I fall to the side, like I can feel every second. The room spins. I clamp my hands on my knees. Something sharp and animal snaps in me. The part that wants to tear out throats. Josh punches me in the chest. Hard. I didn't see the fist coming; it lands, and the pain is an anchor.

"Get your fucking head on straight, man," he says. "She took a small boat. Black clothes, sunglasses, hood. She wasn't taken in a truck. She went willingly. I don't know how we missed it. Gavin called, Corver checked the call logs. He must have threatened her, or Bridget. We need a plan."

A small boat. She chose it. A hundred versions of why tumble through my skull, and I'm dizzy with them: guilt, relief, fury, helplessness. If she went, why didn't she tell me? Why did she think she had to go alone?

I look at Stefan. "Do you have gear here? If not, I'll hit Ballard and grab mine."

Stefan gives that slow, dry grin. "Ah, me son. I've all that an' more, I do." He taps the table with a ring, and the men who move under his orders already shift into lines I recognize.

We march back into the office, and Corver is already back in his world, eyes blue with code. "I'm in a backup office," he says, but he's doing work right now. "Arnie's gone to Tacoma. Gunnar's going to help me move closer when I find the Warehouse I am sure he will end up in if the intel on Natasha is good. I'm pulling every feed."

"Good," I say. "We will pack up here and head that direction. Let us know the location to meet you in Seattle." Corver nods, and the rest of us move out to collect what we will need.

Before I exit, I place my open hand on Sam's chest, feeling his heartbeat hammer against my palm. His jaw tightens, a muscle twitching beneath the three-day stubble that darkens his face. "We get her back," I say, my voice barely above a whisper but hard as tempered steel. My eyes meet his—two mirrors reflecting the same desperate fury, the same raw fear.

"I can't lose her again, Brenden. I won't. It was bad enough the first time." His gaze holds mine for a breath, and I give him a single, sharp nod. I understand. I turn away, boots scuffing against concrete as I fall in step with the rest of the men, their weapons gleaming dully under the fluorescent lights.

We move fast because there's only one direction that matters: forward. Bags are thrown together. Stefan's boats are loaded with the kind of kit that smells like rubber and oil and certainty. We don black and pack light. The chatter is clipped, everyone running on coffee and adrenaline. There's no room to be sentimental in the hull of speed boats hurtling east; that will come later, if we live.

On the way to Seattle, the world goes by in strips of bright sun, which is unusual for Washington this time of year, and industrial coastlines. Corver calls from the backup office; he's already scraping the grid and turning over cameras. Gunnar texts an ETA. Arnie is standing by in Tacoma; we'll bring him in if we need the muscle. Right now, he serves us better by being attached to his screens.

We get to the safe house Corver keeps, a nondescript block building with one of those garage doors you'd ignore if you saw it every day. It smells like electronics and takeout. Corver and Gunnar arrive within the hour, faces set and ready. We are not far from the coast, near a section of warehouses, praying to whatever god might listen that these will be the right ones. They dump laptops, lay maps, and immediately start overlaying feeds.

After two hours, Corver yells, "Found her!" Flipping the screen, the map zooms to a strip of brown warehouses on the east side. "Old industrial lot. One big derelict shed. Looks like the description of where Natasha was rumored to be held."

Adrenaline hits like a second heartbeat. The room gets quieter; the panic crystallizes into a shape we can answer.

"We go tonight?" Josh asks. He's ragged and ready. It's about four in the afternoon right now, so we have a few hours until dark. So now we need to lock in a solid plan.

I run my hand over the map until the lines blur. Kill the chatter, make a plan that doesn't put her in more danger. But we're not kids throwing stones. We do this once, and we do it right.

"Corver, get more eyes on the building. Gunnar, call in anything you need to get now, prep staging. Josh, be ready to move with me to the front. Sam, you're with the exit team. Arnie stays on standby in Tacoma in case we need a diversion." I keep it plain because plain is what people can hold to. Stefan, are you men ready to move with us?

"Aye," is all he responds with, and then everyone begins to move, preparing for what's to come in four short hours.

Corver nods, fingers moving. Gunnar's face is a hard line before he's back on the phone, already double-checking routes.

We have a small window before dark. We shouldn't rush without cover, but waiting is a different kind of danger. I hate that we're counting hours and not bodies. The plan is simple: approach under dark, hit the power to blind their cameras, move quick, get Surry and any others. No heroics. Go home.

We push our gear into waiting sedans and stack like animals ready to spring.

And then my phone vibrates on the table. I see the name light up, and for a second, hope blasts through me like a flare.

*Surry.*

My hand goes for it before reason can tell me not to. The room leans in. I swipe answer and put it on speaker so everyone can hear.

"This is Brenden," is how I answer, since I am positive it isn't going to be Surry.

"You know, I could have called from my phone, but I was hoping that the sight of my sweet wife's name on your phone would give you some hope. Which, if I'm being honest, you shouldn't have. I forgot how great her pussy is. You failed to mention that when we spoke earlier. But these tattoos, they need to go. Which ones do you think I should burn off first?"

Gavin. Fuck this guy.

"Yes, I do know since I've been buried in it for the last few months. And if you even think about touching one of her goddam tattoos I'll drive my boot so far up your ass you will be able to tie the laces with your teeth." I look to Stefan with an apologetic look on my face, but he just waves me away. He knows I'm trying to ruffle Gavin's feathers.

"Ah, yes. About that, I see she is not with child. Are you incapable of creating heirs, Brenden Slater?" Apparently, he has no idea that Surry cannot have kids. What a smart girl not saying anything. That is the best way to get her killed if he thinks she is useless to him.

"No, I'm not. But I also don't do anything to Surry that is against her will. And children would be against her will. You and I are not the same, Gavin. Don't try to relate to me. Or upset me. I know how the rest of your life will pan out. I'm not worried about it."

"Speaking of which, where is my child. I assume Stefan is with you. Do they have my child? He has to be what, ten now? Eleven?" What the actual fuck, this guy thinks she had his kid from back then?

"All I know, is that I won't be telling you shit, sweet cheeks." I am hoping to make him do something dumb. Make a mistake.

Almost instantly I hear a slapping sound and regret my words, and then Surry lets out a yelp. I set the phone down on the table and walk away from it, punching every chair on my way to the wall and back again.

"My handprint looks so excellent on the milky white skin of her ass. Don't you love that as well?" Then I hear the unmistakable sound of a zipper.

I look at Gunner and mouth the words, we can't wait, at him. He shakes his head and closes his eyes before turning to Corver who is already hopping onto his laptop without a word.

"Would you like to stay on the phone with me as I fill her with my seed, or would you like me to save you the embarrassment of fulfilling her needs and hang up first?"

"Let me talk to her. Now."

"Ah ah ah, now Brenden. Don't get any ideas. You can't save her. You don't even know where she is." I'm about to say that yes, I do in fact know where she is, but both Josh and Stefan grab my arms and squeeze, reminding me of the end goal.

"You're right, Gavin. I can't. So can you at least let me say goodbye?"

"Now that is not what I expected. You hear that, Surry darling? He is giving you up. He would like to speak with you."

"He-hello," I hear the most beautiful voice on the other end of the phone. I want to assure her that I am coming, but I don't know what to say without giving away our plans.

"Hey Siren, do you remember the first night we spent together?"

"Yes-" she answers, her voice trembling.

"Did you hear me say that I wish I could bottle your scent to always have it with me?"

"...Yes?" She sounds confused. Fuck, this isn't working.

"I want you to know that I will forever smell your scent on my pillow. Do you understand?"

There is a long pause with no sound except for that of a slapping sort of noise. I don't want to know what it is. I will pay for her therapy for the rest of my life as long as she lives through this.

"I think so." Is all she finally answers me.

"Okay Siren, I love you. Give the phone back now."

"Now, Brenden," is how Gavin begins. "Would you like to stay on the phone, or would you like me to send you a video. I am happy to do either."

"No thanks. I will catch up with you later though, alright?" I end the conversation as if I was signing off with an old friend, hanging up before he can say another word.

The call ends, and for a moment, the whole room is silent, the kind of silence that hums.

My hand is still tight around the phone. Everyone's looking at me, waiting for the cue I can't give fast enough.

The air feels like it's thick with electricity, every breath too hot, too shallow.

Corver's voice breaks it. "Arnie's in position. He says he can kill the power in three minutes."

Three minutes. That's nothing. That's everything.

"Tell him to do it," I say, my voice low, but it cuts through the room like a blade.

Josh grabs his gear. Gunnar's already moving toward the door. Stefan checks his weapon with a calmness that makes me wonder if anything ever rattles him. Me? I'm already halfway gone in my head. The distance between me and Surry is a living thing now, clawing at my insides.

Corver's laptop screen glows, reflecting off his glasses he placed on his nose a while ago, as numbers flicker down. "Two minutes," he says.

I pace the narrow space between the map table and the door. Every sound feels amplified; the scrape of Velcro, the metallic snap of magazines locking into place, boots on concrete. It's the rhythm of preparation, and it's the only thing keeping me from losing my damn mind.

"Thirty seconds," Corver murmurs. He doesn't look up.

The industrial block holding the target warehouse goes black, one floor at a time. The hum of power dies, replaced by a sudden, living quiet, the kind that carries danger.

"That's our cue," Gunnar says, voice a growl.

"Move!" I bark, and the room explodes into motion.

Doors slam open. Engines turn over, muffled under black tarps and night. Stefan's convoy splits, two SUVs heading west, one south. Corver stays behind, headset on, eyes darting across camera feeds as the power cuts ripple through the grid. We leave him the final sedan in case he needs to move.

We're flying through city streets before I even realize my hands are shaking. The headlights are off once we are two blocks away. The city feels hollow. Just our tires, the wet slap of rain that started forty-five minutes ago, and the faint echo of distant sirens.

"Two minutes out," Josh says from the passenger seat.

"Stay low," I reply. "We breach fast, clear faster."

When the warehouse comes into view, it looks like a carcass against the skyline–brown, broken, ribs of rusted metal and shattered glass. I can feel the tension rolling through the car, sharp and electric. Stefan's men are already fanning out through the shadows, ghostlike in their gear.

Corver's voice crackles through the comms. "Snipers down. You're clear for entry."

That's all I need.

"Go."

We hit the doors like a thunderclap. Boots, voices, the deafening crash of impact and the echo of gunfire that follows.

And then it's chaos.

Shouting. Smoke. Flashlights cutting through dust and debris. The air feels too tight to breathe. Every step forward is instinct, not thought. A prayer turned into motion.

I can't see her. Not yet. But she's here.

I know it.

The men that Gavin sent to find me walk me to the all black SUV's that are parked and running near the port. I am surrounded, one in front of me, one behind me, and one on either side. I can't run. But that wasn't what I wanted to do anyways. I have a tiny, but incredibly sharp knife in my shoe. It's in a sheath so I won't cut myself. But I am hoping that it's either small enough they won't notice or they just won't search me. I am hoping for the latter since I also have my small revolver tucked into my bra. If I need to take my clothes off, I can keep it in my bra as I take it off.

"After you, Mrs. Kelly." Says Fuck Face number one. That is what I am going to call all these henchmen. And Fuck Face is the perfect name for each of them. They are all like Gavin. Just as sick and deranged.

"I am Ms. O'Brien. NOT Mrs. Kelly. Never call me that again." I say this in my most stern voice while making direct eye contact. That's when I am poked in the back by something suspiciously hard and pointy. A gun, probably.

I turn around and look at what I will now refer to as Fuck Face number two. "I know you can't hurt me. So fuck off with the intimidation, Fuck Face number two." I turn around and begin walking. They all freeze for a moment before continuing to follow me. I think their new name caught them off guard. I nearly giggle at the looks on their faces, nearly.

I am told to wait with a palm to the chest as one of the Fuck Faces, number three lets call him, slides into the SUV first. I slide in afterward and am forced to the back of a limo-like experience inside this SUV. Unfortunately, there is no music or champagne. A real let down, actually. Another Fuck Face, the first one I think, slides in after me so I am sandwiched between them. Another one shuts the door and goes around to the front passenger seat, and Fuck Face number two goes to the other SUV.

I feel like a celebrity in here. "Is there any champagne?" I ask sweetly to all the Fuck Faces surrounding me. They just stare at me as if I have sprouted a second head. Oh well.

"Hey! Can we turn on the music! I am really in the mood for some The Plot In You!" I look around, and most of them are ignoring me now. The driver looks at me through the rear view mirror. "How about *Don't Look Away*, one of my fave songs," I say to the driver. He shakes his head but in after a minute it begins playing really, really quietly. I begin to hum along, just like Brenden said his mom used to do when she was afraid. She was right, it does help.

The drive doesn't take long, and before I know it, we reach an old, dilapidated-looking building. The surrounding buildings are just as worn down, and I can see the stadium from here. Hopefully, the phone I have stashed in my waistband has told Brenden where I am. I'm glad I turned the service back on before I got off the boat, so I don't need to try and do that now. I know I won't be keeping it long, but I am hopeful they tracked me here. We will see, I guess. But I do have a plan. That plan is to kill Gavin, really, that's the only step I have right now. Death. I mentally shrug at myself and my plan. I know that this is going to be harder than I expect. I haven't seen him in more than ten years. I actually think next month is the eleven-year mark. Holy shit.

"Out," says Fuck Face number one. I do as I am barked at, and begin to exit the vehicle. Once my feet are planted on the ground outside the vehicle, Fuck Face number two asks for my phone. I pull it out of my waistband and hand it to him. He pockets it and then looks at me once more, not saying a word. I look at him with the most deadpan face I possess, and roll my eyes before turning toward the building we are obviously going to enter and begin walking. Might as well greet fate on my own terms.

"Where do you think you are going, Mrs. Kelly?" Yells one of them, and I roll my eyes.

"I am meeting my fate, Fuck Face.." I turn around to see which one before continuing my walk. "Fuck Face number three. Why wait for fate when I can greet it myself?" I berate myself internally because I guess Richie was right when he said I was going to get all self-sacrificing. I reach the doors by the time I am finished explaining to my *security* team, and push the doors open wide before stepping inside.

To my utter disgust, Gavin is standing there. Waiting for me. He looks the same, but more evil. I swear the shit he does sucks more and more soul out of him. He is wearing jeans, a white t-shirt, and lace up shoes. Very weird. I am used to seeing him dressed up a bit more. His brown hair is pushed backward, and he has new tattoos creeping up his neck and down his arms. I see the Irish Mafia on the side of his neck, and I see the Russian Mafia down his left arm. The others I don't recognize, except for one. He has a girl tattooed on his forearm. She is more of an artistic outline, with only three things filled in. Her eyes, they are an emerald green, the same shade as mine. The lips are ruby red and look to be dripping, like blood. Lastly, the throat. There is a slit with blood leaking from it. It's me. It's obviously me.

Before he can say anything, I stride further into the building. It is far different than it looks on the outside. The inside is nicely polished, as if in a secret laboratory. There are at least twenty TV monitors on one wall, all in neat rows of five. Underneath there are rows of desks, like when they show the people who stay on the ground when astronauts go into space. *Houston, we definitely have a problem right now.* Next to them, sitting in a chair, is Bridget. She looks awful, and I am dying to get to her, but I know I have to wait. I turn to look the other way, and I see a few desks with monitors on them and then two hallways. I will need to see if I can figure out where those go.

Finally, I turn back to Gavin and wait. I have nothing to say to him that won't earn me a slap, so I will wait for him to greet me. But he shocks me in his first act after not seeing me for eleven years.

"Surry Marie O'Brien," he starts before dropping to one knee. "Will you do me the honor of joining me at my side, ruling the Irish and Russian Mafia, and making me the happiest man on earth by marrying me once more?" I stand there. Stunned. It felt like forever, but I bet it was only twenty seconds before I double over laughing, I don't know if I have ever laughed this hard.

"You're kidding, right?" That's all I can manage to say between laughs. The Fuck Faces all around look extremely uncomfortable. "Which of these men were around when I was still trapped in that fucking house by you? Did any of them rape me and impregnate me? Why the actual FUCK, Gavin, would I do anything with you? Especially willingly? I have been happy. HAPPY. For the past eleven years. Want to know why?" I stand up fully and regain my deadpan expression. "Because you were dead to me. For all I cared, you were dead. And I moved on with my life. I made friends, I started a career, I met a man who treats me as if the sun shines right out of my ass hole. He loves me, and I lov-" WHACK. He slaps me across the face and then grabs my hair and pulls my face toward his. His loving and thoughtful mask is gone, replaced with the real one. The angry, evil, sadistic one. That's better.

"Oh my Surry, my dearest wife. How you will regret the words you just said to me. Let's go have a chat, shall we?" He doesn't let go of my hair and begins to drag me behind me so fast that I eventually fall down, and he actually pulls my body along the ground by my hair. I try to scream and kick all while holding onto my hair with hopes I will have some left after this. Fuck, it hurts. I'm pulled down one of the hallways to the right that I noticed earlier. Bridget is screaming at him from where she is tied in the chair, and I can hear one of Gavin's men go over and hit her to quiet her. This was a stupid plan. Why did I do this?

My voice has disappeared from all the screaming, so I hold my hair and try to look around, all while I am being actually scalped. The hallways are white with a long glass wall, no. Not a glass wall. There is a girl in there lying on the bed staring straight up at the ceiling. She looks familiar. Before I can place her, I am pulled past the room, then we stop. I look up to see he is punching in a code, 6-9-0 is all I see of the code, but I have a guess as to what it is. A glass panel moves like a door, and he steps in, pulling me with him. He drops my hair, and my head falls and bounces off the cement, making me incredibly dizzy, and I feel a wet heat on the back of my head. Excellent, it's great to start all this off with a concussion.

"Surry, do you not understand the lengths I have gone to get you back from your little meltdown all those years ago? Have I not proved to you that I need you?"

I just stare at him. I have no idea what to say. He is actually insane and there is no reasoning with insanity. I just close my eyes and hold my head where it is bleeding on the floor. I feel him before I hear him, and he is grabbing my arms and pulling me up. I go limp, I don't want him to touch me, but unfortunately, he is much bigger than me and can hold my weight. Before I come to a fully standing position, I am thrown onto a bed. I lay there, knowing what to expect. Just because it is familiar doesn't make it something I can ever get used to. He unties my shoes and takes them off, not noticing the knife I have in the bottom of it, and sets it down on the floor next to the bed I am lying on. Next, he unbuttons my pants and slides them down off my body. I'm left in my socks, underwear, shirt, and coat. I am just praying he doesn't go for my bra until I can stash it in my coat in the room somewhere. But, unfortunately, life is not always full of granted wishes.

"Sit up. Take your coat off. Get fully undressed, Surry." I do as he instructs. Fortunately, I am able to take off my bra and shirt together, so that I can hide the gun in it, placing them onto my coat lightly to ensure no noise. I take my socks off and place them with my coat as well. Now I stand before him, completely nude. He begins to look me over, I am sure noticing the new tattoos, the ones covering the scars he left on my body that he never got to see healed. He only saw the wounds.

"What is this scar?" He asks and points to the one that goes from hip to hip, almost like a smiley face.

"It is from when you put me in the hospital when I finally escaped you," I spat at him.

"Why?"

"Because you all ruined my body. You hurt more than just the outside, you did internal damage, you stupid fuck." His eyes widen. I think he is finally shocked for once in his whole life.

"Where is my child, Surry?"

"Who's to say it was yours? How many men was it that day? Twenty? Thirty? I know I stopped counting somewhere in the teens. You raped me and got me pregnant. Then your men raped your pregnant wife," I pause, waving my index finger in the direction of the hall where we came from and then pointing back to him. He slaps my face again so hard that I fall onto the bed. He then loses it and screams an unintelligible noise before pushing me all the way down on the bed and forcing my thighs open so he can place his knees between.

"Let's call this man you say loves you, and see if he would enjoy the show. What do you say, Surry?" I don't answer, just close my eyes and turn my head.

The next thing I hear is the hollow, digital tone of a phone ringing—that mechanical purr that seems to stretch time itself. I open my eyes, momentarily disoriented by the harsh ceiling light, to find Gavin kneeling between my splayed thighs, his eyes fixed on my exposed center with a predatory intensity that makes my skin prickle. His mouth twists into something between a smirk and a snarl as he holds his phone at arm's length, the blue glow illuminating the sweat beading on his collarbone. The speaker icon glows on the screen, broadcasting each ring that reverberates through the otherwise silent room.

"This is Brenden," he really called Brenden? What the fuck.

"You know, I could have called from my phone, but I was hoping that the sight of my sweet wife's name on your phone would give you some hope. Which, if I'm being honest, you shouldn't have. I forgot how great her pussy is. You failed to mention that when we spoke earlier. But these tattoos, they need to go. Which ones do you think I should burn off first?" I didn't even notice he was using my phone until he said that.

"Yes, I do know since I've been buried in it for the last few months. And if you even think about touching one of her goddam tattoos I'll drive my boot so far up your ass you will be able to tie the laces with your teeth."

Oh my God, Brenden. I internally cover my face. What the fuck is he doing?

"Ah, yes. About that, I see she is not with child. Are you incapable of creating heirs, Brenden Slater?" Please, Brenden, don't say a fucking word. I didn't tell him on purpose. I'd most likely already be dead if he knew my uterus was gone.

"No, I'm not. But I also don't do anything to Surry that is against her will. And children would be against her will. You and I are not the same, Gavin. Don't try to relate to me. Or upset me. I know how the rest of your life will pan out. I'm not worried about it." Ya. He is definitely trying to get me murdered. What the fuck.

"Speaking of which, where is my child. I assume Stefan is with you. Do they have my child? He has to be what, ten now? Eleven?" Gavin really thinks I had that baby all those years ago. I swear, I have never met a more moronic person.

"All I know, is that I won't be telling you shit, sweet cheeks."

Gavin rolls me to the side and slaps my ass, causing me to cry out, before rubbing it. He is staring at the welt, watching it grow on my skin.

"My handprint looks so excellent on the milky white skin of her ass. Don't you love that as well?" He begins to unbutton his pants and pulls the zipper down before pulling his dick out and begins to stroke it between my thighs, the tip barely coming in contact with my entrance. I squeeze my eyes shut.

"Would you like to stay on the phone with me as I fill her with my seed, or would you like me to save you the embarrassment of fulfilling her needs and hang up first?"

"Let me talk to her. Now," is all Brenden growls out.

"Ah ah ah, now Brenden. Don't get any ideas. You can't save her. You don't even know where she is." There is a slight pause on Brenden's side of the phone.

"You're right, Gavin. I can't. So can you at least let me say goodbye?"

"Now that is not what I expected," Gavin says to me. "You hear that, Surry darling? He is giving you up. He would like to speak with you."

"He-hello," is all I manage to get out. I am having trouble finding my voice. This is all too much.

"Hey Siren, do you remember the first night we spent

together?" Obviously, but I am not sure what he is getting at.

"Yes-" I cut short as to not fill in any more details for Gavin to use against me.

"Did you hear me say that I wish I could bottle your scent to always have it with me?" What? No, I have no idea what he is talking about. But I will play along.

"...Yes?" My answer framed as more of a question, what is he getting at...

"I want you to know that I will forever smell your scent on my pillow. Do you understand?" He is coming for me, he is going to save me. But he is trying to do it in a way only I would understand. But I can't reply because Gavin is getting more agitated, and is working his cock faster and more disgustingly in front of me and I can't take my eyes off of it since I don't know what he is planning on doing.

"I think so." Is all I can manage to get out.

"Okay Siren, I love you. Give the phone back now." I don't get the chance to say it back because Gavin snatches it out of my hands.

"Now, Brenden," is how Gavin begins. "Would you like to stay on the phone, or would you like me to send you a video. I am happy to do either." He is prodding at my entrance now with his disgusting body part.

"No thanks. I will catch up with you later though, alright?"

The phone makes the disconnect sound, and I know Brenden has hung up. I knew he couldn't do anything to help me right now. But it took the wind out of me when I heard those three beeps indicating the call was ended. Gavin is leaning over me now, and I just close my eyes. I feel the tip slip into me, and I go to the quiet place in my mind.

I used to have this secret place within my mind when he would get on top of me. I would think about the compound in Oregon. The pool, the huge fields of nothing to run around, catching bugs and snakes. There was the random bunny here and there too. So peaceful. It takes me away so well I barely feel my body. I can tell he is inside me, but not very far.

A buzzing sound shakes me from that place and causes me to open my eyes, feeling him all the way inside me nearly causes me to gag. He halts, unable to continue. The lights go out.

"FUCK!" He screams out at everyone and no one. "WHY ARE THE FUCKING LIGHTS OUT!" I just lay as still as possible, hoping that he will forget what his plans were. A man walks into the room, I notice he doesn't need to enter the code to come in. He looks at me with hungry eyes, being able to see me due to the emergency backup lights that dimly illuminate the room.

"Sir, the power is out but we are unsure why. The surrounding buildings are also out, but the city is fine, so it is only us."

"Fuck." He shakes his head and looks down at me before pulling out and stuffing his dick back in his pants, zipping himself back in. The man looks down my entire body now and licks his lips. The second Gavin is off the bed, I shut my legs and grab the blanket on the bed to cover me. The man looks away and faces Gavin.

"What would you like us to do, sir?"

"Guard the girls' rooms. I will go talk with everyone else. Stay in the hallway and do not move. Do you understand me?" Gavin turns to look at me. "We will be together again once I sort out this little problem." Then they turn and walk away, leaving me in the dark room alone.

I jump up and begin redressing. I notice that my panties are gone; he must have taken them, fucking sicko. I stride into the bathroom allowing myself a moment of privacy. The disgust, the shame, the repulsion, the sadness, the anger. It all glides over me. But I hold onto the anger, not letting it get past me. I take the washcloth from the hanger next to the sink and wet it with the faucet, then wipe between my legs. The more I can get rid of the feeling of him inside me, the more I can focus.

Once clean, I slide all of my clothes on one by one. Fortunately, the gun was still in my shirt so I slide that into the waistband of my pants and walk over to the door. I push it sideways, and it slides right open. This is going to be easier than I thought. I see that the creepy dude, let's call him Fuck Face number five, is not where Gavin told him to stay. Tisk tisk.

I walk along the wall until I am in front of the other girl's room. I look into the room and see she is on the bed, and I have found Fuck Face number five. He is on top of her. I slowly push open the door which thankfully doesn't require a code due to the power outage; thankfully he is facing away from me. I grab my knife from my shoe and sneak up behind him. I catch her eye it hits me all of the sudden. I know her. It's Natasha. I show her the knife, tapping my lips with my finger to indicate to her to be quiet. She just looks away and doesn't say anything as the guard continues to thrust into her.

I am right behind him and refuse to second-guess myself. I take the knife and stab it right into the side of his neck, and blood instantly starts pouring from him. His body stops thrusting, falling to the side of the bed as he struggles to hold his neck. Natasha is pulled with him, but I catch her before she is drug under his fat, ugly body.

His attempts to cover his neck wound are no use though. I got him right in the carotid artery. That's where Papa always told me to stab someone. You'll bleed out too fast to get help or do anything about it.

As he lies there I step closer to the bed, helping her shift back onto it.

"Natasha?"

She looks at me with a surprised expression.

"You're Natasha, right? I am so sorry for what has happened to you. I am Surry. Gavin is my ex-husband. I'm going to get you out of here, okay? Brenden Slater has told me all about you, and I know Corver has been searching for you since we, well, since we saw the video..."

She closes her eyes and nods but doesn't move. She is wearing a dress and nothing else. I see shoes in the corner, so I grab those and bring them over. She hasn't said anything, so I begin to put the shoes onto her feet myself. I know she is in shock. I know exactly how she feels. But I won't let her stay here. She needs out of here just as bad, if not worse, than I do.

BANG.

A gunshot goes off somewhere else in the warehouse.

"Natasha, you don't need to face him, but I can't let you stay here in a room that will lock again if the power comes back on. I need you to get up and walk, okay?" I grab her hand and begin to pull her up very slowly. The longer I pull, the more she comes out of the stupor she is in. By the time I have pulled her to a standing position, she has a fire in her eyes. Good. I need her to be angry. I hold the knife out to her, and she takes it. I reach down to Fuck Face number five's body and grab both the guns and the knife he has. I hand one of the guns to Natasha, stashing the knife in my own pocket.

"Are you ready?" I ask her, looking her in the face, trying to read her expression.

Without looking at me, she nods. "I have never been more ready for anything," she says in her thick Russian accent. "He needs to die."

I nod. "I couldn't agree more," I reply, an ugly grimace on my face. "We need to try and save my friend before we get out, though. Can you help me?" I have people on the way right now to help us. The Slater's in fact."

Her eyes shine slightly in the emergency light, and I know she is desperate to see someone she knows. Someone to save her. "Okay, what's the plan then?"

"Well, I don't really have one. I just got here, and it all happened so fast. But we each have a gun and a knife. I am hoping that'll be enough." I shrug, because I don't really know what else to do.

She looks at me like I might be a little off my rocker, but nods anyway. We don't really have another choice. We sneak out of the room and begin to walk along the walls as quietly as possible. When we reach the end of the short hallway that leads to the larger main room we both look around the corner into the room. There is so much going on. I am not sure how we didn't hear it before. The rooms must be soundproof. That's when I see him. Brenden. He and Gavin are locked together in some weird fight hug. I nearly sob when I see him. But it isn't them who notices us first. One of the fucks who collected me at the port sees me and Natasha and starts running toward us.

"GET BACK IN YOUR ROOMS!"

He starts yelling at us. I look at Natasha, ready to fight my way out of this, seeing if she is as well. She nods, and we both pull our guns out and pull the trigger. We each fire two shots, and he is down on the floor, two holes in his head for sure, and at least one body wound. Now that is out of the way, but we drew attention to ourselves. A few more of the Fuck Faces start running toward us, most likely with the order not to hurt us, as none of them raise a gun to us. We, however, do. We take all of the ones that run toward us out, taking turns firing one bullet at each man, right in the face each time.

Finally, it seems that anyone who has noticed us—is dead. How they all didn't hear that, I'll never know. We stand there, not moving. Taking in what is happening. That is, until I see Bridget. She is sitting in the chair still, her head slumped forward. There is blood dripping from her face, and she isn't moving. Then I see the blood on the wall behind her. She's dead. I am frozen and can't move. She is dead.

The woman who cared for me all my life. Who loved me as if I were her own. She is gone, and I will never get to see her again. Everything I did was for nothing. Coming here. Killing people. Gavin assaulting me once again, and I can't do this. It was all for nothing. I fall to my knees, unable to remove my eyes from her slumped form. Natasha notices and bends over to look at me, seeing where my eyes are looking.

"She would not want you to die with her," she tells me. She's right. But I'm not ready to hear it. I nod, but make no other move to get up.

"Come, we must help. We must get out of here." Natasha

slowly raises her pistol and begins to walk forward into the shadows further, staying against the wall. I breathe deeply, begging to count to five, remembering the only therapy lesson that ever stuck with me.

1...Feel the emotion.

2...She is gone.

3...Process..

4...Anger. Feel the anger. The sadness.

5...Use the anger. Feed it with the sadness.

That's it. I can't give myself any more time. I stand and follow after Natasha. The pistol is now warm in my hand, and I mentally tally how many bullets I likely still have. When I reach her, I lean in close.

"If we can avoid it, don't kill him. I have a plan on how to deal with him." She nods.

BANG.

Another gun goes off. This time, we can see. Gavin has Brenden by the throat and his gun pointed straight in the air. Everyone froze.

"Well, well, well. It seems you have come much sooner than I was prepared for. But don't worry, I will take great care of our girl for you. Where is Stefan? I might as well get this over with if everyone is already here?" At that moment, a man walks in, holding a shadowy figure by the shoulder with one hand behind his back. Dad. How did this happen? How are we...losing? I watch in disbelief. We are really about to...to lose.

Gavin's voice cuts through the air like a blade. "Hello Stefan. Did you see that video I sent you with the Russians?" My dad's silence is deafening. "Should I retrieve Surry so we can get this union back on track?" Gavin's words hang in the air, met with nothing. His face contorts from the lack of reaction he receives.

"No? OKAY THEN." He slams the gun barrel against Brenden's temple, drawing blood. "TIE HIM UP!" I cringe seeing the blood, and then the spittle that flies from his mouth as he screams, veins bulging in his neck. Brenden crashes to his knees. Gavin's eyes are feral now—pupils blown wide, nostrils flaring with each ragged breath. My heart hammers so hard I taste metal. I lock eyes with Natasha, her terror mirroring my own. Following her gaze, I see them—Gavin's men forming a death circle, weapons trained on Josh, Gunnar, and my father's crew. The metallic click of safeties being switched off echoes in the sudden silence.

A hand comes around and covers my mouth, and I try to spin around but can't. I use my peripheral to see that Natasha also has her mouth covered. Between us a blonde head comes into view and starts whispering to us.

"It's me, Corver, don't scream." Just before he removes his hand from our mouths Natasha lets out a tiny sob, and we turn to face him. Corver and Natasha just look at each other before she falls into him, his arms wrapping around her, and he presses kisses onto the top of her head. I can see her shoulders shaking as she begins to fall apart.

I gesture to the others, and Cover looks at me with sadness in his eyes. "What are we going to do about this?"

"Arnie is still over in the other building, I have him in my ear. He says hi." Corver whispers and gestures toward his ear. "We turned the lights out and are the only ones able to get them back on. But through the cameras we could see what was happening to you, and to Natasha, and then everyone else. So I decided I'd better get in here. I have a gas bomb, but I only have one respirator. Do you have any ideas?"

"Actually," Natasha says in her low Russian accent. "I do."

Corver's voice crackles through the comms. "Snipers down. You're clear for entry."

That's all I need.

"Go."

We hit the doors like a thunderclap. Boots slam. Metal screams. The echo ricochets off concrete, folding into the deafening pop of gunfire. The air fills with shouting—guttural, desperate screams that barely register as human—and muzzle flashes strobe across the room like hellish lightning. Smoke billows thick enough to chew, a suffocating gray blanket that burns my lungs with each panicked breath. I can taste copper and dust on my tongue, metallic and gritty, while fine particles of debris coat my teeth and throat, turning my saliva to paste. The deafening thunder of gunfire reverberates through my bones, each blast sending tremors through my chest.

The first man through doesn't make it to the second step. A shot snaps past me, catching him in the shoulder and spinning him sideways. Stefan's men flood in after, shouting positions, but it's chaos—our carefully built plan disintegrating the second we hit the floor.

I move on instinct. Head down, gun up, scanning. Every shape, every flicker of movement could be her—or him. My heartbeat is too loud in my ears, a drum drowning out the rest.

She's here.

She has to be.

Someone yells "clear!" from my left, but it's a lie. A shadow rises behind him, knife flashing, and the scream turns wet and short. I spin, fire, drop the man. No time to think about names. No time to breathe.

"Two on the left!" Joshua shouts through the comms.

I pivot, covering him. I squeeze the trigger—three, four shots— and they're down. We press forward, edging toward the center of the building when I hear it.

Gavin's voice cuts through the mess like glass.

"Come to find the little bird? Bad news, the bird is home, right where she belongs. Now come out and FACE ME!"

My blood runs with ice. The sound of him crawls straight up my spine. Too close—he's in the open, taunting, somewhere beyond the fog of bullets and debris.

I catch movement up ahead. Men in dark gear, moving too cleanly to be improvising. Trained. Waiting. A trap within a trap.

Stefan curses in the comms, accent thick with fury. "They knew we were comin'!"

I don't answer. Can't. My focus narrows. I push forward, firing at the shapes ahead. Two go down, but three more surge forward to take their place. Gunfire tears across the room, hammering the walls. Shells rain on the floor like coins.

Every step forward is through bodies—ours, theirs, I can't tell anymore.

The noise blurs into something unreal. My pulse and the gunfire are one sound now. My breathing syncs with it. *In, out. In, out. Move. Keep moving.*

A body crashes into me from the side, all muscle and momentum. The impact steals my breath, sends me flying. A flash of white light explodes behind my eyes as my shoulder blade connects with the wall first, then my skull. The crack of bone against cement reverberates through my skull—hot, jagged pain blooms outward from the point of impact, electric currents of agony shooting down my spine and into my fingertips, which tingle and go momentarily numb.

I stagger upright, gun clattering from my grip. My hands find it, slick with blood, I can't tell if it is mine or someone else's.

Everything doubles again. The world lurches like it's underwater. Two Stefans, two Joshs, two of everything. I steady on one image and aim for that.

Through the haze, a flicker of movement.

A figure slumps in a metal folding chair next to Gavin, head bowed, wrists bound with zip ties that bite into flesh. My brain misfires like a faulty engine. My chest stops mid-breath, lungs frozen in panic. Surry. The silhouette, the curve of the shoulders, it's a woman. I think, no—as the smoke thins, I see older features, deep lines etched around the mouth, silver-grey hair falling in limp strands across a face that holds the ghost of someone I once knew.

Bridget.

The edges of her shape shimmer and split. Two of her, side by side. I blink hard, once, twice. Still two. *Fuck.*

Gavin steps into the light, calm and steady, like he planned this all along. My throat locks. Nothing comes out.

My legs move before my brain agrees, trying to reach her.

Josh grabs my arm. "Wait, Bren—"

I rip free.

"Now, now, Brenden. Stop right there, or you won't see poor Bridget alive again." His eyes are wild, stretched wide and gleaming.

I glance around, head clearing just enough to see it—we're being funneled, trapped between pillars and machinery. The air stinks of cordite and sweat.

Bridget meets my gaze, gives a small, sad shake of her head. She looks wrecked—face bloodied, hair matted, still wearing the same clothes she left the island in.

I freeze. I know I have to try to save her. Surry would never forgive me if I didn't. I holster my weapon and step closer, hands raised.

"What do you want, Gavin? Bridget's innocent in this. Let her go, and we can talk–just us men. I know you prefer it that way. Women are only good for two things. Food and fucking."

I cringe inside at my own words, but not to him.

Gavin laughs. Unhinged, too loud, too long as he stalks closer to Bridget. "You don't really believe that, do you, Brenden Slater? You think you can charm me? No. I know why you're here. To take my wife." His voice cracks. "But nobody leaves this building tonight unless it's in a body bag. Or a barrel. I don't care which."

He presses the barrel to Bridget's temple, leans close.

"Now, Bridget...what should we do? Keep you alive for leverage? Have Brenden hand himself over willingly?" He grins, the look on his face completely unhinged and feral. Feral men make fearsome opponents. You never know what they are willing to do. "No. That will never due. It sucks all the fun out of it, don't you think?" But she never gets the chance to answer.

He pulls the trigger.

Her head snaps back, the wall behind her painted red, blood and matter spread wide on the floor and wall behind her. Stefan's strangled yell tears through the air. I feel nothing. Just a hollow thud in my chest where rage should be.

Before I can move, more of Gavin's men pour in from the shadows. We never saw them. Guns raised, shouting, herding us toward the center.

Now I can see the screens, they must have a back up power source somewhere we didn't see before. Rows of monitors glowing in the dark. Different feeds: a man assaulting a woman in a small room, my destroyed apartment complex, Surry's place, the Oregon compound. Even the doors–front and back. Cameras everywhere, still running without power. He knew where we were all along.

Fuck.

"Didn't I tell you, Brenden?" Gavin's voice rings, manic. "She always comes back!"

He's feral, wild-eyed, blood smeared across his jaw and white shirt.

"Corver," I hiss under my breath into the comms, forcing breath through my teeth as we're pushed closer to Gavin. Stefan's beside me now. "We could use some extra help."

"Yeah," he answers. "On it. Hold on."

"Hold on?" My voice cracks. "We're outnumbered and surrounded."

Static hums. Then Corver again: "Three minutes. Trust me."

Three minutes feels like a lifetime.

"Copy," I grind out, but my focus stays locked on Gavin's face.

"Hello, Stefan." Gavin turns from me, voice oily. "Did you like the video I sent–the one with the Russians? Should I fetch Surry now, so we can put this union back on track? She's been performing her wifely duties so well since she came back."

His eyes cut to me, waiting for a reaction. I grit my teeth, close my eyes for one second–and pain explodes across my skull.

"No? OKAY THEN!"

Stars burst behind my eyelids as the barrel of his gun cracks into my temple. Warm blood spills down my cheek, soaking the cotton under my vest.

"Tie him up!"

I drop to my knees, vision strobing. My stomach flips. Voices blur together, meaningless noise.

Slowly, sight crawls back. Gavin's face hovers above me, the gun barrel inches from my left eye.

This is it.

I whisper, *"I'm sorry,"* to no one and everyone–to Surry, to her father, to Sam, to my brothers. For not keeping my promise. For being too slow.

Josh is beside me, also on his knees, eyes wide—not on the men in front of him, but past me.

I turn my head. And there–through the haze–she's walking toward us. Surry.

Something dangles from her waistband; her arms cross awkwardly in front of her.

"Gavin, that's enough," she says, voice calm, steady, lethal. She stops ten feet away.

She's talking to him but I can't make out the words, just the rhythm, sharp and cutting. Gavin laughs, spreading his arms like he's welcoming her home.

"Surry—" I rasp, but she doesn't look at me. She takes a single step back, raises her hands.

"Iontas!" (Surprise!)

Fuck, the code word. How does sh–

She throws something small–metal flashing as it spins–and instinct takes over. I reach for my mask, but my hands are useless, trembling.

How the fuck did she get a bomb?

By the time I look back, she's already masked, sprinting at Gavin, pistol in hand.

The detonation isn't loud. But the world explodes anyway.

Light. Smoke. A wave of pressure that swallows everything.

The air folds in on itself. White, then gray. My ears scream with ringing.

Someone grabs my shoulder–Josh, maybe–but the world doubles again, and he's gone.

I drop to my hands and knees, choking on the thick chemical burn of air and blood.

Through the blur, one last clear image: Surry, standing in the center of it all. Mask on. Eyes hard. Unflinching.

She's the calm in the storm.

Then the world collapses into noise, and then black.

**Surry**

      I tightened my fingers around the little cylinder in my pocket until the metal pin bit into my skin. Corver kneels in front of me like he's reading from a manual, but his voice is clinical and steady, which is the only thing I need right now.

"Okay, here is the gas mask, and then the actual gas bomb. Look right here," he says, pointing to the handle with a tiny metal pin and ring. "This is the pin. You will want to squeeze the handle closed, and then pull this out. But for the love of all creatures—"

I raise a brow. Love of all creatures? Natasha gives him the same look and he sighs, starts again.

"For the love of EVERYTHING," he corrects, stabbing a finger at the pin. "Do not pull the pin until you are ready to throw it. Got it?"

I nod, fully planning on ignoring him, and slide the cylinder into my back pocket. Cargo pants: a literal lifesaver right now. I shove the gas mask beside it and pretend not to feel the tremor at the base of my throat.

"Thanks, Corver. What will you do?" I try to make my voice light. It comes out thin.

"I'm going to take Natasha out the way I came in. See if our friends are here." He gives a grin that's half hope, half something darker. I don't know who our friends are, but I'm praying that they're here.

He squeezes my shoulder–quick, businesslike–then lets go. Natasha steps forward, takes my hands, looks at me with those steady blue eyes, and says something in her rough, beautiful Russian.

"Pust' muzhestvo vedët tebya, a strakh ostanetsya pozadi."

"Sounds nice, but I have no idea what it means. Good luck?," I ask, laughing a cracked little laugh.

"May courage lead you, and fear stay behind. But, close enough." She lets go, a half smile on her face, and the two of them melt back toward the cell block.

I stand alone for a beat, listening to my own breath, the way it wheels and thuds in my ears. I pat my pocket, pistol is there; weight is a comfort, an anchor. I tug my pants down a notch, letting the fabric and a sliver of skin do the work I can't: distract, disarm, entice. If I'm going to be bait, I'll play the part.

When I'm ready I pinch the handle, yank the pin. The little ring squeals as metal slides free. I keep my fingers clamped around it, the cylinder hidden between my chest and arms so no one can see.

Then I leave the shadows and walk toward them.

The warehouse smells of old oil and something rotten. Every footstep is loud in the silence around Gavin. He stands too calm, the wrong kind of calm, a man who's already accepted violence as a daily ritual.

"Gavin, that's enough," I tell him. My voice sounds braver than I feel. Seeing Brenden, Papa, Josh, Sam, and Gunnar on the floor, forced to kneel before the man who used to own me makes bile rise in my throat. I fight it down.

"You got what you wanted. Me and Natasha. What more do you get by killing them?" I keep my eyes on my people, cataloging every face for any sign I can do something to help.

He is smiling, but it doesn't reach his eyes. "Oh, Surry. Sweet, stupid Surry. You don't get it. They will always come for you. I can't be king of both my armies until Stefan is dead. So–therefore–they must die."

He says this last part with a casual flick of his wrist, like he's discussing the weather instead of murder. His eyes have a glassy sheen to them, pupils blown wide and dark as bullet holes. A thin line of spittle clings to the corner of his mouth when he speaks, trembling with each syllable. There is no logic in the twitching muscles of his face, only the wild, erratic pulse of a man who not only believes in monsters, but has become one himself.

"Can I–just–say goodbye?" I press for time. I need time. Panic claws at my ribs. My fingers sweat on the cylinder. His gaze slips over my body; the room narrows to his pupils, the white of his teeth, and the slow inhale he takes like a predator smelling blood.

I nod toward my father. This is the second before the breath leaves you; this is the long, three-second silence before a gunshot. I yell the code word sharp as a whip.

"Iontas!"

I fling the bomb high–aiming just above Gavin–and the little cylinder hits the concrete just behind him. Gas wheezes out of it, almost invisible at first, then curls like smoke. He turns to see what I've done; that's my opening. I yank the mask out, jam it over my face, and take a deep breath in through the filter. The world snaps into narrow clarity: sound muffled, edges bright, the chemical tang a second layer beneath everything.

Gavin is choking. He thrashes as the fumes bite; his men cough and scramble for their own masks or stagger away. I run.

I'm under him in two steps. My left hand closes on his shirt; my knee hammers up into his groin knowing exactly where to go. He doubles, a sound somewhere between a sob and a shriek. He coughs—eyes streaming, face flushing scarlet and then strange pale.

I draw the pistol from my hip with my right hand and press the barrel to his temple. Even through the fumes and the protective mask, up this close he smells like sweat, cheap cologne, and rot. Maybe I'm just remembering what he smelled like earlier. Regardless, I cannot get away from him fast enough.

With great pleasure, I tell him, "You will pay for what you've done." My voice sounds small to me, but steady.

I raise the gun and flip it. The butt smashes against the side of his head; Gavin goes limp like a marionette whose strings were cut.

My legs are shaking. The gas fog crawls at the edges of my vision, but I can still see Brenden slumped on the concrete, several large men looping arms under his and hauling him toward the door. My father moves in fast, large and terrible in his own quiet way, standing over Gavin with a gun leveled at the fallen man.

"Don't kill him, Papa. I have plans. But I need to go with Brenden."

He gives me a look-soft, buried under steel-and nods. "We'll take him to Tacoma. Quiet place. No one'll hear."

I step out of the doors, and pull off my mask, allowing fresh air to fill my lungs. As thankful as I am that I had the mask, I am far more grateful to remove it now.

Corver appears at my shoulder with Natasha bundled in a thermal blanket, cheeks raw but blinking, alive. He looks like he's just finished a terrible job and is trying to be casual about it. One of the men rises from near Brenden and steps forward, bowing his head when I glance at him. He takes my hand in both of his, firm and warm and not afraid.

"Who are you guys?" I question. I am positive I have never seen these men before.

"Ms. Surry. We are the Bratva. We serve Natasha." His voice is flat, respectful. The syllables roll in the heavy, unfamiliar way that suddenly feels like rescue.

"You called them?" I say, glancing at Corver, more question than accusation.

Corver shrugs like it's nothing. "Yup. I said I found Natasha, and they came. They wanted to settle the score." He looks down at Natasha with something like devotion that makes my chest ache for reasons I don't have words for.

Brenden groans and flails-awake, angry, and messy. I drop to my knees next to him and shake him by the shoulders gently until his slitted eyes focus on me.

"Brenden, look at me. It's Surry. You're okay." My voice cracks. He reaches for me with hands that are warm and bloody, and I let him clutch me like I am a lifeline.

He breathes out-deep, ragged-and the panic inside me melts into a tired, furious relief. If he is alive, we can do so much more than survive-we can get our revenge.

I lay with him on the ground for a few minutes before looking up at his face.

"If you go, I want to go with you," I whisper to him, my voice barely audible over the chatter. His eyelashes flutter against pale cheeks, but his eyes remain closed. Blood has dried in a thin crust along his hairline. I lean closer, close enough to feel the faint warmth of his shallow breath against my ear. His cracked lips part with effort, and though no sound emerges, I can read the shape they form: "always." My heart lurches painfully in my chest. Even now, broken and bleeding, he is with me.

Behind me, Alec and the other men move with quiet efficiency, dragging bodies, binding hands, applying oxygen. Outside, the warehouse hums with activity–boots, Russian voices, and the wet slap of someone tending a wound.

Sam finds me and scoops me up into his arms like I'm a child, and for a beat, I let myself cry into the curve of his shoulder. It's not the kind of victory anyone wanted, but it's the kind that matters: people breathing, people still here.

I pull away from Sam and wipe my face on my sleeve, swallow, and let my fingers tighten around Brenden's hand beneath mine.

The gas stings my eyes, my lungs, but the ache in my chest is a different thing. Solid, sharp, the promise of the fight to come.

The headlights cut off, and the night swallows us whole. The sign above the building reads **"MATTRESS MAGIC"**, half the bulbs burnt out, so it flickers like a dying heartbeat. The place smells like dust and rain-soaked concrete. Every window is barred, every corner shadowed.

We walk into the old mattress store off 38th and Steele. At night, it feels less like a business and more like a crime scene long forgotten. The kind of place where you could scream and no one would notice. Not because they couldn't hear, but because they wouldn't care. This part of Tacoma doesn't ask questions. Even with the police station down the street, nobody comes when they should.

"Where do you want him, boss?" Josh's voice grunts from ahead of me. He's carrying Gavin like a bag of trash, one arm slung over his shoulder.

We'd made the forty-minute drive in thirty, the convoy slicing through the dark like a string of silent bullets. It was the kind of movement that should've made the news–too many headlights, too much purpose–but I don't care anymore about getting caught. The law stopped meaning anything the day Gavin took everything from me.

"I actually don't know," I admit. My voice sounds steadier than I feel. "Papa, where do we take him?"

My dad gestures toward the back, his face unreadable in the flickering light. "That door there. 'Tis an elevaytor up tae the second level. It's sound-proof an' secure — everythin' ye'd be wantin'."

A chill runs through me at the casual way he says *soundproof*, like it's a feature, not a warning.

Brenden's arm is slung over my shoulders, and though it looks like he's steadying me, it's really the other way around. He's still weak, pale under the bruises, his steps uneven. Every wince he tries to hide slices through me. I tighten my grip around his waist, pretending it's affection when it's really desperation.

"Why does your dad own a mattress store?" Brenden whispers, his breath hot against my ear. The humor is there, buried under pain.

I almost laugh. "I have no clue. Didn't even know it existed until tonight."

He just nods, grimacing with every step. The sound of his labored breathing echoes in my skull like guilt.

"Josh, you good?" Corver calls out from behind us.

Josh doesn't even look back. He waves him off, half a smirk curling at the edge of his mouth. "Got it."

When he reaches the back door, he pulls it open and presses the circular button beside the elevator. The old machinery groans awake with a low chime before the doors creak open. The smell of oil and rust escapes like breath from a tomb.

We pile in–Josh, Gavin, my dad, Brenden, and me. Corver, Natasha, and her men wait behind. The rest, my mom, Hazel, June, Richie, Alisha, and my sister, are still en route. Sam went to collect all of them.

As the elevator rises, the air grows heavier. I can hear the clank of chains somewhere above us. The old gears groan, the light flickers overhead. Brenden leans on me harder now, his forehead brushing the top of my head. He doesn't say anything. He doesn't need to. I can feel the apology in the way he exhales.

When the elevator doors slide open again, the world changes.

The room is sterile, echoing, and wrong. One mattress against the wall, a set of chains bolted into the concrete above it. A single wooden chest sits in the corner–large and deliberate. I'm afraid of what I would find if I opened it. Finally, a metal chair stands in the center of the floor, its arms fitted with restraints.

It isn't a room. It's a stage.

I stare for a long moment before realizing I'm holding my breath. My father wasn't exaggerating–this place was built for pain. The air even feels colder here, like it's been conditioned to watch and not interfere.

My dad walks around, showing everyone what is up here, even showing Josh and Brenden what's in the chest, but I ignore it. I don't want to know.

The elevator groans again, descending. A minute later, it returns with Corver, Natasha, and Alec. Their footsteps echo hollowly on the floor. Josh has already dumped Gavin into the chair and secured the chains tight around his wrists and ankles. When he's done, he slaps him across the face hard enough to echo, then spits on him.

A bloody bead rolls down Gavin's chin, and something inside

me almost–*almost*–feels pity. Then I remember Bridget. The gas. The years.

"Hey," I say quietly, voice cutting through the tension. "Give Natasha and me a moment."

They hesitate. My father's gaze lingers on me a second longer than I can stand, but he nods. One by one, the others step back, gathering near the far wall. Corver catches Brenden before he can stumble, guiding him down to the floor. Brenden tries to protest, but Corver hushes him, looking over the head wounds he received.

Natasha walks to my side. Her face is pale, but her eyes burn with something sharp and dangerous. I take her hand, cold and strong in mine, and we step toward Gavin.

He's slumped forward, eyes closed. The bastard still manages to look smug even unconscious.

"So," I say softly, almost conversational, "did you ever think this is how your night would end, Gavin?" My tone light and airy.

No response. He just looks at us both up and down, blood dripping onto the floor from his chin like slow applause.

"ANSWER US!" Natasha roars. Her fist snaps forward, cracking against his face. His head jerks sideways, more blood and a tooth hitting the ground at once.

The sound–wet and final–makes my stomach turn.

"Damn, girl," I mutter under my breath, forcing out a humorless laugh. "Remind me not to piss you off."

Gavin groans, lifts his head, his lip split, trembling–but he doesn't speak.

I turn to Natasha. "What do you want to do? How much of this do you want to carry?"

She looks back at me, eyes unreadable, and for a heartbeat, I wonder if she's seeing him or the ghost of her father sitting in that chair instead.

Natasha goes quiet. "I don't think I want to be here. You can carry it out. Will you kill him?"

Her question isn't filled with worry or pity. More genuine curiosity about what I plan to do.

"Yes," I answer her simply. "He will be dying for what he did. To you. To me. To all the other women I am sure are out there." It can't just be us that he has done this to. He takes pleasure in hurting women. So what did he do the last eleven years?"

She leans forward, and takes my hands in hers, squeezing gently. Her eyes lock onto mine, and she whispers to me a promise. "The Bratva will always be friends with the Irish as long as I rule."

I smile sadly, knowing we will be the women on top of two of the largest crime syndicates in the United States before long. I whisper back to her, squeezing her hands in return. "The Irish will always be friends with the Bratva, as long as my father and I are at the helm."

She pulls me forward, letting go only to wrap her arms around my shoulders, mine pulling her in at the waist, hugging each other for what seems like the last time. "Give us the justice we deserve," is what she whispers before pulling away and heading toward the elevator, no looking back.

Alec immediately follows after her, but Corver walks to me, giving me a brief hug and a nod, before trailing after them into the elevator, waving at Brenden, then at Josh as he enters, and then down into their future.

"Surry, I'm goin' tae leave ye tae it up here. Ye're in good hands."

My dad cups my cheeks and presses a gentle kiss to my forehead. The warmth lingers even as he pulls back, and my throat tightens. I know I don't need him–but God, I'll always want my dad.

"Thank you, Papa. I'm sorry I messed up the plan so badly."

"Ah now, don't be sayin' that, a stór. Ye had yer reasons. I'm just glad tae have ye back where ye belong." His thumb brushes a tear from my cheek. "Go on now–do what ye need tae do. An' if ye need me for anythin', ye call, aye?"

"Okay, Papa."

He pulls me into another hug, strong and protective, the kind that still makes me feel small no matter how much I've survived. When he lets go, the air between us feels heavier. One last look, one last nod–then he follows the others into the elevator, the doors closing with a soft metallic sigh.

I take a moment to collect my thoughts. Reminiscing on everything that has happened over the last twenty-four hours. Then I turn to look at Brenden, and realize he is going to be here. For the next twenty-four hours. And the twenty-four after that. And for as long as I can see. My tears become happy ones as I laugh, mainly to myself. I really have fallen in love with this man. And it happened so fast, but it feels right. It feels good. It feels... like home.

I clap my hands, and spin around, facing the others. "I think that each of us deserves our chance at revenge. He blew up the shop, and June and Hazel deserve revenge for that. He blew up your apartment, Brenden and Josh were affected by that."

Corver too, but he seems uninterested in anything but Natasha. So he will be avenged, rather than getting revenge himself. I don't blame him for following the woman he has clearly loved for years instead of beating up an evil man.

I begin to circle Gavin, like a vulture circling its dying prey. Shoes hitting the floor and dust rising. Making the entire production look even more sinister than it already was.

"So I say, let's each have our turn." I run my index finger down the side of his face, temple to chin. He will get what is coming to him. From me, from Brenden, and from the rest of us who he decided to hurt.

"So," I pull my hand away and clap my hands together once more. "Who wants to go first?"

"Oh, me!" Yells Josh, coming over and punching Gavin as hard as he can in the stomach. Gavin lets out a wet breath, likely having broken a few ribs. He begins to pant, but I don't look his way again.

"Excellent." I smile.

An hour later, June and Hazel are here with their tattoo machines, tray table set with various inks and needle sizes. It looks like a regular tattoo appointment. Until you see the restraints, the damage inflicted on Gavin from the chemicals, and from Josh's fists. Really it's the whole background in general.

Richie decided not to come. He went home, he said he wanted to see Tommy. He hadn't seen him in so long, that he was ready for a *"reunion."* I knew what that meant, and I knew how much I was looking forward to one of those with Brenden, so I totally understood. He sent me a text with like forty-seven heart emojis, telling me to kick ass though.

"I think," June starts talking while putting the wrap around her machine, "that I will be putting the shop's logo on his chest. It feels fitting, him dying with what he destroyed on his body. What do you think?" She looks to Hazel. Hazel just nods, a wide smile like the cheshire cat plastered on her pretty face, making it look far more evil.

"Well, I've always wanted to know what it was like to tattoo someone's finger nails." That's all Hazel says before she brings up an entire roll of grip tape and begins to wrap Gavin's hand open to the arm of the chair. Once secure, she takes rope and secures it around his hand and wrist for added security. "There," she says. "All set. Ready, you fucker?" Without waiting for Gavin's consent, she brings the needle to Gavin's middle finger and begins to tattoo through his finger nail, wrenching a blood-curdling scream from him as he tries to get away.

"Now, now, Gavin. That isn't the only tattoo. Hold still so I can take a look at your chest. Fortunately, I know the logo really well. I did design it, after all." June keeps talking, looking at Gavin's chest. She had cut his shirt off him before setting up any of her supplies. "Now I'm going to draw on your chest for an outline. So hold still."

A few hours later, and every one of Gavin's fingernails has been tattooed blood red. Or possibly, that's the blood and I have no idea what color she used. Either way, I don't really care. But June, she created a masterpiece somehow. Covering the entirety of Gavin's chest in the logo of Tattoos On The Bay.

Hot pink, black, you can even see the Kraken layered in. It's somehow...beautiful.

"Do you think I can take a picture of this for my portfolio?" June asks out loud, and Hazel and I start cracking up. That has to be the most Juniper thing I have ever heard in my entire life.

"What the fuck, June?" Josh asks, but he can't stifle the laughter that bursts from his chest. Brenden is in the back, hacking a cough from snorting. He was mid-drink when she said that and breathed in the liquid instead of swallowing it.

"Do it, how morbid. I love it," is my answer between fits of giggles. The thought of his tattoo living on without his consent, allowing June's business to continue thriving? It is absolutely karma's way of fucking with Gavin even in the afterlife. And I'm here for it.

June snaps a few pictures, hands steady even though the air feels thick with exhaustion. Then, one by one, they begin packing up their things—ink bottles twisting shut, the buzz of the machine falling silent for the last time. Their movements are careful, methodical. I focus on them because it's easier than thinking about what comes next.

When everything is tucked away, June, Hazel, and I link arms and head toward the elevator. Brenden had asked for a moment alone with Gavin, now that he finally looked steady enough to stand on his own. But not until I made him swear—swear—he wouldn't kill him without me there.

He wants his revenge. Not for his apartment. Not for the pain he received. He want's it for me. The support system of a survivor. He wants that all for himself. So I let him.

We ride the elevator down together, quiet except for the soft hum of the machinery. When the doors open, the air feels colder. The faint smell of dust and oil from the old mattress store wraps around me as I step out to see them off.

My dad had already taken my mom and sister home earlier,

but Samuel and Alisha waited behind for the rest of us. I think Sam's afraid to let me out of his sight—or maybe he's just not ready to see me walk into another fight.

"You doin' okay, a leanbh?" Sam's voice is low, careful. He's always careful with me.

Alisha moves beside me, looping an arm around my shoulders, warm and grounding. She hadn't wanted to go upstairs—didn't need to see any of it.

"Yeah," I answer after a moment, though it comes out softer than I mean it to. "Yeah, I'm as okay as I'll ever be, I think. I just... I want this to be done, Sam. Once he's gone, maybe I can finally stop looking over my shoulder. Maybe I can finally breathe."

They both nod, quiet understanding passing between us. I love them for it—for not needing to fill the silence with false comfort. Just being here is enough.

And even as I look at them, something small and selfish flickers in me—a spark of normalcy. I can't wait for the day they stop pretending there's nothing between them. I want to laugh with Alisha about it, to tease them both like old times. But not tonight.

"I'm gonna head back up," I tell them, forcing a small smile. "If I leave Gavin with Brenden much longer, he'll be dead before I get my turn."

That earns a laugh from both of them, shaky but real.

Sam steps forward, wrapping me up in his arms. "We're headin' back to your place. Waitin' for you there, alright?"

I blink up at him, half-smiling. "You do remember it's Alisha's place too, right? You don't need my permission to go home."

He opens his mouth to argue, and I cut him off with a grin. "Yes, *our* home, Alisha, Hazel, Richie, and myself. *Ours.* Go. I'll meet you there when it's over. Good luck with Richie though. Tommy is there, so I have no idea what you're walking in on when you get there." Alisha and I giggle, and Sam rolls his eyes.

He presses something into my palm—Brenden's keys. His hand lingers around mine. His eyes search my face, worry written all over him.

"We picked up his truck. It's out front. But if you need me, Surry—if anything happens—I'll be back in a heartbeat. Don't hesitate."

"I know," I whisper. "But Brenden's here. And I think..." My voice falters. "I think I might actually be okay."

It comes out like a question, like I'm asking him to believe it for me.

Sam's expression softens. "I think you will be too, a leanbh."

He kisses my cheek, and Alisha pulls me into one last hug before they turn to go, June, Josh, and Hazel close behind them, each taking their own turn to hug me goodbye.

I watch them leave, hands tucked into my jacket, heart pounding quietly in my chest. Their taillights fade into the dark, and the street goes still again.

Then I turn toward the elevator, toward the storm waiting above.

Two men. One who broke me. One who pieced me back together.

And tonight–only one of them walks away.

The elevator dings when I arrive at the upper level, and I step out to a magnificent view. Brenden is standing in front of Gavin, fists clenched, jaw clenched. He looks like a Greek god who just took out his vengeance on a millennia-long nemesis. And damn, does he look good doing it.

I begin to walk toward him, turned on by this version of him. I have seen him fight, I have seen him soft. But vengeful Brenden. There is just something about it. That feral light in his eyes is calling to the one inside of me.

Now that I'm closer, I can see there is blood spatter on his face, shirt, and pants. His knuckles are also split and bleeding. I look at Gavin and find him awake, seething, and bleeding from just about everywhere. The split in his lip is larger now than how Natasha left it, he has a split in his swollen cheekbone, and another above his eye. He is staring at Brenden with more hatred than I have ever seen in my entire life.

"Well. I see you two have gotten on without me." I take the final steps to Brenden, running my arm behind him and hugging his waist, reaching up with my other hand to grab his collar and bring his face down for a kiss. The heat is instant and he devours me. I can taste Brenden, but I can also taste the copper of Gavin's blood. The mixture turning me feral. I run my hands all along his chest, stomach, and back, not being able to get close enough to him.

Brenden bites down on my lip gently, bringing me back to reality and he pulls away. "What do you want to do with him, Siren?"

"I want him to hurt like he hurt me." It's all I say. It's all I have to say, because he knows what I mean.

Brenden's eyes are filled with warmth as he reaches into his pocket, pulling out a black, textured pocket knife, before flicking it open. "I sharpened it just for you," he says, handing it to me handle-first.

"Thank you," I smile up at him, leaning in for another kiss, not getting carried away this time. At that moment, Gavin decides to speak for the first time since arriving here.

"Please, Surry. You know I always loved you. You know I was only doing what was best for you."

"Best for me? Oh, silly, stupid, Gavin. I'm not killing you. Do you see this on my forehead?" Re-purposing the words he said to me in the warehouse, I point to the long scar that goes from my eye up to my hairline. "I am going to give you one of these, and one of all the rest of the scars I now have because of you."

Gavin whimpers as I move to straddle him, sitting down on his lap and grabbing a fistful of hair. I yank his face down to look me in the eyes. His eyes are dull and glassy. He knows this is a lost cause, but he can't help but continue to whine for forgiveness. I guess he did still have a shred of humanity in him, realizing your own mortality will do that, I suppose.

"Do you remember when I dropped that plate all those years ago, and you got so angry you took one of the pieces of the ceramic and cut my face as a reminder to not fuck up?" Gavin shakes his head vigorously, but not in a *no I don't remember* way, more of a *no don't do this* way.

"Well, I do."

I take the blade and press deep into his eyebrow, feeling the initial resistance before the skin gives way with a soft pop. Blood wells instantly, thick and dark crimson, as I drag the knife upward into his hairline. The skin and shallow muscle on his forehead part like wet paper, revealing glistening layers of pink and red beneath. A warm spray mists my fingers as the knife cuts deeper, until the blade scrapes against something solid—the unmistakable grating sensation of steel against skull, white bone visible in the widening valley of the wound.

I nearly gag at the feeling, but then I see the blood begin to pool in his eye. Disgusting, yes. But I can still feel the way I felt when it was *my* blood pooling in *my* eye. The panic I felt at being blinded, and the sheer volume of pain.

Gavin's scream erupted like a siren the instant my blade bit into his face—a high, animal like sound that clawed at the walls. His voice broke when I paused, his chest heaving in ragged gasps, sweat beading where blood wasn't. Then when I finally withdrew the knife, a different sound altogether—a wet, gurgling yell that bubbled up from somewhere deeper, more primal, as if the pain had finally registered in some ancient part of his brain.

And so I continued, reminding him of each one of my injuries that he inflicted upon me, covering him from waist to forehead with fresh cuts to mimic the scars I have had to cover with my beautiful tattoos. I don't touch the tattoo on his chest, leaving that intact, despite the scars I possess on my chest. Instead, I make similar length cuts along his shoulders to make up for those.

Once he is covered, I finally stand and remove myself from his lap, and kneel before him.

"Remember all those times that I was forced to kneel for you, only for you to rape me? Or let your friends rape me?" Gavin shakes his head, full on sobbing now, each cut tearing more and more distress from his throat.

I look to Brenden, "Help me get his pants off." Brenden gives me a weird look but asks no questions. Together we lift his hips and pull down his jeans and boxers. I take the knife and run the sharp point from just below the tattoo, all the way to where his pants used to sit lightly drawing blood along the way. I stand and begin to pull my own pants down.

"What are you-" Brenden begins, until he sees me pointing at the large smiley face scar that goes from hip to hip. A puckered pink scar, slightly curving down as it travels across my lower stomach, from hip bone to hip bone. He steps back, letting me carry on without further question.

"See this Gavin?" But he doesn't look. Brenden walks up, and grabs Gavin by the back of his neck, forcing him to look at me. "See this one? This one you never got to see until earlier tonight when you raped me, again." Brenden freezes, his eyes meeting mine in feral distress. Like a mother animal learning someone hurt her young. I just shake my head. Now is not the time. I can tell him later. Because I now know that I am ready. Ready to be open. Ready to tell him everything.

"Because it was the night I went to the hospital after you and your friends raped me for hours and hours. All this time, you wanted an heir. You thought that if all of them fucked me and filled me with their disgusting cum, that I would *finally* get pregnant. But little did you know, I *was* pregnant that night."

I pause, letting the information sink in. Gavin's face is one of horror. Once I know he understands, I pull my pants back up, and let my shirt fall back into place. I take a deep breath before I continue speaking. This is only the second time I will have said these words aloud. And the first time I said them, was to the magnificent man helping me torture the one who did this to me. Brenden looks at me, his face morphing from anger to pride, and nods.

"That scar, Gavin, is from my emergency hysterectomy. You see," I begin to pace in front of him, watching as his eyes roam my body and his cock becomes harder as he stares at me.

"You all raped me so violently, and for so long, you caused a miscarriage and tore my vagina nearly beyond repair. It was why I was bleeding so heavily."

I pause my pacing, his eyes on my breasts, and his cock pointing directly at me now.

"Because the trauma was so bad, and then the miscarriage, I began to hemorrhage. I lost so much blood, I died on the table at one point. But the doctors, not knowing I had wished I had stayed dead instead of being forcibly revived, had to make a choice. Remove my entire uterus and cervix to stop the bleeding, or let me remain dead."

I stop pacing and look him in the eyes. I want him to feel how I felt. I want him to hurt like I hurt. He took my opportunity to be a mother. He ruined my body. And while I am thankful to be where I am and who I am today, it is still. His. Fault.

"They took my uterus. Never allowing me to have children in the future. Never letting me fulfill my dream of becoming a mother. So, now I think it's your turn. To let you bleed, and wish you were dead."

Gavin groans now, the look of fear in his eyes clashing with his erection. I kneel before him again, his dick too close to my face for me to think.

"Actually, I think we should deal with this first. What do you think Brenden?" I say, pointing the knife to his disgusting dick.

"That, my love, is a fantastic idea. Here, use my gloves. I don't want you to have to touch that thing ever again." The look of disgust on Brenden's face seeing the erection is nearly comical.

I take the offered gloves and slide them slowly onto each hand, extending the excruciating wait for Gavin as he shifts in the chair violently, doing everything he can to get away. But it's useless. And he knows it.

Once gloved, I take his penis in one hand, and the knife in the other, and I squeeze as hard as I can, causing him to cry out in pain. Then I nick it slightly, causing blood to ooze out. Gavin begins to scream and scream, this time not letting up. I continue causing small cuts all over his penis, the erection slowly shrinking into his body.

"Oh come on now Gav, if I remember correctly, you tend to get off on inflicting pain, why the limp noodle?" I say as his cock finally shrinks back into a flaccid, disgusting piece of bloody meat, diverting my attention to his testicles.

The moment I reach to grab one, Gavin begins to shriek like a pig, the sounds so outlandish I laugh, I can't help it, pulling my hand back for the slightest moment. Brenden makes a choking sound in his throat, trying to stave off his own laughter.

I pull myself together, inhale deeply, and then grab one testicle between my thumb and forefinger, the flesh warm and slippery. I make an incision with surgical precision, the sharp knife's edge parting skin with a wet whisper. The insides bulge then burst forth—pearlescent, viscous—like a ripe grape surrendering its pulp when squeezed too hard. Blood wells up, crimson and thick. I reach behind me for the jar of bleed stop powder sitting on the concrete floor, its metallic smell mixing with the copper tang already hanging in the air. I coat the deflated skin sac thoroughly, the white powder turning pink, then red as it clots the testicular artery. It is highly unlikely that he would completely bleed out from this, but I want to keep him slightly lucid. His screams become guttural, animal-like, before his eyes roll back. He passes out, but only briefly—Brenden's open-handed slaps echo like gunshots until Gavin's eyelids flutter open just in time to watch me position the blade against his remaining testicle. His renewed screaming vibrates through my bones as I complete my work. I stand back, wiping sweat from my brow, to admire my masterpiece.

I take the knife one last time, and cut a smiley face on his lower abdomen, just like the one from my hysterectomy. Hip to hip, going into his flesh about a quarter of the blade's length, we now have matching scars on our lower abdomens. Brenden, noticing how deep I cut him, begins to pour Bleed Stop on the wound immediately.

"Why are you stopping it?" I ask incredulously. "That's the cut that killed me. And it's how I planned on him dying too."

Brenden looks at me and grins. The expression is so malicious that even I get nervous. "So, I had an idea...

Once Gavin's wounds were packed, we left him there and drove until the world outside blurred into silence. I let the images of the last hour replay in my head like a film reel soaked in crimson, each frame dripping with satisfaction as the emotions crashed over me in waves. Every time the blade kissed his skin and parted flesh with that soft, wet resistance, a piece of me knitted back together—that raw, jagged place where he'd hurt me suddenly smoothing over, the phantom pain evaporating.

My hands had trembled with power, not fear, as I carved my vengeance into him. I was maniacal, pupils blown wide, breath coming in short gasps, lost in a blood lust that painted my vision red and made my mouth taste like copper pennies. But at the end —when I stepped back and saw my handiwork glistening under the harsh light—it was a baptism. Nothing I did would end his life, though my fingers had itched to press deeper. But everything I did would sit as permanent reminders for however long he has left on this earth. He would sit in that chair, no pain meds to dull the burning, no medical attention to stop the angry red inflammation that would bloom around each wound, just him and his scars searing into him in the exact same places he left scars on me.

I am pulled from my thoughts as the truck pulls into a parking spot at a cheap hotel on the outskirts of town. A place where nobody would ask questions.

Alisha, bless her, had thought ahead—an overnight bag waited for us in the backseat. Clean clothes, toiletries, and everything we didn't realize we'd need. Brenden jumps out, but my body is stuck in slow motion as the weight of the last week pounds against me, the agony, the build, and then the release. I watch this man I am blessed to have run around the front of the truck and up to my door, opening it like we are in an old-fashioned movie where men were still chivalrous. He helps me out, grabbing the bag from the back and unlocking the room.

When we walk in, Brenden heads straight for the bathroom and turns on the shower. The pipes groan to life, steam spilling through the open doorway. He meets me by the bed again, grabs the bag, wordless, and leads me to the bathroom. He helps unpack the bag–lining up toothpaste, hairbrush, deodorant, the kind of small, normal things that make the world feel real again.

Then he turns to me.

His hands, rough and warm, catch the hem of my shirt and lift it slowly, carefully, like I might break. He never looks away. The shirt hits the floor, followed by my bra, unhooked with practiced gentleness. The air is cool on my skin, goosebumps following his touch.

He kneels. Lips trace a quiet path: mouth, throat, collarbone... down to the scars that cut across my hips. His fingers work my buttons loose, his breath warm against my stomach. His tongue laves at the scar, soft and reverent. I step out of my pants and stand before him, bare and trembling, not from fear, but release.

The air between us hums with electricity. It isn't sexual. It's sacred. Worship.

He rises, his lips catching mine again before pulling off his own shirt. Then his jeans. Then nothing between us but air and the heat of the running water.

We stand there for a heartbeat. Just looking. Love, grief, exhaustion, and something wordless passing between us. Then he takes my hand and leads me into the steam.

The shower scalds at first, reddening his skin, and he hisses through his teeth. "Damn hotel water pressure," he mutters, and I laugh. An actual laugh, small but real.

We squeeze into the tub together, too close, too crowded, and neither of us cares. He trades places with me so the spray hits my back, my hair heavy with water. The scent of cheap soap fills the air. I look down at the tub floor and watch as the blood—rust-colored and thick where it's dried under my fingernails and nearly everywhere else, bright crimson where it's fresh—mixes with the scalding water running off me. It creates an abstract dance of pink and clear swirls that spiral toward the drain like watercolor paint. I lift my trembling hands a little, taking in all the dirt, grime, and dried blood of the last twenty-four hours. Flecks of someone else's skin still cling to my knuckles. My gaze drifts back up, scanning the white tile walls, searching for something to wash away the evidence of what I've done.

"Let me," he says quietly, reaching for the washcloth.

He starts at my shoulders, running the cloth across my shoulders, every moment a question. *Does this hurt? Are you still here?* His touch is steady, solid. He reaches my belly and then sinks the cloth between my legs gently. He lathers soap there, as if trying to wash away the feeling. Little does he know, I had tried to do that before as well. We haven't spoken of it, yet. And now is still not the time. He continues down to my feet, before standing back up and rinsing the cloth out.

I turn toward him. "I'm okay," I whisper.

He nods, eyes glassy. Then he spins me gently so the water rinses away the soap. His fingers find my scalp, working shampoo into my hair. I close my eyes, the rhythmic motion lulling me into something close to peace.

Neither of us says anything for a while. Only the hiss of water. Only breathing. Once I am fully washed, he beings on himself, and we trade places so he can get the blood and grime off of his skin as well.

When the water runs cold, he shuts it off and grabs the towels. He wraps one around me first, careful and firm, tucking it at my chest before towel-drying my hair. Another goes around his waist.

We brush our teeth side by side at the sink like we've done this a hundred times. Domestic. Quiet. Strange.

Back in bed, we sit in the soft light, phones in hand. I text my dad and brother short messages, just enough to say where we are and what the plan is. Dad replies that he'll post a guard outside of the mattress shop. Sam tells me to keep him updated. I promise I will.

Across from me, Brenden murmurs into his phone. "Yeah, thanks, man. Eleven tomorrow night. Got it. Appreciate you, Elliot."

He hangs up and slides into bed beside me, pulling me close, skin to skin, a tangle of limbs and warmth.

"Good night, Siren," he whispers, kissing me softly, lingering.

I smile against his lips. "Good night, dear."

He pulls back a little, eyebrows lifting and a small smile tugging at the corners of his lips.

"Dear?"

"My grandparents called each other that," I say, blushing. "It just... fits."

A slow grin spreads across his face. "Then that's what I'll be."

He turns off the light and gathers me closer, my head against his chest. His breathing evens out first. Mine follows. The world outside can wait.

For tonight, I am whole.

We pull up to Point Defiance Zoo and Aquarium the next evening, but not how I've ever seen it. The 5500 utility truck takes up half the back lot it seems, headlights cutting through the marine fog like search beams. Brenden kills the engine. The night goes still.

We'd gone back for Gavin around nine thirty. Dad's guard said he was alive–barely–but that the room smelled like piss and rot. He was still where we left him, tied and trembling. I'd texted Dad an apology for the cleanup before pocketing my phone and helping Brenden wrap the bastard in one of the mattress-store blankets.

Now, as we back up to the loading dock, the ocean wind stings my eyes.

Brenden hops out first, jogging around to my side and pulling open my door with a theatrical bow.

"Here we are, milady."

His grin is ridiculous and somehow exactly what I need.

"Thank you, my lord," I say, taking his hand.

We had spent the day in bed, rotting in front of the television, having food delivered. We didn't bother getting dressed until about seven this evening. There wasn't a point. We explored each other again. I wasn't ready to had sex again yet. I needed a bit more time. More closure. But we touched, tasted, and loved one another. Slowly. Deliberately. Methodically. It was a beautiful day. And tonight, that pain finally ends.

When we circle to the back, Gavin's already awake, thrashing under the blanket. He kicks out, nearly catching Brenden in the ribs, but the ropes hold.

"Sorry, mate," Brenden says mildly. "You won't be getting free this time."

"Do you think anyone will hear him?" I ask. My voice sounds too loud in the empty lot. "Nah," Brenden answers. "The beach is closed at night. Anyone down there's either drunk or too smart to come looking."

He hoists Gavin up and over his shoulder like a sack of wet sand, then takes my hand again as we head for the back entrance.

The metal door groans open to reveal a tall, gangly man with glasses sliding down his nose.

"Brenden! Man, long time!" he says, beaming as if it's perfectly normal to see someone carrying a bloodied, writhing human burrito.

"Elliot," Brenden greets, shaking his hand one-armed. "Thanks again for the favor."

"Oh-oh, wow." Elliot's eyes widen when he spots me. "You're Surry O'Brien. I follow you on TikTok! Uh-your videos are awesome." He blushes hard enough to match the red exit sign overhead.

"Oh! Well, it's nice to meet you, Elliot." I smile despite myself. "Send me a message so I can follow you back."

He nearly chokes. "Right. Yes. Sure thing!"

Brenden coughs to hide a laugh. Elliot takes the hint and gestures us forward.

"This way."

The corridor is long, narrow, and humming with filtered water behind the walls. The air smells of salt, metal, and disinfectant.

"So, how do you two know each other?" I ask, if only to drown out the sound of Gavin's muffled growling.

"Brenden helped my sister out," Elliot says. "Her husband was a Capitol prick who thought hitting her made him powerful. Brenden and his brothers made sure that stopped."

"Permanently," Brenden adds, voice flat. I nod my understanding.

At the end of the hallway, Elliot pushes through a swinging door into a room that vibrates with soft, underwater light. The glass of a massive tank glows faint blue, waves of reflection crawling up the walls. Brenden walks over to the wall near the tank and drops Gavin's body, just straight lets go. There is a loud thud and cracking sound as he hits the ground, but neither of us pay him any mind.

"I'd like you to meet my girl, April," Elliot says, leading us to the edge. "Grey reef shark. Born here. I was there when she was born."

He points at a graceful figure gliding through the water, one fin slightly shorter than the other. "See that? She's my little mutant ninja turtle. Strongest one in the shiver."

A look of confusion spreads across my face. I have exactly zero idea what he's talking about. But before I can ask what the hell a shiver is, Brenden beats me to it.

"What in the actual fuck is a shiver? Like when you're cold?" Brenden looks bewildered, causing me to laugh out loud. Subtlety is not his strong suit, that's for sure.

Elliot laughs along with me for a moment, both of us enjoying Brenden's facial expression.

"Ya, sorry," he begins. "I forgot I'm not talking to other shark nerds. That's who I usually talk to back here."

He pauses as if that's the explanation we require.

I open my mouth, waiting to see if he will continue before I ask. But after about ten seconds, I realize he is not planning on answering.

"So, ya. What actually is a shiver? We legit don't know," I laugh again, this time awkwardly.

"Elliot doesn't seem perturbed, eyes still focused on April. "It's a group of sharks. They're called several things depending on what they're doing. A school, which is a general term for all fish. A shoal, that's for when there is a group near the surface. A frenzy is not technically accurate, but that's what it's called when there is a group feeding. But a shiver is a group of shark, specifically."

"Huh, I guess you learn something new every day after all," Brenden mumbles under his breath.

"Well, she's beautiful," I whisper in Elliot's direction. And I mean it.

Elliot grins, proud as a father. "This is the holding tank, by the way. Closed to the public. Everyone's gone home. So... no witnesses, and they will clean up after themselves. Whatever they don't get, the filtration system will. And no one would ever check that."

"Convenient," Brenden mutters.

"Ready when you are," Elliot says, then looks between us. I think he notices the stress on my face because he claps his hands together before continuing. "I'll just give you two a minute. Knock when you're ready." He slips away toward the adjoining office.

Brenden crouches in front of me, thumb and forefinger tipping my chin up. "You sure?"
My throat tightens. "I think so."

He nods once. No judgment. Just faith. Then he hauls Gavin upright, pressing him against the nearest wall. The bastard's eyes are wild now—more animal than man.

I knock on the office door. Elliot reappears, rolling up his sleeves. Together, he and Brenden drag Gavin closer to the tank's edge, half-lifting him to sit on the ledge above the water. Gavin is thrashing, doing his best to escape their grasp, apparently not realizing where he is.

Elliot's voice is soft, clinical. "You're really ready to swim with my sharks, aren't you?" Gavin freezes, looking to Elliot and then cranes his neck to see behind him. His eyes triple in size, and so do his efforts to get away.

I step forward until I'm inches from Gavin's face. For the first time, I see it—the flicker of fear beneath the arrogance. Real, gut-deep terror.

"This is for me," I say quietly. "This is for Natasha. For Bridget. For every woman you ever hurt." My voice doesn't shake. "You will never touch another woman again. This isn't murder, Gavin. It's taking out the trash."

He starts to speak, sputtering nonsensical words, but I'm already pushing. Brenden and Elliot let go.

Gavin topples backward into the tank. His scream cuts off the instant he hits the water.

For a second, there's silence. Just bubbles and the slow, drifting blur of his body sinking, tied and helpless. Then blood begins to bloom from the wounds that reopened from his thrashing–a dark ribbon spreading through the blue.

The sharks sense it instantly.

Elliot murmurs, almost reverently, "Watch their fins. That stiff, jerky motion? Means they're about to strike."

The first grey reef shark bumps him hard, testing. Another follows, circling tighter. Then the water explodes.

"And this," Elliot states in a reverent tone, " is a frenzy." Brenden and I don't say anything. We just stare into the tank.

Foam. Thrashing. A burst of red clouds the glass.

I flinch but don't look away. Brenden's reflection joins mine in the tank–our faces pale in the glass as chaos turns the water pink.

Gavin disappears beneath the frenzy.

The sounds muffle through the barrier. Dull thuds, the slap of tails, the churn of water. My pulse slows. The noise fades until all that's left is the low hum of the pumps and the whisper of waves against glass.

For the first time in eleven years, the world feels quiet.

The frenzy fades fast. Sharks don't linger–they strike, feed, then vanish. The water calms again, and the blood dissolves into soft, clouded ripples.

Beside me, Surry hasn't moved. She's staring into the tank, face ghostly white in the glass. For a moment, she's completely still. No trembling, no anger, no fear. Just... peace. The kind you don't get in this world without fighting for it.

I take a step back, giving her some well-earned space. She deserves this quiet. Deserves to feel what it's like to breathe without demons clawing at her throat.

When she finally turns, her eyes find mine. They're clear again–storm-wrecked, yes, but alive. Whole.

I reach for her hands, still cold from the glass. "Surry," I say, her name low in my chest. "I know this isn't how it's supposed to go. No candles. No ring. Just us, salt in the air, a shark tank full of karma, and...Elliot." Surry giggles, but it sounds nervous.

Elliot blinks, then nods in understanding. "Right. I'll, uh–leave you to it." He disappears into his office once again, door shutting softly behind him.

I exhale a small laugh, then turn back to the love of my life, my thumb brushing over her dainty knuckles. "But I don't need perfect," I continue quietly. "I just need you. I want to spend the rest of my days worshiping you, laughing with you, fighting for you, loving you."

I take a step closer before dropping to one knee, voice roughening. "Will you do me the immense honor of being my partner for life?" I pause, clearing my throat. It has gone dry with nerves. "Surry, my sweet Siren... will you marry me?"

The sound of the tank echoes off the walls–steady, rhythmic. The glass between us and the water glows faintly, a heartbeat of blue light flickering along the walls, reflecting in her long, beautiful hair.

Just then, a soft melody plays through the speakers. *Jaws*, by Sleep Token, I think. Surry gave me a full history and discography of them today. Thank you, Elliot.

And just like that, the sharks are forgotten. The world narrows to her hands within mine, the warmth of her skin, the peace I never thought I could deserve.

When she whispers yes, it feels like the first sunrise after a decade of storms. I stand, pulling her into my arms and pressing my lips to hers. The kiss is passionate but calm. Romantic, loving, closing a chapter in our lives so we can turn to the next one. It is filled with relief and love and so many other things.

We turn, leaving the aquarium–and everything it buried–behind us.

At last, hand in hand, we step into our own forever.

The End

(For now)

# EPILOGUE
## 2 MONTHS LATER

**Surry**

"Wow, the weather is surprisingly nice today," I say as I look out the window of our new apartment overlooking the city. Brenden and I ended up picking the penthouse in his tallest building. It's massive, but I started making it feel like home the day we moved in. I painted all the walls, black as you would expect. The ceilings I kept bright white to give height to the walls. Although they are already fifteen-foot walls, so it's not like I needed to make them look any taller.

The living room is a mix of black, white, grey, and greens. Deep greens, emerald one could say. Brenden swears that emerald green is his favorite color. The kitchen and the rest of the main spaces follow the same color patterns. But the guest rooms, we have three, each has its own theme. I thought it would be fun, and it would satisfy our different decor ideas. Brenden surprised me with his keen eye for design. I was shocked, actually.

In one room, it is themed all pink. I needed to have a girly room in the house. I don't wear pink, or decorate with it much. But I wanted one room that was entirely pink. I channeled Selene's theme of cotton candy. The walls are a warm blush color, the bedding and rug are a mix of soft pinks, hot pinks, and blacks. The little desk meets vanity is black, with little cutesy decor from different craft stores. The artwork is sweet and lighthearted. Bunnies, birds, a few skulls and random designs, but my favorite is the sign that is the largest. It has a white background, in a black wood frame and in a beautiful cursive that says "Live, Laugh, Lobotomy." Just because it's a girly room doesn't mean it doesn't need a touch of our dark humor.

The second room, Brenden was in charge of. It is very manly. Steel grey, deep blues, and dark greys. It is very cozy and warm feeling in there. Leather and other rough textures are strewn about. The bed is black with blue accent pillows, and the headboard is made of steel.

The final room, we decorated together. It is the perfect mix of us. It is primarily just a deep blue. The walls are painted the dark blue, the headboard, doors, and casings all painted the same color. The bedding is varying shades of dark blue, and the decor is all blue and blue glass. The large floor to ceiling windows lighting up the room. This one is my favorite, because we made all the decisions together.

Brenden came up behind me, wrapping his arms around my middle and placing his nose in my ear. He has been so lovey since I said yes at the aquarium. Yes to forever with the man who loves me more than anyone loves anything, I think. Except for maybe how much I love him. I will always claim to be the winner of that.

Together, we are a formidable pair, and no one should cross us. Or they will see exactly what it is like to have the both of us as enemies.

"It is, I am excited to have everyone over for Thanksgiving today. Your food all looks delicious." I turn my head and kiss his temple, one of the only times I am able to since he is so much taller than me. He is dressed and ready for the day, looking so hot I think I should be burnt just by touching him. He has on black dress shoes, black jeans, and a black long-sleeve silk button-up that is undone to his upper chest with the sleeves rolled up past his elbows. His hair is down in a rare display, as he usually keeps it up in a low bun. But I am sure I don't look as I normally would either.

I've swept my hair into a low, messy ponytail, wisps of bright strands already escaping around my temples. A single fishtail braid winds through it—a small touch of deliberate beauty amid the chaos. My black pointed-toe booties click against the floor with each step, their worn leather creasing at the ankles above my black jeans, torn strategically at the knees and thighs. The plain black silk tank top clings slightly to my skin, its subtle sheen catching the light when I move.

Brenden got me an emerald necklace that catches every hint of light in the room—the center stone must be three carats, deep green like forest shadows, flanked by four smaller stones that graduate down the gold chain like teardrops. When I move, they shimmer against my skin, cool and heavy. It pairs perfectly with my engagement ring—a two-carat emerald that seems to pulse with its own heartbeat, surrounded by black marquee stones sharp as obsidian blades. Lighter green stones and diamonds encircle the center emerald like protective sentinels, all nestled in a gold band that gleams warm against my finger. The weight of it anchors me, a constant reminder of what we've survived together. It is the only piece of jewelry I will never take off ever again. And I don't wear jewelry much as a rule.

"Thank you, I'm excited to show everyone the apartment too. They haven't seen it since we moved in, and it was empty. So this will be really fun. I need to check on the turkey though, make sure it's cooking like it is supposed to. Oh, I forgot to tell you, Richie is spending the day with Tommy, so he likely won't make it."

I step out of his grasp, but he snags my hand and spins me around, placing a very intense kiss on my lips. Unfortunately for him, this black lipstick is not stay proof.

When we part, I laugh at his newly painted mouth and tell him to go wash up, as my parents should be here any moment, before walking away to check on my turkey.

"Well that's too bad about Richie. Has he known the guy long? Are they like actually dating or are they just seeing each other casually?"

"Look at you being good at gossiping today," I say with a wink. "They started talking a while ago, I think Richie really likes him. But we will see, I suppose. I once found his boxers in our kitchen sink. Not Richie's. Tommy's." I give him an exasperated look, then I continue on my mission to check on the food.

With the turkey cooking nicely, I begin to set up the sides that I have prepared for snacking. It is about four pm, and the football game is about to come up, so I ask my Alexa to turn on the television so that it's going when people arrive. At that moment, two things happen almost simultaneously. Brenden steps out of the hall and into the kitchen, and someone begins banging on the door.

We look at each other, wary from everything we just went through only two months ago. Brenden reaches into his waistband and pulls out his 45. Of course, he has that on him. I don't think he has walked to the bathroom without it since we left the warehouse. But I do almost the same thing. I have a 9mm I keep in the kitchen drawer. We don't have any kids around here or anything, so I don't feel bad not locking it up.

We both approach the door, safeties off, and place ourselves strategically by the door. Brenden peeks through the peephole, and sighs before putting his gun back on safe and placing it back into his waistband holster. He winks at me, and I point my gun at the door, but put the safety back on before he opens the door. Whoever it is isn't a threat, but he wants to scare them, apparently. I giggle as he opens the door and shove the barrel of my gun right into Josh's face, who in turn screams like a little girl, causing myself, Brenden, and Juniper to double over laughing. That's what you get for surprising people who have just been through actual hell.

"What the fuck, guys. I almost pissed myself!" Josh screams at us, clutching his chest with one hand, and his crotch with the other.

"That would have been something I would have paid to see," Brenden replies. Completely unfazed by his outburst.

I laugh as I apologize. Behind him, Corver and Natasha walk up. They aren't holding hands or even smiling. So I am not sure what is going on between them. I know that Corver is especially happy that she is free and with him, but I know she has been through so much and adjusting can be difficult.

We greet all four of them and usher them inside, and I take them all to the island to start digging into the snacks I set out, as well as get the remaining food out. We will have a full apartment once everyone is here.

Before Brenden shut the door, Alisha and Sam show up. Together. Brenden told me about how they were when I was gone, and I am desperately hoping I get that I LOVE YOUR BROTHER/I LOVE YOUR BEST FRIEND speech today. It's really all I want for Thanksgiving. Are there Thanksgiving wish lists? If not, there should be. Brenden points them in my direction and they join the conversation. Slowly, everyone else arrives. Selene shows up with my parents, and Gunnar arrives with Hazel and Arnie, which shocked me since I didn't know they were hanging out after the compound.

But I think her and Arnie make the world's most adorable couple. Finally, everyone has arrived and we are all mingling, Brenden and I in the kitchen making sure everyone has the booze and food they need as we wait on the turkey and sides.

"Hey, can I talk to you for a moment?"

Alisha came up and grabbed my elbow, and I looked over at Brenden, and he knows exactly where my head is at, as I am sure his eyes are as wide as mine. I turn back to her and grab her hand.

"Yeah, I wanted to show you the guest rooms anyway. I think you'll love one of them in particular. Just don't puke in it." We giggle as we walk toward the hall.

"Wow, this is beautiful! Why pink?" She asks as we enter the all pink bedroom. She steps in and does a slow 360 spin in the center of the room.

"Well, it's like having my best friend here with me always. Plus, I thought you'd love this room whenever you stay here! Do you like it?"

"Surry, it's beautiful! Yes I love it! But that's not what I wanted to talk to you about."

I knew it, I knew it, I knew it!

"Okay, so what is it? Spill now, bitch!"

"So, I know you aren't blind." I instantly close my eyes and start feeling around in the air, causing her to laugh and smack my arm. "You know what I mean, crazy. I know you have seen Sam and I spending time together. And I wanted to talk to you about it. Before it goes any further."

"Yes. You have my blessing. You have for years. I have always known you loved him. But I don't want ANY details about it. Just that you are happy." I grab her hands and squeeze them, pulling her closer. "My brother is a lucky man to even breathe the same air as you. And to have my best friend become my literal sister maybe one day, I'm in."

"Good, because I know he asked my dad for permission to ask me to marry him. And I think he is going to ask yours as well. And I want to say yes if he does."

My brain glitches, probably because I am screaming and laughing and dancing around. This is by far the best news I have heard in a long time. "FUCK YES!" I scream at her, and Brenden comes rushing in. I point at him, and he shuts the door behind him, looking eagerly between us.

"Sam asked her dad for permission! I told you! I knew it!" He starts grinning like a fool and comes over and squeezes us both, lifting us off the ground, causing more giggles and yelling between the three of us.

"Sam is a lucky man, and you are a lucky woman. I am so excited to have you join this family officially. Thank you for being you Alisha, for loving my girl all these years, and for being the best woman Sam could ever dream of being with."

At that moment, Sam comes in, probably hearing the screaming and noticing the three of us are gone. "What's up in here?" He asks us, keeping his eyes on Alisha.

"Nothing! Want to see the other guest rooms? Come on Sam. Brenden, take Alisha out and get her a drink, please! And send Selene into the room we designed together, will you?"

With that, Brenden kisses the top of my head and then hauls Alisha over his shoulder and exits the room, yelling for Selene on his way. He treats her as if she is his baby sister, and it's hilarious. They fight like cats and dogs, just like the three of us do regularly.

"What is it now? Why is Brenden yelling at me again?" Selene asks as I grab her elbow as well as Sam's and pull them into the room across the hall, before shutting and locking the door behind us.

"So, do you want to tell her or should I?" I ask Sam, with a serious look on my face, acting as though I am upset with him.

Selene, having no idea what's happening, picks up what I am putting down and faces him with a look of pure disappointment. It's quite funny how similar we are, and how great we are at reading each other's thoughts.

"Well, I am not sure what Alisha told you. But I wanted to talk to you anyway," he says while rubbing his hands together.

"Spill," Selene and I say at the same time.

"Well, so, Alisha and I moved in together. She moved into my apartment."

"WHAT!" We both scream at him.

He ignores our outburst and continues talking. "So, things are getting pretty serious. Also-"

Selene plops down on the bed and curls up on the pillows. This bed is so soft, I almost join her. But then I remember my current outfit, and don't want to risk it.

"Also what?" I can't take this suspense anymore. I need him to answer the question already. I know Brenden is chomping at the bit to find out too.

"Also," Sam starts and gives Selene a side-eyed glare when Selene opens her mouth to interrupt, and I slap her leg to get her to shut up. "I want to ask her to marry–"

"I KNEW IT!" Both Selene and I scream at the same time, she jumps up off the bed and grabs me and we do a little happy dance, gabbing Sam and pulling him in to some weird ring around the rosey dance and scream fest we started.

Sam begins to laugh and dance a bit more freely with us as we continue, seemingly with no end in sight. This, I missed this so much. Being with my siblings and celebrating life events. I need to not stay away so long like I had been before all this mess. At least something great came out of it all.

Eventually, the three of us settle and flop down on the bed, forgetting about my outfit and hair worries. All three of us lay across it, shoulder to shoulder, staring up at the ceiling.

"So, is it okay with you if I ask her. She is your best friend, and I wanted to ask for a while. I should have. Because I want to do it today. After dinner."

Selene and I turn and look at each other. Her eyes mirroring mine, filling with tears, and I am sure her heart is just as full and happy as mine. I look the opposite way to see Sam.

"Nothing would make me happier than to have the dessert be outshined by your proposal, Sam. Having Alisha enter this family officially, gaining a second sister. I can't think of anything I would rather have happen today." I reach over and put my arm around him, and Selene joins in and lays on top of us, creating a Surry sandwich or a Sam Sundae. I love puns. We stay like this for a moment and then begin untangling to stand and fix our clothes and hair in the large mirror on the dresser.

We leave the bedroom behind after fixing the comforter, and I run to Brenden. I can't say anything since everyone is listening, but I wiggle my eyebrows at him, signaling good news. He knew it too, I think most, if not all of us, did. And it's about damn time.

Spending the rest of my life with the man I love, gaining a second sister, my baby sister finally healed, and restarting her life. Everything is safe, and solid. I couldn't ask for anything more. Brenden leans down and whispers into my ear, "I love you, Siren." I look up at this man who saved me. Not just from Gavin, but from myself and the never-ending cycle of misery that I endured every moment of every day. He is the person my soul has been looking for. And I cannot wait to begin my forever with him.

### Brenden

Dinner is done, and we are all stuffed to a nearly uncomfortable level. Surrey had gestured wildly toward dessert once she exited the bedroom with Sam and Selene earlier, so I have a feeling that whatever is going to happen, is about to happen. There really is only one guess, though.

I clear my plate and begin to wash some of the dishes so we don't have a mountain of them later on, while everyone settles into the living room with coffee or tea, and they all begin to chat. I clear my throat, and both Sam and Surry look at me. I look Sam in the eyes and slightly nod my head to get him to come over. "I could use some help with the dishes, if you don't mind, Sam." He nods and gets up, assuring both Alisha and Surry that he doesn't mind.

Once he is standing next to me, I say through the side of my mouth, "do you need me to do anything or set anything up, man? I have some champagne I can get out as well."

"Champagne would be great. I'm kind of nervous, though. When do I do it? It feels too relaxed, and everyone is full. But I want to make sure nobody leaves."

"Do it now, help me finish these last few plates, wash your hands, and then we can pour some champagne and you can get everyone's attention with it."

"Okay."

We get to work doing just that, and begin the rest of our lives together as one large, happy family. To think that only a few short months ago, I was prepared to live as a bachelor the rest of my life.

Working and taking care of my brothers, taking jobs as needed. I still take jobs with Josh and Corver, as well as more legitimate ones. We are currently in talks with a company from Tokyo about building a few high rises over there. Josh thinks he and Juniper might go over there together to watch over the project in person. Surry and I are going to start studying under her dad to take over when he retires in a few years. Being the leader of the Irish Mafia was never something I expected. But looking over at this beautiful woman I get to spend the rest of my life with, I couldn't be happier.

This life of mine is not what I expected, but I can't say I would have it any other way.

Turn to the next page for a deleted scene that was too spicy not to show you (hehe).

# BONUS CHAPTER
### NEVER SEEN BEFORE
##### SCENE FROM THE COMPOUND
##### WHEN THEY FIRST ARRIVED

**Surry**

Damn, it was fucking hot out here. I left a bathing suit in my dresser here when I left all those years ago, and I am very happy with my choice.

"Good Lord, girl, are you trying to get everyone to see my chub?" Brenden asks me, eyes trailing up and down my body. Hunger and lust circling within the light blue orbs.

I was lying out in the backyard in this cute little personal pool that I found out in the pool shed. The bathing suit is this cute little emerald green bikini. It matches my eyes, so Alisha made me buy it. It is nearly too small for me now. I was so skinny back then, and while I'm not overweight by any means, I have put on healthy weight since then. The triangles that cover my breasts are at least one size too small, and the bottoms are at least three sizes too small. I've been doing squats, and the bottoms will definitely be leaving red marks when Brenden inevitably removes them.

"Yes, in fact, that is exactly what I wanted. I wanted you and every man in this house to stare at me until all your eyes fall out and your dicks are pointing directly towards me," I said and rolled my eyes. The way his eyes roam me, I can't lie and say I don't love it. My core begins to respond to the look he's giving me. Throbbing heat comparable to that of the sun's.

"Well, everyone else is gone, actually. Most of them went to the store to get some stuff, others left to do surveillance. Josh took the girls to go do some shopping because they didn't get to grab very much before we left. I think Hazel has been wearing the same shirt since we got here." He was right. Hazel had in fact been wearing the same shirt. A black band tee she snagged thrifting one weekend. Bridget had been washing it every night before returning it to her room.

"Oh? Well what would you like to do if we truly are all alone?" I had slipped my sunglasses down my nose, and decided now was the time to push them back up, feigning disinterest. His eyes immediately grew darker, and his hands flexed by his sides. I run my eyes down his body, and holy shit. His dick is straining against the khaki cargo shorts he wears. I'm sure it's painful, because his shorts are a bit too small, and his cock is extra large.

"I don't know, Siren. What would you like me to do about it?" He begins to stalk toward me, slowly. Predatory.

I sit up from my reclined position in the little pool and set my book down. I had just stopped reading right when the two main characters were in their first sex scene, so I was feeling a little needy myself.

Once the book was down, I reach behind my back and pull the strings that barely keep my bikini around my middle. It loosens and I pull the bikini away from my breasts and up and over my head, exposing my nipples that immediately peak from the fresh air rushing against them.

His eyes move down and scan over them. He licks his lips and speeds up his walking. I toss my top onto the ground next to me, before reclining once more in the pool at the same moment he reaches me.

Brenden stops before me, and looks at my bottoms. Leaning down, he tugs on his own, pulling them down to the ground. His erection bounces when it leaves his bottoms, thick and heavy. Every time I see his naked body, I melt into a puddle of nothing but hormones and lust. Now is no different. I feel my jaw drop, but I don't bother closing it. Maybe he'll use it.

He kneels into the small pool before me, and grabs the sides of my bikini bottoms, forcefully ripping them off my body. The sting on my skin is painful, but my pussy is soaking wet and pulsing with need for him. I lay there looking into his eyes, completely naked before him. He places his hands on my knees and widens them, exposing my entrance to him. The look of hunger in his eyes was enough to make me explode then and there.

The water in the small personal pool is low, just reaching my pussy, and I can feel it sloshing around as he moves within the pool with me.

He grabs my hair gently, but with enough grip to get me to sit up, and my face is now eye level with his cock. My mouth instantly begins to salivate. I like my lips, and then my tongue darts out to taste the bead of precum that has gathered on the end of his dick.

He groans, hips jerking forward, and I take the opportunity to open my mouth and allow him entrance. He wasn't prepared to feel my mouth so suddenly and another jerk causes him to slip farther in and touch the back of my throat.

Seeing him melt from barely doing anything always gives me such a large confidence boost. I bring my hand up grab his heavy balls, giving a firm tug before gently beginning to knead them. Slowly, Brenden begins to thrust into my mouth. Gently at first. But the more I hollow out my cheeks, and squeeze his balls, the fast he goes.

His dick barely fits a third of it into my mouth so I use my hand to wrap around some of the remaining length, twisting and rubbing, using my saliva as lubrication. He begins to groan and shudder, before quickly withdrawing. He was so close, I also got to taste his cum as it dripped down my throat. But instead he pushes me back down into a laying position.

He bends at the waist and pulls my hips up, closing the gap between my pelvis and his mouth, returning the sensations I just gave him. He places his hands under my ass and lifts my pussy to meet his face, and begins to devour me. I am instantly moaning his name.

"Brenden, fuck. Oh my God, Brenden!"

The growl that leaves his chest and throat vibrates into me, heightening my desire.

I was truly blessed; this man had one of the longest tongues I had ever seen. Or felt. It moved inside me, eating me from the inside out. His one hand played with my back entrance, entering it slightly, teasing gently. The other hand has me propped up so that I am angled upward. My back arched as he fucked me with his mouth, making me a hot, wet mess.

He removes his mouth from my body and begins biting, kissing, and sucking his way up toward my nipples, slowly lowering my hips back to his own. He focuses on my belly, lavishing it with his mouth, before continuing his journey. He found my left nipple and begins to use his tongue to draw circles around it, slow and lazy.

His hand pulls and squeezes my right nipple, making it even harder than it was before. I reached my hands down and grabbed a fistful of his hair now that I could reach him.

"Brenden, please," I moan. Not wanting to wait any longer.

I began tugging, trying to get him to pull me closer so that I could grind my hips into him. The lack of friction on my pussy was starting to drive me mad. He let out a chuckle with my nipple caught between his teeth.

"Siren, what is it that you need. Will you tell me, please?" He said it so nicely, but the look in his eyes was dangerous. I wanted more of it.

"Brenden," I said in a breathy moan, "I need you in me. I need you in my pussy. Please."

He broke when I moaned the please, still grinding my hips against nothing. He sucked my nipple into his mouth and gave a hard, nearly painful suck, before letting it go with a popping sound. He grabs my hips and pulls me closer, entering me with one fluid motion.

I let out a scream as he impales me, filling me to the brim with his cock in one go. His balls slap against my ass, expressing with sound how completely and utterly full I am with him. It is just what I needed. That is, until he started to move.

He began thrusting into me, so hard that it was sloshing the water out of the pool. I had just filled this thing up, but oh well. This is what I really needed.

"Siren, play with your clit. I wanna see you work yourself up into a frenzy. Show me what you like."

I didn't need telling twice; I ran my right hand down to my clit and began to furiously circle it, instantly sparking a wildfire that was previously just an ember in comparison.

I moaned loudly and reached my left hand up to my nipple. I began to twist it to the point it was slightly painful, tugging once it was painful to add more sensation.

"Good girl, Surry, good girl." He pants his praise to me. Hearing him say my name is something I never knew I needed until I heard him say it for the first time. I instantly begin to orgasm around him. My pussy clenches down so hard on his dick that he has trouble moving, but continues to fuck me as hard as he can.

"Fuck, fuck, fuck me! Please fuck me harder!" I was screaming for him. Brenden was breathing and moaning so loud, I am sure the neighbors that were fifteen miles away could hear us. I know for sure the house staff could. Oh well.

"Yes," Brenden huffs out air. "That's my," he pauses, breathing heavily, before continuing. "Good fucking girl," Brenden finishes praising me in a moany, breathless voice as he fucks me, near violently at this point.

"I wanna hear you scream baby, scream for me." His eyes meet mine, and I can see how close he is to release.

I couldn't do anything though, this orgasm wouldn't end. Maybe I would die like this, I wouldn't even be mad honestly. *Death by orgasm.*

I feel Brenden begin to find his own release inside me, his cock pulsing in time to mine, somehow lengthening my own everlasting release with his new movements. His thrusts become more jagged and rough, it was pure bliss.

Finally, when my body had been through enough my orgasm

finished, and Brenden fell on top of me, getting us both soaking wet in an entirely different way. I was too sated to move or care.

"Damn girl, fuck.." Is all he could say between his ragged breaths. I felt the exact same. Except that this man was so damn large, I couldn't breath. I shoved him to push him next to me, instead of on top of me, his dick popping out of my pussy and cum began to leak out of me. Well, I will really need to change the water after this.

He looks down at his semi-hard dick and total nudity, and back up to me. He then scans my naked body that is covered in marks as if he was trying to brand me as his own.

"Although, I am happy to show everyone what's mine." He looks around the outdoor space.

I rolled my eyes at his claiming remarks. "I am in need of a shower." He reaches over and pinches my sensitive nipple and I screech.

"Quit it, they are sensitive!" But I can't help giggling.

He leans in, nipping at my ear now, "just how I like them." He kisses my cheek and I begin to stand.

"I go where you go, Siren." He grabs all my clothes and his, and walks right behind me as I make my way into the house, butt ass naked, to take a shower with this amazing man.

## ACKNOWLEDGMENTS

I want to thank so many people that this is already getting unwieldy — in no particular order of importance (except one: Cody, you are the most important; sorry not sorry).

**To my readers** — you, the one who just cracked this book open — thank you. You are seriously the best. Thank you for taking a chance on *If You Go*. I hope you loved reading it as much as I loved writing it. Every page you turn is a tiny vote of confidence that keeps me scribbling late into the night.

**To my Alpha Readers:**

Kyla C. **@bound_to_please_** Without you, I would've been stuck circling the same paragraph for months. You caught my logic leaks, laughed in the right places, and told me when to shut up and when to write more. I owe you big.

Felicia B. **@bookish_bennett** Thank you for being my sounding board and ALL the voice notes (even the unprofessional ones hehe)! Your insight, encouragement, and willingness to dive into messy drafts made this story sharper and stronger. I'm endlessly grateful for your patience and your honesty—you kept me going when I doubted myself.

**To my ARC readers** — you brave souls who read draft-me — you made me fall in love with the book world all over again. Your notes, gifs, and enthusiasm made this process feel like a party, and I'll never forget how you cheered me on.

**Huge thank you to Author Sabreena Rodgers** — my copy/line editor and friend. Without you, this book would not be done. Like, ever probably. You absolutely crushed it editing, and all your advice along the way was a lifesaver. I appreciate you more than words can describe. XOXO

**Sage & Fable** — my cover is everything. It's exactly the thing I pictured at 2 a.m. while drinking too much coffee. Thank you for wrapping this book in such a gorgeous outfit and for being magic at what you do.

**Crown & Chaos PR** — Thank you for championing this book with such heart and hustle. Your passion, creativity, and dedication to connecting authors with readers mean the world to me. I couldn't imagine launching without your powerhouse team in my corner.

To **Author EC Garrett** — without you, I literally wouldn't be writing this. You taught me, encouraged me, loved me, and shoved me gently (and sometimes not-so-gently) into doing the work. Starting as your PA was the best decision I ever made — I got into the book world, learned the ropes, and found a lifelong friend. I love you endlessly.

**To my people, my tribe** — The Wellbutrin Club: **Alyssa, Kendahl, Madi, Brandi, Katie** — you are my heart and soul. You show up in ways big and small. You know which battles to fight and which jokes to make when I'm falling apart. I couldn't do life without you. Smut Freaks For Hire: **Breanna, Becca, Brittney, Lainey, Stephanie**— Thank you for being here, listening, reading, and sending me the funniest shit I have ever read (Dobby the Dough Elf).

**To my in-laws,** most of you don't know that I wrote this. Some of you do. And I'm sorry bahaha. I hope you enjoyed at least *some* of it!

**To my sister Megan (and her amazing husband Ricky — yes, I almost wrote "Dick," but I'll leave that little joke here with the bag of dicks you're owed)**— thank you for always making me laugh, for loving Cody and the kids as your own, and for holding my chaos with grace. I love you.

**To my parents** — who, for the record, have no idea I wrote this book and might never know — thank you for teaching me I could be anything. Becoming an author with deranged characters based on myself and my husband may not have been part of your life plan for me, but hey — here we are. (Sorry in advance.)

**To my kids, R, F, and L** — I hope you never read this, but if you do, know that I love you more than I can say. Being your mom is the coolest, messiest, most wonderful job I've ever had. I wouldn't trade any of you for the WORLD!

**To everyone who cheered, edited, lent a GIF,** offered a couch for writing, read an early chapter, or put up with my late-night rambles: thank you. This book is as much yours as it is mine.

**Finally,** to my best friend, the love of my life, my partner in crime: **Cody**. You've walked with me through every storm since 2013. You fought to keep me here when the world and my own brain threatened otherwise. You are my favorite human. We fell in love over ice cream at Cold Stone in weather that absolutely did not make sense for ice cream, and somehow that day made the rest of my life better. You remind me of everything (thanks ADHD), keep me fed, and are so ridiculously hot I can barely concentrate. I could write a whole book about why I love you — and technically, I did. I love you. I know you know.

XOXO

**— MM Tish**

MM Tish is a lifelong book lover turned storyteller, making her debut with If You Go. Married for over a decade, she credits her husband as the inspiration behind many moments woven into her writing. Together, they're raising three incredible children who keep life full of joy, energy, and laughter— along with two dogs, Lugnut and David, who ensure there's never a dull day at home.

Based in Utah, MM Tish finds inspiration in the mountains and the beauty of the outdoors, with fall being her favorite season to soak in the crisp air and colorful landscapes. She's been reading for as long as she can remember, but it was series like Divergent, The Hunger Games, and Harry Potter that truly sparked her love of stories. That passion only deepened when Fifty Shades of Grey opened the door from YA to NA and beyond, shaping her taste for bold, emotional, and unforgettable reads.

Now, with her own words on the page, MM Tish is excited to share stories that blend heart, heat, and honesty. If You Go is just the beginning of what she hopes will be a long journey of creating books that make readers feel, escape, and fall in love with storytelling all over again.

COMING SOON

Book 2 in the Tattoos On
The Bay series

**GO WITH YOU**

Part 2 of Brenden and
Surry's story.

Will they survive the Mafia
as Surry takes over?

When a mysterious partner from Ireland comes to the US, Surry and Brenden are both put through challenges that test not only their resolve as leaders, but their relationship. The Irish do not approve of an outsider becoming the leader of their important venture, and decide that testing is needed, not only for Surry to prove she is the rightful leader of the Irish Mafia, but Brenden as well.

Marrying into the Mafia is not what he had expected, but he will happily accept whatever challenge, and succeed, if that's what it takes to stand beside Surry.
But will he survive those challenges?

Follow Author MM Tish @authormmtish to find out more, see sneak peeks, and fall in love with all of the characters over, and over again.

www.ingramcontent.com/pod-product-compliance
Lightning Source LLC
Chambersburg PA
CBHW021419110726
47901CB00008B/2220